Hannah Hooton grew up in Zimbabwe lifelong involvement with horses and the added authenticity to her books.

Praise for Hannah Hooton

'Group class and makes the grade on my shelves' *Love the Races*

'Move over Dick Francis' *Amazon reviewer*

'Georgette Heyer updated to the 21st century' *Amazon reviewer*

'Whether you know anything or nothing about horse racing… there is something for everyone here' *Amazon reviewer*

'A must-buy for those who love racing, horses and, of course, romance!' *Amazon reviewer*

'A great first novel by a new young author. Easy reading – romance, intrigue and the insight into the racing world makes a nice change' *Amazon reviewer*

'An incredible talent for making completely loveable and relatable characters' *Amazon reviewer*

Also by Hannah Hooton

At Long Odds
Keeping the Peace

Giving Chase

HANNAH HOOTON

Copyright © Hannah Hooton, 2013

All rights reserved

The moral right of the author has been asserted.

No part of this publication may be reproduced, stored in a retrieval system, or transmitted in any form or by any means without the prior permission in writing of the publisher. Nor be otherwise circulated in any form of binding or cover other than that in which it is published and without a similar condition including this condition being imposed on the subsequent purchaser.

All characters and events in this publication, other than those clearly in the public domain, are fictitious and any resemblance to real persons, living or dead, is purely coincidental.

ISBN: 978-1-291-34821-7

Cover image by
Pro Book Covers

"Canal Turn" sculpture courtesy of
www.peggykauffman.com

Published by Aspen Valley Books, 2013

In loving memory of Tessa
(1983 – 2008)

Acknowledgements

I owe much of Giving Chase's creation to the many people who gave up their generous time and knowledge to answer my often naive questions. Not only did the research of this novel introduce me to new friends, but it also opened my eyes to the strenuous but very brave lives that National Hunt jockeys lead.

Firstly, my thanks to my lovely editors Charlotte Dolby, Michelle Foster and Jackie Svatek. And, as always, I am forever grateful to the members of FictionPress for their feedback and support during the sometimes frustrating process of writing Giving Chase.

I am also indebted to the following people who have all contributed in one way or another to the completion of this novel:
Anglia Ruskin University Writers Workshop, Natalie Bell, Debbie Bowden, Jo Crawforth, Hannah Grissell, Diane Jackson, Peggy Kauffman, Diane Kelly, Annabel Kingston, Martin Pennington, Victoria Schlesinger, Dan Skelton, Karen Thacker and Tim Vaughan. I feel I should also credit jump jockeys Mick Fitzgerald, AP McCoy and Ruby Walsh who, although weren't directly involved in my research, provided a much more in-depth and personal viewpoint on National Hunt racing in their autobiographies than I could have hoped to achieve in an interview.

And in conclusion, I would like to express my gratitude to friends and family who have always backed me up, especially when Giving Chase's finish line never seemed to get any closer.

1

Through bleary eyes, Frankie looked at a stain at the base of the toilet. She clung to the rim, two fingers held in a trembling V. They were slick with saliva. She dry-heaved, squeezing her eyes shut as the bile reached only half-way up her throat. Her reflexive gag dragged it up further. Then the overpowering need to swallow pushed it back down again. The sound of voices beyond the toilet wall had her holding her breath but they soon faded and she could resume her task. She directed her fingers into her mouth again, pushing further, touching the soft sensitive skin at the back of her throat. Again, she wretched, this time more effectively and she drove her fingers deeper. The heaves rolled through her body.

Satisfied, at last, that her body had no more to offer, she slumped against the cubicle wall. Blindly reaching out, her hand slapped down on the flusher and she rocked back onto her feet. She let herself out and trudged over to the basins. She gargled then splashed her face. The water was cool on her hot sweaty skin and she closed her eyes in restoration. Looking back up at her reflection in the mirror though, she winced. Her blonde hair was coming loose from her hairband and fell lank over her sludge green eyes. Her cheeks were a blotchy pallid. Frankie let her head fall back and groaned. Never again would she let herself walk past Moulin Raj Indian Restaurant during a three day fast. Ever. A thumping on the door saved her from further admonishment.

'Frankie? You in there?' a male voice yelled from beyond.

'I'll be out in a minute,' she called back.

She pulled her hair free and flicked it upside down to give it some volume. She carefully arranged it around her face to obscure the pale rings around her eyes.

Tom Moxley, jockey's valet and Frankie's flatmate, was waiting outside in the narrow passage alongside Fontwell's weighing room. He held up a set of green and white silks.

'Will you be joining us for the two-ten?'

'Sorry,' she said with a weak smile. 'I had to shed a bit extra.'

He shook his head and looked at her pityingly.

'Why do you put yourself through this hell?'

She shrugged her shoulders and avoided his eyes.

'Diamante's got minimum weight.'

'Has he got any chance of winning?'

Frankie shrugged again.

'He was about forty-to-one on the exchanges this morning and you know their prices are always bigger. And my amateur's claim takes five pounds extra off his back.'

'Will that be enough? Jesus, Frankie. Look at yourself, you look like shit.'

'Thanks.' She took the silks from Tom and walked on. Tom followed close on her heels.

'Sorry, but it's true. Look at what you're doing. You're torturing yourself just to be an also-ran.'

Frankie stopped and looked back defensively.

'Hey, I won just the other week on a horse they said had no chance.'

'Out of how many others?'

She gave him a sour look.

'I love what I do, okay? And sometimes, if you love something or someone, you have to make some sacrifices. Mine was food.'

Tom didn't argue. She knew that given the chance he'd much rather be in her shoes. Instead he was a size twelve and a half and eight inches taller than she.

'Maybe you won't have to do it so much next week onwards.'

She nodded.

'Let's hope. Things are bound to change in some ways.'

'Yeah. Now come on, out of my way. Sir Bradford still needs his boots polished.'

Frankie snorted and stepped aside.

'Go on, shoeshine boy. I intend to land him on his arse in half an hour so you might have some breeches to get the stains out of too.'

Tactics. That's what the game was all about, more so when your starting price was an abandoned fifty-to-one. Frankie swallowed her impatience. That would all be changing soon.

She gave her mount an irritable slap on his neck with her whip and tried to engineer some enthusiasm with a couple of ineffective kicks. Diamante lurched into a jog and, bumping shoulders with one of his fourteen rivals, approached the start.

'You gonna sit midfield?' a fellow unfancied jockey asked beside her.

'Don't think I have much choice,' Frankie replied with a wry smile. 'Either that or at the rear.'

'Speaking of which, look at Bradford's there. He rides so short, it's a wonder he doesn't have more falls.'

Frankie looked towards where he was nodding. In front of them, the line of jostling horses was dominated by the presence of Rhys Bradford - boots polished to a mirror shine - his rear tilted arrogantly high above his saddle.

'So tempting to give it a kick,' the jockey said with a resigned shake of his head.

Frankie pulled her goggles down and collected her reins.

'I'd like to give him an arse-kicking in other ways, although I don't see that happening on this plodder. A bath runs quicker than he does.'

Rhys Bradford swivelled in his irons, catching them both looking at him. His eyes were hidden by the gloss of his goggles reflecting the late autumnal sunshine, but by his sly smile Frankie could imagine the dangerous twinkle in them.

'Admiring the view?' His luxuriant tone was lofty.

'On the contrary, we were just saying how it ruined the view,' she replied.

'Best get used to it. You know it's all you'll be seeing for the next two and a half miles.'

'And you should know not to be so cocksure. Elsie Dee looks over the top to me. She looks like she's going to burn out before we've gone one circuit.'

As if to prove her point, Rhys's mount bounded forward in an explosion of nerves. Rhys barely moved in the saddle. The mare chafed at the bit yet he held the reins like they were spun silk.

'Sweetheart, you couldn't pack water to fight the fires I start.' His smile broadened, sculpted as a yacht's hull. Taunting.

Frankie wasn't quick enough to think up an equally insulting reply before Elsie Dee bolted forward again. The two rows of runners gathered momentum as the starter climbed his rostrum.

'See you on the other side,' her neighbour said, pulling down his goggles.

Frankie nodded and fixed her gum guard in place. A flurry of nerves and adrenalin trembled down her spine. She rose in her stirrups as Diamante, sensing her nerves, broke into a crab-like canter.

Thoughts of Rhys Bradford and his eye-catching rear end vanished as the charge towards the first began. Vaguely aware of the shouts from fellow jockeys and the hectic scrimmaging for position, Frankie guided Diamante towards the better ground, steering clear of the inside rail. The first of nine hurdles was quickly upon them. She dug her knees into her saddle. Diamante scrambled over. Up front, Rhys's mount, Elsie Dee, fought for her head. The grey veered erratically off her line as they cavalry-charged past the grandstand and into the first left-handed turn. Rhys's arse was no longer so high as he moved his centre of gravity backwards.

Watching the battle ahead, Frankie grudgingly acknowledged Rhys's horsemanship as he skilfully brought his horse back in the field and settled it behind three others.

The field ran wide into the back straight, heading for the overhanging trees on the outside to avoid the heavy ground.

Tactics. Her earlier thought came back to her. Pushing Diamante forward and up Rhys's outside, Frankie angled for an inner line. A smug smile tugged at her lips as Diamante's pace didn't falter. The ground was no heavier on the inside than it was on the outside, yet she was stealing a good few lengths on her rivals.

'What the hell are you playing at?'

Frankie's smile disappeared as Rhys's angry shout cut through her concentration. She realised her tactic was taking him with her.

'What?' she yelled back.

'Move the fuck over!'

Rhys's horse shook her head, eager to cover the clear path ahead of her.

'No. The ground's just as good here.'

'I need cover! The others have all gone stand-side!'

Frankie clutched a handful of mane as their horses clashed shoulders and Diamante stumbled.

'That's not my problem! Go around me!' Keeping a wary eye on the fast approaching hurdle, she glared stubbornly at Rhys.

With a sneer in her direction, Rhys pushed down in his stirrups, struggling to ease the favourite back. Frankie looked ahead, annoyed at his interference and focussed on finding a stride. Out of the corner of her eye, she could still see Elsie Dee shaking her head, her mouth agape. The flicker of Diamante's left ear told her he was watching the battle too.

'Concentrate on your own race,' she muttered, tapping him on the neck with her whip.

Two strides out, Elsie Dee cannon-balled forward. Both horses took off in disjointed harmony, clashing against each other in mid-air. Rhys's knee dug into her leg and his elbow sent a sharp jab of pain through her breast. Gasping, she clung to Diamante's neck and lost a rein. Diamante pecked on landing and without his rider to balance him, disappeared muzzle first into the turf. Minus a neck in front of her to save her, Frankie was catapulted by Diamante's backend out of the saddle. Curling up into a protective ball she hit the ground and rolled.

The grass was cool and moist against her cheek, tickling her ear as she lay there, waiting for her lungs to refill with air, listening to the thunder of Diamante's hooves disappear into the distance. For a moment her spirits were dragged south by the thought of the days of punishment she'd put her body through for this race only for it to be over within a minute. On the bright side, said body was not throbbing with pain anywhere.

'Fuck's sake!' an angry and decidedly close voice snapped.

Frankie uncurled. Beside her, Rhys was slowly getting to his feet, his horse nowhere in sight.

'God,' she murmured beneath her breath, 'I didn't really mean it when I said I was going to land him on his arse.'

His shoulders shook with anger. He pulled his goggles down around his neck, revealing dark flashing eyes, and unclipped his helmet. Watching him pull it off and throw it on the ground, Frankie wasn't sure whether he was angry at her for their fall or just angry in general. Falls weren't exactly a rarity in this game after all.

'What the hell were you thinking?' he demanded.

Okay, he was angry at her. Looking up at the rage on his face, the high dirtied cheek bones, the damp dark curls still clinging to his forehead and over his collar, Frankie wondered what life had in store for her next week. If Rhys let her live that long, of course. Her eyes travelled down his athletic figure, so undeniably... well, put it this way: the Injured Jockeys Fund would make a packet if they put him on the cover of their calendar.

'I was riding my race. I can't help it if you can't control your horse.' Gingerly she picked herself up off the ground and tried to brush the grass stains off her breeches. Where his elbow had caught her in the chest seemed to be her only injury and had it been anywhere else, she would have tried to rub the pain away. But here she was not about to show him how much it hurt.

'Damn stupid thing to do,' Rhys muttered. 'Everyone goes stand-side when the ground's like this! You should be done for careless riding.'

On the other side of the running rail, Frankie watched the ambulance and doctor's car pull up.

'Rubbish. I told you Elsie Dee was over the top,' she said, bending down to pick up her whip. She pointed to the paramedics teetering by the rail, unsure whether or not to approach Rhys. 'There's our ride.'

With a last glare Rhys, snatching up his helmet, followed her across the course and ducked under the rail. He shrugged off the paramedics' concerns.

'There's nothing bloody wrong with me. Just take me back to the weighing room. And I'm not riding in the same car as *her*.'

'Suit yourself,' Frankie said, accepting a paramedic's assistance into the back of the ambulance. 'I'll see you bright and early on Monday.'

Rhys stared at her, his expression further fraught now with confusion.

'What?'

Stopping the paramedic from closing the ambulance door, Frankie grinned.

'Oh, didn't Jack tell you? I start work as Aspen Valley's new amateur jockey on Monday.'

2

As Frankie stepped over the Golden Miller pub threshold and into its spacious lounge, she silently praised Jack Carmichael for choosing this venue for their rendezvous. Eight o'clock on a Friday evening would ordinarily see the residents of the West Country town of Helensvale out in force, but the die-hard locals obviously hadn't been able to desert the age-old Plough for this more modern watering hole. A quick glance at the few inhabitants in the cool pine and blue-furnished restaurant area told her Jack wasn't here yet.

Feeling self-conscious, Frankie hastened past the bar in the direction of the Ladies. In the privacy of the bathroom, she looked at herself sternly in the mirror above the basins.

'You've nothing to be nervous about. You've already got the job. He won't withdraw the offer just because you brought down one of his horses earlier. Tonight is just about getting to know one another so you'll be more prepared on Monday.'

The constellation of freckles across her nose bunched up as, catching sight of her neckline, she grimaced. Easing the neck of her dress down, she examined the blackening bruise above her left breast which no amount of concealer could hide.

'Bloody Rhys Bradford,' she muttered, readjusting her cleavage and pulling her jacket further across her chest. She leaned forward and fixed herself with a stern glare. 'You're tougher than he thinks. You'll show him. You –'

The flushing of a loo in a nearby cubicle cut Frankie off. A heavily pregnant girl waddled into the mirror's reflection.

She looked awfully young to be venturing into motherhood but Frankie conceded looks could be very deceiving. Even though she herself was twenty-three, she was still constantly asked for her ID.

The girl smiled in sympathy at Frankie's anxious expression and stopped beside her to wash her hands.

'First date?' she asked.

'Something like that,' Frankie replied, embarrassed at being caught talking to herself and name-dropping while she was at it.

'You'll be fine, I'm sure.'

'Thanks.' Frankie motioned to her stomach. 'When are you due?'

'Two weeks,' she replied, tenderly rubbing her bump. 'We're out for our last night of freedom before the responsibilities of parenthood descend.'

'You make it sound like doom.'

The girl's face creased in discomfort and she moved her hand to the base of her back. Frankie had the sudden urge to be somewhere – *anywhere* – else.

'No, I'm sure it'll all be fine,' the girl replied and a pang of envy shot through Frankie. Why couldn't she be as fearless as this girl obviously was?

'Yes, I'm sure it will be,' she agreed as the girl exited the bathroom. She nodded at herself and squared her shoulders. 'It'll all be fine.'

Pep talk complete, Frankie's freshly-gained confidence made a nimble exit as, following the girl out into the pub, she caught sight of Rhys Bradford ordering a drink. A black biker's helmet perched on the bar counter beside him like a sinister disembodied head. She wavered, wondering whether she could hide in the loos until Jack arrived. Too late, Rhys looked up and saw her teetering in the shadows. Frankie let out a strangled chuckle as his gaze flittered over her then carried onto to survey the rest of the pub.

He didn't even recognise her! Not even six hours ago he'd been effing and blinding at her and now he didn't even have the decency to recognise her! Frankie stopped herself in the midst of her indignation.

Why did she want him to recognise her? She didn't want him to recognise her. Well, maybe when they were working alongside one another every day it wouldn't be so flattering, but right now didn't matter, surely?

Frankie beamed and walked across to the bar. Right now, with her straight blonde hair falling about her shoulders and a pretty midi dress making her look more feminine than the mud-splattered jockey silks and helmet had earlier, being unrecognisable to Rhys Bradford suited her just fine. She even afforded herself a leisurely appraisal of her future work-colleague. He was dressed in hip-hugging charcoal jeans and his dark hair curled over the collar of his black biker's jacket, looking like Darth Vader's evil son.

A pity, she thought as she ordered her drink. He would be rather attractive if he wasn't so arrogant. As it was, one could practically skydive off his ego.

Frankie was just paying Joey, the ponytailed barman, when she heard the pub's main door clatter closed. She took a deep breath before turning around. Some sixth sense which, through evolution, employees have developed to know when their bosses sneak up on them, told her Jack Carmichael had just entered the Golden Miller. She set a confident smile on her face and looked round.

Jack was helping a pretty auburn-haired young woman out of her red coat by the door. His machismo and her petite femininity made them a perfect match. His striking blue eyes travelled around the pub.

The smile she had ready for him froze when his gaze passed her by.

Okay, maybe this being unrecognisable in a dress wasn't such a bonus anymore.

She was just about to call out to him when Jack recognised someone he did know.

'Ah, Rhys,' he said, walking across to the bar with his hand placed protectively in the small of his partner's back. 'Wasn't expecting to see you here. How are you feeling after your fall?'

Standing ten feet away, Frankie opened her mouth and shut it again. How was she meant to announce her existence now?

'No lasting harm,' Rhys shrugged. 'Just annoying really. I reckon we would've won that race if Elsie Dee hadn't been hampered.'

Frankie sucked in her breath and clamped down on her bottom lip to keep herself from interrupting. The audacity of him! Elsie Dee had hampered *her*!

'Well, she's still fresh,' Jack replied. 'We can have another crack in a couple of weeks' time. Can I get you a drink?'

Rhys motioned to his orange juice and shook his head.

'Let me. What are you and Pippa having?'

'We were going to get a bottle and go sit in the restaurant. We're meant to be meeting up with our new amateur, Francesca Cooper –' He paused for another fruitless glance around the pub. 'But she doesn't appear to be here yet.'

Frankie realised this should be her cue, but the stiffening in Rhys's posture made her hesitate.

'Frankie Cooper? The mad thing that brought us down earlier?' Rhys sounded almost panicked. 'Wait, she mentioned something, but I thought – I thought she was just being delusional.'

Frankie couldn't help herself. She gave a bark of laughter which, in the relative quiet of the sparsely-populated pub, sounded a lot louder than she'd anticipated. She covered her mouth with both her hands, feeling an embarrassed warmth tingle her cheeks.

Rhys, Jack and Pippa all looked at her in astonishment.

Frankie haltingly opened her hands to reveal her face. Recognition flooded through Rhys's and Jack's expressions.

'Surprise!' she squeaked.

Jack gave a disconcerted cough.

'Frankie, er – hello. Sorry, I didn't see you there.' He strode over and she took his outstretched hand. She tried not to wince as his fingers crushed hers.

'It's the dress. It works as an invisibility cloak,' she said. 'Nice to see you again.'

'Likewise.' Still holding her hand, he drew her over to the rest of the party. 'Frankie, I'd like you to meet Pippa, my fiancée. And I believe you might have already met Rhys, Aspen Valley's first jockey.'

'We've crossed paths,' Frankie said with a wicked smile. 'Hi Pippa. Rhys.'

Rhys glared at her with undisguised dislike. His black eyes glinted, sending a shiver up her spine.

'Right, well, shall we get a table?' Jack suggested, looking from Frankie to Pippa. 'Rhys, would you like to join us?'

Rhys dragged his eyes away from Frankie to address their boss.

'Thanks, but I won't. I'm meeting someone.'

With Jack gesturing towards the restaurant tables, Frankie shot Rhys a grin as she passed by him.

'Nice to bump into you again.'

Rhys cocked an eyebrow and nodded curtly. *Just you wait*, his expression read.

Their passage towards the tables was punctuated by excited gasps from Pippa.

'Oh, look, Jack!' she exclaimed, clutching his arm and pointing at the far wall. 'They've got my paintings up. There's the one of Aspen Valley and there's that one of Helensvale from the top of the hill.'

'Pippa's an artist,' Jack explained. He pulled out a seat for Pippa as they reached a vacant table, but she wasn't paying any attention.

'Look! There's Emmie and Billy!'

Frankie looked towards where Pippa was pointing. The pregnant girl she'd met in the bathroom was sitting with a young man a few tables away.

'Bloody hell,' Jack muttered. 'Is the whole of Aspen Valley here tonight?'

'I must go say hi.' Pippa looked apologetically at Frankie. 'I'm sorry. Will you excuse me for a minute?'

'Of course,' Frankie replied. 'Take your time.'

With Pippa clattering across the stone floors in her heels, Frankie took her seat opposite Jack.

'She looks a bit above riding weight to be working at Aspen Valley,' she said, nodding towards Emmie.

Jack shrugged.

'For now. Emmie was one of my best work riders until she got pregnant. Lucky for you she did. The new job of amateur was hers originally. She's been working as my secretary for the past five months.'

Frankie again thought how fearless Emmie had seemed in the Ladies.

'Brave girl,' she commented.

Jack's mouth twitched into a smile.

'I'm not that much a tyrant to work for.'

Frankie gasped.

'Oh no! I didn't mean that. I just meant she looks so young and now about to be a parent...' Her voice trailed away, but she was relieved when Jack chuckled.

'Don't worry. I'm just teasing.'

She smiled.

'I'm really grateful for the opportunity you've given me. Riding for you and being a part of Aspen Valley is something I've only ever dreamed of.'

'You're a talented rider. It must run in the family. After all, it wasn't so long ago that I'd given the job to your brother. Then...' This time it was Jack's turn to trail off. He swallowed uneasily. 'Sorry, I didn't mean to bring that up.'

For a moment Frankie struggled to draw breath. She looked down, letting her fringe mask her eyes. Slowly, the iron clasp around her chest loosened. When she looked up at Jack's awkward expression, she was composed once more. On the outside at least.

'It's okay. It's been five years now, believe it or not. Almost to the day. Still feels like it happened yesterday though sometimes, doesn't it?'

Jack ducked his head in surprise.

'Five years already? God, yes. I suppose it must be. Rhys has been with us for five Cheltenhams, if you include last season.'

Frankie grinned. When life seemed to go by at a hurricane pace, she also kept track of the years by Cheltenham Festivals. She recalled as a child her mother once asking her and her brother, Seth, if they knew how many seasons there were in a year and what they were called. Nine-year-old Seth had shouted, 'Yes! I know! I know! There's two: the flat season and the jumps season!'

A pang of nostalgia hit Frankie as she remembered the exuberant boy she had hero-worshipped. She was saved by the reappearance of Pippa.

'I'm back,' she grinned, slipping into her seat beside Jack. 'He hasn't been giving you too much of a hard time, has he?'

Jack looked offended at the suggestion.

'What do you mean?'

'You were a right grump at the start of the evening because of your car –'

'It's not a car. It's a Land Rover.'

'Well, whatever it is, it's broken.' Pippa turned to Frankie. 'That's why we were late this evening. Jack's Land Rover wouldn't start so we had to come in my car.'

'I still think we should have persevered. It was probably just a loose connection somewhere. Whatever condition it's in, it's probably more reliable than yours.'

Frankie watched in envious wonder at the couple arguing good-naturedly with each other. Despite the occasional insult thrown, there was no malice in their tones. She noticed Pippa habitually touching the diamond ring on her finger, her thumb grazing it affectionately.

'Anyway,' Pippa said, bringing their exchange to a smooth decisive end. 'Back to the purpose of this evening. Frankie, how long have you been a jockey?'

'Well, I spent a couple of years riding in point-to-points after graduating from racing school. Then I got a job as amateur for David McKenna earlier this year but then he closed down –' Frankie paused as she realised she'd lost half her audience.

Pippa was looking beyond her, a frown furrowing her forehead. Frankie swivelled round. All she could see was the young couple, Emmie and Billy, sitting, eating their meals. Except... Frankie looked closer at Emmie. She didn't look very comfortable. The girl suddenly gave a gasp and reached forward, pitching over her glass of juice and clutching her side with one hand.

'Oh, God. Emmie!' Pippa said, jumping to her feet.

Frankie spun back around as Pippa's chair crashed to the ground. Her eyes met Jack's. His were wide with fear.

'Oh, shit,' he muttered.

3

At a loss as to what else to do, Frankie followed Pippa and Jack over to the neighbouring table.

'Emmie, are you okay?' Pippa asked. 'Is it time?'

Emmie looked up, her face contorting with pain.

'I think it must be.'

'Already?' Billy said.

'What do you mean "already"? I've been carrying this baby for nearly nine months!'

'I mean all of a sudden like this?'

'I've been getting pains all day, but that one was a bugger,' she muttered through clenched teeth.

The ashen-faced father-to-be continued to stare at Emmie, hands still clenching his knife and fork with a chunk of roast chicken still attached. Frankie sympathised.

'Okay, no need to panic,' Pippa said, her voice wavering. 'Let's get you to the hospital. Billy, is your car outside?'

Billy swallowed and dropped his knife. It fell to the floor with a clatter.

'Yes, but um –'

'What, Billy?' Jack said irritably.

'Well, I might have had a pint or two too many...'

'Jesus Christ!' hissed Jack. 'You're over the limit, aren't you?'

'I didn't think I would be driving all the way to Bristol tonight,' Billy defended himself. 'I thought we'd just go home afterwards... out of sight of any police.'

'Ooooh!' Emmie cried as another contraction took hold. Pippa squeezed her hand until it had passed.

'That's it,' she soothed. She coaxed Emmie out of her chair. 'Never mind about the car. We'll go in mine.'

'Your car?' Jack said. 'It's not exactly the most reliable. We were taking a chance just driving it here from the yard.'

'Well, do you have any better ideas?'

Frankie followed Jack's gaze back to the bar. Rhys was now sitting in the company of a flamingo-legged brunette, blissfully unaware of the drama unfolding behind him.

'He's got his motorbike helmet with him,' Pippa said, reading his thoughts. 'I doubt whether Emmie will go for that. We'll have to take a chance in my car.'

'With all due respect, Pippa, I don't fancy breaking down halfway to Bristol and having to give birth on the side of the A37,' Emmie said.

'Shall we call an ambulance then?'

Emmie shook her head.

'No time,' she gasped. She clutched Pippa's shoulder for support.

'We need someone with a car who isn't drunk then.'

Frankie, standing in the background, drew in her breath as all eyes turned to her. Damn. Some induction this was turning out to be. She took an unsteady step backwards.

'Oh no,' she said, shaking her head.

'But you do have a car, don't you?' Pippa urged.

'Yes, but –'

'And you haven't had anything to drink, have you?' Jack took up the plea.

Frankie hesitated, taking in the four desperate faces before her. Billy still had his napkin tucked into his collar.

'You haven't seen my car,' she tried one last time.

'Does it have four wheels, a reliable engine and steering control?'

'Yes, of course.'

'Then that's three things more than Pippa's.'

Frankie caved, at the same time wondering how they'd managed to drive to the Golden Miller with less than four wheels.

'Oh, dear. Okay. It's parked outside.'

The party exited the Golden Miller, Pippa and Billy supporting Emmie along the pavement. The first spots of rain were riding in on the cool evening breeze. Frankie reluctantly gestured towards the red and white car parked thirty feet away.

'There she is.'

A landslide of horror paled Jack's face and his step faltered.

'You drive a Mini?'

'Come on, Jack,' Pippa intervened, brushing past him. 'Stop stalling.'

The Mini's indicators flashed hello as Frankie beeped the locks open. With Pippa's help, they managed to ease Emmie into the front passenger seat. In his haste to get in the back, Billy smacked his head on the doorframe. He paused to rub his forehead.

'Ow, that hurt,' he mumbled.

'Not as much as this fucking does!' Emmie yelled from within. 'Hurry up!'

Billy clambered in, followed by Pippa. Jack folded himself low and somehow managed to wedge himself into the small remaining space on the backseat.

'Can we go now, please?' Emmie begged. She lent her head back and Billy comfortingly stroked her damp hair.

'We're off, don't stress,' Frankie said as calmly as she could. With trembling hands, she buckled herself in and gave Emmie a quick smile. 'Where are we going then?'

'Southmead Hospital,' Billy provided.

'Southmead?' Jack said. 'That's the far side of Bristol! Why the hell didn't you choose somewhere closer?'

'Because Billy was born there. Now, is there anything else you'd like to object to, Jack?' Emmie growled.

Reversing into the High Street, Frankie glanced at the three faces in her rearview mirror. Their shocked expressions told her Emmie wasn't usually so forthright.

Another contraction had Emmie grimacing in pain again and her hand shot forward to slam into the dashboard. The radio flashed into life. Bonnie Tyler's husky voice swelled inside the compacted car as *Holding Out For A Hero* boomed out of the speakers. Spinning the wheel and putting her foot down, Frankie was vaguely aware of Rhys Bradford and the brunette exiting the pub as they roared by. Their disbelieving stares followed the Mini's full-to-capacity progress down the street.

'Billy, are you timing the contractions?' Pippa asked as they navigated the streets of Bristol in the drizzle.

'Er, about two minutes?'

'No, Billy. You can't estimate like that,' Pippa corrected him gently. 'And they're not as close as that –'

'It bloody feels it!' Emmie groaned from the front. 'Oh God, here comes another. How far away is the hospital?'

'Not far, not far,' Frankie soothed. Despite the low traffic, it had still taken them a good half hour to reach the city and according to the Sat Nav, the hospital was another ten minutes away.

'Quick! Get your watch ready, Billy,' Pippa said as Emmie gave another groan. 'Ready, steady, go!'

'Pippa,' Jack spoke up. 'It's not a race.'

Frankie glanced at him in her mirror. His face was briefly lit by the streetlamps rushing past. He looked stressed but a lot more composed than he had half an hour ago. He had been very quiet up until this point. Frankie conceded he was probably having difficulty breathing, folded up like a contortionist as he was, let alone talking.

'Ooh, this is so not comfortable,' Emmie said with a grimace. 'I need to – I need to –'

Frankie shot her passenger a nervous look as she unbuckled her seatbelt and began to move around.

'What? What do you need to do?' she asked. 'We're nearly there. It's okay. Come on. Just ten minutes more. What are you *doing*?'

With a lot of puffing, Emmie manoeuvred herself sideways.

'It'll be more comfortable if I can just... kneel down in the footwell... and face backwards,' she said. 'My back is killing me.'

'Um, I don't think that's such a good idea.'

Emmie ignored her. In her determination, she kicked the gearstick, knocking the car out of gear and making it complain loudly. Frankie looked down at the tiny footwell, then at Emmie. Emmie wasn't exactly huge but in comparison to the space available, she might as well have been an elephant trying to turn around in a horsebox.

'Look, I really don't think you should do that –'

'There! That's better.' Emmie smiled weakly, now parked backwards with her elbows on the seat.

Turning into Gloucester Road, Frankie noticed Emmie barely move as they negotiated the corner. The girl was wedged. How the hell were they going to get her out?

'How are you feeling now?' she asked.

'Another one's coming.'

'Quick, Billy!' Pippa bounced in her seat as much as was physically possible. 'Where's your watch?'

As Emmie slumped onto the seat with another groan, the others turned to Billy expectantly.

'So? How long was that?' Pippa prompted.

'Well, it's eight forty-nine and fifty seconds... um, what time was it when you said go?'

'Oh, Billy!' Pippa complained, sounding like he'd just ruined a favourite game.

'Six minutes,' Jack said calmly.

'Six minutes?' echoed Frankie. She looked at Emmie in horror. 'How long have you been in labour?'

Emmie grimaced.

'I've been sore all day. I suppose those might have been contractions earlier. I just didn't know since they weren't exactly agonising. Unlike these bastards.'

Frankie put her foot down and the Mini sluiced through the wet with more urgency.

'Didn't you notice anything when your waters broke?' she asked.

Emmie looked at her, nonplussed.

'My waters haven't broken yet. I think I would have noticed *that*.'

'I thought your waters breaking is the first sign that you're about to pop,' Billy said, leaning forward and wrapping his arms around the backrest of the chair so he could see Emmie better.

'Weren't you listening in the antenatal classes, Billy? That only happens in Hollywood. Waters can break at any time during labour.'

Frankie tried to look subtly at Emmie's rear end jammed against the glove box. She really did not want Emmie flooding her car. It had taken four packs of air fresheners to mask the smell when her cat Atticus Finch had thrown up beneath her seat on the way to the vets. She did not want to find out how many packs this would need.

Frankie's heart stepped up the pace when finally a sign for Southmead Hospital was illuminated by the headlights.

'Nearly there,' she informed Emmie.

'About bloody time.'

She stopped the car as they reached the entrance and were met by about fifty different signs for all the hospital wards.

'Shit. Which way do we go?'

'Pink – sign –' Emmie gasped. 'Oh God, it's coming!'

'I see it! I see it –'

'What? You can see the baby?' Billy tried to climb over the headrest.

'No, the pink sign,' Frankie replied. 'Just - um - hold it in. Don't push. We're nearly there.'

The car lurched forward, making Emmie groan again. Driving as fast as she dared, Frankie peered into the darkness looking for further directions. It wasn't looking promising. They came to a T-junction. There weren't any more pink signs.

'And now? Billy, does any of this look familiar?' Frankie asked.

'I think things might have been changed around a bit since I was born here. We're talking twenty-one years ago.'

'Fuck's sake, Billy!' Emmie snarled. 'Stop being a tool. She means the last time we came here to visit!'

'Oh! Okay, um, right, well. I don't remember this bit. I might be wrong though. It was daytime then and things - well, things look different in the dark.'

'Let's back up. We might have missed something.'

'Oh God, no more speed humps, please,' Emmie whimpered. 'This baby's going to bounce out in a minute.'

With a high-pitched whine, the Mini shot backwards.

'Look!' Billy yelled, jabbing his finger against the window.

Peeping out from behind a bush was a discreet pink sign. Frankie spun the wheel and put her foot down, the car almost becoming airborne as they hit another speed hump. Emmie groaned like a dying whale. Drawing up to the maternity unit car park, she read the payment instructions beside the boom and meter.

'We have to pay by the hour. How long do you reckon we'll be?'

'What?' Jack said, craning his neck to see out of the window. 'How the hell are we supposed to know that? Just get the maximum.'

Frankie hefted her bag onto her lap and dipped into her purse for some money. She had a ten pound note and some small change. Peering at the meter, she couldn't see any entrance for notes to be accepted.

'It only accepts coins,' Frankie announced. 'I don't have enough.'

'Everyone empty your pockets,' Pippa said. 'How much do you need?'

'Another seven pounds and forty pence.'

There was a minute of grunting and heaving as the backseat occupants all tried to extract their wallets, digging elbows into ribs and cracking heads.

'I've got two pounds and sixty seven pence,' Billy said, spilling his change into Frankie's waiting palm.

'Here's three fifty,' Jack added to the pool. 'Pippa?'

Pippa looked embarrassed as she turned over her empty purse.

'I – er – just remembered. I gave all my loose change to the charity worker on the way to the pub earlier.'

They sat in compounded silence for a moment.

'Come on!' Emmie screamed at last. 'Someone must have some more money! Or break down the boom! This baby is coming NOW!'

Frankie gasped as an idea popped into her head.

'The ashtray! I always keep change in there! Here we are.'

With a handful of silver and copper, Frankie painstakingly fed the meter, aware that like the last grains of sand in an hour glass, time was fast running out.

At last, the meter disgorged a ticket and they were allowed through. She pulled up in one of the last available parking spaces with a jerk of the handbrake. After helping Jack, Pippa and Billy out of the back, she approached Emmie's door in trepidation. Emmie held out her sweaty palm to be helped up.

Frankie tugged.

Emmie didn't budge.

'Oh no,' Frankie muttered, pulling harder. 'Er, folks, I might need some help here.' She turned to the others standing behind her. Jack was cricking his neck back into place. 'Emmie's stuck.'

'Oh God, here comes another!' Emmie yelled. 'Fucking hell! What the hell is this baby doing in there? Ooooh! Oooooooooh!'

Billy and Pippa took up the case, each grabbing an arm.

'Okay, on five,' Billy said. 'Onnnnnne... twoooooo... threeeeee –'

'Billy, for fuck's sake!' Emmie screamed. 'Just get me out of here!'

Twisting, pulling, grunting and puffing, Emmie suddenly popped out of the footwell. Billy staggered as she collapsed on him.

'Ooh, there they go,' she wailed, looking down.

Frankie, closing the door behind her, followed her gaze and saw the girl's legs shiny with liquid beneath the street lighting. Feeling guilty, she gave a sigh of relief that it hadn't happened thirty seconds earlier.

In the face of everyone's semi-panic, the receptionist inside the maternity unit was amazingly calm. Frankie supposed if she threw a wobbly every time a labouring woman staggered in, she probably wouldn't be that suited to the job. With Emmie and Billy ushered through to the birthing suite, Frankie took a seat beside Pippa in the stark blue bubble-like foyer. Jack continued to pace up and down.

Long minutes ticked by with the silence interjected by muffled groans and wails and frantic buzzers being pressed like an overenthusiastic quiz panel. Four more mothers-to-be tottered in and were led into the torture house. Frankie grimaced and swore that she was never going to have children.

'I wonder if that's Emmie,' Pippa said, concerned etched across her face as a particularly wretched groan pierced the walls.

'Poor kid,' Jack muttered. He fixed Pippa with stern blue eyes and held up a finger. 'All that oohing and aahing you were doing over Emmie's bump and the baby clothes? Do not get any ideas, okay? I'm not putting you through this.'

Pippa gave him a loving smile and reached out her hand to give his a squeeze. Another blood-curdling scream breached the walls and Jack swayed.

'I've got to get out of here,' he said and strode out into the night.

Frankie and Pippa sat in silence for a time, both listening to the activity from beyond, both accompanied by their own thoughts. With every scream, Frankie became more and more certain she would never become a mother. She was sure Pippa must be feeling the same.

'He'll come round to the idea eventually,' Pippa broke the silence.

Frankie looked at her in disbelief.

'You mean you still want to have children after sitting here for an hour listening to all that racket?'

Pippa nodded.

'Not right now, I'll give you that. But when the time is right. I think Jack will be an amazing father.'

'He seems very protective,' she said cautiously. 'Of you, naturally. But of Emmie too, and well, isn't she just an employee?'

Pippa smiled.

'You'll find out soon enough that Jack has a rotten temper but he is very fair – you can ask any of the Aspen Valley staff. He might chew their ear off occasionally, but they'll all admit that they probably deserved it at the time. And when they find themselves in a jam, Jack is right behind them.'

Frankie nodded in agreement.

'He's been very fair to me. There's not that many trainers who'll take on a female jockey.' She grinned, reliving the moment when Jack had offered her the job. 'It feels like a fairy tale that not only have I been given a chance, but I've been given the chance by one of the top trainers in the country.'

'Have you always wanted to be a jockey?'

'I guess so,' Frankie replied with a shrug. 'My dad used to be a jockey and my brother was as well. It seemed the natural thing to do. Do you ride?'

Pippa laughed.

'No. I haven't sat on a horse since I was about six and that was at Brighton Beach.' She flashed Frankie a proud smile. 'I do have a horse though that Jack trains. Peace Offering.'

Frankie forgot how to breathe. She stared at a beaming Pippa.

'You own Peace Offering?' she gasped.

Pippa swelled with pride.

'Yes. Have you heard of him?'

'Of course I've heard of him! He nearly won the Grand National last season but got brought down by a loose horse while leading at the last.'

'He's favourite for the next one too,' Pippa grinned.

Frankie could feel her heart thumping inside her chest. *The Grand National.* Sitting next to the favourite's owner, this was the closest she had ever been to it. She could almost taste it. From riding claimers for a trainer going out of business last month to now working for the yard who boasted the Grand National favourite, Frankie marvelled at the huge leap she'd taken towards her ambition.

Pippa smiled at Frankie's awe and patted her hand.

'Someone once told me that you don't become a jockey without wanting to win the Grand National. Is it the same for you?'

Frankie thought about the question for a moment. Her reasons for wanting to win the National weren't exactly straight forward. They went deeper than just ambition.

'I think although we all have a common goal,' she began hesitantly, 'we all have different reasons for wanting to win it. For me, it's not about personal conquest, about being the best – or in my case, the first lady jockey. My father rode in the National a few times during his career, but he never won it and I know it bugged him long after his retirement that he never quite reached his goal.' She looked up at Pippa who was listening with interest. 'I'd love to win the National for him.' *Or even just get a ride in the National,* she added silently. Anything to make him proud.

Pippa's eyes sparkled and she blinked rapidly.

'That's a lovely reason. Did you know the only reason Peace Offering ran in it last season was to fulfil my uncle – his late owner's – wish? Jack didn't think he had a hope in hell.'

'He'll have changed his tune since then,' Frankie grinned. 'He'll have a strong chance this season –' A stab of jealousy punctured her dreams. '– Especially with Rhys Bradford back on board.'

Pippa gave a mirthless laugh.

'Yes,' she replied drily. 'If Peace Offering were to win the National, then it'd all be down to Rhys's blinding talent.'

Frankie laughed, but cautiously. Was he really that much of a bastard? Despite exaggerating massively to Jack earlier at the Golden Miller about their fall, he'd otherwise been courteous and amicable towards Pippa.

Frankie was trying to decide whether her boss' fiancée and Rhys had a history when the door to the birthing suite was flung open. It bounced off the wall and hit the entrant sideways.

Frankie and Pippa popped up from their seats like toast.

Billy stood immobile, only his Golden Miller napkin rising and falling with his heaving chest. His cheeks were wet with tears.

'Billy?' Pippa prompted gently. 'Is Emmie okay?'

His lower lip trembled then his face crumpled. Pippa rushed to his side and hugged him. Jack entered from outside with a whoosh of the automatic doors.

'What's happened, Billy?' he said.

Billy looked at his boss with weak watery eyes. Frankie held her breath.

'Emmie – Emmie – Emmie's had a baby,' he gulped.

4

As far as first impressions went, Aspen Valley Stables was up there with the best of them, thought Frankie come Monday morning. Snuggled at the base of a wide rolling hillside, the red brick stables were sheltered from the blustery southwest winds.

Not so much from the rain though, she thought, turning her collar up against the misty drizzle. She was greeted by the ricocheting sounds of horses banging their stable doors, keen to get out and stretch their muscles on the gallops. It seemed her enthusiasm to start her new job had made her early. There was relatively few staff wandering around.

Passing along the E-shaped yard, Frankie stopped outside the opposing row of offices and knocked on the Reception door. The windows were dark and she listened dubiously.

'Frankie!'

The welcoming voice didn't come from within but from behind. Jack advanced from further down the yard. A nervous flutter pre-empted her greeting.

'Morning,' he said as he reached her. 'Ready to rock and roll?'

Frankie filled her lungs with damp straw-scented air and smiled.

'I think so. After Friday night I'd say I was ready for anything.'

'Tell me about it. Thank God you were there. Both mother and son are doing well, you'll be glad to know. Although Billy, I'm not so sure about. He's too afraid to hold baby Sam in case he drops him.'

Frankie laughed, remembering Billy's awkwardness during Friday's escapade.

'I'm sure he'll get the hang of it soon.'

Jack looked doubtful.

'I'm not, but he's got a few weeks to practice at any rate. I've given him some leave. Actually, the baby arriving at the same time as you has worked out quite well.' Motioning for her to follow, he set off across the yard. 'Someone's got to look after Billy's horses while he's gone and you need some to keep you busy.' He pointed to a row of five stables directly opposite the offices. 'These are going to be your charges. Only two of them are Billy's – June's got the rest. Your other three are pretty new so I thought it would be good for you all to learn the ropes together.'

Frankie's heart began to thud that little bit harder as he spoke. She, Frankie Cooper, would be in charge of five of Aspen Valley's racehorses. Aspen Valley, three-time National Hunt champions from the last five years! They stopped at the first stable. No horse came to greet them and she peered into the darkened box to see its occupant. A silhouette-like figure watched them from the back.

'Ta' Qali, a newbie like yourself.'

When Jack didn't follow up his initial introduction with anything else, Frankie was gripped in a sudden panic. Should she have heard of Ta' Qali? Was he some multiple Grade One winner and Cheltenham favourite?

Trying to appear knowledgeable, she nodded and murmured an indistinct approval. When she ventured a look at Jack, she noticed him frown. Thankfully, it wasn't directed at her. Instead he was regarding the horse. He held out his hand and clicked his tongue. Ta' Qali took a hesitant couple of steps forward and exhaled noisily as the smell of Jack's hand reached his nostrils.

'A bit shy, is he?' Frankie asked.

'Head shy, yes. We're still trying to figure him out. He's just been retired from racing on the flat. We picked him up at the sales.'

The gelding at last ventured forward into the light of day, his long ears flicking like insect antennas. He was black as an oil spill except for a small sprinkling of white hairs on the bridge of his Roman nose, like someone had knocked over the salt cellar. Running a practiced eye over his large nobbly head, long thin neck and sway back, Frankie hesitated to voice her immediate question.

'Can he jump?' He had to have something going for him because it certainly wasn't looks.

'Well, he did when I rattled the bucket behind him.' Jack smiled grimly. 'He's a full-brother to Sequella, the Goodwood and Doncaster Cups winner.'

Frankie did a double-take.

'This is a full-brother to Sequella?' she said, incredulous.

'Not exactly identical, I know. Didn't show much of her talent on the flat either, but he's got the breeding. I just hope he improves as he matures.'

Frankie put out her hand to stroke Ta' Qali's nose. With a start, he threw up his head and backed away into the security of his stable. Jack shook his head again.

'We'll see. I bought him out of my own pocket. I have to find him an owner before the season's out otherwise we're stuffed.'

Frankie shifted from one foot to the other, unsure whether she was included in this conversation anymore.

'Sorry – *stuffed?*' she prompted.

For a moment, he looked at her blankly then gestured to Ta' Qali's reclusive figure.

'Well, he's no good on the flat. If he doesn't take to jumping then I don't know what to do with him. Look at him, he's not exactly going to win any showing classes nor can he be described as a reliable hack because of his nerves.'

Frankie was sure he wasn't implying he would send the horse to the knackers, but a small ball of apprehension gathered in her stomach on Ta' Qali's behalf. Her belief that, like every human, every horse had a calling in life, probably wouldn't be received with much enthusiasm so she kept quiet.

'Next up. This is Twain, one of Billy's lot...'

An hour later, Frankie finished her last stable. She removed her cap and wiped the sweat from her brow. Turning back to the horse tied to the wall, she patted the mare's steel grey shoulder. She'd managed to muck out her other four boxes without having to resort to securing the occupant, but Blue Jean Baby was so restless Frankie had been forced to take defensive action.

'There you go,' she murmured, slipping off the head collar.

The mare shook her head, which quickly became a whole body shake. The shudder unbalanced her and she flung out a foreleg to stop herself falling over. Frankie shook her head. 'I wouldn't have to tie you up if you could just stand quietly and not knock the wheelbarrow over.'

The mare gazed at her with Bambi eyes.

'Don't look at me like that. Twice you knocked it over,' Frankie reprimanded her. 'And it took me twice as long to do your stable since you walked your crap all over the place. What sort of a lady are you?'

'The box-walking type,' a voice said from the stable door.

A young woman, probably only a few years older than she, smiled at Frankie. She held out her hand.

'Hi, I'm June. You must be Frankie.'

Frankie stepped around the wheelbarrow and shook her hand.

'Yes. Nice to meet you.'

'I see you're discovering the charms of Dory here,' June grinned. 'Walks every last dung ball into shreds then tries to help by tipping what you've already collected back out of the wheelbarrow.'

Frankie gave a small uncertain laugh. Had she just spent the past half hour mucking out the wrong horse?

'Um, I thought her name was Blue Jean Baby?'

'Yup. But it's such a mouthful. Dory's her stable name. We took her hurdling last season. Jumped superbly on her first two starts then completely forgot how the game was played next time out. She's not the sharpest knife in the drawer but she's kind.'

'So Dory as in *Finding Nemo* Dory?'

'Yeah. Word of the wise: she's a bit excitable in her work so we usually put her on the horse-walker for twenty minutes beforehand when her box is being mucked out. That way, you kill two birds with one stone instead of her killing the both of you.'

'Thanks, I'll remember that.'

June winked at her.

'And keep an eye out when she's in the paddock. She likes taking herself off on little adventures. Doesn't always remember the way back.'

That earlier feeling of exhilaration at caring for Aspen Valley horses was swiftly losing its appeal.

'Crikey, she sounds high maintenance,' she said.

The stable lass shrugged.

'Just being a mare.'

A rise in voices outside saw Blue Jean Baby aka Dory push past Frankie to see what the fuss was about. A group of lads and lasses had gathered around a corkboard on the wall between the office and the tack room. Sheets of paper attached to the board were ruffled by a gust of damp wind and one of the lads studying it put out a hand to flatten them. Frankie turned to June questioningly.

'The work list,' June explained. 'Best go see who we've got.'

With a quick smile, she left Frankie to finish up.

'I wonder if I'll be riding you, you crazy woman,' Frankie said to Dory.

The prospect was too much for one jittery mare to take. She spun round and tipped the wheelbarrow over once more.

By the time Frankie had reloaded the dirty bedding and deposited it in the muck heap round the back, the corkboard was deserted. Three sheets listed a table of contents of lot numbers, work riders and horses with the occasional alteration. Written in hand down the bottom of the list was herself: Francesca Cooper. Frankie grimaced. She hated the full version of her name. Why her parents had even called her that, she didn't know. It was so girly and besides, she'd always been called Frankie. Alongside her name in lot order were Twain, Dory, Foxtail Lily, Aztec Gold and Ta' Qali.

'Not liking what you see?' a voice behind her spoke up.

Frankie didn't have to turn around to recognise the owner of the silken tone. She ignored Rhys, aware though that her heart rate had stepped up a beat.

'Not until I turn around,' she replied over her shoulder.

She couldn't be certain, but she was pretty sure Rhys almost laughed. Well, maybe laugh was too expressive a term, 'harrumphed'.

'Touché. What have you got?'

Frankie felt the overpowering yet completely pointless need to show off to him.

'A Festival winner in Foxtail Lily and a full-brother to a Goodwood and Doncaster Cup winner; I think I've got a pretty good deal.'

Rhys stepped into her line of sight next to her and peered at the list, his brows knitted together. His collar was turned up against the drizzle, but apart from that he seemed unaware of the weather. Raindrops swept over his cheekbones into the hollows of his gaunt cheeks before riding along the hard line of his jaw and gathering at his chin to take the final plunge to earth.

'Who's your Cup full-brother?' he asked, curiosity stamping out the arrogance in his voice.

'Ta' Qali. His sister was Sequella.'

Rhys looked at her in disbelief.

'That thing?' he said, pointing towards Ta' Qali's stable.

Frankie squared her feet and crossed her arms.

'Yes.' She might not have known Ta' Qali all that long but no one, especially Rhys Bradford, was going to get away with insulting any of her charges.

Rhys threw back his head and laughed. Frankie glared at him.

'I'm sorry but his dam must have cheated,' he chuckled before heading over to the tack room. His walk was offset by a slight limp. 'Good luck with your "good deals",' he flung over his shoulder.

Frankie bit her lip and watched him disappear through the doorway. Her heart was still thudding. It's just because every time you've met him there's been some drama or other, she told herself sternly. It's got nothing to do with the fact that you find those black eyes so compelling or that he has features so flawlessly defined you just want to stroke them. Put those features on a nicer person, then she might be tempted, but while they belonged to Rhys Bradford? No way.

Would those unsettling looks he gives you have the same effect if the person was kinder, the voice in her head questioned? Would that delicately pouting mouth be so captivating if it wasn't always set in that mocking smirk?

'Oh, shut up,' Frankie muttered. With a sigh, she concentrated once more on the corkboard. Who was he riding anyway that made him ridicule her horses?

'Ah, okay.' She felt a fraction less bumptious of her defence. Rhys only had three rides this morning: Romano, a high-class handicap chaser, Virtuoso, a previous Cheltenham Gold Cup winner, and Dexter, another Festival winner. Foxtail Lily's success in the Champion Bumper five years ago hadn't gone down as one of racing's most historical moments, so in comparison, yes, Frankie supposed Rhys did have a reasonable excuse for looking smug.

Jogging along the track aboard Twain towards the main gallop, Frankie forgot about the rain. In front of her, beside her, behind her the famous red anoraks of Aspen Valley Stables burst through the gloom.

Wait until I tell Dad about this, she marvelled. The ceaseless chatter of a dozen riders filled her ears, interrupted only by equine snorts and clarion whinnies. A thin mist draped across the hillside making the all-weather track disappear into the sky. As they neared the gate that led onto the gallop, Frankie studied the leader. Unlike the others, Rhys rode alone, silent, uncommunicative and to make him even more glaringly estranged he wore a black jacket instead of red.

The distant growl of a car engine caught her attention and she watched Jack's silver Land Rover disappear into the mist, bumping over the uneven road up the hill as he prepared to watch his horses train. His words of instruction drifted back to her.

'Twain could do with a confidence booster, so start three back. Apart from Rhys's horse at the front, the rest are just having a canter. So give Twain a push, let him feel like a winner by passing the others. He can be lazy so keep him up to his work. Try be alongside Romano after three furlongs. Then have his head in front by the five. Rhys knows you're to go past so don't worry about it turning into a race.'

That didn't sound too difficult.

Frankie gathered her reins as they swung onto the all-weather surface. Ahead, Rhys was waiting for the entire string to step out before setting off. His horse tossed its head, snatching at the reins and crab-stepping. Sinister in his dark riding outfit and unflinching authority, Rhys at last pulled down his goggles and released his mount. Romano gave a small rear and plunged forward, flicking synthetic sand into the faces of his stablemates.

Twain needed little urging to break into canter. But as she lowered her posture over his withers and asked for more, his response was lethargic. Needles of cold rain stung her cheeks and she took a deep lungful of cold air, knowing this would test her fitness if she was to pass Rhys already flying ten lengths ahead. Scrubbing with her hands and pushing with her body weight, she felt the big-boned chestnut at last begin to lengthen his stride. The horse beside her began to drop back and the quarters of the one in front bunched and released as they climbed the hill.

By the time the three furlong marker whooshed past, Twain wasn't the only one breathing hard. Frank's throat burned dry and just the moist wind offered any relief to Frankie's hot face. Rhys's horse galloped just ahead of them. Frankie again lowered in the saddle, her focus unwavering on the rider before her. Twain's rats' tail-mane whipped her face but she didn't feel it. They were gaining. She glanced across as they drew level with Romano. Hunched over his horse's neck, Rhys tilted his head sideways. A smile twitched his lips.

'Making you work for your money, is he?' he shouted above the rush of wind.

'I wasn't expecting an armchair ride,' Frankie yelled back.

'Well, what are you waiting for?'

Setting her jaw, Frankie pushed for more speed. Out of the mist, the four furlong marker whipped by. She frowned. It *felt* like Twain was giving more. It *felt* like they were galloping faster. Yet still Rhys's leg juddered beside her own. And all the while he sat motionless aboard his horse. Frankie pulled her goggles down around her neck so she could see better. Only then did she notice Rhys letting his reins slip through his gloved fingers.

The bastard! With a renewed intensity, she scrubbed her hands up and down Twain's outstretched neck. She was running out of track to get ahead. Jack's instructions resounded in her mind, muffled by the roaring wind.

'Get his head in front... It won't turn into a race.'

So much for that, she thought furiously.

A growing despair rose inside her as the 5 on the next furlong marker became more distinct. Romano still galloped easily beside Twain. Frankie's chest tightened as she gasped for air. They flashed past the marker. She sagged in her saddle, her muscles thankful for the reprieve. The white boards marking the end of the gallop loomed and pricking his ears, Twain slowed to a ragged trot.

'Not strong enough to get past?' Rhys taunted her.

Anger swelled inside Frankie.

'What?' she cried. 'That was bullshit! You stopped us from going past!'

Rhys pushed his goggles up over the peak of his helmet, revealing his shadowed eyes, goading her, mocking her.

'Such language from a girl.' He smiled as they rode through the top gate onto the path that would lead them back down the hill. 'Because – let's face it – that's what you are: a girl. And sadly, girls just aren't strong enough to be jockeys.'

Frankie opened her mouth to retort but couldn't find anything suitably stinging. Too late, the headlights of Jack's Land Rover cut through the mist and the trainer pulled up next to them. Frankie and Rhys stopped as Jack leaned out of the window.

'This was meant to be a confidence booster for Twain, Frankie. I thought I asked you to go past Rhys, not sit alongside him.'

Here was her opportunity to land Rhys in it, but something made her pause. She looked at Rhys. He raised an expectant eyebrow.

She hesitated. He wanted her to say it. He wanted her to be a tattle-tale, to pass the buck.

'I'm sorry, Jack. I just wasn't able to get past.'

Jack looked miffed and Frankie saw him wrestling to keep his patience.

'Well, don't let it happen again. When I ask you to do something, it's for a reason.'

Frankie hung her head, genuinely sorry. She wondered if Rhys's stunt had caused any lasting damage to Twain's confidence.

'Yes, Jack.'

He turned his attention to the riders behind them, effectively dismissing them. Frankie felt her spirits sink to her heels as she tapped them against Twain's sides.

What a way to start her job at Aspen Valley. So much for the joyful, sparkling career she'd been fantasising about. She'd failed before she'd barely got started. Twain bumped against Romano as they walked by. Rhys stared at Frankie, his expression a mixture of amazement and – dare she say it – *guilt?*

To her relief, none of her remaining lots included Rhys, probably because her mounts weren't of the same calibre as his Festival winners. However, her spirits picked up after her rides on Dory and Ta' Qali. She enjoyed the challenge Dory presented her with. Dory was so narrow it felt to Frankie as if she was balancing on a drum-majorette's baton as she pirouetted all the way to the gallops. Nevertheless, once on the move, the mare was enthusiastic and if anything, a little too keen. Frankie's arms felt of orangutan-lengths (though less hairy) by the time they'd managed to pull up. Jack's nod of approval was enough to bring a smile back to her face and for a short while she forgot about Rhys's foul play.

If her rides could be compared to the Three Bears with Twain being too lazy and Dory being too keen, then Ta' Qali was just right. He didn't pull, he didn't lag, he just cantered up the hill with his long ears wobbling to and fro and his bottom lip flapping then pulled up sweetly at the top.

'You're special, Ta' Qali,' she told him as she unsaddled him in his stable. She ran her hand along his steaming neck and over his swayed back. Ta' Qali shivered. She grinned. 'But boy, are you unfit. Look how you're sweating. What say we give you a few rounds on the horse walker to cool off, eh?'

Grabbing a head collar from outside the door, she went to slip it over the horse's neck. She stepped back in surprise as Ta' Qali threw his head and shied away.

'Sorry, I forgot you were head shy,' she said. With a more gentle approach, she secured the head collar and turned to lead him outside. She gasped as she was met by Rhys standing in the doorway. He held out a simple leather strap looping together a circular metal bit.

'You'll need a Chifney with him,' he said, not quite meeting her eye.

'Don't be ridiculous, he's the quietest horse here.'

Rhys looked at her for a long moment then shrugged.

'Suit yourself.' He dropped the piece of tack on the ground and turned on his heel.

Frankie frowned at his departure. Was this just another taunt to show that girls weren't as strong as the guys? It was an odd way of doing so if it was because surely she and Ta' Qali would just prove him wrong? Pulling on the lead rope, she stepped forward to pick up the anti-rearing bit lying in the straw. A cry slipped from her lips as Ta' Qali reared away from her and the rope burned her palm. His bulk loomed over her, his belly exposed as he rose higher and higher. Instinctively, Frankie side-stepped out of the way of his hooves. When he touched down, she was ready to grab the head collar.

Beneath her firm hold, Ta' Qali trembled. Frankie trembled too. Her knees were weak with fright. It wasn't because he'd reared; she'd had plenty of experience with horses rearing on her. It had been so unexpected though. What had brought it on? She gulped and looked at the Chifney clutched in her hand. Her gaze lifted to the doorway and the dark figure of Rhys Bradford limping away. Her eyes widened. Maybe he *did* have a conscience, after all.

5

That evening, energised by her first day at work, Frankie met Tom outside the Golden Miller. With a quick grin, she linked her arm through his and they entered the pub together. Apart from her father and Seth, she didn't know any other male whom she trusted so completely. He was also the only guy she'd been able to maintain a platonic relationship with without being labelled a cock-tease. Even through their late teens there had been no slip up at any of the parties they had both got hammered at. Tom had moved from London with his elderly parents to Bristol in time to attend sixth form college with Seth. Both crazy about horses, Seth, at five feet eleven, had just snuck under the realistic height restriction for a jump jockey, but Tom, who at seventeen was already six feet tall, settled for the next best career: being a jockey's valet. Now twenty-eight, Tom had thankfully stopped growing and had been Frankie's best friend for the past ten years and flatmate for the last four.

'They used an awful lot of pine to build this place,' Frankie remarked as they approached the vacant bar.

'*Pine*-fully so,' Tom replied. 'Would you like a pine or a half-pine of lager?'

Frankie snorted.

'I think I'll settle for a Pine-a Colada, thanks.'

Once Tom had placed their order with Joey, the smiling barman, they leaned their backs against the bar in comfortable silence.

'I know this place is new and everything, but why do you reckon it's so quiet in here tonight?' Frankie said.

Tom gestured towards a poster on the wall.

'Poker night. Whereas the Plough, I believe, is having a pool tournament tonight.'

'Don't tell Mum. She'll be down here in a flash.'

'A flash or a flush?'

Frankie laughed.

'God, you're full of those homophobe things tonight.'

Tom stared at her.

'Full of *what*?'

'Homophobes – no, hang on, that's not the right word. Homo – words that sound the same but mean different things.'

'Homophones I think you mean.' Tom cleared his throat and scowled at his feet.

'Frankie, there's something I've been meaning to tell you –'

'Hey, Tom!'

The pair looked round as his name was called. Donnie McFarland, Aspen Valley's second jockey, raised a hand in greeting while trying to gather up four drinks. 'Care to join us for some poker? We could use another player at our table.'

'Thanks, but I don't play cards.' He gave Frankie a mischievous grin. 'But Frankie here does.'

'You play poker, Frankie?' Donnie asked, somewhat sceptically.

'What were you going to tell me?'

'It can wait.' He held up a finger when she opened her mouth to object. 'Honestly. Now's not the best time.'

She hesitated again, this time looking at Donnie's dubious expression. Her fortnightly game of Texas Hold 'Em with her mother was hardly hardcore enough to take on a table full of whisky-fuelled testosterone.

'I don't know –'

'Go on, Frankie,' urged Tom. 'You're always saying you want to be treated as an equal.'

Rhys' sexist remarks from that morning flitted through her mind. Squaring her shoulders, she beamed at Donnie.

'Sure I do.'

While Tom remained behind waiting for their cocktails, Frankie followed Donnie round to the poker tables.

'Look who I found lurking by the bar, lads! Frankie's come to join us for some cards.'

Frankie's breath caught in her throat. Lounging in his chair, his dark hair curling over his forehead, Rhys looked up in surprise.

Feeling conspicuous, Frankie wrung her hands then suddenly aware of the image she was projecting, she whipped them down by her sides. Stay cool, she told herself.

'Hello, Rhys,' she said.

'Frankie,' he nodded in solemn greeting. He looked her up and down. 'No need to stand to attention. Take a seat.' Hooking his foot around the chair leg, he pushed it out for her to sit down.

Frankie swallowed and took her place next to him. Where was Tom? She could really do with his moral support right now. Craning her neck to see over the restaurant-bar partition, she could see him chatting to a bored-looking Joey.

Rhys shuffled the cards as Donnie counted out some chips for her.

'I take it you know how to play Hold 'Em?' Rhys asked, raising a flyaway eyebrow.

Frankie smiled sweetly and wiped the sweat from her palms onto her jeans beneath the table.

'You bet.'

Rhys gave a half smile (either that or he had wind).

'Oh, I do.'

Frankie tried not to admire his long strong fingers and toned forearm as he deftly dealt the cards to her, Donnie and the two other men at the table. She was about to pick up her cards when she noticed the others only bend theirs to peek at them. Damn, she hated it when they did that. She could never remember what her cards were if they were always faced down. She took a quick look. Okay, maybe this time it wouldn't matter. She wouldn't get far with a two of spades and seven of diamonds anyway.

Three hands, two folds and a failed bluff later Frankie was regretting her decision to play. With Rhys to her left, she was very aware of him methodically collecting the pot on each occasion. Each time he reached forward to take his winnings the scent of seductive cologne tickled her nostrils. This was not conducive to her game concentration.

As Donnie dealt the next hand, Frankie's heart gave a flutter when she bent her cards back. Two queens! Much the best hand she'd had so far. She glanced up to see how the rest of the table were receiving their cards. The man sitting opposite her, named Carl, pushed out his lower lip sceptically. The other man, Richard, looked preoccupied with snuffling into his handkerchief. On her right, Donnie was smiling coyly. She looked at Rhys. His deadpan expression altered a fraction as he raised an eyebrow at her.

When the betting reached Donnie, he raised the stakes. The crooked smile was still there but Frankie noticed his foot wasn't tapping like it had on the two other occasions he'd had good hands. She decided to take a chance. She re-raised. One by one, each of the players matched her bet. She didn't know whether to be glad or not yet. The first three community cards were turned over and Frankie held her breath. Two threes and a five, giving her two pair. It wasn't the strongest hand but it had potential. Her focus turned to Rhys once more. Was it because she felt he was her most likely opposition or was it because she was finding some bizarre satisfaction in being allowed to study him without coming across as a weirdo? Rhys's eyes, black as coal pits, flitted over each of the players as he made his own assessments. The shadows beneath them and the cheekbones one could base-jump off made him attractive in a haunted-by-demons kind of way. Considering he was a jump jockey, his nose was surprisingly straight in comparison to Donnie's mangled features. His eyes came to rest on her and Frankie felt like she'd been zapped by a live wire.

'Frankie, are you still playing this round?' he asked.

Her attention snapped back to the game, realising that they were waiting on her. Embarrassed, she pushed forward her raised bet.

The fourth community card was turned, revealing a six of clubs. Frankie felt her throat contract and she tried not to swallow. Her two pair was looking vulnerable now. She decided there was nothing for it and raised again. Rhys considered her for a moment then pushed his cards forward in defeat. Frankie felt the world caving in on her as Donnie raised his bet, calling her bluff. She bet again and waited for the fifth and final community card to be turned.

Yes!

She tried to keep the quiet thrill in her stomach under control as the bland features of the queen of hearts looked up at them. A full house! It wasn't the strongest of hands, but it certainly wasn't the weakest. Richard folded, leaving Donnie and Carl to match her bet. With a smile bordering on a smirk, Frankie revealed her hand once the pot was accumulated.

'Fuck it,' Donnie muttered and threw down a straight. Carl's three of a kind came nowhere close.

'Frankie wins with a full house, queens full of threes,' Rhys announced. He gathered the cards and offered them to her. 'And your turn to deal.'

Frankie could almost hear her adrenalin humming as she took the pack. Although her hand had won on merit at the last card, she had bluffed her way through most of that hand. And by the glint of amusement in Rhys's eyes, he knew it.

Tom's arrival coincided with the dealing of the next hand. He drew up a chair and sat just behind Frankie, softly humming Kenny Rogers' *The Gambler*. Frankie peeked at her cards. Eight of diamonds and nine of diamonds. Her pulse quickened and her skin tingled with warmth. Another potentially good hand.

By the first three community cards, Frankie's heart rate was bordering on critical. Already Carl and Richard had folded. And with a ten and a queen amongst the first four community cards both bearing the diamond stamp, she knew she was in a good position. Tom had stopped humming behind her and she wondered if his face might give her game away. She daren't look to check. Both Rhys and Donnie raised their bets. Frankie followed suit. The fifth and final community card was turned and Frankie's heart lurched. She concentrated on keeping her breathing steady as the desired jack of diamonds smirked back at her. There, she had it! Just about the strongest hand in poker. Frankie couldn't remember the last time she'd drawn a straight flush.

She looked at Rhys. He was regarding her thoughtfully. Frankie raised a challenging eyebrow at him. The only thing that could beat her now was if he held a royal flush. She barely noticed when Donnie folded. She was only aware of Rhys's eyes boring into hers as he raised the stakes. She took a deep breath and pushed all her chips forward.

'All in,' she announced.

A ripple of respect flowed from the folded players as they waited for Rhys's response.

'I'll match that,' he murmured. A dangerous twinkle sparked in his eyes. 'Actually, I'll raise that. If it's all right with you, Donnie, I'll stake my next first choice ride when we're in the same race.'

Donnie shrugged.

'Fine by me,' he said.

For a moment, Frankie's confidence wavered. What if he *did* have the king and ace of diamonds needed to complete a royal flush? Oh, well, it was too late to back out now. And what had she lost - a bit of pride and thirty quid?

'I don't have anything else to offer,' she said. 'I can't very well offer you a third string ride.'

A small smile curved Rhys's lips.

'Consider it a bonus, being the new kid and all that.'

Frankie's jaw went slack. He was either the best bluffer in town or he must definitely have a royal flush. She shrugged.

'Okay then.' She turned over her cards. 'A straight flush.'

Rhys's expression flickered in doubt for the first time that evening. He looked at Frankie with an intensity that could put airport security out of work. He flipped over his cards, giving them a cursory glance before looking back at her. Frankie tore her eyes away to look at his cards. A pair of kings, which when combined with the community cards would have given him four of a kind. No wonder he had been so confident. He must have thought she was bluffing her way through as she'd done in the previous round.

'Ah, mate,' Donnie said. 'You're screwed.'

Frankie gulped. If only her mother could see her now! She would be so proud! Frankie couldn't contain the grin which spread across her face. Rhys leaned back in his chair, arms folded, making her wonder if he would honour his 'bonus' bet. Then a flicker of a smile tugged at his mouth. He withdrew his wallet from his pocket, extracted a scrap of paper and picked up a worn-down pencil already on the table. Then he began to write.

"*I, Rhys Bradford, do solemnly swear to surrender my next first choice ride to Frankie Cooper...*"

6

Frankie's first ride for Aspen Valley coincided with Exeter Racecourse's curtain raiser meeting of the season. She had three rides on the card: Aztec Gold in a three mile steeplechase, Asante in a novice hurdle, and Dust Storm – her poker game 'bonus' – in the feature race. With the early October sun bathing the undulating course, she jogged the last two hundred metres of the home stretch, dressed in a thick tracksuit, in an attempt to burn off the extra two pounds she was over.

Feeling like she'd run a marathon, she ducked under the running rail and made her way past the barren grandstand, where only the bookmakers setting up their stands and the busy ground staff were in attendance. Her throbbing pulse had more to do with her ride aboard Aztec Gold in three hours' time than her exertions though. She'd taken a quick peak at the racecard when she'd arrived and had felt a full body flush when she'd seen *her* name alongside Jack Carmichael's. It made her wonder if she'd ever get over working for the king of National Hunt. She knew she wasn't expected to win today, but just by association her forecast odds had shortened into joint fourth favouritism. Naturally, Rhys, riding South of Jericho, was the clear favourite.

She wondered, as she climbed the steps to the weighing room, how he would treat her in this rematch now that they were on the same side, so to speak. Greeting the valets and stewards she recognised, she stepped onto the scales, tensing as she waited for the needle to swing round and settle.

'Urgh. Bloody hell,' she groaned. Despite the energetic run around the course and skipping two meals, she was still one pound over Aztec Gold's featherweight.

'Looks like it's the sauna for you,' Tom said with a wide grin as he passed. Frankie tried to bat him across the head, but he held up the saddles in his arms for protection. He knew how much Frankie detested the sauna. Not only was it energy-sapping but it was also full of naked men. Frankie tried to look on the bright side. They were fit naked men, but naked, nonetheless. Racing might be changing to accommodate female jockeys, but they hadn't gone so far as to give them separate saunas yet.

Neither had they done much in the way of changing rooms, she mused a few moments later. Trying to pull off her sweater and leaning against the bench, she managed to crack her elbow against the opposite wall.

Finally, feeling ever so slightly vulnerable in just a towel, she hazarded her way to the sauna door. With any luck there wouldn't be anyone in there. It was still early, after all.

The first thing that hit her was the hot steam, punching the air out of her lungs. The next was the sudden hush in conversation, like a radio had been turned off. Frankie gulped. Six cocks – no, six *jocks* looked in her direction. Frankie focused hard on looking at their faces. Evan Townsend, Mick Farrelly, Tony O'Hare, Gary Hudson, Donnie McFarland – crikey, usually one would have to subscribe to see things like that – and Rhys Bradford. Frankie faltered. Rhys looked horrified at her entrance and swifter than lightning – Rhys lightning – he'd whipped a towel over his crotch. The ill-concealed discomfort on his face as his haste made him unnecessarily forceful almost made Frankie laugh. Then she realised a woman walking in on a group of naked men and bursting out laughing might not be received with much enthusiasm. Averting her eyes, she hurried over to a space, now just as keenly aware of her own state of undress.

Paranoia and claustrophobia set in. At this rate she'd have lost that wretched pound in thirty seconds. Glancing up beneath her fringe, she noticed Rhys was still the only one to have made an effort to cover up. Where to focus her eyes? Everywhere she looked seemed unnatural. She stared up at the ceiling. Yet still, even if she didn't look at Rhys directly, she was still aware of his toned chest and its sprinkling of black hair, his abdominal muscles disappearing beneath the towel to his groin and the single track of hair from his navel.

She frowned. This is ridiculous, she scolded herself. There's nothing in this room that you haven't seen before – with the exception of perhaps Donnie's donger. You are an adult, not some silly teenager.

'This is a nice surprise, Frankie,' said Donnie, making no attempt at modesty. 'Early bird catches the worm, eh?'

Frankie forced a cool smile onto her lips.

'No worms worth catching in here,' she replied.

To her relief, this was met with raucous laughter. Though she dared not look, she thought it might have even raised a smile from Rhys. With the tension somewhat eased, the conversation she had interrupted resumed.

'And so I say yes,' Welshman, Evan, went on with his story. 'Of course I can look after him for the holidays. He's only fifteen, my nephew. I know some good films the likes of he would enjoy and what have you. Maybe show him the local arcade. So I leave him watching *Toy Story* to go racing at Newton Abbott. When I come home he's on the couch with a girl! At it like rabbits, I tell you! I mean, what do you say to that?'

From the corner Frankie was most aware of, Rhys spoke up.

'How about "have you got any tips"?'

Again, the sauna reverberated with laughter. Even Frankie managed a giggle. She looked at Rhys, impressed that he possessed anything remotely resembling wit. As his compatriots roared, a smile tugged at his mouth, his humour more introverted.

Two hours later, his manner was decidedly reversed as, lining up for the start of the three-mile chase, he bullied his way to the front. Frankie sat astride Aztec Gold, two pounds lighter. The cool breeze had a refreshing effect after her dreaded sauna experience and the weak sun bounced off her psychedelic jockey silks. She felt as if a My Little Pony had thrown up over her. The familiar clench of fear knotted her stomach muscles. Eighteen fences between her and the finish line. Eighteen opportunities to mess up. It wasn't the falling that scared her. It was the split second prior to falling when you knew the inevitable was going to happen.

The field pressed together and jogged towards the start. Frankie found herself being pushed back in the hustle for position. With a snap, the tape whipped back and the horses plunged forward. Frankie hardly had a moment to assess their position before the first of two plain fences was upon them. The early leaders crashed through the top of the jump. In a fluent leap Aztec Gold was over and galloping towards the next. With one such confident jump behind, the thrill which fear had obliterated moments earlier, swelled inside Frankie.

Veering to the right in search of the perfect stride, Aztec Gold bounced over the next like a seasoned hurdler. Riding high in her stirrups, Frankie watched South of Jericho, Rhys's mount, swing the field round the bend. Quickly upon them was the first open ditch. Aztec Gold took off half a stride early. The fear returned. Frankie flung herself forward so as not to impede her mount. Aztec Gold reached over the fence. She breathed a sigh of relief when they touched down safely.

By the time the field had rounded the home turn for the first time, Frankie was still only two from the rear. The crackling commentary floated over to them as they straightened up to face four more fences. Aztec Gold popped over them so neatly they passed two other horses in mid-air.

Frankie felt the rush of the grandstand noise greet her as they passed the winning post and swung away for the final lap of the course. She nudged her mount up alongside Donnie on Aspen Valley's second string. In tandem, they cleared the next. Donnie looked across at her and grinned, his blue gum guard not doing his battle-scarred face any favours. For a moment, Frankie saw only Donger McFarland. The hiss of flying birch as the leaders tackled the next fence brought her sharply back. They hit the jump hard.

With her heart beating that little bit faster, she recovered her position. On their outside, Mick Farrelly was riding his horse along with intent. The second open ditch loomed. Frankie saw her stride and asked Aztec Gold to lengthen. To her right, Donnie was on the same stride. Out of the corner of her eye, she saw Mick, to her left, was half a stride wrong. His horse suddenly veered inwards. Aztec Gold puffed as his opponent rammed his shoulder. Frankie didn't have time to check him. The ditch was under them. Unbalanced, the trio took off together. Frankie felt like the meat in a ham sandwich. Mick's horse bumped them again as they landed and in a domino-effect, Aztec Gold ricocheted into Donnie's horse. Aztec Gold scrambled for a foothold. Donnie and his horse disappeared in a nosedive. Frankie hauled at the reins and threw her weight back to counterbalance her horse's momentum. With relief, she felt him find a level footing and right himself. The bump had knocked the stuffing out of Mick's horse and she saw him stand up in his stirrups in surrender.

Aztec Gold galloped on round the highest point of the course and began the descent down the backstretch. Frankie eyed the three horses in front. Rhys was a good ten lengths clear and, by his immobile posture, looked to be going strong. The jockeys in second and third were lowered over their horses' necks in varying degrees of animation. She might not be able to catch Rhys and South of Jericho, but runner-up would be nice, especially in her first ride for Aspen Valley. But there were another eight jumps to tackle. On a downhill slope the next two fences came fast. Less than a mile to travel and the gap between herself and the third horse began to shorten. Frankie pushed for more. When Aztec Gold jumped flat over the next open ditch, the birch dragged his momentum from him. Maybe she had less horse under her than she'd thought.

As they entered the home straight with only four fences left to take, the third-placed horse was running erratically, a sure sign of exhaustion. The pair overtook them in mid-air three from home. Gritting her teeth, Frankie put her head down and drove Aztec Gold forward for all she was worth. Her chest tightened painfully with the effort. When she steadied for the second last, she saw Rhys well clear. There was no chance they'd catch him unless he fell at the last. The rolling hindquarters of the second-placed horse taunted her four lengths ahead. Yet try as she might, try as Aztec Gold might, they couldn't close the gap.

Aztec Gold jumped awkwardly over the last, his energy reserves teetering on zero. The roar of the crowd urging them home barely registered to Frankie. Far more concerning was the thunder of hooves coming from behind. She ducked her head to look behind. Evan, that of the promiscuous nephew, was making a late bid from the rear of the field.

Frankie knew she couldn't win, second place was also out of her grasp, but she'd be damned if she was going to forfeit third.

'Come on, Aztec!' she tried to yell, but only a croak broke from her burning lungs.

Like a weary climber grasping for higher and higher rope, Evan's horse began to inch up beside them. The horses bumped shoulders. Frankie's toe dug into her opponent's girth. Aztec Gold refused to give way. With one last effort, he lengthened his stride, pulling a nose clear. But with fifty yards still to go, it wasn't enough. Evan's horse pegged them back once more then their momentum carried them past.

As they staggered over the finish line, Frankie slumped in her saddle. For a moment, disappointment dragged her south, more so perhaps because she knew Aztec Gold had given everything. But then the reality hit her. She had just completed her first race as Aspen Valley's jockey and had come fourth! She hadn't fallen off. She hadn't made any terrible blunders. And starting fourth in the betting, they hadn't done any worse than expected. A grin split her face as she pulled up a grateful Aztec Gold. She leaned down, pressing her cheek against the horse's sweaty neck.

'Triumph in defeat, my boy. Triumph in defeat.'

Two more races down the card, Exeter's cheering grandstand loomed on Frankie's left as she urged Dust Storm along the last hundred yards of the run-in. She stood up in her stirrups and punched the air as they galloped past the post, three lengths clear of their nearest rival. She clapped her mount's chestnut neck and whooped in ecstasy. Even though it was only a nondescript handicap hurdle they had won, those three golden words glowed through her body.

They had won.

She had won. And in no small way was it thanks to Rhys. The foggy snorts of the runner-up neared as she pulled Dust Storm up. She turned to see Romulus, Aspen Valley's second string bearing down on them. She looked at his rider, an uneasy feeling gathering in her gut.

Rhys pulled down his goggles. Frankie gulped. Apart from looking exhausted, he looked disgusted – with himself and with her.

Dust Storm changed down to a ragged trot and Rhys and Romulus pulled up alongside. Frankie opened her mouth to say something – she wasn't sure what. To thank him? To apologise? But then Rhys granted her a grudging smile that made Frankie sit down in the saddle with a thud.

'Remind me never to play poker with you again,' he grinned before swinging Romulus towards the track gateway.

Frankie watched him jog away, her body and brain numb. It might have been the shock that he was being so unnaturally gracious in defeat, especially considering Dust Storm should have been his ride. It might equally have been the joy of winning her first race for Aspen Valley. But as Frankie let her horse trot down the chute back to the paddock, she knew in all honesty, that that rare smile – she wouldn't have known he had teeth before if it wasn't for his gum guard – had changed her opinion of Rhys Bradford from this moment onwards.

7

When she opened the front door to her parents' house later that afternoon, she could hear the racing on the lounge television battling for supremacy with the hair dryer in her mother's home salon. She entered the lounge where her father was concentrating hard on listening to the racing presenters discussing the upcoming race. Distracted, Doug Cooper looked up from his armchair.

'Hello, Frankie.' He proffered a whiskery cheek for her to kiss.

She struggled to keep the excitement, which had been bubbling inside her, under wraps. She wanted to appear cool, to wait for him to ask.

'How've you been?' she asked.

Doug grunted and shrugged.

'They're about to jump off in the Arc. You?'

Frankie's shrug was a carbon copy of her father's.

'Pretty good. Bit of a hectic week, I guess. Then of course, racing at Exeter today.'

She sat on the arm of his chair and nonchalantly picked at a scab of mud on her jeans. She stole a discreet glance at Doug, waiting for him to press her for details, but saw he'd returned his attention to the television. Her spirits drooped but she quickly forgave him. The Prix de l'Arc de Triomphe was one of the biggest flat races in Europe and featured high on every racing fan's list of Must Sees. She bit her lip, resisting the urge to interrupt. No, it was no use.

'I won today. For Jack Carmichael – you know, my new boss.'

He gave her a bright smile.

'Well done, honey.'

Frankie sat on tenterhooks, wanting to relay every stride of the race, but equally she wanted an interested audience and Doug's focus had already drifted back to the horses parading in the leafy Longchamp paddock.

'I started at Aspen Valley on Monday. There's over a hundred horses in training there,' she tried again, disgusted with herself for sounding so obnoxious. 'I've got five really nice types to look after.'

'That's nice. Are you enjoying it?'

At last, an unprompted question! Yet contrary to launching into her week's adventures, a shawl of disappointment wrapped around her. Yes, she'd got what she wanted: her father's attention, but she felt cheated that shed almost had to force it out of him.

She shrugged like an insolent teenager.

'Yeah, it's not bad.' Then as she thought about her past week - her race on the gallops against Rhys, Ta' Qali and the Chifney Rhys had given her, the poker game, Dust Storm's win - the excitement returned. 'There's bag loads of quality in the yard. Jack's a master at training. He knows all the horses inside out - well, almost. He says he's still trying to figure out Ta' Qali. He's one of my horses. He's a full-brother to Sequella!'

'Mmm. Sequella's old stablemate Caspian's going to jump off in the Arc in a few minutes. I've got fifty quid on him.'

'Then there's Dory, or rather Blue Jean Baby. She's got a screw loose, but boy, can she jump. Then I've got Foxtail Lily. She won at Cheltenham a few years back. And Twain...' Frankie's voice drifted into the ether. The horses on the television were cantering down to the start and she'd lost Doug again. 'Is Mum downstairs?'

'Yeah, but Mrs Banks is down there too, having her hair done.'

'Oh, maybe not then.' Mrs Banks was lovely but a terrible gossip, and Frankie didn't trust herself to speak in Mrs Banks' presence. 'Me and Dust Storm beat Rhys Bradford today.'

Doug looked up so fast, he nearly gave himself whiplash.

Frankie didn't care how arrogant Rhys was, at least his name had got Doug's attention. In fact, the Arc field were being loaded into the starting stalls and Doug was still staring at her. He even looked a little pale on closer inspection.

'You know Rhys Bradford, right, Dad? He also works at Aspen Valley. He's obviously their first string jockey. He was champion jockey a couple of seasons ago, won the Gold Cup on Virtuoso. Dad, are you okay?'

'Yes, I'm fine,' he replied, abruptly turning back to the television. The race had already started, but Doug didn't appear to be taking any of it in.

Frankie wavered.

'Was it something I said?'

'No, no. I thought Rhys Bradford had retired after he smashed up his leg last year, that's all. But steer clear of him, Frankie. Those Bradfords are bad news.' He sighed wearily and looked over at the mantelpiece above the stone fireplace. Frankie sagged as realisation dawned on her. It wasn't her job or Rhys Bradford or the fact his bet in the Arc appeared to be trapped at the back of the field that was upsetting him. She followed his gaze to the photographs on the mantelpiece. She was in some of them, in family shots, and there was one of her smiling gap-toothed and freckled in her third year school portrait. But the majority of the pictures were of a boy, honey-blond like Frankie, and lanky, always grinning at the camera. There winning the 13.2hh and Under pony race at Ascot; there clearing a sparkling red and white show jump on their old pony, Toffee; there standing with the winning owners when he won his first point to point. Throughout the photos, Seth's boyish good looks matured from skinny seven-year-old to strong twenty-three-year-old. And there the photos abruptly stopped.

'Do you know what else was this week?' Doug asked.

Frankie hung her head and nodded. The thrill of starting at Aspen Valley with all its champions seeped away to be replaced with an acute sense of guilt.

'I didn't forget,' she muttered.

Doug turned to her, his eyes almost accusatory.

'I didn't see any flowers on his grave. Didn't you go see him?'

'Dad, I was busy with the new job. I couldn't get there on the day. I did light a candle for him though.'

'It's just one day a year, Francesca. One day! And you couldn't even find the time to pay your respects to your brother. Seth always made time for you!'

All of a sudden, Frankie felt close to tears.

'He would also understand that I've just been given a massive career boost – the same one that he got before his accident – and that maybe that might take priority.'

Doug stared at her, bewilderment swimming in his eyes.

'Priority over your own brother?'

Frankie looked away. She gave a defensive shrug.

'He's dead. I've visited his grave every anniversary for the past five years. This year I lit a candle. What's the difference?'

An awkward silence fell. Frankie swallowed the lump at the back of her throat, but daren't look at her father in case his hurt triggered the waterworks. With the hairdryer now switched off downstairs, the commentary from the television blared around the house. 'Caspian makes a late charge! He has the lead! He's got it! Caspian wins the Arc de Triomphe! The Epsom Derby and Champion Stakes winner adds *another* Group One to his tally. He must surely clinch the Horse of the Year title with that!' Doug and Frankie sat in stony silence.

'How much did you win?' she asked eventually.

'Two hundred and twenty-five,' he replied without enthusiasm.

'Maybe I should go see Mum,' she began, but her mobile phone vibrating in her pocket stalled her exit. She twisted on the chair arm to retrieve it.

Number withheld.

'Hello?'

'Hello, Frankie? It's Pippa Taylor. Remember me? We met at the Golden Miller.'

'How could I forget?' Frankie gave Doug a brief look then took herself into the kitchen for some privacy.

'I saw you won today. Congratulations! Jack tells me it was only your third ride too.'

'Oh, um, thank you.' A small frown creased Frankie's brow. This was going a bit beyond the call of duty, wasn't it? Yes, she was thrilled she had won a race so soon into her partnership with Aspen Valley, but it wasn't an earth-shattering event for anyone else and certainly didn't warrant her boss' fiancée ringing up. Maybe Pippa was the exception to the rule though, she reconsidered, remembering how Pippa and labouring Emmie had appeared very good friends.

Pippa gave a nervy laugh and Frankie rethought again. Maybe this wasn't the norm. Her blood froze. Was she being fired, but Jack didn't have the balls to do it himself? She *had* fallen off her second ride. These irrational thoughts broke a cold sweat over her body.

'You're probably wondering why I'm ringing,' Pippa said.

'A little, I must admit.' She pushed the kitchen door to. If she was going to get fired she would probably cry and she didn't want her father to witness her tears.

Pippa cleared her throat.

'Do you remember the conversation we had that night at the hospital?' she asked.

Frankie wildly sifted through her memory bank. Most memories of that night involved Emmie howling in pain, Emmie getting stuck in the car and poor Billy getting his head bitten off.

'Er...'

'We were talking about Peace Offering; about the Grand National and your reasons for wanting to ride in it.'

'Oh yes. I said I wanted to win the National for –'

Through the slit in the door, Frankie watched her father slumped in his armchair. The tired lines on his face seemed etched deeper as he mourned the loss of his son once more. How could she ever make him smile again?

'For your father,' Pippa provided. 'And I thought that was a lovely reason – the best, in fact. It's got nothing to do with personal conquest or personal gain. It seems to me everyone wants to win for *themselves*. But you don't. Your reasons are completely unselfish.'

Frankie's cheeks tinged with heat.

'Well, I don't know about that,' she said. 'I mean, there would be some sense of personal achievement.'

'How would you like to ride Peace Offering in the Grand National?'

Frankie's vital organs shut down. Her lungs refused to draw in oxygen. She was sure her already fragile heart had given up the ghost. Her brain couldn't connect basic thought sequences together. Had she heard correctly? She couldn't possibly have.

'Frankie, are you there?'

'Ye-yes, I think so. Sorry, Pippa, could you repeat what you just said? I think I might have misheard you.'

Pippa laughed.

'I said would you like to be Peace Offering's jockey in next year's Grand National?' she said, her voice slow and deliberate.

'Really?' Frankie laughed in joyous disbelief. 'Oh my God, yes! Yes, most definitely I do! Are you sure? No – don't answer that. Oh my God!'

'I watched the racing today. I saw you take a fall. Yet you picked yourself up and dusted yourself off then came back and won the next race. That's a very brave thing to do, in my opinion. And I think you need that to ride in the National.'

Frankie's whirring thoughts barely registered what she was saying.

'You want me to ride Peace Offering in the National?' she squeaked. A sudden thought occurred to her. 'What about Jack? What does he think about this? What about Rhys?'

'Hmm, yeah. Jack and Rhys,' Pippa said evasively. 'Well, I haven't actually told Jack yet. The National's still a few months away. I'm going to wait for the right moment, I think.'

Frankie's spirits sank. Jack would surely overrule Pippa when he discovered what they'd agreed to. Pippa was quick to fill in her despondent silence.

'Peace Offering's my horse though, remember. I'm free to choose whichever jockey I want to ride my horse. Rhys might need to employ someone to polish his trophies every day, but Jack certainly wouldn't have hired you as an Aspen Valley jockey if he didn't think you were good.'

Confidence restored once more, Frankie grinned.

'Oh boy, Pippa. Thank you! Thank you so much!'

Their conversation over, Frankie stared at the kitchen cupboards without seeing them. Her phone lay limp in her hand. Then it hit her. *She was going to ride the favourite in the Grand National.* With a gasp, she burst back into the lounge. Doug looked up, startled.

'I've just been given Peace Offering to ride in the National,' she cried.

Doug blinked at her, his face a mixture of shock, delight and fear.

'The National?' he choked out at last. 'Are you sure?'

'Yes! Isn't it amazing?' Frankie sprinted to the doorway leading to the basement salon and hollered down the stairs, 'Mum! Mum! Come quick!'

'Not the Foxhunters Chase for amateurs?' Doug said. 'You might be getting confused. It's run over the same course, but the National has mostly *professionals* riding in it.'

'No, she definitely said the National. That's the race Peace Offering's favourite for.' Frankie skipped around the room.

'But –'

'What's happened? What's wrong?' Vanessa Cooper clung to the doorframe trying to get her breath back. Her thick dark curls were held back by a bandana reading *"I rocked with Rod – Wembley '78"* and her too tight jeans were unfashionably torn.

'I've been given Peace Offering to ride in the National,' Frankie squeaked. 'Isn't that wonderful?'

Vanessa looked overjoyed and confused at the same time.

'Who's given you a peace offering, darling? That certainly is wonderful!'

'No! Peace Offering, the horse! The favourite!'

'The favourite?' Vanessa echoed in delight. 'I'm so proud of you, Frankie! Come here and give me a hug!'

Frankie ran to her mother, receiving a half-rugby tackle. Finally extricating themselves, they turned to Doug, still sat stonily in his chair.

'Doug, for goodness' sake, congratulate her!'

Frankie laughed.

'Don't worry, Mum. He's just in shock. *I'm* still in shock.'

Doug collected his senses and got to his feet. He held out his arms formally and Frankie fell into them.

'Well done, Frankie. I just hope – I hope...'

So absorbed in the promises and opportunities the future now presented, Frankie didn't register Doug's fixed gaze on the mantelpiece photographs nor what he was trying, but failing, to say.

And none of them registered Mrs Banks stood at the foot of the stairs, her ear upturned to catch all the drama.

8

The following morning, Frankie was welcomed by a mist-cloaked Aspen Valley Stables. Security lights still glowed in the half-light and staff looked ghostly as they trundled wheelbarrows across the yard to muck out their stables. Frankie headed straight for the shed of barrows. She paused, however, as she neared the offices. Beyond the thick white walls she could hear the muffled tone of raised voices.

'She's just an amateur though!' Rhys's voice boomed through Jack's office window loud and very clear.

Frankie wobbled to a stop. She pulled an uneasy face. That sounded ominous. She tip-toed on and let herself into the Reception. The sound of Jack and Rhys's voices were much clearer in here although still muffled. It sounded as if Jack had Rhys in a headlock. She looked questioningly at Kim, Aspen Valley's frighteningly efficient racing secretary. Kim raised her eyebrows and lifted her palms in a *don't-ask-me* gesture.

Frankie didn't need to. Jack's office door was wrenched open. Rhys strode out like a grumpy steam train. She could almost see the smoke huffing from his ears. A second later, his eyes lasered in on her. Frankie began to realise how a first-time matador must feel when faced with an angry bull. She reckoned her red Aspen Valley jacket wasn't helping matters. She took a step backwards. Rhys steamrolled towards her, looking murderous. He stopped a couple of paces away and held up a finger. His black eyes gleamed with rage, his nostrils were flared and his lips were white as he sucked them against his teeth.

Frankie hadn't ever seen anyone so angry. The contrast to the heart-stopping smile he'd given her yesterday was bewildering. Her mouth opened in a mute attempt to say something. It came out as a croak. What was she supposed to say? *Hi Rhys, good weekend? Looking a bit misty on the hills today. Please don't kill me?* Whatever she'd done wrong, she was meant to already be aware of it and she had a strong suspicion Pippa's phone call yesterday might have something to do with it.

The silence mounted as Rhys continued to hold that trembling finger to her face. His chest rose and fell. He didn't appear able to talk either.

The office telephone cut shrilly through the tense air. All three of them jumped. Rhys seemed to come out of whatever battle his emotions had been fighting before. A low growl shook from his throat. Without saying anything, he brushed past a frozen Frankie and slammed the door behind him as he stormed outside. Once she and the furniture had stopped trembling, Kim's polite and professional voice broke the quiet.

'Good morning, Aspen Valley Stables.'

Frankie and Kim's eyes met as the secretary held the phone against her ear without really listening to the caller.

'I'm afraid Mr Carmichael is in a meeting right now. Is it something I can help with?'

Frankie looked at Jack's half-open door and took a deep breath. She gumshoed across the grey carpet and looked into the office. Jack was standing behind his desk with his back to her, looking out of the window. His hands were shoved deep into his pockets and his shoulders were rounded in a reef knot of tension. Frankie tapped on the door. He turned and, seeing who it was, strode towards her, pointing at her. Frankie was glad there was a desk between them.

'You! Just the person I was looking for!'

She swallowed as she ventured into the centre of the room. She'd only been in here twice before and it still felt a little overawing. The desk and surrounding furniture were of a dark heavy wood. Jack's black leather chair lurked like a third presence in the room. Along one wall a wide display case flashed rows of gold, silver and bronze prizes. Judging by the size of the lock attached to it, Frankie felt she was punching way above her weight.

'Is something the matter, Jack?' she said, unable to keep the tremble out of her voice.

Jack stared at her.

'The matter? Yes! You could say that. Something is very *much* the matter!' He swung round the side of the desk and snatched up a newspaper which had been lying folded in a wire tray. He held it up for her to read, giving it a shake for good measure. '*This* is what is the matter.'

The *Racing Post* newspaper looked battered, but as Frankie stepped forward to read it she noticed it was only today's edition. A photograph taking up a good portion of the front page showed her standing up in

Dust Storm's stirrups as she crossed Wincanton's finish line. Her clutched whip was raised in a victory salute. Frankie cringed. She really needed to rethink the colour of her gum guard. That red and yellow one blaring from her hollering mouth just looked grotesque.

In the second that it took her to take this in, her focus travelled to the accompanying headline:

LADY AMATEUR TO RIDE GRAND NATIONAL FAVOURITE

Frankie's heart sank. Something told her the right time to tell Jack that Pippa had spoken of had certainly not yet arrived and that this headline was something of a shock for him. She briefly read the first paragraph.

> *Amateur jockey, Francesca Cooper, had good reason to celebrate yesterday when winning the 2.10 at Wincanton. Despite Dust Storm being just her first winner for the Aspen Valley stable, a close friend to Ms. Cooper confirmed that she has been given the ride on next year's Grand National favourite, Peace Offering (antepost 10/1). Cooper was said to be surprised and overjoyed at this opportunity to become the first lady jockey to win the 173-year-old steeplechase but was not available for comment...*

Ohhhh boy. Frankie blinked at the paper, not quite ready to look up at Jack yet. So she'd guessed right about Rhys's speechless fury. But how on earth had the papers got hold of it so quickly? Did Pippa have a unique sense of humour and this was her idea of a joke? Some people loved breaking dramatic news –

Frankie stopped dead in her miniature analysis of her boss' fiancée. She thought back to that whirlwind moment in her parents' lounge and almost groaned aloud. In her mind's eye, she saw Mrs Banks standing at the foot of the salon stairs, primly touching her new perm, deceptively uninterested. Frankie wanted to kick herself – and Mrs Banks. How could she have been so stupid? She might as well have gone straight to Twitter and saved Mrs Banks the bother.

'Oh, dear,' she said, finally looking up at Jack.

Jack looked at her wildly and shook the paper again to refocus her attention.

'Oh, dear? That's all you have to say? What the hell are they talking about? Have they made it up or have you made it up? Because I certainly don't recall telling you you could ride Peace Offering in the National.'

Frankie bit her lip. Her eyes flittered away from his. His voice, lowered to a thicker, more cutting timbre, was just as terrifying as his shouting. Was she about to land Pippa in the dung heap by telling Jack the truth? Was she about to break up her boss' loving relationship?

'What are they talking about, Frankie?' Jack's voice shook.

'Uh, well, you weren't really meant to find out like this.' She ventured a look at him and saw confusion. 'I only found out about it yesterday, see, when I was visiting my parents. And it came as such a surprise when Pi- when I found out that I kind of got a bit excited and told my parents. Unfortunately, Valerie Banks was also in attendance.'

'Valerie Banks?' Jack looked at her, incredulous. 'You told this bullshit to Valerie 'The Voice' Banks?'

Frankie filled her lungs with air and a healthy dose of courage. There was no way she could keep Pippa out of the firing line.

'It's not bullshit,' she said quietly. 'Pippa rang me after I won yesterday and offered me the ride.'

'Pippa rang you?' Jack echoed. 'My Pippa?' When Frankie nodded, Jack threaded his fingers through his hair. 'What the hell did she think she was doing? And she offered you Peace Offering to ride in the National?'

Frankie nodded. Jack shook his head.

'But *why*?'

Frankie's pride took a sock to the right.

'She said she thought I rode a good race yesterday and that she liked my attitude.'

Jack looked at her, helpless.

'Pippa really went behind my back and did this?'

Her own swirling emotions settled on pity for him. He looked confused, betrayed. This powerful man looked hurt. Frankie gave him her most reassuring smile.

'She was going to tell you –'

'Well, she'd have to eventually, wouldn't she?' he said bitterly.

'She was just waiting for the right time. Her call to me might have been done on the spur of the moment. She wasn't keeping it from you purposefully.'

Jack stood with his hands on his hips, the newspaper still scrunched in one fist. He drew in a ragged breath.

'Like hell she wasn't.' He snatched up his mobile from his desk and jabbed at the keypad.

'Wait, Jack,' Frankie said, reaching out her hands. She could see her boss' relationship swirling down the plughole. 'Don't do this. Look, I don't have to take the ride –'

'Shut up, Frankie. This is between me and Pippa,' he growled, holding the phone to his ear.

The office was suddenly filled with Puccini's *O Mio Babbino Caro*. They both looked up in surprise. Pippa stood at the door, holding up her offending mobile. Jack's face turned an angry red. He slammed down the phone and Maria Callas's melody was cut short.

'What the hell is going on?' he said striding over to her.

Pippa smiled apologetically at both of them.

'Can I get you some chamomile tea, Jack?' she said.

Jack, in the process of closing the door, slammed it instead. The display cabinet rattled.

'Fuck's sake, Pippa! Don't patronise me!' he shouted.

Frankie quailed and inadvertently took a step backwards. Pippa, on the other hand, seemed to rise to his challenge.

'Then calm yourself down. We're not going to discuss this with you roaring your head off.'

Jack glared at Pippa, every muscle in his body straining.

Oh God, shuddered Frankie. He's going to break up with her and it's going to be my fault. Then in wide-eyed fascination she watched Pippa's handling of Jack's temper. All she did was stand and wait, returning Jack's glare but with a softer, more patient look.

At last Jack exhaled, the vein in his neck sunk back and his body visibly relaxed.

'Thank you,' Pippa whispered. She took Jack's hand in both of hers and kissed his palm.

'Frankie, please can you give us a couple of minutes?' Jack said.

'Of course,' Frankie said, already halfway to the door.

'No. Wait,' intervened Pippa. 'Sorry, but I dragged Frankie into this. She should stay.'

'Really, I don't mind waiting out-' She hesitated at Pippa's meaningful look. 'Or I could just wait here.'

'Let's all sit down, shall we?' Pippa suggested. She wheeled Jack's chair from behind his desk and positioned it next to the two visitors' chairs. Frankie sat in the chair furthest away from Jack. The trainer remained standing.

'Jack?' Pippa prompted gently.

Jack swallowed and took his seat.

'What are you doing here?' Jack said. 'How did you know I knew?'

'I got a call from Emmie, who'd got a call from Billy. He'd seen the headlines and heard you shouting. Wasn't what he was expecting on his first day back at work, I can tell you.'

Jack leaned his elbows on his thighs and looked at Pippa, bewildered.

'Why did you keep this from me?'

'Jack, I love you. And crazy as I might be, I love your temperament too -'

'I'm not a fucking horse -'

'I know you can get very upset sometimes and I knew this - er - *piece of information*, might upset you. So I was just trying to protect you.'

Jack looked at her in disbelief, his brow furrowed as he squinted at her.

'Protect me? From who? You?'

Pippa looked guilty.

'I guess so.'

'Well, it's madness. Frankie's already said she isn't going to take the ride.'

Frankie opened her mouth and shut it again.

'I heard that,' Pippa said drily. 'She only said it because she thought you were about to kill me.'

Jack looked at Frankie, offended. Frankie shifted uneasily in her seat. She'd so much rather be shovelling horse shit right now.

'Well, maybe not *kill*, but I thought your, um, relationship might be in danger.'

Jack averted his eyes, darting a wary look at Pippa. He hung his head and massaged his temples with his thumbs.

'Can somebody explain to me why the hell Peace Offering now has a different jockey? And don't go giving me some cock and bull story about your attitude, Frankie. You're a nice girl, we know that. Nice people don't win the National though. No offence, but Rhys is a better and more experienced rider than you are right now.'

'Didn't Frankie beat Rhys yesterday?' Pippa said.

'Yes,' Jack answered patiently, 'and she did ride a good race. But some might argue that Rhys rode a *better* race getting Romulus to finish second. Come on, Pippa. You're not daft when it comes to racing. You must know Peace Offering has more chance of winning the National with Rhys aboard.'

For a moment, Frankie's pride cringed. Her cheeks flamed red with humiliation, but Jack didn't appear to notice.

'There must be something you're not telling me here. Is it Rhys? Have you got something against him?'

'No,' Pippa said. Jack gave her a suspicious sidelong look. 'Okay, so he's not my favourite person, but that's not the reason I jocked him off. And to be honest, what God-given right does he have to ride Peace Offering?'

'He's Aspen Valley's first jockey,' Jack said through gritted teeth. 'It's his job to ride Peace Offering.'

Pippa sighed.

'Whatever. Rhys isn't the reason.'

'Then what is?'

Jack's voice, softer and more searching, made Frankie realise just how distressed this was making him. She swallowed. She knew she couldn't let Pippa fight her corner by herself.

'She – Pippa also said she liked my reasons for wanting to win the National,' she said reluctantly.

'What? Don't you have the same reasons as every other jockey? What reason could possibly top the one that reads *Champion jockey determined to win after ten years trying?*'

'I do want to win like every other jockey – at least I think I do. But you know my father was a jockey. He never won it. And I want to do it for him.'

'That's all very touching, Frankie, but the National is a hard race. There is no room for error or sentimentality. Do *you* think you could win the National?'

Frankie hesitated. With the question put so bluntly, she forced herself to look at the reality rather than the dream. Okay, she wasn't terribly experienced. Okay, this would be her first attempt at the Aintree fences.

It would be a pretty big ask for her to win on her debut. And okay, of course, she was female. Apparently, women were at a disadvantage being of the "weaker sex" as it took a man's strength to haul a horse around a steeplechase course.

She lifted her chin.

'Yes, I think I could.'

Jack looked unconvinced.

'The National is still six months away. I can get fitter, stronger,' Frankie said.

'And what she lacks in experience now she can make up for during the lead up,' Pippa said, taking up the case.

Frankie nodded, buoyed by Pippa's support.

'Given the right horse and a bit of luck, I don't see why I shouldn't have a chance of winning.'

'Come on, Jack,' Pippa urged. 'One chance, that's all we're asking.'

Jack looked from one to the other, reluctant defeat creeping into his eyes.

'You'll change my world around,' Frankie whispered.

'I thought I'd already done that by giving you the job here,' Jack muttered.

Whatever this was code for, Pippa interpreted it as favourable. She leapt to her feet and threw her arms round Jack. Jack accepted her kisses, a reluctant smile breaking as he cradled Pippa in his arms.

'Okay, Pippa. Okay, Frankie. You win.'

Frankie felt like kissing him as well, but managed to contain her joy to a beaming smile.

'Thank you. I won't let you down.'

Jack shook his head.

'Don't make those sorts of promises. The National's not as straight forward as that.' He budged Pippa to the side of his lap and pointed a finger at Frankie. 'But I do expect you to make peace with Rhys. He's just been given one of the most public humiliations of his career thanks to your girls' stunt.'

Frankie nodded, absorbing just what she'd done to Rhys. Guilt wrapped around her.

'I'll make it up to him,' she said, really meaning it.

'Okay, then. Go on, you've got horses to muck out and ride and you're already late.'

*

That night, Frankie lay back against her pillows. A rumbling ball of soft fur, otherwise known as Atticus Finch, purred in her ear. The reflection from her dim bedside lamp danced over the framed photograph she cradled in her fingers. Tenderly, she traced the horse and rider in the picture and returned the smile Seth directed at the camera. He was heading a string of work riders, lolling confidently in his saddle with one hand on his thigh. Frankie couldn't remember who'd given her the photo or who'd taken it, but it summed up Seth beautifully. A leader, confident, laid back, always with a friendly smile.

'I wish you were here for all this, Seth,' she whispered. 'It's been such a whirlwind – or a Dust Storm. When we won... it was so much more than a race. We'd won for Aspen Valley.' She smiled at the memory then shook her head in wonder. 'I remember when you got the job there first. I thought my ribs were going to break, you hugged me so hard.' Frankie tilted the frame so the light no longer reflected off the glass and studied it again. All the work riders were wearing Aspen Valley jackets except for one further back. Her gaze travelled past the photograph to her open wardrobe where her own red jacket hung. She looked back at Seth's smiling face. 'It's insane how things can change so suddenly. Fate has weird ways of guiding our lives. I'm there now. Just how you wanted to be. Just how you *were*. And I'm riding in the Grand National. How crazy is that?'

It occurred to her for the first time to study the faces of the other six or seven riders in the picture. Now that she was at Aspen Valley, she might recognise some. The rider immediately to Seth's left Frankie could now name as June. The two behind were unfamiliar and the third was looking down so she couldn't see his face. The others further back were out of focus so Frankie had to squint to see their faces. She looked at the rider wearing a black jacket instead of a red one. His blurry features were in shadow, making him harder to identify. Frankie's jaw slackened. She stared at the photograph for a long moment before replacing it on her bedside table with a shaking hand. She flicked off her lamp and let her head fall back. Atticus Finch extended a foreleg, spreading his paw pads in an almighty stretch before flopping it across her collarbone. She stared at the ceiling and gave a short laugh of disbelief. She wonder what Rhys would have to say if she told him she'd had a photograph of him beside her bed for the past five years.

9

The cold north wind that had arrived over the weekend continued to gnaw at the yard's brickwork over the next few days. With all her lots ridden, fed and mucked out, Frankie joined a cluster of staff gathered in the tack room. She turned over a bucket and sat beside June, gratefully accepting the cup of Thermos tea she was handed.

'You've been the talk of the town this week,' June winked.

Frankie blushed. Now that reality had begun to reassert, her National revelation was becoming a bit of an embarrassment. Thrilled as she was to have the ride, she wasn't particularly proud now of *how* she'd got it.

'The news wasn't meant to be broken quite so soon or in such a manner.'

'To hell with that. What better way, I say. It's not every day you get given the ride on the National favourite.'

Frankie stared at the milky liquid in her mug, cupping her fingers around the china to absorb as much heat as possible.

'I-I know, but still,' she stammered. 'It wasn't very fair on Jack or Rhys.'

'You're not feeling sorry for Rhys, are you?' June said.

Another member of staff leaned in.

'Not sorry enough to give the ride back.'

The room was filled with everyone's laughter – everyone's, that is, except for Frankie's. She smiled politely. The door opened, letting in a gust of biting air and extinguishing the laughter. Rhys stood, his hand clenched on the doorknob. He faltered as all eyes came to rest on him. Frankie's heart skipped a beat.

'You want some tea, Rhys?' someone eventually said.

His eyes flickered from face to face, his brows dipping when he passed over Frankie. He shook his head and gestured to a metal box strewn with odd pieces of tack and riding gear.

'Pass me a whip, will you.'

With a deft hand, he caught the item as it was tossed to him then turned on his heel and walked back into the cold.

'My pleasure,' someone muttered.

Frankie didn't know what to think. Was it because she felt guilty at so publically humiliating him or was it that lingering sweet spot she harboured that made her feel compassion for him? She took a gulp of tea which burnt her throat then handed her mug to June.

'Be back in a sec.'

Rhys was headed for the car park, his habitual limp buffeted further by the wind. Frankie ran after him.

'Rhys!'

He looked behind then seeing who it was, shook his head and carried on walking. His black Audi's lights flashed as he beeped open the locks.

'Rhys, wait!' Even when she'd caught up to him, he still continued on, his head down, hands thrust deep into his black jacket pockets. 'Just stop for a moment –'

'Why, Frankie?' he said, suddenly turning on her. 'Why should I waste my time listening to anything you have to say?'

She frowned at him.

'I'm sorry, okay? You weren't meant to find out through the papers. I didn't mean to humiliate you.'

'You've no idea, do you?' He shook his head. 'You think that all that's happened is a little embarrassing blip, don't you?'

'No – I mean, I don't know. It could be just a blip if you allow it.'

'This isn't just a blip, Frankie! This is the National! And I've been jocked off by some new upstart – some girl!'

'Oh, so it wouldn't be so bad if I was a guy, is that it?'

Rhys' eyes glittered as he glared at her.

'You want the truth? No, it wouldn't be so bad if you were a guy. It wouldn't make it much better, but there you go. That's what you want this to be about, don't you? You want to blame it on sexism, because sexism is such an easy shield to hide behind. When you fuck everything up, you can just hold up your hands and say "Oops, silly me. It's only because I'm a girl." And the crazy thing is everyone believes you. To the extent that when I get jocked off in favour of a girl, it makes me look like a completely useless wanker.'

Frankie ground her teeth and matched his glare.

'Well, you're not doing much to dispel that image right now. I came over to apologise.'

'Don't apologise.' He brushed past her and she hurried to keep pace. 'I don't want your apologies. I don't want your pity. What good is it to me?'

'I don't want you to hate me, Rhys!'

Rhys opened the door to his car.

'You should've thought of that before you took my ride then, shouldn't you? You can't have your cake and eat it.'

He got in and slammed the door, effectively ending their conversation. Frankie kicked the gravel against his tyre and turned to walk back. She heard the Audi fishtail behind her before the wind carried a cloud of dust over her head.

At dusk that evening, Frankie pulled up outside the narrow Victorian house in Helensvale she shared with Tom. Noticing all their neighbours had their bins out reminded her tomorrow was collection day so she squeezed through the side gate to the back of the house to retrieve theirs. She could never remember if it was black or blue bin day and usually relied on Tom to sort those things out. Taking the rubbish out was a man's responsibility, after all, wasn't it?

No, she told herself sternly. She remembered Rhys' earlier words and repeated her mantra that she couldn't fall back on feminism if she wanted to be a jockey. In a man's world, you had to act manly. She let herself in through the backdoor into the kitchen to get the bin bag still in use. Tom was sat in the dark at their small breakfast table, the light from his laptop illuminating his face. He nearly fell off his chair when, in a false baritone, Frankie yelled,

'Hi honey. I'm home!'

'Jesus, Frankie! You scared the life out of me.'

Frankie flicked the light switch and Tom shied away from the brightness. She took his wrist and felt his pulse.

'No, you're still alive. What are you doing sitting in the dark?' She peered down at the laptop screen but Tom slammed it shut before she could read anything.

'Nothing important. I just lost track of time.' He got up and put the kettle on.

'Tea?'

Frankie shook her head.

'No, thanks. I'm going to take the rubbish out.'

Instead, she reached into an overhead cupboard and removed a bottle of cider vinegar. It wasn't the rubbish she had been referring to but she knew it tasted just as unappetising. After mixing a small measure with water, she pinched her nostrils shut and downed the liquid. Her taste buds cringed away from the vile taste and she had to concentrate hard on controlling her gag reflex.

'Bleurgh,' she said, wiping her mouth with her sleeve. 'That is so rank.'

Tom shook his head.

'That stuff will rot your teeth,' he informed her.

Frankie shrugged.

'What do I need teeth for? I don't eat food.'

'All this wasting can't be good for you.'

'Sure, but at least with this stuff I do get to have the occasional meal. It breaks it up faster.'

A meowing from the doorway stopped her and she squatted down to greet the fluffy grey cat that sauntered in.

'Hello, Atticus, my darling,' she cooed. 'How are you?'

Atticus arched his knobbly back as she stroked him and wound himself through her legs.

Starving! he wailed. He fixed Frankie with pleading yellow eyes and she obediently stood up to get him some cat food.

'He's lying,' Tom said, plopping a tea bag into his mug. 'He ate most of my spaghetti bolognaise and he's had his own dinner.'

Atticus Finch gave Tom a resentful look and flicked his tail at him.

'Really, Atticus,' Frankie scolded. 'You mustn't lie like that. Do you think cats are the only animals apart from humans that consciously lie?'

'Wouldn't surprise me,' Tom replied. 'I don't know why you dote on him so much. He's such a grumpy bugger.'

'He's old,' she argued. She turned back to the cat who was still looking at her hopefully. 'Old men are allowed to be grumpy, aren't they? Yes, they *are*. Yes, they *are*. Yes, they –'

'How's work going? Everyone was talking about you at Warwick today.'

Frankie shrugged.

'The usual – had a fight with Rhys, jumped Ta' Qali over a couple of crossbars, Jack's pleased with me, Rhys hates me.'

'I wouldn't take it personally. Rhys hates everyone.'

'Yes, but it's usually passively that he dislikes everyone. There was nothing passive about the way he was talking to me this morning.'

'What did he say?'

'He jumped down my throat when I tried to apologise to him. Said I should man up.'

'Is that why you're taking the rubbish out?'

'Exactly.'

'Wow. Maybe we should organise some more of these chats with Rhys.'

'Very funny.' Absently, she watched Atticus flounce out of the room, shooting feline V-signs at his humans with his tail. His dramatics didn't register with her. 'Don't you think he's being unfair?'

'Frankie, you did jock the guy off his best chance in the Grand National.'

'Yeah, but – it wasn't like I was gunning for his ride right for the beginning. I was just as shocked as anyone when Pippa called me. Dad took ages to recover from it.'

'But it'll be worth it, won't it?'

Frankie gave him a dubious look.

'Truth be told, I don't know. Rhys looks like he wants to kill me the whole time, and Dad doesn't appear all that ecstatic about it either. You would think he would be considering I'm doing this for him in a way.'

'Does he know you're doing it for him?'

'Yeah. Well, I think he does. He must surely do. Yet he could barely raise a smile when I said I got the ride.'

'He's an old man. Didn't you say old men were allowed to be grumpy?'

Frankie pouted. Tom wasn't taking her seriously.

'He's not that old. He's only about fifty-five or something.'

'You can't blame your father too much, Frankie. Wasn't it Seth's anniversary last week too? You know he always goes through a dip at this time. You not putting flowers on his grave might have just aggravated things for him.'

'Tom, you're meant to be on my side,' Frankie reminded him, annoyance creeping up on her. So far he had defended Rhys's corner and her father's. What about hers?

'I know and I am. I just think you should give him a break.'

'But what about my job at Aspen Valley? He must surely realise how momentous that is!'

'Yes, and you've got plenty of time to hog the limelight.'

'Tom!' Frankie gasped, shock and indignation rising in her voice.

'What? All I know is that you've been given this once in a lifetime opportunity and you haven't stopped complaining about it since you've stepped through the door.'

'I have not! You asked me how work was. I had a fight with Rhys, okay? Did you want me to lie?' She glared at Tom.

Tom glared back.

'I thought you were going to take the rubbish out?' he said finally.

Frankie thumped her glass down on the table and ripped the bin liner out of the bin. She held it open, ignoring the whoosh of gag-inducing smells and raised a challenging eyebrow at Tom.

'Care to step inside?' she said.

Tom clicked his tongue and, snatching up his laptop, stomped out of the room. With vicious tugs, which ended up splitting the seam on the bag, Frankie stomped in the opposite direction.

Angry and hurt, she dumped the rubbish bag into the wheelie bin and dragged it down the path. She never fought with Tom. He was always so easy-going. Nothing ever irked him. Ever since Pippa's phone call she seemed to be alienating everyone she cared about. Not that she cared for Rhys with the same affection that she did Tom - it was more of a physical affection - but nonetheless, it wasn't fun when your crush hated your guts.

She wrestled the bin through the cramped gateway in the dark and wheeled it into position at the front of the house. She paused with her hands still on the plastic handles, gazing out over the small green opposite the house. A yellow light illuminated the deserted skateboard ramps and swings beyond the bushes. Maybe she was being too self-involved. Maybe Doug was upset with her because she now had the job originally intended for his son.

She thought of Seth and immediately felt guilty.

'I do miss you,' she whispered into the silence. He had always bolstered her confidence. He'd never turned his nose up because she was a girl. Frankie acknowledged she probably wouldn't be a jockey if it hadn't been for Seth. She exhaled, the cold autumnal air clouding into foggy vapour in front of her. She suddenly felt very alone.

Just as suddenly, it was gone as she noticed a solitary figure walking a dog across the shadowy green. The dog scampered ahead, bounding onto the skateboard ramp and thirstily lapping at the puddle gathered at the base. Its owner followed at a slower pace, a slight limp in his step, his hands thrust into his pockets.

Frankie stiffened. Even before he stepped into the glow of the street lamp, she already recognised Rhys. She edged backwards, careful not to make a sound. But such was her unfamiliarity with putting the bins out, she forgot about the abandoned flowerpots lined up against the gate. Frankie registered ice cold water as she stepped in one of the pots before she crashed to the floor. Rhys stopped in his tracks. Frankie dived for cover behind the wheelie bins.

Heart thumping, she peeped through the gap between them. Rhys was looking her way. She whipped out of sight again and sat with her back against the bin, uncomfortably aware of cold water now seeping through her jeans. How, she wondered, could her life have been so pleasantly Rhys Bradford-free for twenty-three whole years yet now he was on her radar wherever she bloody went?

10

Peace Offering broke into a lethargic canter and Frankie flapped her legs against his ribs. She was finding the thrill of riding the Grand National favourite slowly being sweated out of her. With the Becher Chase, the stage for her mount's seasonal reappearance, less than a fortnight away, the Aspen Valley team were working hard on getting their performer fit. Jack quizzed Frankie more thoroughly about the feel she got from each ride on him than he did about any of her other horses and he checked him over after each gallop. Frankie wondered if this special attention was because Peace Offering was the Grand National favourite or because Peace Offering belonged to his future wife. Maybe it was a bit of both. All she knew was that Virtuoso, their antepost favourite to win another Cheltenham Gold Cup, barely got a look in.

'Come on, you lazy bugger,' she muttered as Peace Offering threatened to slow to a trot.

'Keep him up to his work, Frankie!' Jack yelled from the middle of the schooling paddock.

Uncomfortably aware of Rhys watching from the fence Frankie obediently kicked again and slapped the horse's bay neck. Peace Offering flicked his ears and carried his head awkwardly. Around the paddock's outside lane, they approached the first schooling fence. Peace Offering was lagging so badly they were practically beneath the fence before he took off. He scraped through the brush and only another slap from Frankie on the other side stopped him from breaking into a trot.

Frankie gritted her teeth, aware that the rest of the small string was being held up because of them.

'Come on, wake up!' She booted him forward, hearing the swish of Peace Offering's tail lashing the moist air. The next fence beckoned. 'A big one this time, come on. Give it some air.' She thrust with her hips, shovelled with her shoulders, scrubbed with her fists. Peace Offering grudgingly lengthened his stride, but still decided to put a short one in before take-off.

Jack called them over once the exercise was finished. Frankie couldn't quite meet his eyes as they halted beside him. The trainer's damp jacket collar was rucked up around his neck and his nose was red with cold. Without a word, he parted Peace Offering's lips to inspect his gums. He felt the horse's pulse under his elbow for a few seconds then stood back and looked up at Frankie.

'Did it feel as bad as it looked?'

Frankie looked down at her gloved hands and nodded. There was no point in lying.

'Maybe he's just having an off-day,' Jack muttered. 'Horses get them just as much as we do.'

Frankie didn't like to say Peace Offering was having more of an off-month than day. If he was a person, his employers would be sending him off to the company shrink to talk through his problems.

'I'll get the vet to come out and check him over,' Jack continued. 'He might be running a temperature. Maybe he's picked up a low-grade virus or something.'

'Maybe,' Frankie agreed. 'Or he might be finding it hard to get fit this season.'

Jack sighed.

'He's still only nine though. Granted, he'll be ten in the New Year, but it's not like he's some old codger.' He thrust his hands into his pockets and frowned at Peace Offering. The horse tossed his head and watched the rest of his string walk away from the paddock. 'We'll see what Warnock has to say first. Who have you got next?'

'Ta' Qali.'

'Good. I want to see how he goes. I want to give him a run when we go up to Aintree.'

Frankie's foot slipped out of the stirrup. She stared at Jack.

'On Becher Chase Saturday?'

'Well, he won't be in the Becher Chase obviously. There's a good novice hurdle the same day.'

Frankie tried not to show her doubt. She was quickly falling in love with Ta' Qali. He might have a terrible stable manner, but he was an angel to ride. Having said that, he was still only learning the ropes.

'Ta' Qali's a smart horse, Frankie. You and him have been coming along great in the school. He's ready to run.'

Frankie gulped. She didn't like to question Jack...

'But at Aintree?' she said, her voice shrinking.

Jack gave her a grim smile.

'I know. Not ideal. There are some easier races at Uttoxeter the same day. But you, Rhys and Donnie will have a full day already. Running him in the novice hurdle at Aintree is the only way Rhys will get to ride him.'

Frankie's heart took on water. She knew it shouldn't, but she'd dared to hope that since Ta' Qali was her responsibility at home that it would remain so at the races too. The reality was that Rhys – and Donnie, for that matter – would get first choice for every ride in the stable regardless of who looked after it. Unless she beat him at poker again, that is.

She chanced a look at Rhys, standing slack-hipped with his arms resting on the fence. Dark eyes, indistinguishable beneath his brows, regarded her right back. Frankie quickly dropped her gaze.

'Right, get this boy back to his stable,' Jack said, giving Peace Offering a resigned pat. 'Standing around in the cold won't be doing him any good if he's under the weather.'

His words ran through her head as she walked Peace Offering through the mist and back to the stables alone. She tried to tell herself he was right. He was a training genius, after all. He must be right. Frankie didn't know why she couldn't completely believe him though. No matter how many excuses she and Jack came up with – viruses, fitness, off-days – she knew it was something else. Something quite simple really. Something which only a rider can distinguish by the feel they get when astride. It wasn't anything complicated or life-threatening –

Catching Rhys' eye, she gulped. His lithe body exuded a predatory stillness. His watchful eyes followed her passage past him. Very subtly he tilted his head, his manner curious. A shiver stole over Frankie. That barely perceptible movement warned her he had more than an inkling of what was going through her mind.

11

Bonnie Tyler was cut short partial-eclipse of the heart in the car park of Helensvale Community Centre where Frankie helped out with the local Girl Guides group. Cursing as she nearly turned her ankle in a shadowed pothole, Frankie stumbled in the dark towards the gothic wooden entrance doors. She winced as the the door gave its best haunted house impression when she pushed it open. The shift and shuffle of two dozen starched uniforms turned to watch her late arrival and she raised her hand in a quick apology. She hurried across the parquet flooring to take her seat beside Victoria, a fellow Guider in Charge. Satisfied that she wasn't anyone more exciting, the semi-circle of girls turned back to the woman addressing them.

'You're late,' Victoria hissed. 'What kind of example are you setting?'

'I know,' Frankie whispered into her shoulder. 'What have I missed?'

'Just Mrs Vickers from the council talking about careers advice. She makes shifting paperwork sound like Disneyland. Lying cow.'

'Well, we don't want to dash their dreams just yet.'

'Where've you been anyway?'

'Got held up at work Oh, look sharp, Queen Bee's giving us the eagle eye.'

Frankie and Victoria straightened in their plastic chairs as Bronwyn, the matriarch of Guides in Charge frowned in their direction. The end of Mrs Vickers' speech was received with polite applause from the Guides apart from Harriet and Mischa who were too busy plaiting each other's hair. Bronwyn got up and thanked Mrs Vickers for sharing her knowledge.

'Now girls, if you'll get into your patrols, we'll start on tonight's Go For It activities: the GFI Top Job!'

The small community hall was filled with girlish chatter and giggles as they all grouped together. Frankie noticed an unfamiliar girl standing uncertainly at the back. She was tall for her age, which Frankie estimated to be no more than thirteen, with lank brown hair and round shoulders.

'Who's that?' she asked Victoria, careful not to point.

'New girl. Cassa Preston. Just moved here from Norfolk with her mum. Parents were in a sticky divorce. Mum's a nurse, father's a doctor.'

'Looks like Cassa's the casualty.'

'I've put her in Starfish Patrol. Her mum's here as well acting as a helper.' Victoria motioned to a woman with coifed blonde hair talking with Bronwyn.

'Right. I'll go see to Cassa then.'

Frankie approached the girl with a welcoming smile. The poor thing looked like she'd just stepped into a snake pit.

'Cassa?'

Cassa gulped and nodded.

'Hi, I'm Frankie. It's great that you're able to join us. Have you been to Guides before?'

'Not really,' she said, looking at her feet.

'Okay. Well, I bet you're going to have lots of fun here. Have you heard of Go For Its before? They're like badges except bigger.'

Cassa mumbled something inaudible. Frankie put her hand on Cassa's hunched shoulder.

'The Go For It we're starting tonight is Top Job so we all get to discuss what we want to do in the future and do lots of fun activities. Come meet the rest of your patrol. You're in Starfish and the other girls are really nice so you don't need to be nervous.'

Cassa attempted a smile and let Frankie steer her towards a huddle of five girls aged between ten and fourteen.

'Hi Frankie!' they chorused.

'I saw you sneak in late,' one said, triggering giggles from the others.

'Thanks for that, Harriet. I do like your hair in plaits. Did your mum do them for you?'

Harriett blushed to her roots and the patrol snorted.

'Let's get started. Everyone, this is Cassa. Cassa, this is Harriet, Mischa, Louise, Charlotte and Tammy.'

Cassa gave an awkward wave and seemed to shrink even further into her uniform.

The patrol sat down and waited for Frankie to read out their first activity. Frankie flicked through the sheets she had hastily printed off before coming out tonight.

'Okay, first of all, what do you guys want to be when you leave school?'

Eleven-year-old Charlotte's hand shot up.

'A vampire,' she said, beaming at Frankie.

Frankie narrowed her eyes, trying to decide if she was being serious or not.

'You can't be a vampire, Charlotte,' Mischa said.

Frankie smiled at the wizened knowledge of their oldest patrol member. 'How are you going to make any money? Being a vampire isn't a *career*, silly. It's a fact of life.'

Frankie rethought her judgement of Mischa.

'Charlotte, vampires aren't real,' she said.

Charlotte's lower lip sagged like a pink slug.

'I want to be a vampire.'

'But –' Frankie hesitated when she saw Charlotte's lip quiver. 'Okay, we'll let it slide for now. Who else?'

'I want to be a chef,' Harriet piped up.

Thank God, an achievable career prospect.

'Lovely, Harriet! Do you like cooking?'

Harriet scrunched up her nose.

'It's okay, I guess. I want to be a TV chef like Gino.'

Frankie felt a twinge of embarrassment that this was Cassa's introduction to the apparently delusional Helensvale Girl Guides group.

'Fine. Louise?'

Louise transferred a boiled sweet from one cheek pouch to the other.

'A fashion designer.'

'That sounds exciting. Why?'

'Because clothes are so expensive in the shops. If I designed my own then I can get a discount on them when Mum and I go shopping at Debenhams.'

Frankie considered pointing out the obvious flaw in Louise's grand plan, but decided at ten years of age, Louise was entitled to keep her theory.

'Okay. Tammy?'

'A lawyer.'

'Any particular reason?' Frankie was almost too scared to ask.

'Because I can help put criminals in jail.'

Hurrah! Frankie rejoiced silently, a plausible career with justifiable reasons.

'Mischa?'

Mischa Banks batted her striking blue eyes and addressed the other girls as if she was bestowing them with a rare pearl of wisdom.

'I'm going to be a journalist so I can tell tales and get paid for it.'

'Very impressive,' Frankie said, unsurprised. 'Cassa?'

Cassa licked her lips and scanned the parquet floor for cracks.

'I'd like to be a singer.' She looked up to check everyone's reaction. Frankie watched her focus on something over her shoulder, saw the panic suddenly fill the girl's eyes. 'Or a nurse. I want to be a nurse.'

Frankie screwed round in her chair to see what could cause this sudden change in career path. Cassa's coifed mother was smiling down at them.

'Hello, Mrs Preston, I'm Frankie.'

'Hello, Frankie. Nice to meet you. You'll have to excuse me, but I'm still learning everyone's names.' Mrs Preston squatted down beside their patrol. 'I see you girls don't have a leader to help you so I thought I'd come over and see how I might help. What you would like to be when you grow up, Frankie?'

Frankie blinked. The rest of Starfish Patrol sniggered. Mrs Preston looked genuine enough.

'A jockey I guess.'

'A jockey?' Mrs Preston said with a gasp. 'But that's a boy's sport and so dangerous.'

Frankie looked at the patrol. They were all grinning at her with the exception of Cassa who looked like she wanted the crack she'd found in the floor to swallow her up. The temptation to string Mrs Preston on was overridden by pity at Cassa's embarrassment.

'Sorry, Mrs Preston, I'm really a Guide in Charge here. My day job is actually riding racehorses.'

From her squatting position, Mrs Preston steadied herself with her hand on the floor.

'How old are you, Frankie?'

'Twenty-three.'

'Twenty-three? Good grief! I'm terribly sorry. You – you just look so young.'

'That's all right. People always make that mistake.'

Mrs Preston straightened up, looking embarrassed.

'Well, I'll leave you to it then. Cassa, are you enjoying yourself?'

'Yes, Mum,' Cassa replied obediently.

'Good. Well, cheerio.'

'How's the new job going, Frankie?' Tammy, the future lawyer, asked once Mrs Preston had made her hasty departure.

'Good, thanks, Tammy. I've got five beautiful horses to look after every day.' Frankie thought back to her very productive morning schooling Ta' Qali over his first baby hurdles. The poor thing hadn't known what to make of the jumps at first, but after half an hour had been bouncing over the two combinations like a flea.

Charlotte's voice interrupted her thoughts.

'Do you get vampire horses?'

'No, Charlotte.' Frankie made a mental note to write to the author of that *Twilight* series and ask her to put in large print, preferably capital letters, at the front of the book that ALL CHARACTERS ARE FICTITIOUS. She referred to her activities sheets again and read aloud their first task. 'Right. "You are in a hot air balloon which has flown off course. You see a deserted island up ahead but you are low on fuel and too heavy to make it. Bearing in mind..."' Frankie frowned at the paper. Crikey, who wrote this stuff? '"...Bearing in mind the careers each of you have chosen and the challenges you are going to be faced with on the island, which two people do you throw out of the balloon and why?"'

The girls chewed their lips as they weighed up who they would murder first. Mischa turned to Cassa in grave seriousness.

'Are you a singer or a nurse?'

Cassa darted a look around to see if her mother was in sight.

'A singer.'

'Then I'd throw Cassa and Louise out,' Mischa concluded.

Cassa looked horrified at the thought of being thrown out of a hot air balloon. Louise looked insulted.

'Why would you keep a vampire over a fashion designer?' she said.

'Is there a Debenhams on the island?' Mischa asked Frankie.

'I doubt it, Mischa. There's just you guys living rough until rescue comes.'

'And we don't know when that'll be?'

'No.'

'Then I'm definitely keeping the vampire.'

Charlotte beamed. Frankie decided to play along with the fantasy for a while longer.

'Aren't you worried she'll eat you?' she said.

The girls gave Frankie a long-suffering adults-are-so-dim look.

'Vampires don't eat you. They just drink your blood.'

'They still kill you though.'

'Only bad vampires do,' Mischa explained. 'Charlotte will be a good one. And she can talk telepathically to Edward Cullen so he can come rescue us sooner.'

That was it, Frankie would definitely be writing to Stephanie Meyer. She couldn't believe they were having a serious careers discussions involving vampires.

'And the others which you've chosen to keep?' she prompted.

'Well, I'm not going to be thrown out because I'll have to write the newspaper story about how we survived – well, how most of us did, anyway. Harriet will have to cook for us and Tammy will have to stay so that once we're rescued we can use her to sue the hot air balloon company.'

Frankie had to admit she had a point with the last one.

12

On her way home from Newton Abbott the next day, Frankie sat in dejected silence beside Tom, who'd been kind enough to take on driving duties providing he didn't have to listen to Bonnie Tyler. She'd had three rides that afternoon, had wasted for days and lain in the bathtub for two hours that morning to get down to the featherweight in the feature handicap chase, yet she'd finished well down the field. She was tired, weak and miserable and just wanted her bed.

Their last clash of horns had faded to the back of Frankie's mind. She had more pressing concerns to stress over. Peace Offering took number one spot and as much as it irked her, riding a close second was Rhys's latest tactic which was to completely ignore her existence. When their paths had crossed, his gaze would flit over her with as much attention as a boy racer passing a speed limit sign.

Damn this crush, Frankie scolded herself. And damn Rhys for looking so damned sexy when he's angry.

'Frankie, can you keep a secret?'

The soberness in Tom's tone made her look at him in surprise.

'What's up?'

'You remember that night a couple of weeks ago when we argued –'

Frankie batted him away with her hand.

'Forget it. Truly, Tom. You were right about what you said. I was being selfish about wanting all the attention.'

'No. It was a horrible thing to say. You were obviously dealing with Seth's anniversary in your own way and I didn't make it any easier for you. You just walked in at the wrong moment, that's all.'

Frankie frowned at him, puzzled. She vaguely recalled Tom had been sitting in the dark, working on his laptop. The memory sharpened, Tom had slammed the screen shut when she'd tried to see what he was looking at.

'What do you mean?' she asked.

Tom gripped the steering wheel until his knuckles turned white. He exhaled.

'I've decided to try find my parents,' he said at last.

She looked levelly at him for a cautious moment.

'You don't mean your parents down in Weston-super-Mare, do you?' she said.

Tom shook his head.

'No, my *real* parents. My biological parents.'

'Wow.' Frankie didn't know what else to say. 'Erm, why now?'

Tom shrugged, not taking his eyes off the road in front.

'I don't know. Just things like have you noticed I'm getting grey hairs at my temples? I've only just turned twenty-eight! And Dad didn't go grey until he was fifty-odd. You know what I mean? There's things about me which I've inherited from someone and I don't know who and what they are. I want to know if there's a history of heart disease in my family. Will I go bald? Am I the only one in my family able to bend my finger back like this?'

Tom demonstrated, making Frankie shudder.

'Urgh. Yuck. Don't do that. I get the picture.'

'And when you ambushed me that night in the kitchen, I was just reading an email from an adoption agency forum thing. And there weren't any matches to me.'

'What does that mean though?'

Tom looked downcast.

'It means my parents don't want to find me.'

'No, don't say that. You don't know that for sure. They might be really non-techie people who don't know what an internet forum is or they might be missionaries in deepest darkest Africa or South America or somewhere where they don't know the internet exists. Do you know their names?'

He shook his head.

'No. But I've written to the Social Services and asked for my original birth certificate to be sent to me. That should have their names on it.'

Frankie reached over and squeezed his hand, a sparkle lighting her green eyes.

'This is so exciting, Tom,' she breathed. 'You could be the son of some massive celebrity – haven't I always told you you look like Colin Firth? Or you might be tenth in line to the throne or something.' She searched Tom's face for some enthusiasm. 'Aren't you excited?'

Tom gave an undecided nod-shake of his head.

'I'm a bit apprehensive, to be honest.'

Protectiveness swelled inside Frankie.

'Well, you're not going through this alone. Why didn't you tell me sooner that you were doing this?'

'I dunno. I guess I feel a bit guilty about the whole thing. It feels like I'm betraying Mum and Dad by going looking for my birth parents.'

'Have you told them?'

'No. Mum's not well and you know, I might not find anything. I wouldn't want to distress them unnecessarily.'

The initial novelty of finding a brand new family wore off Frankie pretty rapidly as she realised the psychological burden Tom was carrying. Going behind your parents' backs with something so colossal must take a lot of the excitement out of the hunt.

'Wow, I don't know what to say,' she muttered. 'I'm here, if that's any consolation. Like, if you need someone to offload on. God knows I dump enough of my troubles onto you.'

Tom flashed her a smile and leaned over to squeeze her knee.

'Let's talk about something else. How're you getting on with Lord Bradford? He's got to be the most unsociable person I have to valet.'

Frankie looked pained.

'Can you keep a secret too?'

''Course.'

'I'm having trouble with Peace Offering at the yard and I've got the feeling Rhys knows what's going on.'

'You think he's up to something?'

'Oh no, nothing like that.' Frankie took a deep breath. 'I mean I don't think Peace Offering likes me. Simple as that. But I don't know what to do differently. Jack's had the vet out to check him over, etcetera, but there's obviously nothing wrong with him health-wise. Then I see Rhys watching us from the sidelines and there's just something about him that makes me think he knows what's going on.'

'Has he said anything?'

'God, no. The last time we spoke properly was when I tried to apologise and he bit my head off. He acts like I don't exist now.'

Making their way up the steps to their front door, Frankie was still complaining about Rhys.

'He just blanks me every time I try to talk to him,' she said. 'And bloody Donnie doesn't help matters. He keeps grinning at me when Rhys is around like this is all some big joke put on for his amusement.'

'I wouldn't take any notice of Donnie,' Tom soothed, digging out his house keys. 'He can be a big dickhead sometimes.'

Frankie's thoughts strayed back to Exeter Racecourse's sauna.

'You can say that again,' she murmured.

Tom grinned at her. He pushed the door open for her to enter.

'Made an impression on you, did it?'

Frankie bustled into the warmth of the hallway, rubbing her arms.

'He could demolish buildings with that thing. *That's* the impression it makes.'

Tom laughed and followed her in.

'Yet you're not falling at his feet.'

'Size ain't everything. Anyway, that's not the sort of thing that attracts me to men. I like a bit of refinement, a bit of mystery.' Her mind's eye went through Rhys's attributes. 'And dark hair, dark eyes, someone with a bit of danger about them.'

Tom stopped leafing through the Indian and Chinese takeaway menus he'd retrieved from the mat, and stared at her.

'Frankie, you've got the biggest God-awful crush on Rhys Bradford, haven't you?'

Frankie pulled up short. Okay, yes, she could admit to herself that she found Rhys more inviting than most other members of the opposite sex, but she wasn't sure she wanted to admit it publically.

'I don't know about that,' she said evasively.

'How has it taken me this long to realise? *He's* the reason you're so miserable, isn't he? It's not because you didn't have any winners or because Peace Offering's not going for you. It's because Rhys isn't talking to you.'

Frankie gave a grudging shrug. A knock at the door stalled her reply reply. Their next door neighbour stood on the step, a broad smile on his ginger face. He held up a brown envelope for Tom.

'Just saw you arrive back. This came for you earlier. I had to sign for it.'

'Thanks,' Tom said, taking the letter and closing the door again.

'Ooh, that looks official. Is it for me or you?' Frankie asked.

Tom's face became grave and he tapped the Do Not Bend envelope against his palm.

'It's for me. It's from Social Services.'

Frankie followed as he strode through to the kitchen at the other end of the hall. Rhys Bradford was wiped from her thoughts. The kitchen light flickered on and Tom sat down at the table and stared at the envelope. Frankie slipped into the chair next to him.

'Your birth certificate you mean?' She could feel her pulse drumming and could only imagine what his was doing.

He nodded.

'The original one, yes.' He licked his lips and teased the envelope flap away from the sealing gum.

Frankie held her breath and leaned closer.

Tom pulled out a sheath of paper and booklets. He dropped the latter carelessly on the table and sifted through the rest. He withdrew an A5 sheet of thick paper.

He sucked in his breath. His hands were shaking and Frankie had to crane her neck to read the certificate. Tom exhaled with force and dropped it. He ground his chair back and stood up with a muffled cry. Frankie shot him a concerned glance then picked up the paper.

'Born on the thirtieth of September, 1985,' she read aloud. She looked up at Tom as he paced around their kitchen. 'Okay, that sounds right. Mother: Adelaide Mann.' She looked up again, beaming. 'That's great. We know who your real mother is now.'

Tom stopped pacing and looked up at the ceiling, his hands on his hips.

'Read on,' he commanded with a vague wave of his hand.

'Father – oh, this is a bugger. They've forgotten to fill this bit in. They've left your father's name blank by mistake.'

Tom looked at her, pained. Tears filled his eyes.

'It isn't a mistake, Frankie. It means they don't – *she* doesn't know who my father is.'

13

The first winter frosts staked their ground at Aintree in the early hours of Becher Chase Saturday. Frankie shivered with cold as she exited the heated weighing room alongside twelve other riders, but she was sweating beneath her body protector. In just under an hour, she would be tackling the most famous steeplechase course in the world on a horse she was convinced didn't like her.

Added to her nervous excitement was Ta' Qali about to make his debut in National Hunt racing. She followed Rhys, in his red and white chevroned silks across the parade ring, trying to ignore the yearning she felt to be wearing those colours instead of Roosevelt's blue and yellow. She smiled to herself. It brought a completely different meaning to the phrase "wanting to get into his pants". The thirteen horses skirted the ring, their rugs pulled back to cover their loins. Most of them walked round calmly beside their handlers, now and then skittering out of line if something in the throng of bystanders spooked them.

The first horse Frankie recognised was Ta' Qali. She felt a deluge of disappointment spill over her. Sweaty foam fringed his saddle pad and girth. With his newly-donned sheepskin noseband hiding the white marking on his nose, the big black horse was an imposing presence. Billy, his handler for the day, struggled to keep him on the path. He was flung from side to side like a leaf in a gale as Ta' Qali tossed his head and reared forward.

Jack was frowning at the horse's antics and barely acknowledged Frankie's and Rhys's arrival by his side.

'Don't know what the matter is with him,' he muttered, at last registering them. 'It's not like he's never been to a racecourse before.'

'Did they have a bad trip up?' Rhys asked.

Jack shook his head.

'Billy said he wasn't the quietest, but nothing exceptionally drastic.'

The bell sounded, summoning the jockeys to mount. Ta' Qali bolted, dragging Billy with him. Jack turned to Rhys.

'Keep him prominent, but try get some cover. Hopefully he'll settle down when he's on the move. Frankie, you do the same, but keep to the inside where the better ground is.'

Frankie's Becher Chase worries were replaced with concern for Ta' Qali as they cantered away from the stands towards the start. He wasn't settling beneath Rhys. The jockey was having to use all his strength to keep him to a canter. Down at the start, Rhys was shaking his head almost as much as Ta' Qali. Ta' Qali wouldn't have looked out of place at a heavy metal concert. With each head bang, he flung gloopy foam from his mouth onto his rider. The starter plodded over to his rostrum while runners circled behind.

'What the hell's wrong with him?' Rhys growled, wiping a string of equine saliva from his thigh.

Frankie bit her lip. She almost wished Ta' Qali acted like this at home. At least then she would be able to give Rhys some advice on how to deal with him.

'Maybe he's been stung by something?'

Rhys gave her a disparaging look.

'Seriously?'

For once, Frankie didn't blame him. Unless there were wasps carrying stings full of Meth flying around, it was an unlikely reason for his behaviour. On the bright side, that was the most Rhys had said to her in two weeks.

The starter called them forward. Frankie pulled her goggles down over her eyes and tried to focus on her own race.

The tape snapped away and the horses surged forward in a cavalry charge to the first hurdle. Frankie took up position on the rail behind the two front runners while Rhys wrestled with Ta' Qali on her outside. The pace was hot yet even that didn't settle the horse. He flung up his head, half taking off in mid-stride and smacked Rhys square beneath the eyes.

Frankie cringed at the dull thud of impact. So much for the sheepskin noseband lowering his head carriage.

Rhys growled and wiped away the thin stream of blood from his nose.

'You okay?' she yelled.

Rhys jabbed a gloved finger at the first in a line of three hurdles ahead.

'Just concentrate on your own goddamned race.'

Frankie tried not to take it personally. She could just make out Rhys's eyes watering behind his goggles. That smack must've hurt like a bastard.

Roosevelt lengthened his stride as the hurdle ranged closer then put in a short one, rapping the jump hard with his knees. Frankie sat tight, aware of Ta' Qali jumping high and left. They bumped shoulders on landing. Roosevelt, the lighter of the two, bounced sideways and Frankie clung to his mane.

They jumped the second, then the third in tandem. Roosevelt now jumped left as well, anticipating the impact from his stable companion.

'Frankie, what are you doing?' Rhys yelled out. His cheek was smeared with diluted blood. 'Fucking go on ahead. This thing is gonna bring us both down in a minute.'

Frankie hesitated. She didn't want to be told how to ride. On the other hand, he did have a valid point. She lowered herself in the saddle and Roosevelt edged clear. As they passed the stands for the first time, she became aware of the steeplechase course on their inside. The hurdles looked like trotting poles in comparison. The worries of her upcoming ride on Peace Offering reappeared now that Ta' Qali had disappeared from her line of sight. The wide pool at the base of the water jump glinted in the sunlight, foreboding, winking at her. Frankie didn't like the look of that jump one bit.

14

Frankie had come to think of the Golden Miller as a quiet place to unburden the soul, where Tom would be sat in his usual spot in the corner with his beer and Joey would be leaning his elbows on the spotless counter with a cloth slung over his shoulder, listening to him. The restaurant area would murmur with in-between mouthfuls of dinner conversation and the glass cleaning machine hidden beneath the bar would rattle and beep when it finished its cycle.

Not so, Becher Chase Saturday night it would appear. It wasn't exactly heaving, but a good crowd were there to interrupt Tom and Joey. Including Rhys and Donnie, she noted.

Tom frowned at her when she stopped before him.

'Your hair's green.'

Frankie plonked herself down on a neighbouring stool.

'I don't know what they put in the water jump at Aintree. Is it that bad? I didn't have time to wash it.'

Tom wiped his top lip and shook his head.

'Nah. Just don't stand under the light. How are you feeling?'

Frankie shrugged.

'At least it was a soft landing. Did you see what happened?'

Tom shook his head.

'It's got to be one of the simplest fences in the whole race,' she said. 'He got in close to just about every other fence worth standing off of then he decided he's friggin' Pegasus at the one fence that you need to get in close to make the spread.' Frankie chewed her lip, reliving how each disjointed jump Peace Offering had made over the monstrous Aintree fences had wedged her heart further and further up her throat. Then after he had lost his backend in the water and deposited Frankie into its sub-zero depths, all she could compute was the relief that *it was over*.

She shook her head in shame. Her eyes locked onto Rhys's across the bar and she quickly looked away. 'Now Pippa wants to meet up tonight. I don't know if she wants to jock me off - I wouldn't blame her if she did - or commiserate with me.' She gave herself a mental shake, reminding herself that she wasn't the only one with problems. 'How's your day been?'

Tom sipped his drink and gave a wry smile.

'Heard back from the adoption people this morning.'

Frankie held her breath. She tried not to look too excited – she would be over the moon if her best friend's father was Colin Firth – but Tom wasn't exactly dancing on the tables.

'I got them to look on the Contacts Register for Adelaide Mann. That's where people put their details in case the adopted child ever comes looking for them.' Tom wiped the condensation from his beer glass, looking at it with a mirthless smile.

'And?' Frankie leaned forward.

'She's not on it. Just like with the internet forums. She's just not interested.' He paused. 'Your hair looks green again. Lean back out of the light.'

Ignoring him, Frankie reached out and squeezed his hand. She couldn't think of anything to comfort him with. Unlike internet forums, Adelaide Mann must certainly have been aware of the Contacts Register. Tom blinked with increased rapidity.

'I mean, I'm not trying to be the son she didn't want or anything, I just want to know who I am; who my father is – or was. Is that such a selfish thing to want?'

'Maybe she wasn't in a good place when she had you. She might have felt so guilty that she didn't want to be found – I know I'd be feeling bad in her shoes. And her hormones will have been all over the place, you know what they say about pregnancies. But people change, she might want to be found now. She might have been really young back then, and now, as an adult, she might think differently.'

'She was twenty-two. Old enough in my book to be pretty set in her ways. I looked at the census records. There haven't been many Adelaide Manns born here. There was one from 1908, which I doubt very much will be the right one, then two more who both died before I was born. Then this one was born in 1962. It has to be her, don't you think?'

'If she's English. You might not necessarily see the birth records of someone born in Australia or America who immigrated over here. Or Mann might have been her married name.'

'Which would mean that since my father's name isn't listed on my birth certificate she had an affair.'

Frankie despaired.

'These are just speculations though. We don't know the whole story yet.'

Tom grunted and took another swallow of his beer. He nodded to the Golden Miller's entrance behind her.

'Whatever. I think your date has arrived.'

Frankie's stomach belly-flopped with dread. She swivelled round to see Pippa shrugging off her coat and walking their way.

'Hi, Pippa,' Frankie said with false cheer.

Pippa beamed at her.

'Sorry I'm late. What can I get you to drink?'

'No, let me.' If Pippa was about to jock her off the Grand National favourite she was going to do her damnedest to keep her sweet.

'Oh, okay. White wine then, please. I'll go grab us a table. Bar or restaurant?'

'I don't mind.' Yes, anything to keep the owner sweet.

Pippa grinned.

'Bar then. Less far to go for a drink.' She turned away and laid claim to a nearby table. Frankie gave Tom a look that showed her nerves.

'You'll be fine,' Tom said. 'She doesn't look like she's about to trash your dreams.'

'Shh, she might hear you,' Frankie replied out of the corner of her mouth. She caught Joey's eye and he came over. Even with an apron and cloth, he looked more like a ballet dancer than a barman.

'Hi Joey. White wine and a vodka and orange, please.'

'Don't you want something stronger?' Tom said. 'You look like you're about to go to the chair.'

'I did go to The Chair, but I fell at the next fence,' she drawled. 'Maybe I'll have a Pina Colada.'

'Not something I'd share with the world,' a deep voice said behind her.

Frankie's neck hairs stood on end. She looked across the bar to where she'd last seen Rhys. Donnie was sitting alone, watching her with that annoying grin on his face. She instinctively moved out of the bar's overhead light so she wouldn't look quite so green.

'And what is so wrong with a Pina Colada?' she said, turning to face Rhys.

A blackening bruise curved over his nose to his narrowed eyes.

'You know what I'm talking about. What happened out there with Peace Offering today?'

Was that alcohol she could smell on his breath? Surely not. She was pretty sure he didn't drink. Then again, she recalled the miserable look on his face earlier, watching all the other jockeys file out to take their ride in the Becher Chase. All but him. After Frankie and Peace Offering's poor display, it had probably been knocking around his head that he could have done a better job.

Aware of Pippa sitting within earshot but apparently studying the Golden Miller's menu, Frankie crossed her arms. She surveyed Rhys and the purple bruise which swelled uncomfortably over his nose to his eye sockets.

'I might ask you the same question about Ta' Qali.'

Rhys shrugged.

'That had nothing to do with me. He was acting like a crackpot before I got on him. I think under the circumstances we didn't do too badly.'

Damn. She had to concede he was right. Despite Ta' Qali's unsettled run, he'd still managed to finish sixth – only three places behind she and Roosevelt.

'Well?'

She looked towards Joey. He was still mixing her cocktail. She should have stuck to her original order.

'Jack says he was probably just ring-rusty. He needed the run,' she said, tilting up her chin and flicking her fringe off her face.

Rhys's eyes glittered onyx black.

'Really? I could perhaps see his point if you'd gone two and a half miles *then* started to make mistakes. But you were both struggling from the outset.'

Frankie hazarded a look at Pippa. Peace Offering's owner was now gazing into the distance.

'And those watching from the sidelines probably wouldn't have noticed what the TV viewers were able to see close up.'

Frankie swallowed uncomfortably.

'Which was?'

'You were scared shitless and Peace Offering had no confidence in you. That was why he fell.'

There was a definite tang of whiskey fumes in the air between them.

'Rhys, stop it. I know it doesn't seem fair that you've lost the ride on the National favourite but –'

'But he's not favourite anymore, Frankie. Haven't you heard the latest antepost betting? After you abandoned ship and Skylark went on to win, *he's* become favourite. Peace Offering's price is drifting like a barge.' He smirked in the face of her shock.

Joey came over with her drinks and Frankie slapped a ten pound note down on the counter.

'Save your breath, Rhys.' She gathered her order and gave him a flippant once over. 'Doubtless you'll need it to blow smoke up someone else's arse.'

She hoped Pippa didn't notice the rattle of the glasses as she set them down on their table. Even more, she hoped she hadn't overheard her confrontation with Rhys. She looked back as she sat down. Rhys took a swaying step towards her and Pippa. She braced herself. With a quiet sigh, she noticed Tom coolly motioning Rhys to go back to Donnie. He thought twice then walked back to the other side of the bar.

Frankie exhaled. For the briefest of moments she relaxed, but then it returned. If Rhys had been able to see how scared she'd been earlier then Pippa, who had been watching the race from the grandstand, might have seen it too.

'So are you feeling okay after your inopportune bath?'

'Yes, thanks. One of the softest falls I've had.' She giggled nervously. 'Which sounds odd considering the course we were jumping.'

'Oh, good. I was worried it might have shaken you up.' Pippa took a sip of her wine. 'You know – first ride on Peace Offering, first ride round the National fences. It would rattle me, that's for sure.'

Frankie nodded and tried to appear as confident as she could muster.

'It turned my hair green instead of white,' she grinned.

Pippa laughed. Then, like a sail losing its breeze, she stopped. Her face took on a serious expression.

Frankie's heart thudded in her ears.

'Jack said Peace Offering probably needed the run,' she rushed.

'Hmm.'

Frankie got the impression Jack might have said a fair few more things on their drive home from Liverpool. He'd been supportive of her after her fall, but she'd got the distinct impression he was still in the Rhys Bradford camp.

'It took him a few runs to win last season,' Frankie tried again. It had only taken him one run to become favourite for the National, she added silently. And just one to revoke that title.

'True, and it's not like he has an unblemished record to protect – far from it, in fact,' Pippa agreed.

Frankie nodded, willing Pippa back into her camp.

'We'll definitely improve on this run. The National's still four and half months away.'

Pippa looked up, concerned.

'You're still happy with riding him then, after today?'

Frankie nodded with more conviction. She refused to dwell on Rhys's judgements.

'Yes. Definitely.'

'Well, I'm happy if you're happy,' Pippa said with a wide smile. 'I understand the reasons why you want to win the National, just so long as *you're* happy with those reasons.'

Frankie's mind flitted to the phone call she'd made to her parents when she'd got home after racing. Doug had spoken to her, had asked if she was all right after her fall and had then handed her over to Vanessa to discuss Sunday lunch plans. He hadn't said it, but Frankie knew he was disappointed. He would have seen the race on television – his daughter riding at Aintree, his daughter who hadn't even managed to get round a third of the course. She had to dispel that disappointment. She was going to make sure that Doug Cooper would, for once, be proud of his daughter.

15

Sunday lunch was turning out to be not as disastrous as Frankie had envisaged. It might have been because the Coopers were more focussed on salvaging what they could from the pork belly presented by Vanessa than on Frankie's performance at Aintree the day before.

'I was only following Heston's recipe,' Vanessa said, watching Doug saw through the meat. 'It said to cook it for nine hours.'

'But at what temperature?' Doug rubbed his tired jaw.

Vanessa pouted. She crossed her arms over her tight-fitting James Bond T-shirt, obscuring the words "I'd snog Pierce but I'd shag Daniel."

'I thought it was a typo when it said ninety-five degrees. I mean, who cooks anything at such a low heat? I thought it must have meant one hundred and ninety-five.'

Frankie snorted.

'You've outdone yourself, Mum. At least there won't be much fat left for me to burn off for next week.'

'I ruined a perfectly good casserole dish trying to make this. One which was given to us as an anniversary present. I don't find that very funny.'

'Given to us by the Becketts,' Doug said.

Vanessa pulled a face.

'Maybe not such a tragedy then. Susan Beckett probably put a curse on it.'

'Who are the Becketts?' asked Frankie through a mouthful of leather.

'Old friends,' Doug said. He exchanged a wicked smile with Vanessa. 'Until your mother offered to do Susan's hair.'

'Ooh, that sounds ominous,' Frankie grinned at her mother's pained expression. 'What happened?'

'I don't know why she couldn't just laugh it off like any normal person,' Vanessa said. 'I was trying to be generous. She had some local television interview at an animal sanctuary and her usual hairdresser was down with the 'flu so I offered to do it instead.'

Doug leant in conspiratorially and waggled his knife.

'She slipped while doing Susan's fringe. Made her look more like Captain Spock.'

Frankie gasped in delight.

Vanessa shrugged and tried to make inroads into her dinner.

'I lent her a wig.'

'Yes, love, but it got eaten by an alpaca live on air.'

Frankie choked on her giggles. Vanessa kindly leaned over and thumped her between the shoulder blades.

'Don't bother with the pork anymore, darling. I don't want to be held for homicide.'

'Shall I make us a salad?' Frankie suggested.

'Go on then. I got some lovely big tomatoes at the market the other day.'

Peering into the fridge, Frankie equipped herself with lettuce, cucumber and feta cheese. She rummaged around for the tomatoes. She looked suspiciously at five vegetables leaning drunkenly against the back of the bottom tray.

'Tomatoes or red peppers, Mum?' she called out.

Vanessa appeared at the doorway. Frankie held up a pepper and her mother's face brightened.

'Yes, those are them – oh, dear, they are peppers aren't they? I did think they were a funny shape. Never mind, we can have peppers in a salad, can't we?'

Frankie grinned and tossed one into the air. Beneath the glare of the kitchen light she set about chopping and deseeding the fraudulent vegetables.

'Frankie,' Vanessa said in a concerned tone. 'I don't want to alarm you, but...'

Alarm bells in Frankie's head immediately began to whirl.

'What?'

'Well, your hair looks ever so slightly *green* in this light. I didn't notice it before.'

Frankie held her ponytail so she could see it and grimaced.

'Damn, I thought I'd managed to get it back to normal this morning. I fell off at the water jump at Aintree yesterday.'

Instead of deepening concern, Vanessa looked relieved.

'Oh, that's all right then. I can give you some tint if you'd like to help it along. We saw your race on TV.' She looked over her shoulder into the lounge. 'Didn't we, darling?'

Frankie peeled off the frills of lettuce into the salad bowl and listened for Doug's reply. She could just make out a grunt.

'It was such bad luck,' Vanessa continued. 'And Channel 4 had really made quite a deal about you riding beforehand.'

'Really?'

'Yes, because that horse you were riding was the Grand National favourite – although between you and me, he didn't look like the favourite for anything the way he was jumping. Anyway, they took a trip down memory lane and showed a clip of your dad on some horse that was a Grand National favourite from years back.'

Frankie rushed to the door to look at her father sitting in his easy chair.

'Is that right, Dad? You and I were both on TV? Who were you riding? I didn't know you rode a National favourite! Did you ride him in the National too?'

Doug gave his wife and daughter squashed in the doorway a look of long-suffering.

'Crowbar. In the Charlie Hall Chase. And yes, he was the National favourite. But no, I didn't ride him in the big one.'

'I remember him!' Frankie said. 'Well, I've heard of him obviously because he went on to win the National. But I didn't realise you'd ridden him before!' Her heart swelled with pride. 'Why didn't you ride him in the National?'

A muscle leapt in Doug's jaw and he looked away from Frankie. He drummed the arm of his chair with gnarled fingers.

'Because somebody else rode him instead.'

Frankie opened her mouth to ask more questions, but felt her mother's hand on her shoulder.

'Why don't we have a game after lunch?' Vanessa suggested, nodding to the card table. 'Loser has to load the dishwasher.'

Frankie shut her mouth, taking her mother's hint. She smiled, understanding – although, not quite.

*

Using Vanessa's collection of glass stones as betting chips (yellow worth a fiver, green worth a tenner and blue worth fifty each), they sat down to the serious business of mother-daughter poker.

Frankie laid down her small blind of one yellow stone and dealt them both their two cards.

'I'm afraid I can't ask you back to talk at my Guides meeting,' she said.

Vanessa looked crestfallen.

'Why ever not, darling?'

'You remember how you came along to help on the crafts night to show them how to make mosaics with glass stones?'

Vanessa nodded.

'Well, when you told them we use the glass stones for playing poker and then proceeded to teach the group how to play, that didn't go down too well with the mums.'

'But it's just a card game,' Vanessa protested.

'I know, but I think the mums were expecting tales of how their darling angels can now make pretty mosaic patterns, not how they were now experts at Texas Hold 'Em.'

'Well, that's just silly in my opinion. There's such a stigma about poker,' she tutted. 'And I'm also going to raise you twenty.' She dropped a couple of green stones onto the table.

Trying to keep a straight face, Frankie looked at the cards on the table then at her hand. A pair of sixes wasn't going to get her very far. She shook her head and folded. Vanessa grinned and revealed her cards.

'You had nothing!' Frankie cried. 'Really, Mum. You're a complete shark.'

Vanessa winked and collected her winnings.

'So, are you settling in okay with the job?'

At ease now, Frankie regaled her with stories of her first weeks at Aspen Valley, not putting too much emphasis on horses' or people's names. It constantly amazed Frankie that despite being married to an ex-jockey for nearly thirty years and having raised two racing-mad children, Vanessa still knew next to nothing about the sport. 'What about the people you work with? Are they nice?' Vanessa asked.

With a pair of kings in her hand and one already on the table after the first turn, Frankie raised the stakes before answering.

'They seem nice enough. Jack is so respected there, he's almost like a god. June works next door to me so I probably know her best. She's been there years apparently. She's cool, except...'

'Except?'

'I dunno. She's really friendly. It's just that sometimes I feel she's too friendly.'

Vanessa fiddled with her stones and matched her bet.

'Is she a lesbian?'

'No, I don't mean it like that.' Frankie turned the last two cards and grinned in anticipation. 'I mean her friendship feels a little false. I don't know. I can't explain it.'

'Don't look a gift horse in the mouth. Right, what have you got? I've got four of a kind.'

Frankie's smile disappeared.

'What? I thought I had you with a full house.'

'Darling, you've been grinning like an idiot this entire hand. You're easier to read than a nursery school pop-up book. Have you ever heard the expression "poker-face"?'

Mildly disgruntled, Frankie gave her mother most of her betting stones.

'I managed okay when I beat Rhys.'

'Rhys? Who's Rhys? I don't think I've heard his name mentioned before.'

'Rhys Bradford. He also rides at Aspen Valley.'

'Bradford?' Vanessa looked up in surprise.

Frankie frowned. She knew Rhys was a bit of a head-turner, but if she mentioned his name much more, both her parents would be in neck braces at this rate.

'Yeah. Have you heard of him? Dad gave me the same reaction when I told him a while back that we worked together.'

Vanessa pulled a nonchalant face and retrieved the cards she'd dropped.

'Name sounds vaguely familiar.'

'Well, he is quite well-known,' Frankie said. 'He and Jack just about swept the board at Cheltenham Festival a couple of seasons ago. Then he went and broke his leg at Kempton's last Boxing Day meeting. Horse was killed, poor thing, and it was one of the stable stars. And then of course, he was the one who got jocked off Peace Offering when Pippa gave me the ride.'

'Hmm. That was unlucky,' Vanessa replied absently. 'Is he nice?'

Frankie made a non-committal noise.

'I don't really know. I'm not his favourite person in the world, although I wish he'd hurry up and forgive me. He *is* quite good-looking.'

'Be careful, Francesca. Jockeys are bad news.'

'You're married to an ex-jockey, Mum. Should I be concerned?'

'No, of course not. Your father's different,' she said airily. 'Why don't you marry Tom instead of lusting after jockeys?'

Unsettled, Frankie snorted.

'Mum! I'm not *lusting* after Rhys. Besides, Tom and I are just friends. Best friends. Kissing him would be like kissing a brother.'

'But he's not your brother,' Vanessa pointed out. 'Why don't you bring him round some time? Tell him if he agrees to learn poker, I'll cut his hair for free.'

'Mum, I'm not sure I want you bribing my friends into taking up a gambling habit.'

Vanessa sighed and looked at her pityingly.

'See? Everyone's got a stigma about poker.'

Frankie couldn't wait to get home that evening. Not only was she still starving, but curiosity over her father's association with Crowbar was eating her up. Once she'd refrained from bringing the subject up again, Doug's earlier good mood had eventually resurfaced. He'd given her a warm kiss goodbye.

'Take care of yourself, Frankie,' he said, patting her arm. Frankie had hugged him hard. She could see he was trying so hard not to be disappointed in her Becher Chase flop. He must have been terribly embarrassed that the two of them should have been shown on television and while he had gone on to win his race, she had bailed out on the first circuit. She still wanted to know who he'd lost the Grand National ride on Crowbar to though.

A note on the kitchen table informed her Tom was at the Golden Miller if she cared to join him.

'You're spending an awful lot of time down at the pub, Tom Moxley,' she murmured.

Atticus Finch jumped up onto the table and demanded a fuss then food.

Once she'd opened a sachet of gourmet cat food for him, he turned his back on her.

'You're so fickle, Atticus.'

Feeling guilty about carbohydrates, Frankie made herself a chunky peanut butter sandwich and a cup of coffee. It wouldn't do to be doing detective work on an empty stomach. She thought of the leathery pork which her insides would be working hard to digest and the small salad.

'Well, maybe half-empty,' she conceded, biting into her sandwich and stomping upstairs to her bedroom.

She sat cross-legged on her bed and switched on her laptop. She logged on to the *Racing Post* website and searched for Crowbar's form history.

No records found

'Damn,' she muttered. 'Too long ago, I suppose.'

She smacked her lips together as she thought where else she could get the information before settling on the usual search engines.

Grand National winners, she typed in.

She clicked the top link and waited for the page to load. All one hundred and sixty-eight winners were listed. Frankie scrolled down the page to the correct date. A crunchy bit of peanut butter lodged in her throat and she coughed. With a lurch, her coffee splashed over her keyboard. The laptop gave a whirring sigh then the page faded to black and the power button blinked red for the last time. But Frankie had seen all she'd needed to see...

Crowbar (5/1 fav) – Trainer: Ron McCready. Jockey: Alan Bradford.

16

The frosts which had accompanied the October Becher Chase meeting gave way to a wet November. Returning home from work one evening, Frankie hummed tunelessly along to Bonnie Tyler, the volume turned up to drown out the rain lashing down on the Mini's roof. She peered through the windscreen to where her headlights searched for an empty parking space.

'Come on,' she muttered, aware of her passage taking her further and further down the street away from her house. Then between wipers, she spied a space not far ahead. Another car coming in the opposite direction was also slowing. Frankie chopped down on her indicator aggressively. 'Oh, no you don't. It's on my side of the road.' She put her foot down and the Mini zoomed forward.

Suddenly, out of the shadows, a dark shaggy form bounded into her path. Frankie kicked the brake and the tyres squealed in alarm. A thud followed by a yelp made her wince. The rain and the parking space forgotten, she leapt out of the car and rushed round the bonnet. In the hazy glare of the headlamp, a dog lay in front of her left bumper. It raised its head and whined.

'Oh, darling,' Frankie cried, rushing forward. 'Are you okay? You poor thing. I –'

'Jasper!' a voice from the adjacent park yelled out. 'Jasper!'

Frankie froze.

Rhys came half-running, half-limping into sight. He stopped when he saw Frankie.

'What the hell were you doing?' he demanded, bending over the spaniel.

For a moment, Frankie was too taken aback to say anything.

'I didn't see him. He just came out of nowhere.'

With the rain plastering his clothes to his hunched back, he gently felt the dog's limbs. Jasper whimpered as his hands ran gently over his shoulder.

'You were speeding,' Rhys accused.

'I wasn't!' She could feel tears welling up, shock and remorse for hurting the dog - even if it was Rhys's dog - rising in her chest. 'I was looking for a parking space.'

Rhys looked up at her, his face glistening with raindrops. The bridge of his nose still bore the bruise inflicted by Ta' Qali.

'I've got to get him to a vet. He might have broken something.'

Frankie nodded animatedly.

'Let me take you -'

Rhys stood up defensively.

'No! Just leave us alone. Can't you see you've already done enough damage!'

Frankie's lip trembled before a fiery indignation overtook her.

'Rhys, for Christ's sake! Can you stop hating me for just two minutes and let me help you? You were the one who didn't have him on a bloody lead. Now, come on. My car's right here. What were you planning on doing - carrying him in the rain all the way to the vets?'

Rhys glared at her.

'Fine. Let's get him inside.' He wrenched off his jacket and tried to manoeuvre Jasper onto it. Frankie stepped forward to assist but the dog raised its lips to show small pointed teeth.

'Just let me to do it, okay?' Rhys snapped.

Trembling, Frankie hurried round the car to open the back door. Rhys followed with Jasper in his arms and gingerly placed him on the seat.

'Do you know where the vet surgery is?' he said.

Frankie nodded. Atticus Finch had made sure of that.

With Bonnie Tyler muted, they drove in tense silence through Helensvale's gloomy streets. Every few moments, Rhys leant through the gap between the front seats to check Jasper and comfort him. His arm brushed against Frankie's. She could feel him shivering.

'Is he okay?' she said, trying to see the dog in her rearview mirror.

'I don't know,' he muttered. 'How fast were you going?'

Frankie tried to collect her distressed thoughts. She had slowed right down until she'd tried to beat the other car to the parking space.

'I-I don't know. Not fast, I don't think.'

Rhys sat back in his seat with a sigh and muttered under his breath. Frankie made out the words 'trying to make my life a misery' and 'can't ride or drive'. Her patience snapped.

'Stop it! Right now! Just stop it!' She turned to him in anger. 'You know what, I'm sick of your bloody attitude! If you want to waste your energy hating me, that's your problem but –'

'You've given me good reason to hate you!'

'No, I haven't! I didn't ask to ride Peace Offering. Pippa offered him to me. What was I supposed to do? Turn it down?'

'He was my National ride,' growled Rhys.

'Since when? You didn't ride him last season –'

'I was injured!'

'And now that you're not, you see it as your godly right to ride him? Did you ever stop to think *why* Pippa decided she didn't want you riding her horse?'

'Pippa knows fuck all about racing.'

Frankie laughed humourlessly. All the angst that had been building up in misguided guilt for taking his ride poured out of her.

'It's her horse! She can do whatever the hell she wants with Peace Offering. So I got lucky. And all you can apparently do is stand around and hate me for it. Well, you know what? Suck it up, Rhys.' She banged her palm on the steering wheel. 'Build a fucking bridge and get over it!'

Rhys looked at her, his eyes wide at her outburst but his lips still drawn back in a snarl. She glared back at him.

'I've tried to apologise. I've tried to be nice because, believe it or not, I was actually sorry I took the ride off you –'

Rhys huffed.

'Yeah, right.'

Frankie raised a finger to silence him.

'But now I'm not. You wanna know why? Because I'm sick of feeling guilty about something which isn't my fault.' Her mind flashed back to Crowbar's Grand National result. 'What's more, you don't have any bloody right being angry with me even if I did get your ride. Your father did the exact same thing to my dad!'

'What?'

'Yeah. My dad rode Crowbar in just about every race he'd won yet *your* father stole the ride on him in the National.'

'That doesn't surprise me,' Rhys muttered.

Frankie immediately took that as an insult to her father.

'What is that supposed to mean?'

Rhys's eyes glinted in the darkness as he glared at her.

'What my father does is his business, his problem. He's got nothing to do with me.'

'Oh, how very convenient,' she said sarcastically.

'Actually, no!' Rhys exclaimed. 'It's fucking inconvenient. I wish he'd never got the ride on Crowbar. And not because of your father – I don't give a damn about your father – but I wish my father had never won the National! At least then, he wouldn't taunt me with it. Do you know what that's like? It doesn't matter how many championships I win, doesn't matter how many Cheltenham winners I get, as long as he's won the National and I haven't then I'll never be as good as him!' He flung himself back into his seat and stared moodily out of the window.

Frankie's hands trembled on the steering wheel. From the backseat, Jasper whined. Rhys sighed and turned to the backseat to stroke him.

'Sorry, boy,' he said gently. 'We're not shouting at you.'

'We're here,' Frankie announced a few moments later. The rain still flooded down, making the early evening seem even later, but thankfully the surgery lights were still on. Rhys got out of the car and tried to lift Jasper out.

Frankie, her anger drained, did the same.

'Let me help.'

'I can do it.'

'No, you can't. Just let me –'

'I *said* I can do it,' Rhys said firmly.

Frankie licked her lips and took a step back.

'Okay.'

Rhys could do it, albeit with difficulty. They hurried for cover beneath the entrance's overhang.

'You don't have to stay. We can manage fine,' he said.

Frankie wanted to shake the stubbornness out of him.

'But how will you get home? I want to know if he's going to be okay.'

For the first time, Rhys looked a tiny bit repentant.

'I'll figure it out. Just go, please.' He paused. Frankie could see him wrestling with something within. 'Thanks,' he added.

'You're welcome,' she said with a weak smile.

Turning her collar up uselessly to stem the downpour, she ran back to her car.

17

The rain which had battered Helensvale on Tuesday evening was jeopardising Exeter's Friday meeting a hundred miles south. Frankie jogged to catch up with Rhys as the thirteen jockeys trooped out of the weighing room into the wet.

'How's Jasper?' she asked.

Rhys looked at her guardedly.

'Just bruised, the vet said.'

Frankie closed her eyes.

'Thank God. I couldn't forgive myself if he'd had to be put down.'

Rhys grunted and lengthened his stride to pass her. Jack was waiting for them in the grassy centre of the parade ring hunched beneath an umbrella. As he briefed her, Rhys and Donnie on their rides, Frankie stole a glance at Rhys. His eyes were fixed on Jack's leather brogues. Nodding intermittently to show he was concentrating on what was being said, his face was otherwise devoid of emotion. Only the tapping of his whip against his gleaming boot betrayed any nervous energy. Frankie silently cursed the owner of Blue Jean Baby for choosing black and royal blue stripes as his colours. It was making Rhys look sexier than he deserved credit for. Slowly he became aware of Frankie watching him. His gaze travelled from Jack's footwear to Frankie's, then up her unflattering pink and orange checked silks to her face.

He raised one flyaway eyebrow in question.

She hastily looked away and by accident caught Jack's eye.

'You got that, Frankie?' he said.

Frankie cleared her throat, stalling for time, trying to gauge what sort of mood Jack was in. Could she afford to tell him she hadn't heard a word of what he'd been saying about her mount, Media Star? No, Jack looked pissed off already.

'Got it,' she beamed. Blinking rapidly, she ignored Rhys's look of pathetic disbelief.

Frankie stood high in her stirrups, letting the lanky chestnut gelding, Media Star, bowl around the far turn of Haldon Hill in the direction of the start. Low lying cloud and the thick brush of trees bordered the outer running rail and blocked her view of Dartmoor. The dull drum on the heavy ground of approaching horses made her twist round. Frankie grinned. Dory aka Blue Jean Baby was carting Rhys. With her head so high that Rhys practically had her ears in his mouth, the grey mare thundered towards her lesser-fancied stable companion like she was auditioning for a re-enactment of the *Homeward Bound* ending.

Joining the other runners circling in front of the three-mile start, Frankie's more sympathetic side got the better of her.

'Watch out for her jumping,' she said, jogging a couple of paces apart from Rhys. 'She fly-bucks when she's having fun.'

'Thanks for the tip,' Rhys replied, his voice dripping with sarcasm.

Pride wounded, she replied with an indifferent shrug and turned Media Star away from him.

The starter mounted his platform. Jockeys began scrimmaging for position as they jogged towards the tape. Donnie, aboard the joint favourite, pushed in front of her and Frankie found herself jostled back to the rear. The tape whipped back and the horses plunged forward.

The first plain fence was quickly upon them. Pinned in on all sides, Frankie barely had time to see the jump. Media Star hit it hard. He flung his head up and Frankie instinctively pushed back to counterbalance their forward momentum. Her reins sluiced through her fingers. On landing, she found herself upsides Rhys on a very keen Dory. The two stablemates galloped stride for stride down the backstretch.

Frankie didn't have time to evaluate Dory's progress. Media Star was running in snatches and was in danger of clipping heels with the horse in front.

They rose over the next, disjointed and jarring. Out of the corner of her eye, she saw Dory soar over, flicking up her heels like she was jumping the wall in a Puissance competition. Rhys clutched at the mare's neck to stop himself shooting over her head. Frankie grinned. Dory wasn't letting her down.

Rhys looked across at her as they charged towards the next. She was filled with satisfaction at his disgruntled acknowledgement.

They met the first open ditch together and while Dory put in a huge leap, Media Star added an extra half stride and paddled through the top of the birch.

Frankie shook her head as she regathered her reins.

'Many more jumps like that and your race'll be over by halfway,' she muttered to her mount. She urged him up on the inside of Dory to regain lost ground. Rounding the tight turn into the homestretch, Rhys looked over at her again. He opened his mouth to say something then changed his mind and focused on his race again. Frankie eased back on the reins as Media Star almost cannoned into Donnie up ahead. Rhys turned to her again, this time his face etched with impatience.

'What are you doing?' he yelled.

Frankie glared at him, annoyed by his interference when she was struggling to find a rhythm.

'I'm trying to settle him!'

'I can see that. What are you doing on the inside? Take him wide.'

Frankie threw him an impatient look.

'What?'

'Take him wide like Jack said!'

She looked at him suspiciously. Was he trying to sabotage her race? Rhys looked exasperated.

'I'm not fucking with you! Didn't you listen to Jack? He said take him wide so he can get a good look at his fences.'

Frankie hesitated.

'But I'm saving ground here,' she argued.

'Bullshit. You're losing ground because he's kicking the birch out of all his jumps. Let him see his fences and he'll find a rhythm!'

Her brain buzzed as she juggled her options. The first of four quick fences was approaching. She had to make a decision before she reached it. One last look at Rhys's demanding face and she made up her mind. She squeezed the reins, feeling Media Star respond with juddering alacrity. Letting Dory stride on in front, she angled him to the outside.

The next jump loomed and Media Star, with a clear view, pricked his ears. Seeing a stride, he lengthened beneath Frankie and took off. Frankie whooped. There was no feeling quite like it when you met a jump perfectly. They bounded over the next three like a beach ball and were rewarded with the cheering of the packed grandstand.

The pair passed the winning post four from the rear and set out on the final circuit with a swinging stride. The open ditch at the highest point of the course found out two runners and Frankie easily steered around the jockeys curled up protectively in the pockmarked turf.

Ahead, she could still see Rhys riding high above Dory's withers on the heels of the leaders. Passing their starting point, Frankie was encouraged when Media Star put in a big jump six from home. She didn't need to press for more speed. The rest of the field were already coming back to them, the jockeys hard at work to keep up the pace.

Skidding round the turn once more into the home straight, Frankie crouched lower in the saddle, her sights set firmly ahead. The rain peppered her cheeks with increased force. Four out and they drew level with the fifth-placed horse. Three out, Donnie's horse met it completely wrong and practically came to a halt on landing. Two out, Media Star passed the second and third horses. Come the last, only Dory's steel-grey quarters and Rhys's shapely behind were all that spoilt her view of the finish line.

Media Star twisted over the fence and grunted as he landed. His hooves plugged into the boggy ground before he laboriously galloped on. He didn't have much left in the tank. Flicking her reins at him, she rocked back and forth in the saddle. Media Star stuck his neck out in the race for the line. The noise of the screaming crowd drifted over to them as they drew up alongside Rhys and Dory. Leaning into one another, the two stable companions battled out the final two hundred yards.

Frankie threaded her whip to her outside hand and let it fall on Media Star's flank. Beside her, Rhys must have reached his maximum tally because he had his whip put away and was urging on his horse with hands and heels.

The shouts of the grandstand grew louder and more urgent as the ground between them and the red finish lollipop fell away. Media Star and Dory raced together, their heads bobbing in unison. Frankie's jaw ached as she gritted her teeth and drove for more speed. Fifty yards to go. She momentarily lost her rhythm as her foot entangled with Rhys's. Dory edged a head clear. Twenty yards to go. Media Star strained to draw level again. They thundered across the finish, locked together in battle.

Adrenalin roared through her body as Frankie stood up in her stirrups. She thought they might have nailed Rhys and Dory on the line, but she couldn't be sure. She turned to Rhys to see if he knew.

Rhys pulled his goggles down, his eyes energised and shining. With a benevolent smirk, he lifted his hand and signed an 'L' on his forehead.

'That's for running over my dog,' he said.

Frankie grinned.

By the look on his face, he had enjoyed that finish just as much as she had. And despite the official result which echoed from the loudspeaker confirming Blue Jean Baby as the winner, she knew she was no loser.

18

Frankie was determined to look on the bright side of having to drive a Kars-A-Chiefs' courtesy car and to park two streets from home in the drizzle. One: there was little chance of bumping (literally) into Rhys and Jasper this far from home and Two: Jasper was on the mend. A busted headlight was a small price to pay in comparison. And although it was raining, at least the temperatures had stayed relatively mild. Now into December, the National Hunt season was hotting up and as yet, not one single meeting had been lost to frost or snow.

Clipping the outside rear hubcap against the curb, Frankie managed to wedge the unfamiliar Vauxhall Astra into a parking space. She tried not to think about her beloved Mini sitting in a dirty Bristol garage surrounded by dismembered automobile body parts. She prayed that the Bonnie Tyler album jammed in the CD player wouldn't count against the car's assessment.

She zipped her Aspen Valley anorak up as far as it would go before opening the car door and stepping out into the murk. With her hands planted firmly in her pockets, she hurried across the road in the direction of her street. She jogged a couple of steps at the thought of a cup of hot tea and a toasted crumpet (a few hours on the cross-trainer should see that away fine). What's more, Tom had gone to London for the day to see a Social Services advisor about tracking down his birth parents and had sent Frankie a text twenty minutes ago saying he was only just leaving to come home. That meant she had the telly to herself for two and a half hours minimum.

Atticus Finch sat framed in the lounge window on the sill above the radiator. He watched Frankie jog up the steps to the front door with disparaging yellow eyes.

'Hello, Atticus!' Frankie called, tapping on the pane. 'Ready to watch some *Come Dine With Me* on Catch-up?'

Atticus Finch blinked at her and flicked his knobbly grey tail. He licked his lips, Frankie guessed not because he was anticipating the eating programme, but because he associated her presence with food.

She shook her head happily and dug into her jeans pocket for her keys. She pulled out the courtesy car key attached to a grimy cardboard stump. But no house keys. Frankie's blood ran cold. In her mind's eye she saw herself giving her Mini's keys to the Kars-A-Chiefs receptionist in their puny front office. Resting her forehead against the cold damp wood of the front door, she recalled blissfully handing over her house keys on the same key ring.

'Oh, shit,' she groaned.

Standing beneath the relative shelter of the door canopy, Frankie dismally considered her options. She could drive all the way back into Bristol and retrieve her keys, but she doubted whether the garage would still be open by the time she'd got through rush hour traffic. Besides which, she didn't really fancy driving all that way again.

She could go sit in the Golden Miller and wait for Tom to get back from London. As soon as that more attractive option occurred to her, she dismissed it. The Golden Miller was closed this evening as they prepared for some singing talent competition starting tomorrow.

Her only other option was to sit here and wait for Tom's return. Frankie looked out from the front step over to the green and skateboard park, blurry in the early evening rain. She groaned again and slid down the door to sit on the step. Two and a half hours, possibly more. Okay, she could do this, she told herself. She tucked her hands into her armpits. If it got really cold she could always run back to the car and sit in there for a while.

The streetlamp opposite the house buzzed and flickered into life as the dusk faded to night and the seconds drifted into minutes. A plaintive meow sounded to Frankie's right. Atticus Finch balanced precariously on top of the rickety garden gate that led down the side of the house. He leapt down and joined Frankie on the step, rubbing himself up against her legs. He looked up at her with round questioning eyes.

What are you doing sitting out here in the cold and wet? he seemed to ask.

'I forgot to separate my house keys from my car keys.' She sighed and stroked his bony back. 'Wish we could both fit through the cat flap.'

Atticus looked at her with disdain then sat down to begin the arduous task of cleaning himself with loud juicy slurps.

As the green became more indistinct in the sinking darkness, Frankie stretched out her cramping legs and considered repatriating to the courtesy car. Her movement triggered the security light above her head, bathing her in a deceptively warm golden light.

Uneven footsteps and canine breathing from the pavement made her look up. Frankie's heart did its customary triple beat. She did her best impersonation of a tortoise and tried to withdraw into her Aspen Valley jacket. The limping figure and his equally-limping dog passed by and she breathed a sigh of relief. But, of course, a bright red anorak wasn't exactly the best camouflage. A moment later, the figure stopped. He remained frozen, his focus still on the pavement five metres ahead of him. Slowly, he turned towards Frankie.

Frankie attempted a cheerful smile.

'Evening, Rhys,' she said.

Rhys continued to stare at her, his black curls plastered against his forehead. Jasper came loping on three legs back down the pavement to see what was keeping his master. Then, seeing Frankie sitting in the glow of the security light like some spiritual apparition, he bounded up the steps to greet her. Atticus hissed and whipped over the garden gate to safety.

'Frankie,' Rhys managed at last. 'What are you doing sitting out here in the rain?'

Frankie ruffled Jasper's brown and white speckled ears and fended off his friendly licks.

'I see you've forgiven me,' she said to the spaniel, letting the smell of damp dog clog her nostrils. She looked up at Rhys. 'My car needed its headlight replaced after its run-in with Jasper and I forgot to take my house keys off the key ring.' She felt a lot more stupid telling Rhys than she had telling Atticus.

Rhys surprisingly didn't look as disgusted though.

'Are you planning on sitting out here all night?'

'No. Tom's on his way back from London right now.'

Rhys moved a couple of steps closer to the path leading to her door.

'When does he get home?'

Frankie shrugged and avoided meeting his eye.

'Soon, I'm sure.'

'Oh, right,' Rhys said doubtfully.

'He texted me about an hour ago. Said he was just leaving.' Frankie took her mobile out of her pocket and looked at the time. 'Oh. Actually, make that only half an hour ago. It feels like longer.'

'It's going to take him ages to get back at this hour,' Rhys said.

'I'll be fine. I'm not actually getting that wet under here. And if it does get worse, I can always go sit in the courtesy car the garage gave me.'

Rhys nodded and an uncomfortable silence settled. Frankie dropped her gaze and scratched Jasper behind his ears. He panted happily in her face.

'You're bigger than I remember. Is he a Springer Spaniel?' she asked in an attempt to break the awkwardness.

Rhys's mouth twitched into a smile.

'No. He's just a big Cocker.'

Frankie laughed. Jasper tried to lick her cheeks and she fended him off.

'Jasper, stop that,' Rhys commanded.

The dog turned at the call of his name and lolloped down the path and down the street again.

'Well, goodnight then,' Rhys said clumsily.

'Goodnight.'

Rhys walked a couple of steps down the pavement then stopped again. Jasper's bark from further down the road made him take one more hesitant step.

Frankie tried not to watch him. She picked at the dried mud on the cuff of her jacket.

Rhys spun on his heel and marched back up her path.

'Would you like to come wait at mine?' he rushed.

Frankie stared at him in surprise.

Rhys looked away, embarrassment etched in every line on his face.

'Really?' Frankie managed at last.

Rhys shrugged.

'I live ten minutes away. Seems stupid to let you sit out here.'

Frankie contemplated turning him down. What horrors would the evening entail if she and Rhys were alone in each other's company for long? Then she considered the rain, now falling with more persistence, and the nose-diving temperature.

'Okay,' she said, surprising herself and Rhys. 'Thanks.'

19

Rhys swore beneath his breath as he unlocked the front door to his home and Jasper bulldozed past him into the front room.

'He doesn't seem any worse for his run-in with my car,' Frankie said.

Rhys grunted, flicking on the lights to reveal a comfortable modernised Georgian living room. Jasper headed for a beanbag in front of the fireplace and belly-flopped into its depths. Rhys gestured vaguely to two obese sofas.

'Make yourself at home.'

Frankie smiled her thanks and, feeling his eyes following her movements, walked across the creaking oak floorboards. She perched on the edge of one sofa, her hands clasped and looked up at him. Rhys stood stiffly to the side of the room.

'Excuse the mess,' he mumbled.

Frankie looked at her surroundings. A flat screen television hung above a DVD cabinet. A couple of what Frankie hoped were Jasper's toys lay on the floor and a coffee table hosted a shaggy pile of *Racing Post* newspapers and a winding tower of books.

'Mess? You should see mine and Tom's place if you want to see mess.'

Rhys attempted a smile.

'Would you like a drink? I don't have any alcohol. I, um, don't drink very often.'

Frankie nodded fervently. She needed a couple of minutes alone to find her bearings.

'Yes, please. Tea if you have any.'

'Last I checked tea doesn't contain hard liquor so yes, I do have tea.'

He exited the room through an archway at the rear of the lounge. Left to her own devices, Frankie removed her grubby trainers. A waft of smelly feet invaded the room and she hurriedly kicked her shoes beneath the sofa and waved the air in a futile attempt to disperse the odour. She padded around the room, brushing her fingers over a Mumford and Sons CD case lying on top of a stereo system. The mantelpiece above the fireplace supported an array of bronze horses, some framed landscape photographs and a solitary twenty-eighth birthday card. Frankie peeked at the inscription inside.

Dear Rhys, Happy birthday. Mamà.

She moved on to examine the photos. She was mildly surprised to see none of Rhys himself. In fact, in a room which boasted an entire wall of photographs in addition to the mantel, there were no people in them at all. Except for one, standing alone on a side table beneath a lamp. A beautiful Latino woman smiled at the camera. The fine lines at her eyes and mouth and the slight creping at her throat were the only giveaway signs of her middle-age. Frankie didn't need to look too closely either to tell she was the one who had written the birthday card. Although Rhys didn't share her smooth coffee-coloured skin, they both had the same straight narrow nose and deep-set eyes.

'Ha,' Frankie muttered. 'I knew those cheekbones couldn't be British.'

She moved to the adjoining wall, avoiding Jasper who was enthusiastically chewing on an old riding boot while keeping one boiled-egg eye on her. The blown up photographs hanging here looked professional. A derelict sea jetty at sunset; a bunch of sunlit daffodils stemming from crunchy snow; a grey heron wading through shallow water.

'Tea,' Rhys's voice interrupted her from behind. He put the mugs down on a side table separating the two sofas and sat down with a grunt. Frankie watched warily to see if her hidden trainers were still making their presence known. He wrinkled his nose. Maybe she could pin the blame on Jasper.

'These pictures are amazing,' she said in an attempt to distract him.

Rhys looked embarrassed.

'Thanks.'

Frankie's mouth fell open in surprise.

'These are yours?' she said. 'You did these?'

Rhys shrugged and blew on his tea.

'Photography's a hobby. We all need hobbies, right? It can't all be horses, horses, horses. What's yours?'

Now it was Frankie's turn to be embarrassed.

'Girl Guides. I help out once a week.'

Rhys's mouth twitched into a smile.

'Not poker club then?'

Frankie's laugh rattled, an octave too high. The mention of poker brought back memories of the night she'd won the ride on Dust Storm. And her win on Dust Storm she automatically associated with being given the National ride on Peace Offering. She wanted to broach that subject with Rhys about as much as she wanted a hole in the head.

'Your tea's here.'

She still wanted to look at the photos, but to appear polite she reached for her drink where its steam was blurring the picture of the Latino woman on the table.

'Is that your mother?' she asked.

Rhys nodded. Frankie took a slurp of tea and burnt her lip.

'She's gorgeous.' A moment of panic followed as Rhys must surely know of his similarity to his mother. Would he think she was implying she thought he was gorgeous too? But following it up with a defensive *You don't look like her at all* would also come across as insulting as well as a blatant lie. She looked at the picture's lonely human significance in the room and figured he must be close to his mother. 'Does she live nearby?'

Rhys shook his head.

'She's back living in Spain with my stepfather.'

'Oh, that's a pity.'

Rhys shrugged.

'Not really, no. My stepfather's a prick.'

Frankie could imagine Rhys being a nightmare stepchild too, but kept that to herself.

She turned back to the photographs on the wall, this time noticing a couple with horses in them. The first she had no trouble recognising. It was a shot of a tank-like racehorse crossing the Cheltenham finishing post with Rhys in red and white silks aboard.

'Virtuoso's Gold Cup,' she murmured. 'What a day that was.'

'Were you riding that day?' Rhys frowned.

Frankie shook her head.

'No chance. I've never ridden at the Festival. I'd love to though. There's so much history in that course.'

Dreams of perhaps having her first Cheltenham ride for Aspen Valley followed her to the next photograph. The horse was unsaddled and there were no distinguishing jockey silks to identify him by. It was obviously an Aspen Valley resident because she recognised the stabling in the background, but the tall dark bay horse in the foreshot didn't look familiar.

'Who's this?' she asked, turning back to Rhys.

Rhys's face sobered.

'Black Russian. I took that photo a couple of weeks before last year's Christmas Hurdle.'

Frankie remembered that Boxing Day meeting with clarity. She had watched it on television at home and along with thousands of others had witnessed Black Russian and Rhys leading the field only to fall at the last. Black Russian had been killed instantly and Rhys had been flung into the ground like a rag doll.

'I'm sorry,' she said, giving him a regretful smile. 'That was when you broke your leg, wasn't it?'

Rhys nodded.

'For the second time, yes.'

'Is that why you limp?'

Rhys took another sip of his tea before answering.

'Yeah.'

Frankie hesitated, unsure whether continuing this vein of conversation was wise.

'Does it still hurt?' she ventured.

'No.' Rhys shook his head and placed his mug back on its coaster. He patted the seat next to him. 'Come sit.'

Again, Frankie hesitated. Rhys patted the seat again.

'Come. I want to show you something. I'm not going to bite.'

Frankie could think of much worse things than being bitten by Rhys. Once settled beside him, he stretched out his legs.

'See?' he said, pointing at his feet. 'My right leg is about an inch shorter than my left.'

Frankie leaned forward to look at his black socks more carefully. A gurgle of laughter escaped and she clapped her hand over her mouth.

'Sorry, I didn't mean to laugh. It's not funny, not funny at all.'

Rhys allowed a self-effacing smile.

'At the time, maybe not. I broke it in three places. Hurt like a bastard. Then the doctors proceeded to put a full set of Meccano in to fix it. I was out of the saddle for nearly four months.'

'God, that's awful,' Frankie said, staring at Rhys's leg. She wondered if she would have the nerve to race ride again after such a horrific accident. 'Do you ever get scared? Like, do you worry that you'll fall and break it again knowing how sore it was last time?'

Rhys gave another of his indifferent shrugs.

'I was a bit nervous when I first got back up. But it's perfectly healed now – well, almost if you discount the fact that if I stand on my left leg I'm five foot eleven and if I stand on my right I'm five ten. After four months off the circuit I just wanted to get back into it so bad, fear was secondary.'

Frankie looked at Rhys with newfound respect.

He fidgeted under her admiring gaze and gestured to her tea left idling.

'Your tea's there. Better drink it before it gets cold.'

They sat in silence, only Jasper's toy-gnawing and occasional ear-scratching interrupting their thoughts.

'Are you going to the Aspen Valley Christmas party?' she asked.

'Hmm. Maybe. I don't know.'

'I've been told it's quite the highlight of the season bar Cheltenham and Aintree.'

'So I hear.'

They lapsed into silence again. Frankie wondered what he was thinking. His tension was almost palpable. She daren't look at him, especially in such intimate proximity. He drummed his fingers on the arm of the sofa.

'That night in the Golden Miller,' he blurted, 'after the Becher Chase – I-I'm sorry for the way I behaved.'

Frankie stared at him. Had Rhys just apologised? To *her*? She opened and closed her mouth like a beached bass.

'I'd been drinking and I don't often drink – you can tell why. I'm not exactly the happiest of drunks.'

'Ookaaay,' Frankie said, her eyes still the size of saucers.

'And that stuff I said about you being scared – well, it was your first time over the big fences and I guess you were allowed to be scared. You're allowed to be scared anyway, never mind when facing Aintree for the first time.'

Frankie was about to accept his stumbling apology when his last comment stopped her short.

'*I'm* allowed to be scared?' she repeated. 'Why, because I'm a girl?'

'What? No,' Rhys said irritably as if this was the first time he'd noticed she was female. 'I mean I understand if you are. Scared that is, not a girl.' He gestured to her body, hastily averting his eyes from her chest.

'Why would I be scared?' she asked with caution.

'Because maybe you associate falls, and perhaps even just riding, with danger.'

'I-I don't understand.'

'Sorry, I'm not saying this very well,' Rhys sighed. 'I'm talking about Seth.' He paused and Frankie stared at him in astonishment. 'I'm just saying it's okay if his accident scares you a bit when you're riding.'

'Seth?' she echoed.

'What happened to Seth was a freak accident. It could've happened any time, any place.' Rhys at last managed to meet her gaze with a consolatory grimace.

Frankie's throat contracted.

'How can you say that?'

'Well, because of-of...' Rhys frowned. 'Were you told what happened that day?'

Frankie forced herself to relive the moment her parents had come into her bedroom and broken the news to her that Seth had been killed. She had been reading *To Kill A Mocking Bird*, her favourite book at the time. So unexpected had the news been, it had literally taken her breath away. No hints, no sense of foreboding. One moment he had been alive, the next he was dead. It was months before she was able to comprehend that he was never coming back.

'They said he'd had a fall while working one of the horses and had hit his head.'

'Do you want to know the full story?' he asked gently.

She looked at him, wide-eyed, feeling more scared now than she'd done before any race.

'H-how would you know?'

'I was there when it happened.'

Frankie swallowed the swollen lump in her throat. Did she honestly want to know the intimate details of her brother's death? Her parents had been so vague about his accident that every time she had probed for more, to understand what had happened, she had been made to feel like she was after the gory details. She didn't blame them for that. They just didn't want to go over such sensitive ground. And nowadays the accident was hardly ever referred to.

Maybe it would be less upsetting if she just stayed ignorant. She didn't know for sure if Seth's accident had anything to do with her fears before racing, but mightn't she be risking losing her nerve completely by hearing the whole story? On the other hand, here she was, five years on, with a first-hand witness offering to fill her in on those missing puzzle pieces she'd so often wondered about.

She nodded.

'I want to know, please.'

'It was the beginning of the season,' Rhys began. 'Most of the horses were still doing roadwork before going back into full training. We were taking a string out onto the back roads through Windale Forest. It was a sunny morning, but it had rained the night before so the roads were still wet. Seth was leading the string on Thunder Chief. We were riding two abreast. I was a couple of horses back.' Rhys paused as he too relived the moment. 'The roads were quiet and we were trotting. Seth was laughing up ahead. Then a muntjac deer jumped across the road. Came out of nowhere. The horse June was riding upsides Thunder Chief spooked and gave him an even bigger fright. He slipped on the road and went down. Seth didn't stand a chance of throwing himself clear. It happened so fast. He hit his head and when I - when I -' Rhys swallowed hard and took a deep breath. 'When I felt for his pulse, he was already gone. It was so quick. I doubt whether he would even have realised what was happening.'

Tears slipped down Frankie's cheeks unchecked. She continued to stare at Rhys long after he'd finished. At last she knew. That niggling feeling of unanswered questions had finally abated and all thanks to the most unlikely source.

Rhys twisted his mouth in regret when he saw her tears.

'I'm sorry,' he muttered.

She gave a watery smile.

'Thank you for telling me,' she whispered.

Rhys stared at the rug, back to his awkward manner and nodded briskly.

'No problem.'

He rose to his feet.

'Would you like some dinner?'

Frankie brushed her cheeks dry with the back of her hand and sniffed. She opened her mouth to refuse, but Rhys spoke first.

'It's not much, just some mushroom risotto, but you might as well have some. I've got to eat and I certainly can't have my dinner while you sit there starving.'

An hour later, with low-cal, high-carb risotto put away, Frankie's mobile beeped. She dug it out of her jeans pocket and opened a message from Tom.

'It's from Tom. He's probably wondering where – oh, okay. Maybe not,' she corrected herself as she read the text message. 'His connecting train has been delayed. He's not going to be home for another hour he says.' She hazarded a look at Rhys to see how he was digesting the news. His face was expressionless. 'Sorry.'

Rhys transferred his dinner plate from his lap to the side table.

'What sort of films do you enjoy?' he asked.

Frankie beamed with relief that he didn't seem in too much of a hurry to kick her out. As long as it was a fairly modern film she wasn't fussy.

'I don't know. I've a pretty wide taste.'

He got to his feet and limped over to the DVD cabinet.

'What about *On the Waterfront*? Marlon Brando. Have you seen that?'

Crikey, every time a coconut.

She shook her head prompting him to pull out the DVD. He looked sheepish as he tapped the case against the palm of his hand.

'It's one of my favourites.'

'Let's watch it then,' Frankie replied. She could survive this. *On the Waterfront* was a classic, after all. She pulled her feet up beneath her and made herself comfortable against the arm of the sofa.

Rhys slotted in the DVD and switched on a side lamp before turning off the mains. In the semi-darkness, as the credits began to roll, he came and sat next to her.

Despite being mightily impressed by how attractive Marlon Brando had been in his younger years, Frankie felt her eyelids getting heavier as the film progressed. Lulled in and out of consciousness, she vaguely registered the words "*I coulda been a contender. I coulda been somebody*" and then the credits rolling once more before sleep overtook her completely. She murmured as a blanket was laid over her. She pulled it up to her neck and nestled down further into the sofa. She didn't stir as Rhys switched off the light and crept out of the room.

20

Frankie woke to a lungful of bad breath and a wet cheek. Jasper's doleful brown eyes lit up when his morning kiss had the desired effect. Frankie groaned and pushed his nose out of her face. She rolled over onto her back. Then she froze. In the semi-darkness of dawn her eyes darted about her. The clink of cups and plates from the kitchen made her jump. She stared at Jasper again, still hovering over her.

'Shit, Jasper,' she whispered.

Tunnelling under a blanket she hadn't recalled wearing last night, she pulled out her mobile phone from her pocket. 5:40am. An envelope flashed in the corner of the screen. Frankie clicked on it. A message from Tom appeared.

Where are you?

'You probably wouldn't believe me if I told you,' she murmured.

Giving Jasper another shove, she sat up and rummaged beneath the sofa for her shoes. She stood up and shivered, then on second thoughts wrapped the discarded blanket around her shoulders. A yellow light seeped through the lounge's rear archway and Frankie followed it into the kitchen. Jasper trotted ahead like a proud host. Her heart began to pummel her chest when she heard Rhys greet the spaniel.

'Did you wake her like I asked?'

Frankie turned the corner, seeing Rhys, dressed in a black Adidas tracksuit, squatting down face-to-face with Jasper. His hair was tousled and his face still creased from sleep. A kettle rasped on the worktop behind him.

'He did.'

Rhys looked up at her cocooned in the blanket he'd laid over her the night before. Frankie gave an embarrassed smile and looked down at the floor tiles.

'Sorry I fell asleep.'

'I'm more upset you fell asleep during *On the Waterfront*. That film's a classic.' He straightened up. 'Tea?'

Frankie unsuccessfully tried to bite back a smile at Rhys's offended expression and shook her head.

'I'd better get home. I'll be late for work otherwise.'
Rhys nodded.
'Are you riding at Wincanton this afternoon?'
'Yes. Only the one though.'
'Probably see you later then,' he said.

Frankie nodded. The kettle behind Rhys clicked off. Out of sight, it made his head look like it was steaming. He looked uncomfortable.

'Well, thanks for letting me stay,' she settled on a casual tone. 'And sorry again.'

He followed her out of the kitchen and to the front door. In the narrow entrance hall, Frankie couldn't meet his eyes. Her lungs contracted and her blood decided to use her veins as an Autobahn. Rhys opened the door for her. Frankie stepped out onto the landing.

'Frankie –' he began, his tone urgent.

Did she detect a note of desperation in it too?

'Yes?'

Rhys shifted from five-ten to five-eleven. He pointed vaguely at her body.

'The blanket? Can I have it back?'

Her face became the tollgate for her express-travelling blood. She could even feel her eyelids burning. She unwrapped herself and exchanged the blanket for her Aspen Valley anorak.

'Where've you been?' Tom's tone was indignant when he answered Frankie's knock on the front door. Frankie bustled in, keen to get out of the cold. She tried to pinch the slice of peanut-buttered toast which Tom was holding aloft, but he whipped it out of reach.

'Rhys Bradford's.'

Tom's jaw slackened. Frankie's inner mischief demon rubbed its hands together. She snatched the toast from Tom and made a dash for the kitchen.

'Rhys Bradford?' Tom echoed behind her. 'As in Rhys "I Hate the World and All Who Live In It" Bradford?'

'The very same,' she mumbled through a mouthful.

Tom appeared at the kitchen doorway. Frankie offered him his half-eaten breakfast back and he took it like a post-traumatic shock victim. She delved into the laundry basket and extricated a clean pair of jeans.

'You and Rhys?'

Frankie shrugged.

'Well, you know how I feel about him.'

'Yes, but up until about ten days ago you were saying he hated your guts. You ran over his dog, for Christ's sake.'

'Not on purpose.'

'How on earth did you – you know?'

Frankie grinned and tried to bat the worst creases out of the jeans.

'You really want all the intimate details?'

Tom looked everywhere but at her.

'No, but I do want to know how you got to a point where there *are* intimate details.'

Frankie pretended to examine her nails. They were blunt and still dirty from yesterday's work.

'A scarlet woman never reveals her secret seduction techniques.'

'Frankie! Are you being serious? You can't be. You've had fewer pricks than a brand new dartboard. You're not scarlet – you're more of a-a rose pink when it comes to seduction.'

Frankie wrinkled her nose.

'I hate pink.'

Tom held out his hands in exasperation.

'Frankie, where were you all night?'

She paused. It was worth stretching this out just to watch Tom's expression, but she also wanted to find out how his meeting had gone with the Social Services advisor.

'I was at Rhys's,' she said again then held up her hand when Tom rolled his eyes. 'I was. I forgot my keys to the house and he walked by when I was sitting waiting for you to come home. He invited me round to his flat; we had dinner. Then he put on an old black and white movie and I fell asleep on the couch. The next thing I knew it was morning.'

Tom still looked aghast.

'He got you to watch an old movie?'

'It was the only way I could get him to release me from the headlock.'

Tom swallowed.

'I worry about your sanity, you know.'

Frankie gave him a loving smile and stole the last of his toast on her way to the bathroom.

21

That evening's Guides meeting ended on a good note for Frankie. She loved the Showtime Go For It challenge. Everyone had dressed up in costume, plastering each other in makeup before taking to the stage with dramatics and song. It was fun, but by the end she was exhausted. One of the last to step out through Helensvale Community Hall's creaking door, she was surprised to see Cassa Preston, still dressed in her purple sequinned tutu, which Louise from Starfish Patrol had helped design, sitting on the bottom step of the hall. With just a leotard top for protection, Cassa's gangly body was trembling with cold. She was trying to punch a number into her mobile phone, but her hands were shivering so much she kept having to start over.

'Cassa?' Frankie said, squatting down beside the girl and placing a gentle hand on her icy shoulder. 'Is your mum picking you up?'

Cassa shook her head.

'She has to work the graveyard shift tonight at the hospital. She told me to call a taxi.' Her breath fogged in front of her face, making her features appear even more dismal.

'Do you live in town?'

Cassa nodded.

'South end of Helensvale.'

Frankie looked at Cassa thoughtfully. Tonight, for the first time, she'd felt she was making progress with her. Dressed up in a slightly ridiculous outfit, Cassa had sparkled without her mother's supervision and had joined in the singing and acting with gusto. Frankie remembered the first meeting Cassa had attended and how she'd said she wanted to be a singer, but had changed her mind when Mrs Preston had appeared. Frankie was intrigued.

'Let me give you a lift home then,' she said. 'I probably don't live too far from you.'

Cassa looked at her hesitantly and Frankie nodded to her phone.

'Come on, I'm not a stranger. You can text your mum if you like and tell her I'm giving you a lift – and saving you some money.'

Cassa smiled and stood up. Frankie was encouraged to see she trusted her enough not to message her mother. They walked across to the Vauxhall Astra still on loan from the garage. Seeing the car sparked Frankie's memory.

'We've just got to make a slight detour. My housemate, Tom, will be at the pub and he's got the keys to our house.'

They pulled out of the Community Centre's car park and headed down Helensvale's High Street towards the Golden Miller. Frankie was aware of Cassa sitting beside her as relaxed as a stone sculpture.

'Did you enjoy tonight?' she asked.

'Yes, thank you.'

'I thought you would. You said in the GFI Top Job that you wanted to be a singer.'

Cassa sent her a sharp look.

'It's okay,' Frankie said. 'I'm not about to tell your mum. Although I don't see why wanting to be a singer should be a problem. From what I heard tonight you've got a really good voice.'

Cassa's big eyes glinted in the darkness.

'You really think so?'

'Of course. You've got soul. Who's your favourite singer?'

Cassa shrugged her bony shoulders.

'I don't know. I guess I listen to a lot of Adele.'

'Good taste,' Frankie said. She attempted the chorus to *Set Fire to the Rain* and Cassa collapsed into the corner of her seat in giggles. Frankie smiled, happy to see her relax.

A couple of minutes later, she yanked the handbrake up. In front of them, the Golden Miller looked surprisingly busy. Not heaving, but livelier than usual.

'Right, won't be a sec.'

'Look! They're having a singing competition,' Cassa gasped, pointing at a big poster on the door.

'Oh yes, I forgot that was starting tonight. God, I hope Tom's not entering. Do you fancy a go?' She grinned at Cassa as she went to unclip her seatbelt. The humour drained from her face though when she saw Cassa seriously considering her suggestion.

Cassa looked at her like a timid kitten.

'Do you think I could?' she whispered.

Entrusted to her care at a Girl Guides meeting, Mrs Preston would not look kindly on Frankie taking Cassa to the local pub and entering her in a karaoke competition.

'I was just kidding, Cassa. It's not a good idea.'

'But you said I was good.'

'You are, but...'

Cassa's eyes bore into hers, desperate for her approval, self-confidence hanging in the balance. Frankie teetered. What harm would it do? Mrs Preston didn't have to find out and the Golden Miller was a family pub.

'All right, then,' she said at last. She hesitated again as Cassa scrabbled to open the door. Leaning behind, she retrieved a black overcoat lying on the backseat. 'Just wear this, okay? And don't tell your mother about this.'

Holding Cassa's hand, Frankie weaved her way through the crowd to the bar which, in the dim lighting, gleamed like a crown. Tom was sitting in his usual spot at the far corner of the bar. Nobody noticed their entrance, listening instead in grimacing fascination to a stable lad giving a particularly painful rendition of Kaiser Chiefs' *I Predict A Riot* on a specially rigged stage in the restaurant section. Joey, the bartender, was leaning on the pine bar chatting with Tom. Beneath the sunken lights within the bar's overhang, Joey's blond ponytail shone almost white. Tom creased up at something he said, but stopped laughing when he saw Frankie.

'Evening all,' she beamed. 'This is Cassa. We were hoping she could have a go in this karaoke competition thing. Joey, is there an age limit?'

'Sixteen, I think.'

Half relieved, Frankie was about to express what a shame that was when Cassa piped up.

'Lucky I had my birthday the other week then.'

Frankie opened her mouth to object, but closed it again when Cassa squeezed her hand. Her eyes pleaded with her. Frankie swayed. It was just the one evening, Cassa obviously really wanted to do this and she *did* look old for her age.

'Yes, isn't it just,' she said.

Tom narrowed his eyes at her, but Joey didn't notice her hesitant reply. Instead, he slapped an entry form onto the bar.

'All you need to do is fill this in and since you're still under eighteen, we need an adult's signature.'

What harm could it do, Frankie asked herself again? Ha! Signing something that was untrue could potentially be very harmful. But Cassa was already carefully filling in both of their names.

'Just sign here,' she said, pushing the pen into Frankie's hand. 'Please.'

Frankie was just underlining her signature when the stable lad finished his song. A panel of three judges, which she hadn't noticed before, then proceeded to rip him to shreds.

'Oh, God. What am I getting us into?' she murmured.

Twenty minutes later, Frankie had sunk a vodka and orange and was feeling more at ease with her new stint in fraud. She and Tom moved closer to the stage as Cassa's name was called out.

The vibrant hum in the room quietened as thirteen-year-old Cassa Preston took centre stage. Her sequinned tutu peeped through the unbuttoned front of Frankie's oversized coat. Frankie held her breath. Cassa licked her lips and passed the microphone from one hand to the other. The running piano introduction to Adele's *Someone Like You* flooded the room. Raising the microphone trembling to her lips, Cassa began to sing. Hesitant at first, she gradually found her rhythm. Her rounded shoulders straightened as she belted out the chorus. The overcoat didn't seem half so big anymore.

Frankie's breath shuddered through her and her eyes prickled with tears. She darted a look around. The Golden Miller was captivated by the heartbroken melody and strength in Cassa's voice. The final piano chord fell and for a moment the room remained quiet, like the moment following an earthquake. Then the ovation began. Frankie bit her lip and clapped her hands until they stung.

'My God,' Tom yelled above the noise. 'Where did you find her?'

'Girl Guides,' Frankie yelled back, beaming with pride.

Cassa stood, smiling uncertainly beneath the spotlight. As the cheering subsided, the judges passed their verdicts. The third, a man who Frankie noticed had been particularly nasty to the previous contestants, sat with his arms crossed. Frankie figured he was trying to pull off a Simon Cowell, but not quite nailing it in his flat cap.

'Cassa,' he said. 'How old are you?'

Frankie's heart stopped. Her eyes inadvertently strayed to the exit.

'S-sixteen,' Cassa whispered into the mic.

The judge frowned and Frankie closed her eyes, waiting for her short-lived life of crime to end.

'You're at school?' he prompted instead.

Cassa nodded.

'So Wednesday nights you're presumably at home doing your homework?'

'I g-go to G-girl Guides.'

He regarded her with over-acted condescension.

'Not anymore you're not! You're through to the next round!'

The patrons of the Golden Miller in their tweed jackets cheered their approval. But Frankie didn't hear them. She turned to Tom, who was applauding along with them.

'What does he mean "the next round"?' she exclaimed. 'I thought this was a one-night karaoke competition!'

'Oh, no.' Tom shook his head. 'This is huge, one of the Golden Miller's big ideas to bring in customers. They're doing their own *X Factor-cum-Helensvale's Got Talent* competition except with pub votes rather than phone votes.'

'Jesus Christ Almighty, what have I done now?' Frankie groaned.

22

Frankie sat in the salon chair wearing an apron while Vanessa tugged through her newly washed hair with a comb. With her fringe scraped back, Frankie watched her mother in the mirror critically examining her split ends. Their eyes met.

'Let's do something a bit more daring,' Vanessa said with a twinkle in her eye.

'How daring?'

'Well, your fringe is so long now, it's not even a fringe. It's just a – a –'

Frankie waited for her mother to find a kind way to insult her.

'A mess?' she suggested.

'Yes,' Vanessa said, inspired. 'And we need to take off at least two inches to get rid of these split ends, so why not take it a bit shorter? Have a bob with bangs.'

'A bob?' Frankie said, horrified at the thought of all of her hair being chopped off.

'Not a short short bob. Just about here above the shoulders.' Vanessa held up the serpent of wet hair. 'See what lovely shoulders and neck you have. You'll look divine.'

Frankie chewed her bottom lip thoughtfully. She did want to look good, to make an impression tonight at the Aspen Valley Christmas party. She airily bypassed the image of Rhys which sprung into her head, but in the end couldn't deny it; it was *him* she wanted to impress.

She imagined herself sauntering into the yard – she was still a bit hazy as to where exactly on the premises the party was being held – and her gaze locking with Rhys's. She would smile coyly and become immediately distracted by other people wanting to be in her company. Rhys would limp over – no, she scrapped that fantasy – Rhys would *walk* over, pass her a glass of champagne. He would smile that crooked smile that lifted only one side of his mouth, a dimple indenting his cheek and say -

'Darling, I really do feel you should use a better conditioner for your hair.'

Frankie blinked back to the present as Vanessa interrupted her daydream.

'Hmm?'

'What conditioner do you use?'

'I don't use conditioner.'

'There you go then.'

'Come on, Mum. I'm a jockey, I've got bigger things to worry about than what hair products to use. Besides, I wear a helmet all the time.'

Vanessa sighed dramatically.

'That's no excuse. Jockey or no jockey, every woman should take care of herself.'

'God, you make me sound like a bag lady.'

'That's unfair on bag ladies,' Vanessa said, waggling some scissors at her in the mirror. 'Given the chance I'm sure they would take more care of their appearance.'

Frankie surrendered. She supposed an extra ten minutes a day applying some moisturiser and pampering her hair wouldn't hurt. At the back of her mind, she concluded Rhys would probably never notice her if she didn't put in some effort.

'I do want to look good,' she said.

Vanessa eyes twinkled and she snapped the pair of scissors together.

'I am going to make you look drop dead gorgeous.'

Humming along to Rod Stewart, Vanessa got to work, measuring, snipping, sliding her fingers through Frankie's blonde split ends. Frankie watched her work, feeling a stab of panic every now and then when a long lick of hair would spill into her lap. A question kneeled on her tongue, begging to be asked. Frankie waited until Vanessa had put the scissors down before attempting it. She didn't want a Captain Spock like Susan Beckett.

'Mum, why didn't Dad get to ride Crowbar in the National?'

Vanessa paused and looked at her in the mirror. She secured a wad of Frankie's hair onto her crown with a clip and shrugged.

'I can't remember. It was all such a long time ago.'

Frankie wasn't convinced.

'How come Alan Bradford got the ride? Is that why Dad hates the Bradfords so much?'

'I don't know, Frankie. They were rivals. Maybe that's why they didn't get on.'

'But Dad's still friends with other ex-jockeys.'

Vanessa stopped snipping and looked at Frankie, resigned.

'Your father and Alan Bradford didn't see eye-to-eye, that's all. It happens.'

'But what caused it? Dad gets so sensitive whenever I even mention the name Bradford. It had to have been more than just simple jockey rivalry.'

'Frankie, honey. All of that happened nearly thirty years ago. It's in the past, don't go digging it up now. What went on was between your father and Alan Bradford.'

Frankie recalled Rhys's outburst on the way to the vets.

'He doesn't sound like a very nice person,' she said. 'I don't think Rhys gets on with his dad either.'

'Really?' Vanessa said airily. 'Are you and Rhys friends, dear?'

'I don't know,' she replied in complete honesty. 'We get on better than we used to, I suppose. He wasn't terribly pleased when Pippa gave me the ride on Peace Offering or when I ran over his dog.'

Standing square behind her, Vanessa pulled Frankie's hair through her fingers, measuring its lengths.

'But now he's forgiven you?'

Frankie shrugged, causing Vanessa to remeasure the lengths.

'He must have. I stayed the night at his place the other day – *ow*,' she complained as Vanessa pulled her hair.

'Sorry. Are you and Rhys Bradford, um, you know – *dating?*'

Frankie sighed. Oh, if only.

'No. I got locked out of the house and Tom was in London so he let me sleep on his sofa.'

'That was very nice of him,' Vanessa said, the words sounding like they were being strangled from her.

'Yeah, it was, wasn't it?' Frankie said, almost proud of Rhys. She contemplated whether she could confide in her mother. Although Tom knew about her crush, he wasn't very helpful when it came to building on it. On the other hand she wasn't sure if her mother would approve, even after saying everything was in the past. 'I like him,' she said at last.

Vanessa spun her round in the chair so she could work on Frankie's fringe and pumped the chair higher. Once she'd finished, she looked her daughter in the eye. Frankie hadn't seen her so solemn before.

'I thought you might,' Vanessa finally said with a sigh.

'Why?'

'Well, you were a bit in awe of him when you first started working with him, weren't you? He's a stylish rider and he's good-looking. I suppose I'd worry if you didn't fancy him.' Her usual joviality was back and Frankie grinned.

'He is sexy, isn't he?'

'I'm not saying anything more.' Vanessa leaned forward and snipped the last stray strands of her fringe away. She gave her daughter a mischievous smile. 'But jockeys are the best shag you'll ever have.'

'Ew, Mum!' Frankie squealed. 'Too much information!'

Vanessa stood up straight, looking smug.

'Just saying.' She spun Frankie round again and looked at her in the mirror. 'Is he going to be there tonight?'

'I don't know. I hope so,' she added sheepishly.

'Well, we are going to make you irresistible.'

'Don't you disapprove?'

'Would it make any difference?'

Frankie pulled a doubtful face.

'Maybe.'

'Frankie, it's your life. I'm not going to tell you how to live it. And if he's as nice as you say he is then why would I want to stop you? Now, a few highlights here then we can shape your eyebrows now that we can see them. Rhys Bradford won't know what hit him.'

'I don't want to look like I've made too much effort,' Frankie said in a sudden panic. 'It's only a staff Christmas party.'

'A party's a party, my dear.'

'So I've been told. Pippa's organised the whole thing. She did last year's party and apparently it was a blast.'

'Remember to drink lots of water if you're going to be drinking booze.'

'Yes, Mum.'

'And remember to use protection if you –'

'*Okay*, Mum! I am twenty-three. I have learnt these things.'

Vanessa unhooked the hairdryer from beside the mirror and looked at Frankie in mock horror.

'What? You mean you're not a virgin?'

'Mum, please.'

'Okay, okay. Sorry. So I know about David Grenton,' she said, naming Frankie's boyfriend from her teens.

'Actually David was number two,' Frankie said with a sly grin.

Vanessa switched on the dryer and began to pull Frankie's hair down in an inward curl around her shoulders with a round-brush.

'Scandalous!' she said, raising her voice above the roar. 'And to think a daughter of mine could be such a Jezebel.'

Frankie grinned.

'May I remind you that you are currently "grooming" me for such a deed?'

Vanessa winked at her.

23

Frankie pulled into Aspen Valley's car park at a quarter to nine that evening. Stepping out into the drizzle, she wished she'd worn something more suited to the weather. Instead, she had to rely on just a High Street rip-off of one of Victoria Beckham's dresses and a pashmina shawl to keep the cold and rain at bay.

She followed the sound of booming music along the muddy walkway between the hay barn and the indoor school to the latter's wide entrance at the far end. She realised her fantasy earlier was way off the mark as soon as she stepped over the threshold. The air was warm and musty with the mixed scents of horses, sand and perfumes. The vast building was lit by coloured lights whizzing across the tin ceiling. It seemed the whole of Aspen Valley's fifty odd staff and their partners were inside, sitting on jumps and barrels stacked at the sides. At the far end a DJ was nodding to the beat of a dance track behind a barricade of music equipment, and tables on either side bore punch bowls and crates of drinks. Even though she felt overdressed and her hair still didn't feel quite her own yet, she noticed most of the girls had also made an effort to don a more feminine look. Two of the seasonal workers from Poland were necking in the shadows beside the doorway while others danced in a clearing in the middle of the school.

She looked around frantically for a face comfortably familiar for her to approach without seeming weird. No, it was too dark. Making a conscious effort to stand up straight, she walked across to the one of the drinks tables. Alcohol was always a good place to start when feeling self-conscious.

She helped herself to a plastic cup of punch and feeling less conspicuous with a drink in her hand, turned to survey the other attendees. Rhys was nowhere to be seen and her excitement sunk a level. She recognised June standing not far away in conversation with three other lasses. She hesitated. Her eyes left that group to seek out other allies. At last, she saw Pippa sitting on a jump along the far wall, chatting with Billy and a slimmer-looking Emmie.

*

'Hey, Frankie!' Pippa cried above the music as she came within earshot. 'Come join us. You remember Emmie, don't you?'

'Hi,' said Frankie, still feeling a little shy. 'How've you been?'

'Urgh, you know, sleepless nights, lots of puke and dirty nappies,' Emmie shrugged. 'Mum's babysitting tonight and giving us the night off.'

Pippa patted the pole next to her.

'Come sit, Frankie. I like your hair. Have you had it cut or have I just never noticed?'

Frankie gratefully sat down so she didn't feel so like a freak show in front of a seated audience.

'I just had it done. My mum's a hairdresser.'

'Wow,' said Emmie. 'She's good. You look like a royal.'

'Speaking of which,' Pippa said. 'We were just talking about whether his lordship, Sir Bradford, is going to grace us with his presence. Donnie's just arrived.'

Frankie felt like pointing out that a lordship and a knighthood were two completely different things and neither necessarily constituted royalty, but then again she also wanted to know if Rhys was going to attend.

'Did he say he was coming?' she asked.

'Jack didn't hold out much hope,' Pippa replied. 'He didn't come to the last one.'

'In his defence he was holed up in hospital with a smashed up leg,' Billy piped up.

'Oh, yes. I forgot about that.'

'Where's Jack?' Frankie asked.

Holding her WKD aloft, Pippa pointed into the throngs of people.

'Over there talking to Donnie. Have you seen Donnie's girlfriend? She's stunning. Yet Donnie looks like he got into a fight with an angry tractor. He must have a great sense of humour or something.'

'I think "something",' Frankie grinned. 'Or to be more precise probably ten inches of something.'

Pippa gasped and she and Emmie stared at her, wide-eyed. Billy looked horrified.

'Ten inches? Are you serious?' Pippa squeaked. 'How do you know? Did you and Donnie have a thing?'

'No, but sadly we do sometimes have to share the same sauna at the races.'

'I don't know if I'd call that particularly sad – oh, hello,' Pippa interrupted herself, focussing on the doorway. 'I don't suppose you know what *his* measurements are?'

Frankie followed her gaze.

Rhys stood in the doorway, looking much like Frankie had felt when she'd first arrived. Dressed in dark jeans and a black dinner shirt undone a couple of buttons, he scanned the indoor school. Frankie's mouth watered.

'No,' she said, answering Pippa's question beneath her breath. 'But I would love to find out.'

As the night barrelled on, Frankie became less conscious of Rhys standing on the sidelines in company with Donnie. Buoyed by alcohol and the general cheery atmosphere, she laughed as Billy pulled her round the sandy dance floor and tried to match his Gangnam style moves. Any reservations she had about her own dance skills were put to bed by Billy's own inept rhythm. Hanging onto each other as the song ended, they stumbled back to Pippa and Emmie and collapsed in a heap of giggles onto the jump.

'Having a good time?' Pippa yelled in her ear.

'Great time!' she yelled back. 'You?'

'Brilliant. Seems everyone's enjoying themselves.'

'Cheers to that,' Frankie said, raising her cup of punch to tap against Pippa's.

Pippa cheered and whooped as Jack was dragged onto centre stage by inebriated stable lasses to dance to a sixties track. Frankie clapped with everyone else, laughing at her boss' reluctance. Not for the first time that night, her gaze drifted over to Rhys. Coloured lights lit up his face and she saw a small smile on his face as he too watched Jack.

Pippa nudged Frankie with alcohol-induced forced.

'Why do you reckon he even came?' she said, nodding in the jockey's direction.

'What do you mean?'

'He hasn't danced once all night. He's just stood there drinking poxy orange juice.'

'He doesn't drink,' Frankie replied. 'And he's probably riding tomorrow at Chepstow.'

'Bleurgh,' Pippa said, fobbing a hand in his direction and nearly falling off the jump. 'Party pooper.'

A hazy wall of defensiveness rose in Frankie.

'Maybe he's just shy. Nobody's exactly dragged him onto the floor like they have Jack.'

Pippa looked at her, eyes not quite focussing.

'I bet,' she said, swinging her drink up and pointing at Frankie, 'he wouldn't dance even if the Duckegg of Chambrish asked him to.'

Frankie licked her lips in contemplation and glanced over at Rhys again. Alcohol lent her courage – or stupidity, but that word had ceased to exist after three strong doses of punch.

'How much?'

Pippa flung her head back and tried to focus on Frankie.

'Kate's here?'

Frankie grinned.

'No. I mean how much if I got him to dance with me?'

Pippa's head lolled from side to side as her brain tried to process what Frankie was saying.

'Ten quid – no, twen'y!'

'You're on.' Frankie downed the last swallow of her drink and handed an open-mouthed Pippa the empty cup.

Walking not quite as steadily as before around the outskirts of the school, she approached Rhys. She wiped the sweat from her palms on her dress and tossed her new hairstyle back. Donnie was first to spot her advance. He said something in Rhys's ear. Frankie gulped as Rhys turned to watch her as well. She suddenly felt very sober and not quite as confident as she had on the other side of the arena. Donnie grinned at her sudden faltering steps. Rhys just watched her, not smiling, but thankfully not sneering either. Frankie's eyes whipped around, trying to find a get out clause. There was none. She gulped again. She was beyond the point of no return.

'Hello, Frankie,' Donnie said as she drew to a stop before them.

'Hello, Donnie. Hello, Rhys,' she said politely.

'Frankie,' Rhys greeted her with a nod.

They stared at each other. Frankie didn't know what to say – well, she did, but didn't have the guts to say it just yet. She licked her lips and tried to smile.

'Having fun?' she asked.

'Yeah, not bad.'

Adrenalin whizzed through her body as the moment of truth arrived. Donnie's grinning face was not helping matters. In the ultraviolet light, it looked like he'd swallowed a piano. Frankie felt about fifteen as she focussed solely on Rhys.

'Would – would you like to d-dance?'

The lights played off Rhys's face. Was she imagining it or did she see a trace of pity in his eyes? Oh God, he was going to turn her down. How would she survive the walk of shame back to Pippa and the others?

Donnie said something in Rhys's ear, shielding his mouth so she couldn't lip-read. Frankie wished he would go away. Rhys's gaze flickered away from Frankie to look levelly at Donnie. She held her breath as he returned his focus back to her. The corner of his mouth twitched.

'Sure. Why not?'

Frankie staggered backwards. In a daze she let Rhys take her hand, his touch warm on her palm, and allowed herself to be led to the makeshift dance floor. Open mouths and wide unfocussing eyes followed their passage. Frankie didn't blame them, she was working hard on not adopting the same expression. Rhys stopped in the middle of the floor and bridged his right arm for Frankie to step into his personal space. Rhys's eyes glinted.

'You realise everyone's watching,' he murmured in her ear.

Frankie was having difficulty computing the fact Rhys's hands were on her body, never mind what everyone else was doing.

'Are they?' she said, gazing unseeingly over his shoulder.

Michael Bublé saw this as a good time to sing *Save the Last Dance For Me*.

'Shall we really give them something to watch then?' he said, swaying demurely from side to side.

'What?' She didn't have time to think what he might mean by it though.

Rhys deftly swung her round and brought her spinning back into his arms. Frankie stared, saucer-eyed at him. Following his lead, she stepped back three steps then forward.

'My God! You can dance!' she said, looking down and watching his snaking hips and flicking feet.

Rhys's eyebrows rose and he treated her to a sexy smile.

'My mother would make me take lessons whenever I visited her in Spain. Can you cha-cha?'

Frankie shook her head.

'Want to learn?'

Frankie nodded.

'Let's just do the basic steps then. Left foot behind the right – no, left, you wally.'

Frankie snorted. She tried again and lost her balance. Only Rhys's arms supporting her saved her from falling over.

'Oh God, I've got my work cut out for me here,' he groaned, making her laugh. 'Now, listen to the music. Can you hear that triple beat?'

Frankie listened.

'Yeeeaaahhhh,' she said dubiously.

'Now step on the spot like this.' Rhys's hips snaked as he shifted his weight to the beat. Frankie's mouth fell open. Rhys had metamorphosed into Johnny Castle. 'Now you try it.'

Frankie stepped like a wooden soldier. Rhys grinned.

'Bend your knees. Let your hips absorb the movement,' he said. 'Yes, that's better. Right, left, right. Now you've got it.'

Frankie giggled uncontrollably as she jigged up and down on the spot.

'Okay. Now let's try a step. It's the same as before on one, step back on two, stay the same on three – no, don't step back on three. Try it again. Listen to the beat in the music. One, two, three. And again, one, two, three. Ow! Don't step forward on three. Just step in place. Look at me, don't look down.'

As Frankie gradually found her rhythm, she felt like she'd been transported into *Dirty Dancing*. Any minute now, Billy was going to whip out a *Time Of Your Life* vinyl.

'Good. Now step forward in the same way starting with your right, step in place on four and five. Let it carry you forward again for six, seven, eight and one. Don't look down.'

Frankie had difficulty in tearing her eyes from Rhys's grinding groin.

'You can dance,' she said again faintly.

Rhys laughed for the first time.

'So will you after I'm through with you. You ready to go again? One, two, three...'

Something about the rhythm, the beat, the way Rhys's body taunted hers into following his lead, made Frankie feel sexy and dare she say it, *womanly*. With a deft flick of his wrist, he spun her round and catching her, dipped her backwards. Frankie squealed with glee. Others around them cheered and clapped. Frankie forgot that moments ago she'd been as nervous as hell. Holding his hand in a looped arc, she rocked back and forth, following, backing-up, teasing and twirling. She'd never thought she'd ever learn to dance. But here she was doing it, and doing it with *Rhys*, no less.

The song came to an end and Frankie fell against Rhys in exhausted bliss.

'That was so fun,' she said breathlessly.

Perhaps encouraged by their attempt at Latino dancing, the DJ switched track to *La Bamba*. Obviously a hit with Aspen Valley, everybody bounded in to dance including Billy, Emmie, Pippa and Jack.

'Wanna keep going?' Rhys murmured in her ear.

Her glittering eyes was answer enough and with a smirk, he spun her out and with one arm around her back and the other held out wide, he danced beside her. With another twirl they danced the other way. The room spun around Frankie, faces and lights were a dizzy blur as she kept step with Rhys. Why had she waited so long to ask him to dance? Hell, Pippa could keep her twenty quid now. She'd even be happy to pay *her* twenty quid, even fifty if Atticus didn't mind having basic brand cat food for the next fortnight.

Completely out of breath and with a stitch in her side from laughing so much, Frankie begged for mercy after ten more minutes of being twirled around like a washing machine on spin cycle.

'I'm dying,' she panted, one balancing arm clinging to Rhys.

'Do you want some air?' he asked.

'Good idea,' she nodded.

The doorway was squashed with smokers sheltering from the pouring rain. Although the coolness of the December night was a relief, the air was hardly fresh. Frankie stood squashed up against the doorframe.

'I had no idea you could dance so well,' she said, raising her voice above Jennifer Lopez's.

'What?'

'I said I HAD NO IDEA YOU COULD DANCE SO WELL.'

Rhys nodded.

'Thanks. You weren't so bad yourself after a while.'

'What?'

'YOU WEREN'T SO BAD YOURSELF AFTER A WHILE.'

Frankie frowned, wondering why Rhys should be telling her she wasn't sober after wine. She hardly ever drank the stuff. She shook her head.

'I've been drinking punch, not wine.'

'What?'

'I'VE BEEN DRINKING PUNCH –'

Rhys cut her off with a shake of her head.

'Neither of us can hear fuck all next to these speakers.' He craned his neck to look up at the saturated sky. He looked back at Frankie, a twinkle in his eye. 'You wanted to cool off, right?'

'Yes,' she nodded.

He grinned.

'Come on, then.' He grabbed her hand and ran into the rain.

Screaming, Frankie was pulled after him. The icy rain soon drenched her hair.

'Rhys!' she shrieked, but was only laughed at in response.

Running and sliding along the muddy path, Rhys skidded to a halt next to the hay barn door. Pushing the big sliding door open, he pulled Frankie inside. It was dark inside with only a thin stream of light from the open doorway highlighting the mountains of bales. The air was heavy with the scent of hay.

'We're soaked,' Frankie said, looking down at their dripping clothes in the dryness of the barn.

'It's not that bad,' Rhys said, twisting a stream of moisture out of his shirt. 'You don't feel half as hot as you did two minutes ago though, do you?'

Looking at Rhys with his short curls slicked to his forehead, his cheeks pink from exertion and his shirt moulded against his chest, Frankie felt that was debatable.

She was suddenly very aware of the fact that she was alone with him. Not only that, they were on speaking terms too. More than speaking terms even. Dancing terms was in a completely different stratosphere. Rhys appeared to cotton on to this fact at the same moment. He swallowed, his Adam's apple bobbing. Frankie mirrored his glance at the doorway. The rain was pelting down, hammering on the roof of the barn and drowning out the music next door. She shivered as a cool whisper of wind threaded past and she crossed her arms for protection. Rhys raised his hands and rubbed her forearms.

'Sorry,' he said, 'I didn't quite think this plan through.'

His hands were hot on her skin. Frankie bit her lip.

'That's okay.'

Rhys's eyes shifted to her mouth. He swallowed again. His grip on her arms tightened. He looked solemnly at her then turned away with a mirthless exhalation.

'I'm sorry. I don't know what I'm doing.' He dragged his fingers through his hair. 'This isn't what I usually do. I mean this is crazy – here with you and me,' he said, pointing to the both of them.

'Do you always live sensibly?' Frankie ventured. Her heart was doing its best to battle its way out of her chest. She had come this far, she wasn't going to walk out of here without giving it her best shot.

Rhys paused to think for a moment then nodded.

'Yes. I like things to be in order. But this is – this is –' He gestured to her, his eyes travelling over her body where her dress clung to her. He took a deep breath. 'This isn't orderly.'

'Order is meaningless without chaos,' she replied with a coy smile.

Rhys stopped breathing. He stared at her. She didn't know if the penny was taking its time to drop in his head or whether he was trying to think of an excuse to get away. She stepped closer to him. Rhys licked his lips. He raised his hand and cupped her cheek. Frankie closed her eyes, revelling in the soft warmth. She heard the crackle of hay breaking beneath his feet. A gentle pressure on her lips, a tang of masculinity tickling her nostrils. He cupped her other cheek and the pressure on her lips intensified. She breathed in a ragged breath, parting her lips to accommodate his kiss. He drew back and Frankie opened her eyes. Christmas was twelve days early.

They stared at each other. Rhys looked slightly shell-shocked. Frankie reached out a trembling hand and hooked her fingers into his shirt. She gently tugged him towards her again. Before closing her eyes once more, she thought she saw a ghost of a smile flicker over his mouth.

Frankie soon realised hay barns were overrated when it came to romantic escapades. The force of Rhys's body pressing against hers pushed her backwards into a stack of bales. The sharp blades scratched her head and her neck.

'Ow,' she muttered.

Rhys pulled away and looked around them. He gathered up a couple of horse rugs dumped by the doorway and threw them on to the uppermost bales. Precariously balanced, he climbed the mountain of hay then leaned over and offered his hand.

'You coming?'

Frankie kicked off her heels.

'I certainly intend to,' she said, taking hold.

Actually, maybe rolls in the hay weren't so oversold, she decided on second thoughts. Especially when the filtering light from outside bathed Rhys Bradford for her perusal. The rugs might be a bit smelly, but they were thick and up there on top of the bales, they had privacy and, rurally-speaking, penthouse views. Rhys's hands expertly unzipped her dress and peeled it away from her skin. Frankie thanked God she had chosen underwear which was in a relatively healthy state.

That sprinkle of black chest hair peeking from his open shirt which had tantalised her all night, she now marvelled at being in a position to actually touch. The buttons undid easily, one revealed his sternum, two his contracting abs, three his belly button, four the pathway of hair which disappeared beneath his belt. Rhys shook off his shirt, flicked open his belt and shed his jeans. Holding her by her shoulders, he kissed her mouth, trailing down her throat to her chest. His tongue continued its exploration of her body, sending tiny starbursts of sensation whizz-banging through her.

Frankie gripped his back, feeling his muscles roll beneath her hands as he lowered himself over her. His skin was deliciously hot against hers. He pulled the strap of her knickers lower and pinched the soft skin of her hip between his teeth. On her back, Frankie gasped as her body reacted in favour. His hands trailed over her breasts, his calloused thumbs circling her nipples. He knelt before her, unembarrassed by his pyramid briefs and, holding her beneath her knees, pulled her down towards him.

Frankie swallowed hard and let her head fall back. Hands which had cajoled victory after victory from the most reluctant of horses proceeded to work their magic on her. Frankie could feel another victory for Rhys Bradford mounting inside her. Christmas wasn't the only thing coming early this year. As he moved against her, her lungs seemed incapable of holding in the oxygen she sucked in. No, she couldn't let it happen too fast. Hell, she'd waited long enough for this moment, her body could bloody well wait a short while longer and get some lengthier satisfaction.

Her gaze flickered down to his groin. Say eight inches lengthier. She sat up and met Rhys's kiss, cradling his head, rocking forward so she straddled him. She felt the hot heat of his erection against her inner thigh. The friction of his stubble tenderised her lips as she dropped them along his jaw and down his neck. She trickled her nails over his chest and abdomen and dipped beneath his briefs.

Rhys Bradford ceased to be her work colleague and rival, but a man, hot-blooded and aroused. He tugged at her knickers, tearing the lace. Caught up in his haste, Frankie bucked out of the last of her clothing. With Rhys kneeling before her, she sank down on his lap, wallowing in the feeling of raw and unbridled passion. Rhys guided himself into her. Looping her arms around his taut shoulders, she pushed against him. A rising trot soon became a canter, and a canter a gallop. Losing balance, she fell back with Rhys still in attendance. She shifted higher and higher up the rugs as Rhys sought to send each forceful thrust deeper and deeper into her.

Frankie grabbed handfuls of hay to contain the rush and with little purchase, her desire whipped beyond her control. She cried out. Rhys pinned her hands above her head and drove harder than he had his closest Cheltenham win. His clasp on her hands tightened as he too passed the line, spent, slick, but oh so victorious.

24

Frankie was woken by a wisp of hay tickling her nose. She opened her eyes, taking a moment to remember where she was. Having fallen asleep to the drum of rain on the roof and the booming of music, everything now was eerily quiet. It was still dark, water was dripping somewhere and the distant dawn chorus of birds drifted through the doorway. The impatient bangs of horses knocking their stable doors with their knees, demanding their breakfast, told her it must be close to dawn. She shivered. Beside her, Rhys lay with one arm around her, the other behind his head. At some point during the night he had put his jeans back on. He was staring up at the ceiling. Frankie breathed him in.

'Hey,' she whispered.

He turned to look at her, causing their bed of hay to crunch beneath them.

'Hey, yourself,' he said, his voice thick like melted chocolate.

Frankie smiled at him, wondrous at her bedmate.

'Did you sleep okay?' she asked.

'On and off. You?'

She nodded.

'What time is it?'

'Twenty past five.'

Frankie sat up like a meerkat.

'Shit. I've got to be mucking out in an hour.' She scrambled around for her clothes. 'Where's my bra? Oh, bugger it.' She shook the hay and dust out of her dress. The material was still damp and a 7.0 magnitude shiver ran over her body as she pulled it on. Rhys lay with both hands supporting his head, his eyes following her manic scramble.

'Do you want a hand with your zip?' he said after watching her struggle for a moment.

'Yes, please.' She turned her back to him and swept her hair out of the way, extracting a stray strand of hay while she was at it. She did not want to see a mirror any time soon.

Rhys sat up and tugged her zip up. She thought she felt his lips brush the top of her spine, but it was so fleeting it could have been a draft.

'There you go,' he said.

Frankie turned back to him, torn between the urgency to get home and ready for work and a longing to stay with him. Whatever it was that had happened last night, she didn't want it to end. But a niggling feeling told her that as soon as she walked out the door, things were going to change.

'Thanks,' she said.

They continued to look at each other in silence until a human voice outside interrupted them.

'All right, all right,' the voice said. 'I'm getting your food ready now. Just have some patience.'

'I'd better go before I get caught.'

Rhys smiled for the first time.

'Caught?'

Frankie hooked her hair behind her ear, finding another piece of hay, and gave a short uncertain laugh.

'You know what I mean.'

He nodded. Delving beneath the horse rugs, he pulled out her purple bra. She bundled it into her pashmina shawl with an embarrassed thanks.

'Get going then. I'll follow you out in five.'

'Okay.'

She hesitated, not knowing if she could kiss him goodbye or not. She wanted to, but in the half-light of morning, she was back to being Frankie, Aspen Valley amateur jockey and Rhys was back to being... well, *Rhys*. Without the brazen boost of alcohol, he was no longer Latino dancer and sex god. Still damned sexy, but Rhys, nonetheless.

'Bye,' she said, barely above a whisper. She went to make her shaky descent from their hay bale penthouse. She was about to let go and jump the rest of the way when Rhys's hand covered hers.

'Hey,' he said.

She looked up at him kneeling above her. He leant down, raised her chin with his fingertips and kissed her.

'I'll see you later,' he whispered.

Frankie bit back the grin that threatened to reveal her morning teeth.

The coast looked clear when she peeked out. Down the muddy alleyway between the hay barn and the indoor school she could see the clear sky lightening to indigo over the gallops. The clouds were paintbrush slivers in the distance and their forsaken bounty now glistened on the frosty ground. Frankie made a dash for the car park. Horses neighed and she heard a door slam in the yard beyond. She peered round the corner as she reached the end of the barn. Her car was parked about twenty metres away. It had been the closest she'd been able to get last night, but now it sat alone with just a couple other cars to keep it company. One of them, she noticed, was Rhys's black Audi Spyder.

'Morning, Frankie,' a voice said from the yard entrance.

Frankie's foggy breathing stopped.

With saddle cloths flung over one shoulder, Billy grinned at her.

'Oh, hi, Billy,' she said, pinning a smile to her face.

'Gonna be frosty this morning, don't you reckon?'

Frankie nodded, not quite believing he was acting like she hadn't just rolled, quite literally, out of bed and was still in her decidedly crumpled party dress. She resisted the urge of looking back to the barn entrance. She hoped Rhys could hear her talking and know not to walk out.

'Yeah, I reckon so. Yes.'

'You riding at Chepstow this afternoon?'

'If racing goes ahead, yes.'

'Touch wood. I'm leading up Ta' Qali and Smoking Ace for Rhys.'

'Let's hope so then,' she said, inching towards her car.

Billy stood, hand on hip, looking like he was settling down for a good chatter.

'I hope Ta' Qali behaves better than last time. He was a nightmare in the parade ring at Aintree.'

'He was a nightmare for Rhys to ride too. Jack's declared him with ear plugs today to see if it makes any difference.'

'Ha! That'll be fun trying to get those in. The bugger won't let me near his head.'

'Yeah, well, good luck with that. Anyway, I've got to, um, go. I'll see you later.'

'Okay,' he said, a mischievous smile still on his face.

Released at last, Frankie continued on her way.

'Oh! Frankie, I think you dropped something.' Billy stepped forward before she could stop him and picked up her bra.

Her cheeks went from Arctic to Saharan as she held her empty pashmina. Billy looked just as mortified. Then as things began to slot into place and he looked across at Rhys's car, he gave her a knowing grin.

'Way to go, Frankie,' he said, handing her her underwear.

Frankie gave him a look.

'Thank you, Billy. I've got to go now.'

Racing fans had turned up in droves for Chepstow's first sunny meeting of the season. Buoyed by a win in the amateur's race on the card, Frankie settled back in the weighing room to watch the two mile novice hurdle starring Ta' Qali on the television. She listened to the racing presenters go through the form of each of the runners, waiting patiently for the camera to show her horse.

'Number Six on the card is Ta' Qali,' the presenter said. 'Just his second start over hurdles. Was sixth on his debut, but got very agitated beforehand and never really settled for Rhys Bradford who is back aboard today.'

Frankie let out a quiet groan as Ta' Qali filled the screen. He was in a muck sweat already. His coat looked starry and a white lather was smeared between his hind legs. Pushing against his shoulder, Billy battled to keep him on the path. Ta' Qali skittered sideways and threw his head into the air. Frankie noted his odds had drifted from twelve-to-one out to sixteen – unheard of for a first string Aspen Valley horse.

Her heart skipped a beat as she caught her first glimpse of Rhys since her earlier departure from the hay barn. Jack legged him up into the saddle then had to skip out of the way as the horse bounced sideways. The trainer looked grim. His strategy to settle Ta' Qali with earplugs obviously wasn't going to plan.

He was right. Frankie watched the race with ever-deflating hope. Rhys jumped Ta' Qali off smartly to take the lead, hoping perhaps that he'd settle in front, but it made little difference. Ta' Qali ran with his head in the air, his foaming mouth agape under Rhys's strong hold. By halfway, he'd burned himself out. Knowing the race was out of their grasp, Rhys pulled him up four flights from home.

Frankie turned away, uninterested in the final result, and began tying the yellow silk cap of Bold Phoenix's ownership to her helmet.

Out on the course, the sparkling green of the Welsh landscape and the crystal blue sky regalvinized Frankie. The crisp country air breathed energy into her bloodstream as she cantered Bold Phoenix down to the two and a half mile start. The chestnut gelding, flashy with his white face and four white socks, pointed his toe and pricked his ears at the puffballs of sheep grazing in the adjacent field. Down by the starter's rostrum, Frankie circled with the other ten runners and found herself alongside Rhys on Smoking Ace.

'Hey,' he said. 'What do you say to buying me a drink tonight if I beat you?'

Frankie smirked right back at him.

'And if I beat you?'

'I'll buy you a drink.'

'May I remind you you are riding the five-to-two favourite. Bold Phoenix is only a fourteen-to-one shot.'

'Fine,' Rhys said, pulling down his goggles. 'A drink *and* dinner.'

Enjoying this new side to Rhys, Frankie gave him a flirtatious smile.

'Risky. You're prepared to put your diet on the line?'

Rhys lowered his goggles so she could see his black eyes glinting.

'There's a number of ways I can think of to work the extra pounds off afterwards.'

Frankie couldn't help the somersault in her stomach. She wasn't one to play games, but she wasn't going to let Rhys think he had it on a platter. She adjusted her goggles over her eyes and raised an eyebrow at him.

'How right you are. But if you *do* decide to go jogging after dinner in the dark, remember to put on your high vis jacket.'

His chuckle followed her as she straightened Bold Phoenix up and jogged him towards the starting tape. It was lost in the jockeys' cries of '*Hyah!*' as the starter let them go.

By luck more than anything else, Frankie found herself just where she wanted to be, on the inside stalking the leaders. Bold Phoenix jumped as his name suggested over the first plain fence and Frankie took a tug on the reins as they met the rising ground. The rain-softened turf was already ploughed up from the two previous steeplechases and she was aware of the question mark over Bold Phoenix's stamina.

The second, an open ditch, loomed and again Bold Phoenix gave it plenty of air. The cries and cheers of the grandstand rose as they jumped the three fences in front of it and passed the winning post for the first time. Around the far turn, Bold Phoenix ran wide and forsook his inside position. The grey head of Smoking Ace nodded into Frankie's peripheral view, blowing clouds of foggy air through his nostrils like a steam train.

'You a vegetarian?' Rhys yelled.

Frankie frowned as her focus wavered.

'No,' she yelled back.

They entered the back straight and jumped the next together.

'Do you like Indian?'

The second open ditch intercepted her reply and Bold Phoenix pecked on landing.

'Rhys, can we discuss this later?'

His wicked grin made her shake her head and she cajoled Bold Phoenix forward to chase the leaders six lengths ahead, and more importantly past Rhys's distracting dinner plans.

Actually, an Indian didn't sound such a bad idea.

A plain fence was quickly followed by the water jump. Bold Phoenix flew over with little trace of slowing up. Frankie grinned. She would be back here in three weeks' time for the Welsh National in which Peace Offering was no doubt an entry. She just hoped he would jump as co-operatively for her then as Bold Phoenix was now.

Over the second last in the back straight and the ground began to fall away in descent. One of the leaders over-jumped and crumpled on landing. With a quick glance to her left to make sure she wasn't cutting Rhys off, Frankie guided Bold Phoenix closer to the inside to avoid the horse heaving itself back to its feet.

'Easy does it,' she murmured to her mount.

He cocked an ear back and took advantage of her quiet riding to take a breather. A flock of gulls grounded up ahead flapped into the air as the thunder of galloping hooves neared them. Their squawks followed the strung-out field skimming the rail into the home stretch.

'Go on now, my boy,' Frankie whispered. She lowered her posture and pumped her hands alongside Bold Phoenix's chestnut neck. The honest pace was starting to take its toll on the leaders and Frankie felt a glimmer of hope swell inside her chest. But the danger, she knew, was not what was in front of her. It was what was behind her and by the ever-nearing drum of hooves on sodden ground, she knew it was coming fast.

They straightened up for the final five fences. Bold Phoenix made his second mistake of the race and Frankie clung to his wither strap to keep her balance. The leaders were coming back to her with more rapidity than she'd anticipated and she angled out to get a clear view of the next open ditch.

The horse in second jumped awkwardly and unshipped his rider. Between hard riding, Frankie looked up. The undulating home straight of Chepstow Racecourse beckoned. Three out and they were over safe. She ducked her head down again and rocked in the saddle, asking Bold Phoenix to defy his outside odds. But as they drew up to share the lead, the flagging leader began to drift wide. Frankie pushed harder. Bold Phoenix leaned into the challenge and held his line. They were in the clear.

With gum guard (now a fashionable white) bared, she rode towards the roar of the crowd up the centre of the course. She pulled down her muddied goggles and the chilled wind stole tears from her eyes. The second last fence bumped closer and closer into view. Bold Phoenix gave a small groan as he put in a gallant leap and his hooves plugged into the muddied landing ground. A familiar grey head appeared on their inside.

'Dammit!' Frankie cursed into Bold Phoenix's mane. She hadn't meant to give away her inside position. Rhys was no longer in the mood to discuss appetisers. Smoking Ace was all out. 'Come on Phoenix!' she yelled. 'I've got a meal ticket at stake here!'

Bold Phoenix, it would seem, did not want to see his rider go hungry. He responded to the challenge. The two stable companions took the last as one. Frankie didn't look up. Rhys didn't let up. He might be one helluva generous ride in the hay, but he wasn't giving her an inch on the racecourse. Frankie raised her whip and brought it down on her horse's flank. More from the sound of the slap than the feel of it, he surged forward. The grandstand redoubled their hollers as he drew clear.

'Go on, Phoenix! Go! Go! Go!' Frankie cried through gritted teeth.

A clear neck became half a length. A half-length stretched to a full one as Smoking Ace gave up the battle. Bold Phoenix galloped wearily across the line and Frankie slapped his mane in delight.

25

Despite alluding to an Indian dinner, Rhys treated Frankie to a meal at the Golden Miller.

'Would you like some wine?' he asked as they reached the bar.

'I thought you didn't drink,' Frankie said.

'I don't. I was asking you if you would like some.'

Frankie dropped her gaze, embarrassed.

'Oh, sorry. No, I won't then.'

Rhys gave her a wry smile.

'It's okay, you know. I'm not an alcoholic, drink just doesn't agree with me.' He picked up a wine list to peruse its contents and murmured, 'It only takes one glass to send me over the top. It's just remembering if it's the ninth or tenth that's the problem.'

Frankie snorted.

'A vodka and orange then, please.'

Rhys raised the wine list to attract the barman's attention. Joey was chatting to a couple of pretty girls further along.

'Hey, Joey. Can I get a vodka and orange and an orange with ice?'

Joey flung his habitual dish cloth over his shoulder.

'Sure thing.'

Frankie watched him carry on charming the girls while he fixed their drinks.

'Wait a minute,' she said under her breath, frowning at one of the girls. 'Isn't that Donnie's girlfriend?'

'Certainly is,' Rhys replied.

Frankie looked around for Aspen Valley's other jockey. Donnie was nowhere to be seen. His girlfriend, however, did not appear to be lamenting his absence.

'Crikey. Donnie better watch out.'

Rhys gave her a mischievous smile.

'Why?'

Frankie nodded discreetly at Joey and the girls.

'Well, look at them.'

Rhys snorted.

'I don't think Donnie's got anything to worry about, Frankie. Joey's gay.'

'Seriously? I would never have guessed.'

'Hey, Frankie,' Joey called from down the bar. 'How's your little superstar friend? Is she gonna be singing on Tuesday? It's the second round, you know.'

Frankie regathered her wits.

'I don't know, Joey. We'll have to see.' For starters, she didn't know how they would convince Mrs Preston to let her daughter sing in a local pub.

'Who's your little superstar friend?' Rhys asked.

'Just someone from my Girl Guides group.' Frankie checked to make sure Joey was over by the fridges and out of earshot. 'She shouldn't really be singing in this thing. She's underage.'

'So I'm not the first to be led astray by you?'

She gave a mirthless laugh. 'I didn't know this singing competition was going to be Helensvale's answer to *X Factor*. I thought it was just a one-night karaoke competition.'

'Well, I hope you weren't thinking last night was just a one-night-stand.'

Frankie pinched her tongue between her teeth and looked down.

'I don't really know what to think about last night,' she mumbled.

Rhys gave a leisurely stretch and leaned his elbows on the bar. He cocked his head to one side to catch her eye.

'I think last night was possibly the best Aspen Valley party I've been to.'

'That's not saying much,' Frankie giggled. 'They've only ever had one before, so I hear, and you weren't there.'

'Ah, yes. I was just getting myself comfortable for a two-month stint in hospital. Jack told me he and Pippa threw the party to try cheer everyone up after the accident. I think Pippa threw it to celebrate.'

Frankie hesitated. She didn't want to pry into other people's affairs, but she was intrigued by Rhys's and Pippa's cold treatment of each other.

'I take it you and Pippa don't get along.'

'Not so much. It's nothing personal. We're just very different.'

Frankie let it go.

'It must have been torture having to stay in hospital for so long.'

'I was sky high a lot of the time. While the rest of Aspen Valley were downing Pina Colada cocktails, I was downing morphine and ibuprophen cocktails.'

'Did they come visit you?'

'Jack did pretty often.'

'What about your parents?'

Rhys pursed his lips and looked into the distance.

'My mother would have if she could. But she was in Spain. It was Christmas. She had other family commitments. Once she knew I was going to be okay, there was little point in her coming all the way over. There was nothing she could have done to make my leg heal any faster.'

'What about your dad?' she said, with a certain degree of caution. Both Doug and Vanessa didn't have very many nice things to say about Alan Bradford, but she wanted Rhys's take on things. He must surely know him better than her parents did.

Rhys shot her a quizzical glance and shrugged.

'Oh, he called to check on me. Once we got that straight, he then gave me a lecture on what I'd done wrong.'

Frankie was instantly indignant, perhaps more so through compassion. But she'd also watched the race.

'But it wasn't your fault,' she said. 'Anyone could see that.'

Rhys's eyes followed Joey scooping ice into a glass at the far end of the bar.

'There's a few people who would disagree with you there. Some argue Black Russian shouldn't have been running at Kempton. Better yet, he should've been running free like God intended.'

'He's a racehorse though. It's in their blood to race.'

'I'm not disagreeing with you. But everyone's entitled to an opinion. The antis stuffing theirs down our throats didn't help at the time though. A bit like rubbing salt into a fresh wound.' He stood up straight as Joey returned with their drinks and asked him to put it on a tab.

She happily accompanied him to the seated area and felt such a lady when he held out a chair for her. She couldn't recall anyone offering her a chair before, except for the time the doctor at Uttoxeter Racecourse had after she'd suffered a concussion.

She and Rhys both studied a menu, and leaning over the table, thin wisps of aftershave tickled her nostrils. Glancing up, she noticed the curls at the base of his neck were still wet from a recent shower. Although it was silly and she'd done the same, she was pleased he'd made the effort to scrub up after racing for their date.

'What are you going to eat?' he said.

Frankie smiled slyly.

'Well, since you're buying –'

'Bear in mind you only beat me by a length and a quarter,' Rhys said, raising a cautionary finger.

'I'll skip dessert.'

Rhys grinned.

'Dessert is on the house. Just not this house.'

'I'll have the chef's special then,' Frankie said, leaning back with her decision made.

'So will I. Joey, can we order some food?' Rhys called out. There were few enough people in the pub for his voice to be heard clearly at the bar.

'What can I get you?'

'Two chef's specials. Oh, and hold the olives on one. Cheers.'

Hearing his order, Frankie laughed. Rhys frowned at her.

'What's so funny?'

Frankie raised her hands in wonder and shook her head.

'Sorry. It's just that – well, I don't usually do what we did last night quite so soon.' She felt a blush creeping over her cheekbones. 'But it didn't feel so soon because it was like I'd known you for years. Which I have, but really, I've only known *of* you. Thinking about it now, I don't know you very well at all. The olives, for example.'

Rhys frowned to himself and thought it over for a moment.

'Okay. What do you want to know?'

For such a private person, Frankie felt Rhys was being especially open with all her questions. This could be fun.

'Favourite food,' she challenged.

'Smoked salmon and cream cheese.'

'Favourite band?'

'Gastric. That way I don't have to diet so much,' he said without skipping a beat.

'Favourite singer then?' Frankie laughed.

'Mumford and Sons.'

'Guilty pleasure,' she said, sending him a sidelong look.

Rhys exhaled as he considered his answer.

'Got to be cherry-flavoured lollipops.'

'Seriously?' she giggled.

'Seriously. They're a great sugar-booster.'

'Have you always wanted to be a jockey?'

'Pretty much. My father had me up on a horse before I could walk. Besides, I wasn't one for schoolwork or anything academic.' He gave her a self-effacing smile. 'While some people drink from the Fountain of Knowledge, I only used it as a mouthwash before changing my gum guard. My turn now. Have you always wanted to be a jockey?'

'I guess so,' Frankie shrugged. 'I didn't always know what I wanted to be, but when I did, it was always going to involve horses.'

'Your dad must've got you started then.'

Frankie smiled as the memories flashed in her mind.

'Actually, no. It was Seth. Seth knew right from the start that he was going to be a jockey. Dad bought us a pony, a little thoroughbred-cross called Toffee. Seth used to tear around on her, whereas I was more into show jumping at that stage. I wanted to be like Pat Smythe and jump for Britain. Then when I read Jilly Cooper, I *really* wanted to be in the British team.'

Rhys chuckled and raised an arrogant eyebrow.

'Is that why you switched then? Discovered jump jockeys are a lot better looking than show jumpers?'

'Are you including Donnie in that statement?'

Rhys put up his hands in surrender.

'Okay, so he's got a nose like a blind carpenter's thumb. What about the rest of us?'

Frankie pretended to be undecided.

'Hmm. You're not bad, I suppose. You don't get fat jump jockeys at any rate.'

'True. That show jumper guy, Pete Whitehead – he's got more chins than a Chinese phonebook. It's a wonder his horse can get off the ground.' He smiled as Frankie laughed, as always his humour less exuberant. He raised his glass of orange juice in a toast. 'Anyway, congratulations on riding a treble today.'

Frankie gave him a puzzled look as she raised her own drink.

'Thanks, but I only rode a double.'

Rhys clinked his glass against hers.

'Last time I checked, the day hadn't ended.'

26

Snowflakes were drifting on the wind the following evening when Frankie returned home from work. Humming *It's Beginning To Look A Lot Like Christmas* she let herself into the house and closed the door firmly before the cold could invade.

'That you?' Tom's voice called from the kitchen.

'No, it's Santa.'

'Aren't you meant to use the chimney then?'

She padded through in her socks to find Tom sitting at the kitchen table which was littered with scrunched up pieces of paper. Atticus Finch was batting one paper ball in between the chair legs.

'And have you been a good boy this year?' she asked Tom.

'Define good for me.'

Frankie laughed and squatted down to fuss Atticus. Atticus wasn't in the mood to be fussed. She stood up again.

'Want some tea?'

'If you're making some.'

'What are you doing there?' she said, nodding to the pad of paper in front of him.

'Trying to write a letter.'

'I know in this day and age of emails, some might find it difficult, but you look like you're really struggling there,' she said, pointing at the balls of paper.

'It's a tricky one.'

Frankie dropped two teabags into mugs and leaned against the counter, waiting for the kettle to boil.

'How so?'

'I'm writing to Adelaide Mann.'

Frankie's hand slipped off the counter.

'Seriously? You've found her?'

Tom shrugged and chucked down his pen.

'I don't know. Remember I told you I could only find one Adelaide Mann who could've been my mother? Well, I got her address on the electoral roll so I'm just writing to her.'

Tea forgotten, Frankie stared at him.

'Wow. What are you going to say though? Hello, merry Christmas. I think you may be my mother?'

Tom shrugged.

'That's what I've been trying to decide. It's not exactly the sort of letter you want to receive at Christmas time, is it?'

'Maybe it is. Maybe she's been waiting twenty-nine years for that letter.'

'Twenty-eight, thank you very much.'

'Sorry. Do you want some help?'

'I don't know. I think I've got it now. Listen to this:

Dear Ms. Mann,

My name is Tom Moxley. I am writing in the hope that you may be able to help me. As a baby I was given up for adoption by my mother, whose name happens to be Adelaide Mann. Although I have enjoyed a happy childhood and love my adoptive family very much, I am now searching for my birth parents. Apart from my birthdate, which is the thirtieth of September, I have very little information by which to go on so I am writing to ask if you are the same Adelaide Mann who gave birth to a baby boy twenty-eight years ago.

How does that sound?'

Tears leapt to Frankie's eyes. She couldn't help it. Maybe too much sex was playing havoc with her hormones, or maybe it was the time of year. Maybe it was just the lonely tone of Tom's letter that caused such a rush of emotion inside her. She blinked hard. Tom needed her strength, not her tears. She gave him a watery smile.

'I think it's beautiful.'

'I don't know,' Tom muttered. He made to tear the paper up, but Frankie stopped him.

'No, don't. Please don't. I think it's lovely, really I do.'

'You don't think it's too formal? Or too casual? Or just too basic? I've been trying to get the right tone, but nothing seems right.' Tom threaded his fingers through his thick hair. 'I mean, how do you write a letter like that?'

Frankie poured boiled water into their mugs and came to sit down with him. Thoughtfully, she dipped the teabag in and out of her mug. If it was her, what would she have written? She had no idea. She looked at it from the other point of view.

'I think,' she said, pausing to choose her words carefully, 'if I was her, and I received a letter like that, it would be the most special gift. It's not too formal, and it's not too casual. You can tell that you haven't done this on a whim. It sounds like you're speaking from the heart, from a son looking for his mother. And it has just the right amount of formality about it because even though she might be your mother, she is still a stranger, so it's polite as well. I think you should send it as it is. Don't try to be someone that you're not.'

Tom sighed.

'What if it is her? What if she doesn't want to know? She wasn't on the Contacts Register, after all.'

Frankie bit her lip. He was right. Contacting someone who'd not given any indication they had wanted to be contacted was risky, but...

'You won't know unless you try,' she said gently.

Tom rubbed his face and looked at Frankie with desperate eyes.

'I just want to know why, you know? I don't necessarily want to become best buddies with her, but it would be nice to know who she is, who my father is. Do I have any brothers or sisters? Is that asking too much?'

Frankie shook her head and covered Tom's hand with hers.

'I think you should send it.'

Tom took a deep breath, folded the letter and slipped it into an envelope. He sealed it and Frankie noticed his hands trembling.

'Do you want me to post it for you?'

'Would you? I don't know if I would be able to go through with it if I was faced with the post box. It's like the point of no return. Once it's in the box, it's on its way.'

'Unless you accosted the postman.'

'Thanks. I appreciate it.'

'No problem. I'll do it on my way to work tomorrow.'

'Have you been busy at work or something? I haven't seen you in days, it seems.'

Frankie opened her mouth and shut it again.

'Has Atticus been fed? Atticus, are you hungry, baby?'

'Frankie,' Tom warned. 'You're avoiding the subject. What aren't you telling me?'

27

If Frankie had any doubts about whether or not Cassa had forgotten about the Golden Miller's singing competition, those were firmly put to bed at the following evening's Girl Guides meeting. After packing up the hall and waving goodbye to the last of the girls, she was about to switch off the lights when Cassa appeared from the toilets, changed into jeans and Ugg boots from her uniform.

'Frankie, would you give me a lift home tonight? Mum's got the late shift again.'

'A lift home is all you're after?' Frankie said, fixing Cassa with a suspicious eye. 'Odd that you've changed your clothes just to go home.'

Cassa wiggled her feet and gave her a pleading look.

'Please, Frankie. It's the next round. I have to be there.'

Frankie sighed and switched off the lights. She ushered Cassa out into the crisp night and heaved the heavy doors closed behind them. Since being voted through on the last occasion, Cassa had appeared a much happier Girl Guide. Her confidence was up and she was now a livelier participant at the meetings. Frankie was torn between encouraging this new side to the girl and remembering her responsibilities towards her.

'How does your mother feel about you singing in the competition?' she asked without hope.

'She's fine with it,' Cassa said.

Frankie gave her another distrustful look. Out in the sub-zero temperatures, she could tell Cassa was holding her breath.

'You're lying to me,' she warned, 'like a cheap Japanese watch.'

Cassa giggled.

'Come on, Frankie. All I've ever wanted to do is sing.'

'That's what showers were designed for.'

'Pleeeease.'

Frankie sighed. Oh, how she wanted to help Cassa pursue her dreams. What could be more satisfying? She knew what it was like to have a dream. But what about the risks? What if the judges voted her off? Her confidence would come crashing down and it would be Frankie's fault. What would Mrs Preston say if she found out? Frankie would surely be fired from Girl Guides, in much the same way Vanessa had been banned – for being a bad influence. Was helping a young talent follow their ambitions such a crime though?

'You're not putting me in an easy position, Cassa,' she said at last.

'Just one more time. That's all I'm asking. I have a song ready. I've been practising it ever since they put me through.'

Curiosity got the better of Frankie.

'What's the song?'

'*At Last* by Etta James.'

Frankie's heart ached. She loved that song and with Cassa's husky tones, she would love to hear her sing it. She wavered.

'Just this once, okay? Even if they put you through to whatever round is next, it's the last time. It's too risky, Cassa. Your mum would kill us both if she found out.'

Cassa jigged up and down on the spot and crossed her heart.

'Promise,' she grinned.

Frankie shook her head and nodded to her car, standing covered in silvery frost in the car park.

'Come on, then. But if you become a big star because of this and end up making millions, I expect a cut of the profits, okay?'

Frankie's heart dropped with dread as she pulled up outside the Golden Miller. Through the windows she could see the pub was packed to the rafters. She hoped the Prestons were still new enough to Helensvale not to have made too many friends. If word got back to Cassa's mother – well, Frankie daren't think of the consequences.

'You sure you're ready for this?' she asked Cassa, pausing outside the door.

Cassa looked less sure of herself now that she'd seen the crowd. Nevertheless, she nodded.

'Okay then. Here goes.'

They stepped inside the warmth of the pub just as a cheer went up for the contestant walking onto stage. Frankie shouldered a path to the bar with Cassa close on her heels. Tom was in his usual spot in the corner but it was seeing Rhys, standing further along nursing his customary orange juice that made her heart skip a beat.

Joey gave a cheer and left his bar duties to greet them.

'Thank God you're here. I thought you weren't going to make it.' He winked at Cassa. 'All set to knock 'em dead?'

Cassa gave a hesitant nod. Joey clapped his hands together.

'Great. I'll let them know you're here.'

Not letting go of Cassa's hand – she wasn't sure if it was for her own reassurance or for the girl's – Frankie edged her way along the bar.

'Hello, Rhys,' she said.

Rhys's expression broke into a smile.

'Hey, Frankie. You all right?' He spotted Cassa hovering beside her and his eyebrows lifted in question. 'Who's your friend?'

Frankie shook her head at his devilish smile. He knew full well Cassa was her fraudulent Girl Guide.

'Cassa, I'd like you to meet Rhys, my –' The words choked in her throat. What exactly was Rhys to her? Boyfriend? Or was it too soon to assume that? Lover? Or was that too much information for a thirteen-year-old? Friend? Or would such a casual reference offend Rhys?

'Rival,' Rhys said. He put out his hand to shake Cassa's. 'Frankie and I are both jockeys.'

'Hi,' Cassa said, hiding her chin shyly in her shoulder and taking his outstretched hand.

Although relieved Rhys had helped her out of a potentially awkward moment, nonetheless, her spirits sunk a couple of degrees. Her nerves were already wound tight and it would have made her feel so much better if he'd said 'boyfriend' or shown some form of affection towards her.

Never mind, she told herself. There was plenty of time for that to change. It had only been three days since the Christmas party, after all. And not so long ago, Rhys would have sneered at her presence. This was progress, she reminded herself.

She looked across at Tom and their eyes met. He looked glum. What was he thinking? She thought of the letter she'd posted with a silent prayer earlier. Was that it? Knowing that by tomorrow, Adelaide Mann of Bethnal Green, London, would more than likely have read his letter? And now with Joey busy serving customers, he had no one to distract him from his thoughts.

'I'm just going to go see Tom,' she said.

Rhys looked accommodating.

'Let's all go over. Looks like he's got more room where he's at.'

*

Tom mustered up a smile at Frankie's approach. A wry twist was added to it when he noticed Rhys in tow.

'So it's true,' he said, loud enough for only Frankie to hear.

'Shush, Tom,' she hissed.

When she'd told him last night that she was seeing Rhys on a more personal level, he hadn't believed her at first. Once she'd convinced him, he'd then started asking why and how come. Frankie hadn't been quite so convincing after that, since she herself wasn't so sure. Every objection Tom raised had been valid. Why was Rhys seeing her when he'd so obviously resented her taking his ride in the National? Frankie's argument that a lot of water had flown under the bridge since then (this December was making a bid for the wettest on record) hadn't entirely removed Tom's doubts. She would ask Rhys - eventually. Right now though, she was quite happy to carry on in blissful ignorance.

'All right, Rhys?' Tom said.

Rhys nodded.

'All right, Tom.'

'Hello, you,' Tom said to Cassa. 'I remember you from the last round.'

Cassa beamed at her newfound fame.

'How's it been going tonight?' Frankie asked.

'Competition's a bit tougher than it was before.' Seeing Cassa's smile fade he added, 'But nothing like the standard you set. You could sing *Old MacDonald* and still beat the rest.'

Confidence restored, Cassa moved a little out of Frankie's shadow.

Cassa was applauded on to the Golden Miller's rigged up stage. The noise made it seem as if there were twice as many people in the building. Frankie's knees were weak and her heart was hammering. She prayed Cassa was coping better than she was. The introduction to *At Last* sliced through the clapping and another small cheer went up from those who recognised the classic blues track. Cassa looked so alone on stage, Frankie wanted to push her way through the crowds and sing it with her. On the other hand, she also wanted her to be a success and that would never happen if they were to duet.

She watched Cassa take a deep breath and raise the microphone to her lips. So far removed from the Girl Guide who had been crafting Indian elephant mobiles out of plastic milk cartons just a couple of hours before, Cassa's low sultry voice now rolled through the pub. Another cheer went up and distracted, her voice wobbled. She looked over at Frankie, her eyes filled with panic.

Frankie nodded, urging her on.

'You can do it,' she whispered.

Whether Cassa could lip-read or not, the message must have got through.

A smile reappeared on her face as she hit note after note. She even had the courage to remove one of her hands from the mic to gesture with the song's lyrics.

Frankie felt a warm arm slide around her waist. She smiled to herself and pressed her hand over Rhys's, holding it close. She saw Tom out of the corner of her eye pause as he lifted his glass and frown at the gesture. Frankie was on a cloud too high to care though.

Cassa finished the song, almost sinking to her knees as she belted out the last line. The Golden Miller erupted into cheers. There was no doubt in their minds that Cassa was through to the semi-finals. Frankie's resolution swayed again. Maybe they could risk another round.

28

Later that evening, Frankie lay wrapped up in Rhys's duvet, tired but one hundred per cent sated. Rhys lay beside her with his arms crossed behind his head. She traced her finger along the firm contours of muscle, silvery in the moonlight, which ran from his arms to his chest. He was lean, naturally, but not as skinny as other jockeys she knew from the weighing room. He looked like an Arabian thoroughbred, slender, athletic and beautiful. Again, she wondered why he had chosen to be with her of all people when he could have had his pick of his female fans.

She chewed her lip as she remembered her conversation with Tom. His disbelief was unsettling to say the least. She sighed inadvertently.

'You okay?' he asked.

'I was just thinking.'

Rhys lifted himself up onto one elbow to look at her properly.

'What about?'

A curl of hair hung out of place over his forehead. A small smile broke her frown. She realised that, if she wanted, she could stroke it out of the way. She could touch him, kiss him, and chances were good he wouldn't have her done for sexual harassment. But the question still remained though: *why?*

She opened her mouth to ask, but bit her lips closed again. She didn't have the courage to ask him. What if he said something she didn't want to hear? What if this was just a fling to him? While her heart felt like a contestant in a cheese rolling competition, tumbling deeper and deeper towards – well, *something*. She was wary of calling it love. Love surely didn't happen this quickly, but whatever it was, it was strong and completely addictive.

'Nothing important,' she said, shaking her head.

Rhys frowned at her. With a tender hand, he reached out and threaded her hair behind her ear.

'Tell me then.'

Frankie couldn't look him in the eye and say it. She gazed up at the ceiling.

'What are we doing, Rhys?' she said, finally brazen enough. She swallowed and closed her eyes, waiting for him to put a stake through her heart.

'What do you mean?' His question was guarded and Frankie forced herself to open her eyes and look at him. He'd stopped stroking her hair.

'I mean what does "we" mean to you?'

Rhys hesitated.

'That's a pretty weighted question so early on, don't you think?'

Frankie grimaced.

'I know, but I have to know. I'm sorry. It's just that – well, like I said before, I'm not in the habit of starting things off by sleeping with someone and then getting to know them. Usually, it's the other way round.'

Rhys was silent for a long moment. Even though he was barely touching her, she could feel his body had tensed.

'Are you regretting what happened?' he said.

'What? No, no. Not at all. I'm just a little unsure of where things are going.'

'Maybe we should just live in the moment and enjoy it, instead of looking ahead.' Rhys ran a curved finger down her cheek. 'I'm not going anywhere soon.'

Frankie managed a weak smile and Rhys brushed his finger along her lips, tickling her.

'Why?'

Rhys tilted his head back a little and frowned at her.

'Why what?'

Frankie gave a mirthless chuckle.

'Why me, I guess is what I'm trying to say.'

'Strange,' Rhys mused. 'You never struck me as being the insecure type.'

Frankie shrugged. She waited for him to answer her question.

Rhys exhaled, blowing the wayward curl on his forehead to the side.

'You're a nice girl. You're pretty. We have a lot of shared interests. You know what you've signed up for. Not everybody can handle dating a jockey.'

'That's the thing though. We do have a lot of shared interests. Riding Peace Offering in the National being one of them.'

'Isn't a guy allowed to change his mind?'

'To be completely frank –'
'Which you are.'
Frankie allowed him a wry smile.
'– to be frank, it's one helluva U-turn. You used to hate me. That morning in Jack's office – I've never seen anyone so angry. Yet nothing has changed to make you *not* hate me.'
'You sure about that?'
Frankie paused to reconsider. As far as she was aware, she still had the ride on Peace Offering.
'Yeah,' she said dubiously.
Rhys sat up to face her.
'You remember that night when Jasper ran in front of your car?'
'How could I forget?'
'And in the car we were arguing and you lost your temper with me because I was acting like a spoilt brat?'
Frankie half-nodded, half-shook her head, remembering that conversation, but not willing to admit Rhys had acted like a dickhead.
'You told me to suck it up, buttercup. And you were right. There I was moping around thinking how I'd been so hard done by and blaming you for it all. When really, it wasn't your fault at all. You hadn't gone kissing Pippa's arse trying to get the ride. She'd just given it to you. So when I stopped blaming you for that, I saw that actually you weren't such a bad person.' Rhys looked down into his lap with an embarrassed smile. 'You're really quite a good person. And when I saw you at the Aspen Valley party – *well*,' he chuckled, 'you looked gorgeous. You looked so happy, so full of life.'
'I was also rather drunk.'
'Regardless, there you were mixing with other people, socialising, laughing with everyone. It might not seem like a big deal to you, but see, I'm not like that. I can't talk to people like others do. I can never think of the right thing to say. So I keep to myself and well, you know what people think about that.'
Frankie's heart swelled. Not only in relief to put to bed those niggling doubts, but also compassion for Rhys. He was right. People did think he was arrogant. Had it all been a cover-up to hide his shyness? She pulled herself into a sitting position and leaning forward, she kissed his lowered head. He looked up to meet her next kiss and she wrapped her arms around his neck, letting the duvet slip from around her. Rhys held her

tight. His skin burned against hers and he kissed her again. As he lowered her back into the pillows, his kisses becoming more demanding, Frankie felt like an Air Supply song.

29

'Merry Christmas, Mum! Merry Christmas Dad!' Frankie shouldered open her parents' front door, her arms cradling a small but precarious pile of presents.

Vanessa appeared from the kitchen wearing a Santa hat and a scarf of tinsel around her neck. In one hand she held a mince pie, in the other was a flute of champagne.

'Merry Christmas, darling!' she carolled before disappearing back into the kitchen. 'Doug! Frankie's here!'

Frankie stamped her feet on the mat to unstick the snow from her soles. The Cooper home was welcomingly warm with the sound of Christmas tunes and the tang of hot mince pies and roasting turkey in the air. She hustled into the kitchen and was accosted by Vanessa with another Santa hat for Frankie.

'Ow, Mum. Easy on the scalp,' Frankie winced. 'You bring new meaning to Brut force.'

'Hello, Frankie,' Doug said, joining them from the lounge. He too was wearing a Santa hat.

Frankie stretched out her lips to greet her father over the presents. He gave her an enthusiastic smacker and laughed.

'Come on through. Put that lot under the tree.'

'D'you want some bubbly?' Vanessa asked.

Frankie wavered. She would love to share Christmas with her parents getting sloshed, but racing didn't stop for anyone. There would still be horses needing their supper on Christmas Day and tomorrow it was off early to Kempton for their Boxing Day meeting where she had two rides on the card.

'Not just yet, thanks, Mum,' she called over her shoulder.

She knelt before the small silver tree in the lounge and let her gifts tumble gently onto the carpet to join the rest. She missed the big trees they'd used to have when it would take her, Seth, Vanessa and Doug an entire evening to decorate. Now just a few of her mother's own crafts dangled from the wire limbs and the old angel sitting at the top had a crooked halo and torn wings.

With a quick peek over her shoulder to make sure her parents were still out of sight, she checked the tags on the other gifts to see which ones were hers. A small present, the size of a ring box, wrapped in gold foil caught her attention hiding behind the tree. Her fingers stilled over the attached tag. She sighed as she read the single-word inscription in her father's writing: "*Seth*".

She heaved herself to her feet, wondering what Doug did with all the unopened presents that he gave her brother. And more curiously, what was in them? She moved to the mantelpiece to look at the rows of Christmas cards. One of them was from Gracie, the girl Seth had been dating when he'd died. Frankie shook her head. It was sweet of her to remember the Coopers even after five years, but did her season's greetings mean that she hadn't moved on either? She moved the card to the side so she could see a photo of her brother.

'Merry Christmas, Seth,' she murmured.

If Christmas was a time for indulgence then Frankie hoped hers would be with winners. It certainly couldn't be food. Watching her mother throw back the champagne and mince pies made Frankie even more envious and determined to ride well tomorrow. With Doug subtly monitoring the cooking over Vanessa's shoulder, Frankie was more gutted than usual when she could only take a couple of slices from the huge bird. It was roasted to perfection. She went to take a scoopful of Brussels sprouts then remembered she might be spending the night at Rhys's later so tipped most of them back.

Her parents looked sympathetically at her sparse helping, but neither said anything. They had been there before, no doubt, when Doug was a jockey.

'This looks lovely,' Frankie said brightly. 'Thanks, Mum.' She gave Doug a discreet nod of thanks too and he winked in acknowledgement.

'Let's tuck in then,' he said. 'There're presents to be opened!'

Lunch was followed by a quick refill of glasses (Frankie had caved midway through the meal) before they regathered in the lounge. Vanessa weaved over to the tree, lost her balance and sat down with a bump.

'Whoops, maybe I should just sit down here and pass these to everyone.'

'Open that one first, Mum. That's from Tom.'

Vanessa picked up the gift and tore away the wrapping.

'Ah, Tom,' she said, touching her chest. She showed the album of Rod Stewart's Christmas songs to Doug and Frankie. 'Bless his heart. I don't think I have a Christmas album of Rod's. How is he?'

'Who? Rod?'

'No, darling. Tom.'

'He's okay. Spending Christmas with his folks down in Weston.'

'Well, please tell him thank you very much and there's a present here somewhere for him too. Now, here's one for you.' Vanessa stretched across the carpet to hand a pillow like present to Frankie.

Frankie ripped off the wrapping with zest and pulled out a heavy duffel coat with a fur hood. She leaned over and kissed her father and blew one to her mother.

'Thank you. I could do with a new coat.'

'Doug, this one's for you.'

Vanessa handed him a small present, which hadn't come from Frankie's bundle. She and Vanessa waited eagerly for him to reveal it.

'Cufflinks!' Doug cheered. 'A horse on this one and this one says –' He peered through his glasses at the other cufflink, '– "Hung like a".' He squinted at a beaming Vanessa. 'Huh? Oh, right. I get it. Thanks, lovie. Ha ha.'

Frankie was saved from having to admire his present by the Big Ben-tuned doorbell.

'I'll get it,' she said, shaking wrapping paper from her lap. 'You expecting anyone else?'

'No, unless it's Santa,' Vanessa said. 'And if it is, tell him he's a good few hours late.'

Laughing, Frankie jogged down the hall in her socks and opened the front door.

A courier man, dressed in thick motorcycle gear with his helmet visor clipped back, stood holding a wide flat box.

'Delivery for Miss Cooper?' he said.

Frankie's heart bounced around her chest for a moment.

'Yes, that's me.'

'Sign here, please.' He passed her a clipboard and pen and pointed to a space beside her name. 'Thank you. Merry Christmas.'

'You too. Thank you!'

'Who is it, darling?' came her mother's voice from the lounge.

Frankie came back into the lounge, proudly holding aloft the box.

'That was a courier. It's for me,' she said faintly. She sunk onto the sofa and ran her hands over the silver and blue paper. It looked professionally wrapped.

'What is it?' Vanessa said, crawling forward on her hands and knees away from the tree.

'I don't know.' Maybe it was because it was so immaculately wrapped or because the paper looked so expensive, but Frankie took extra care to tug the tape free.

'A giant pizza?' suggested Doug.

'Dominos have certainly upped their customer service if it is,' Frankie replied.

With the paper finally cast aside, Frankie slid open the lid. She gave an involuntary gasp.

'What is it?' Vanessa asked again.

Frankie reached into the box and lifted out a beautifully styled Burberry jumper from a bed of fine tissues.

'Wow,' she breathed.

Vanessa, still on all fours, looked up with her mouth open.

'Who's it from?' she said, finding her voice at last.

Still holding the jumper up, Frankie squirmed in her seat to find a card or a note. Doug plucked a small card from the tissues.

'"To keep you warm when I'm not there. RB",' he read.

Frankie's mouth fell open in amazement. How could she ever have doubted Rhys's resolve? This present must have put him back at least five hundred pounds. You could buy a second-hand car for that.

'Who's RB?' Doug asked.

Frankie's grin faded. Oh yeah, she'd forgotten this bit might happen.

'No one,' she said vaguely and busied herself putting the jumper back in the box.

'It can't be no one if he's sending you designer clothes.'

Frankie shrugged and tried to play it coy.

'Ooh! Ooh!' said Vanessa. 'Let's guess! Who has those initials, Doug? Russell Brand? Richard Burton?'

'Isn't he dead, Mum?'

'Oh yes. Um - *oh!*' As obviously the right person entered her mind and she was about to shout it out, Vanessa remembered where she was. She froze with her open smile fixed in position.

Doug looked from his wife to his daughter in frustration.

'Who? You know who it is, Vanessa. Tell me! I don't know anyone with those –' Doug also stopped in mid-sentence. He ran his tongue over his teeth, almost in a grimace.

Frankie inched further away from him on the sofa and discreetly moved the expensive wrapping paper out of his reach.

'It's Rhys Bradford, isn't it?' he said.

Half-hiding behind the fluff of the jumper, Frankie nodded. Doug looked panicked. His eyes darted from his daughter to the box to his wife.

'But what is he doing sending you expensive gifts like that?'

'Well, um,' Frankie began. She attempted a consolatory smile. 'Rhys and I have been seeing a bit more of each other in past days.'

'Seeing more of each other? As in dating each other?' Doug's face took on a distinct red hue.

'I guess you could say that.'

Doug leapt to his feet and away from Frankie as if she'd just opened up a box of anthrax.

'You're dating Rhys Bradford.' He said it more as a statement than a question, as if he was trying to get it into his head. He looked at Frankie in disbelief. 'Why? How? I thought you hated him?'

'Well, no, not really. I mean, sure, at first he wasn't my favourite person in the world, but lately – well, lately I've seen a different side to him. And I think I maybe misjudged him.'

'But it's Rhys Bradford!' Doug cried.

The pom-pom on his Santa's hat bounced around as he flung his arms out, making him look like one very unhappy elf. This conversation was never going to have gone well, but it still caught Frankie unprepared. She was torn between her loyalty towards the new Rhys – the *real* Rhys, and the addictive need to please her father.

'Rhys is good though, Dad. Really he is. He makes me happy. That's what you want, isn't it?'

'Yes, of course I want you to be happy! But couldn't you have found happiness with someone else?'

Frankie bit her lip, resentment that Doug thought she'd had a choice in this matter, that she'd purposefully fallen for Rhys just to spite him.

'You don't know him, Dad. I don't know what happened in the past with Alan Bradford, but Rhys isn't like that. He hates his father.'

'That means nothing though!' Doug said, ripping the Santa's hat from his head and flinging it to the ground. 'You can see he's just like Alan just in the way he rides.'

'Doug –' Vanessa tried to intervene, but he ignored her.

'He's arrogant, he's cocky. I mean just look at that note! What does he mean by "when I'm not there"? Are those the occasions when he's warming someone else up?'

'No –'

'I know his type better than you think, Frankie! The Bradfords are all the same. They only know how to look after one person and that's themselves.'

'Stop it, Doug!' Vanessa exclaimed.

Doug and Frankie both stared at her in surprise. Vanessa rarely raised her voice except in song.

'And you knew about this?' Doug said, redirecting his anger. 'How did you know this – this *gift* was from Rhys Bradford?'

'Don't go getting all cross with me, sunshine. Just because I'm quicker than you at name games doesn't mean I was in on it.'

Still brained, Doug looked back to Frankie then crept over to sit beside her again. He looked at her imploringly.

'Frankie, honey. I've never tried to tell you how to live your life, but you're making a mistake here. I'm not saying this because of my past, I'm saying this because I love you and I don't want to see you hurt. Please don't do this.'

Frankie sighed.

'Dad, please don't ask me that. I'm not going to get hurt, and if I do, so what? That's what life and love is about, right? You can't hide away from it just because it might turn around and bite you on the arse later on.'

'Love?' Doug looked horrified. 'Who said anything about love? You're not in love with him, are you?'

Frankie repeated the question to herself silently. A flutter in her stomach and a tingling of warmth made her cheeks glow and she hid the tiny smile that tugged at her lips.

'I guess I am a little bit,' she said.

'Jesus Christ!'

'Rhys is good, Dad. You have to trust me on this one. I know what I'm doing.'

'Do you, Frankie? Do you, honestly?'

Frankie licked her lips. Was she ever particularly certain of anything she did? So often, things that seemed a great idea at the time didn't appear so attractive later on. But she'd survived this far without too much damage.

'I do,' she whispered. She searched Doug's face for some sort of consent or blessing, but all she saw was remorse.

'I just don't want you to get hurt.'

'I know, Dad.' She leaned over and kissed her father's cheek. 'And I promise nothing bad will happen. He makes me happy. And that seems to make him happy. We're happier together.'

Doug hung his head in resignation.

'I hope so, honey.'

Deciding this to be an opportune moment, Vanessa clapped her hands from her kneeling position on the rug and beamed at Frankie and Doug.

'Shall we open some more presents?'

30

As a way of conciliatory gesture, Frankie wore her parents' duffel coat gift to Kempton Park the next day. There would be plenty of occasions in the future for her to wear her Burberry jumper for Rhys. Today she had just the two rides, but such was the quality of the field, she felt privileged to have even those. She was on Asante in the first on the card, a novice hurdle, then she was aboard Romulus in the Christmas Hurdle to be pace-setter for Rhys's and Donnie's mounts, Dexter and Dust Storm. She knew her chances in that race were about the same as the temperature outside, a bone-chilling minus three, but she was quietly hopeful that Asante might run into a place in the novice hurdle. Though he never particularly stretched himself at home, she was sure he had more to give. He would have to give if she was to get anywhere close to a place.

Frankie was welcomed into the warmth of the weighing room by the buzz of Irish and English accents with a sprinkling of French. Kempton's Boxing Day meeting always pulled in the best horses and jockeys even from beyond British shores. Frankie was also well aware that she was the sole amateur riding throughout the whole card.

She nipped into the main changing room on her way to the lady jockeys' to deliver Tom's present. Rhys was sat on the bench in just his breeches, pulling on his boots. Above and behind him hung six different sets of silks which he would wear through the course of the day and his saddles. Frankie felt a bit like she'd pitched up at an airport to go on holiday with a friend and found that they'd bought along three suitcases while she'd only brought a hold-all.

Rhys looked up and smiled. A lollipop stick stuck from the side of his mouth. He slapped his hands to the left of his chest.

'You're breaking my heart, Frankie,' he said then gestured to her wardrobe. 'I'm disappointed.'

'I got this from my parents. After your gift arrived yesterday, I figured I should wear this as a peace offering.'

'You'd need to get a lot hairier and walk way better on all fours before you'd get close to that.'

'Eh?'

Rhys flapped a hand.

'Never mind. Didn't your parents appreciate it much then?'

Frankie didn't want to hurt his feelings – what worse feeling could there be than when, in the first straits of love, you found your potentially future in-laws hated your guts? Or maybe she was getting a bit ahead of herself here. But just in case...

She gingerly stepped onto the tightrope between truth and deception.

'Mum thinks it's lovely.'

Rhys gave her a sober look and took out his lollipop. His tongue was red.

'And your dad?'

'Well, Dad's a bit of a tricky customer. I've always been his girl, if you like, and I think because he's been a jockey he knows about the usual promiscuity, so he was a little... *protective*. Yeah, protective.' There, that didn't sound so bad.

'Did he give you a hard time?'

Frankie saw the first signs of regret in his eyes and she gave him a reassuring smile.

'No, he was fine. How did you get my parents' address, by the way?'

Rhys gestured behind her.

'From that fella over there.' She turned to see Tom walking by the other side of the tables. 'Do you want to come by my place later?'

'Come on, Rhys,' Frankie laughed. 'You're riding the two favourites in the two biggest races today. You're bound to want to celebrate later.'

'I certainly am. And I can't think of a better way than with you.'

Frankie's heart flapped like a butterfly's wings.

'You mean that?'

Rhys grinned at her, looking like Hannibal from *The A-Team* with the lollipop stick between his teeth.

'I'll catch you later,' she told him.

'Not too soon, I hope. Jack will have a hernia if Romulus beats Dexter. Poor guy's already crippled with nerves. Thinks the Christmas Hurdle has a hoodoo on him.'

Frankie remembered today would be the first anniversary of Black Russian's fatal fall. It would also be the first anniversary of Rhys busting his leg.

'You feeling okay?' she asked.

Rhys pulled on his vest and body protector. With the white long-sleeved vest tight over his shapely arms and chest and the dark blue of his body protector beefing him up, he reminded Frankie of a superhero. Perhaps one whose special power was to turn into some superfast stallion. He reinserted the half-sucked lollipop into his mouth. Okay, maybe not such a superhero, after all.

'Yeah. Don't worry about me.'

Worrying Rhys was the last thing she was doing two and a half hours later. She stood up in her stirrups as Romulus rounded the home turn and stopped urging him on. The puffed-out horse slowed immediately. There were still two hurdles to take, but he had reached the end of his race. Frankie strained to make out the commentator's echoing voice yelling the other horses home. She held her breath as the leaders met the last hurdle and it seemed the packed crowds had as well. A fresh roar tumbled from the grandstands as Rhys sent Dexter further and further clear. Frankie sat down in the saddle as Romulus slowed to a jog then a walk.

'Well done, Rhys,' she murmured. She smiled. 'Well done, Jack. And well done you,' she added, patting her mount's steaming neck. 'You played your part in that victory too. You set a great gallop. Good boy.'

Through leaden eyelids, Frankie looked across at the alarm clock on the bedside table.

3:44

She lay quietly, contented, still a little druggy from sleep. She listened for the deep breaths of Rhys sleeping beside her. He was breathing, yes, but he didn't sound asleep.

'You still awake?' Frankie looked over at him and stretched.

In the darkness, she could make out the flutter of his eyelashes as he blinked.

'Yeah. Did I wake you?'

'No,' she mumbled, snuggling into his shoulder again. 'You okay?'

Rhys lay on his back, looking up at the ceiling.

'What do you dream about?' he said after a pause.

Frankie raised her head alertly. That was the last time she was eating cheese-on-toast before bed.

'Was I talking in my sleep?'

'No, nothing like that. I mean day dream, like consciously.'

Frankie rolled onto her back to contemplate the ceiling as well. She tried to zone in on one dream, to picture herself succeeding. But even though she could feel the buzz of success, she couldn't see herself. She could only see her father's beaming face, full of pride, applauding.

'I guess I dream about making my dad proud. How about you?'

Rhys looked quickly across at her then back at the ceiling. The shaking of his head made the pillow rustle.

'No, I'm sorry. I shouldn't have asked you if I was never going to answer that myself.'

'Come on,' Frankie said, giving him a playful smack on the chest. 'I bared my soul. Now it's your turn.'

Rhys sighed. He didn't answer.

Frankie thought he was going to remain unresponsive when he broke the silence.

'Have you ever dreamt,' he began slowly, 'of being the first to skirt The Elbow at Aintree for the run-in? After defying death over thirty jumps and four and a half gruelling miles in the biggest steeplechase in the world, you look up. All you see on the horizon is that red lollipop by the finish and a smooth pathway of green grass between you and it.' Rhys held up his hand as if he could touch it. 'No more big scary jumps, no other horses. To your right is this black booming mass of people cheering you on. And as you gallop up and over the line, you have time to absorb those tiny particles of history in the making.' His hand flopped down again onto the duvet. 'And you know that you have been part of it.'

Frankie continued to gaze at him with her mouth ajar.

'Wow. Something tells me you've thought that one through on more than one occasion.'

Rhys gave her a mischievous smile.

'Sometimes I add a loose horse or two to make it more exciting.'

Frankie giggled. Then she sobered. She was only just beginning to realise how her dreams had shattered Rhys's.

'You want to win it so bad,' she whispered.

Rhys waved her away with his hand.

'No more than the next guy.' He rolled onto his side so he was facing her. 'Including you.'

Grateful to see he wasn't sinking into depression, she returned his smile.

'So I'm just one of the guys now, am I?'

'Believe me, what I am about to do to you I have absolutely no interest in doing with the other guys.'

Frankie giggled as Rhys ducked beneath the covers. His hair tickled her ribs and she squirmed. He trailed kisses over her stomach before burrowing up and gently holding her hardening nipple between his teeth.

Frankie pushed her head into the pillow and closed her eyes.

'Rhys, no,' she moaned. 'I've got to get up early tomorrow. We don't have time.'

Rhys's black curls appeared from beneath the duvet, shortly followed by his face.

'"Time is a companion that goes with us on a journey. It reminds us to cherish each moment because it will never come again. What we leave behind is not as important as how we have lived".'

'Look at you, Professor Bradford of the Philosophy Department. Whose words of wisdom are those? Aristotle?'

'No, Captain Jean Luc Picard in *Star Trek*.'

Frankie rolled onto her side in giggles. When she'd recovered, she turned back to him. She could see him smiling in the darkness.

'Can I ask you a favour?' she said.

'Depends on what it is. You should know I don't do violence and while it's okay for some people, I really don't go in for foot fetishes.'

'No, it's nothing like that.' She hesitated. 'You know I help out at Girl Guides?'

'Yeah,' Rhys said guardedly.

'Well, we organise these events for them, themed events. They're kind of like badges but they're called Go For Its.'

'Okay.'

'I'm meant to be organising a couple in the new year. One's called Lights, Camera, Action and the girls get to learn about film production and acting and stuff like that.'

'Frankie, I know Hollywood is missing out on its next leading man while I'm over here, but I'm a jockey. What favour could I possibly do?'

Frankie stroked his cheek, bristly with shadow. He would make such a sensuous leading man.

'Well, you're a bit of a film buff and you do all of your photography. I thought maybe you could come along and teach them about how a camera and tripod and things work.'

Rhys groaned.

'No, Frankie. No, no, no. I couldn't, I'm sorry. I'd be the worst teacher. And I very much doubt whether I could tell them anything about cameras that they don't already know.'

'Of course there is. No one takes photos like you do without knowing a thing or two about – I don't know what you'd call it – framing and lighting, I guess. Please. It'll be fun. Everyone gets to dress up as a movie character.'

'Oh God, no.' He lay his arm over his eyes then peeped from beneath it when she didn't respond. Frankie gave him her most doe-eyed look. Rhys covered his eyes again.

'Say you'll think about it?'

Rhys sighed.

'I'll think about it.' He raised his arm to look at her again and pointed a finger. 'That is not a "yes" though. It's a "I'll think about it".'

Delighted that he hadn't given her an outright "no", Frankie snuggled deeper into their bed.

'That's good enough for me.'

Rhys curled up behind her, neatly fitting his body against hers and nuzzled her neck. Frankie felt like purring.

'Now this is what I call a quality Rhysy-spoon,' she murmured.

'Except that sausage and eggs are off the menu,' Rhys replied. He kissed her neck. 'Sweet dreams.'

31

By the time Frankie received a sleepy text message from her mother wishing her a happy new year, she was already driving across the Severn Bridge into Wales with Rhys. There had been no huge celebratory bash for her the night before. She had toasted in the new year and shared a kiss with Rhys on the stroke of midnight, but that was all. Okay, and she'd had a shag, but that had come later and hadn't been particularly New Year-related.

She needed to be sober and wide awake for New Year's Day. She had to ride Peace Offering in the Welsh National, up against his old foes Skylark and Okay Oklahoma and last year's Grand National winner, Faustian. Skylark was favoured to repeat his Becher Chase triumph over Peace Offering and adding to the pressure on Frankie's shoulders, her parents had promised to attend.

Frankie looked up at the sky as they pulled up in the car park and got out. Low cloud hovered over the surrounding hilltops. She sucked in a lungful of the frigid air.

'You coming for a run?' she asked Rhys.

Rhys exhaled noisily. His hair was still tousled and purple smears of sleep-deprivation shadowed his eyes.

'If it's pounds you need to lose, we could always have a fast fuck in the sauna.'

Frankie slung her bag over her shoulder and began walking towards the course.

'Nice try, sunshine. I've got to walk the course before the big one.'

'Ah, yes. You're riding Peace Offering, aren't you?'

It wasn't a question as such, Frankie knew. Rhys was well aware of her four rides today. And despite his reassurances that he was okay with her riding Peace Offering, she still felt the horse was an uncomfortable topic. She dreaded to think how she and Rhys would cope come Grand National Day in April. Right now, she didn't want to think about it. Dare she say it, but she'd even prefer her own company. She had plenty on her plate already without having to worry about hurting Rhys's feelings.

'I'm going for a run,' she said. 'I'll see you later.'

The first of Frankie's rides came aboard Dory in the three mile Beginners' Chase. Ordinarily, Frankie felt she would have been in with a chance. Dory was a good jumper and she had a decent of foot. But Aspen Valley was triple-handed in this race and Dory was the weakest of its three entries.

'I wouldn't change you for the world,' she said, ruffling Dory's silver mane as they cantered down to the start. 'Let's show these boys how to do it, eh?'

The turf was thick and the ground heavy underfoot. Frankie knew conditions weren't ideally suited to Dory's daisy-cutter action and from where she was sat, the six walls of birch which severed the backstretch seemed insurmountable. She glanced across at Rhys, sat astride Faulkner in his blue and grey-striped silks. He looked focussed; his goggles were already down even though the tape still hadn't been drawn across the course.

The first droplets of rain began to fall as the starter climbed his rostrum. Frankie went to pull her goggles down.

'Shit,' she hissed.

'What's up?' Rhys asked.

'I forgot to bring spare goggles. These won't be any use in the mud. Dammit! Jack wanted me to drop her in at the back too.'

The starter called the runners forward and the field grouped together. Dory bounced sideways.

'Do you want a pair of mine?'

Frankie looked at the starter, at the bright orange ribbon of tape up ahead quivering in the wind. Dory pulled her out of the saddle and bounded forward. Frankie shook her head.

'No time,' she said as her mount surged past Rhys's.

'Okay. Keep her wide then.'

'She'll never get the trip if I take her wide. Not in this ground.'

'Well, keep her handy then.'

At the starter's cue, the tape lashed back and the nine runners plunged forward. Dory was away smartly and Frankie settled her in third. The first of two plain fences was quickly upon them and Dory put in a giant leap. Frankie grappled at the mare's mane as her impetus threw her forward.

'Dory,' she growled, pushing herself back into position. 'Please don't do that.'

Dory twitched her ears, but obviously hadn't paid any attention. She'd spied the next fence and was keen to get to it. She edged into the lead. Another Puissance leap put them a length and a half clear. Dory pricked her ears and quickened away. Frankie gently worked the reins, dislodging the bit from between her horse's teeth.

'Come on, honey. You might be enjoying yourself now, but you've got another three miles to go yet,' she murmured. 'Come on, ease up.'

She took a quick peak across her shoulder. Jack would kill her. She was doing the complete opposite to what he'd instructed and she was only now beginning to realise just how significant dropping Dory out the back would be. There she could settle, but here at the front she would be out of puff in just one circuit.

'Bloody hell,' Frankie growled.

She sawed more insistently on the reins. Goggles or no goggles, she had to get Dory to settle.

As they rounded the home turn for the first time, Frankie was relieved to hear the rhythmic huff of heavy breathing and dull drum of hoofbeats nearing her from behind. Within seconds the field had surrounded her. A sod of mud was flicked up by passing hooves and hit Frankie square between the eyes. Blinded for a moment, she dragged her gloved fingers across her goggles. Through the brown smears, she could just make out the next fence approaching. A small flurry of panic rose from her gut. She had slowed too quickly. Now Dory was getting bumped from all sides.

The cheering of the crowds washed over her. Doug would be watching.

The new leaders prepared to meet the third fence. Another onslaught of muddy turf hit her in the face. Like a bank of warm air meeting a cold front, a hurricane of fear swirled through her body. Frankie dragged her goggles down around her neck so she could see. Two and a half strides. The horse in front took off, dispatching a clod of earth with his hindfeet.

Slap!

She squeezed her eyes shut to dislodge the stinging pain. Dory took off and with her reins flapping loose as Frankie lost her grip, the mare soared over the jump, adding in an extra kick out of exuberance and love of the game. Frankie didn't stand a chance. She didn't know where the ground was, where the sky was. Where were the rest of the runners? She hit the landing side of the jump in an untidy Jenga pile of limbs. Pain shot up her arm from her hand. Frankie rolled over and groaned.

*

'Does this hurt?'

The on-course doctor gently manoeuvred Frankie's wrist up and down. Sat in Chepstow Racecourse's medical room, Frankie hissed through her teeth.

'No, it's fine as long as you don't do that.'

The doctor gave her a weary look. She probed her thumbs around Frankie's arm. Frankie gritted her teeth so hard she was sure they would crack. This could not be happening to her. She could not have fallen off Dory and broken her arm. She had to ride Peace Offering in the Welsh National in just over an hour's time.

'Just give me a couple of painkillers and I'll be fine,' she insisted.

'You know I've been doing this a long time,' the doctor said. Her unlined face told a different story, but Frankie waited for her to continue. 'And in my experience, you lot never let on just how much pain you're in.'

Frankie gave her a sulky look, which the doctor ignored.

'Looking at this,' she nodded at Frankie's dirty wrist, 'you're not riding anywhere except to hospital for X-rays.'

'It's honestly not that bad. It looks worse than it really is. I stub my toe and my whole foot swells up. Please. I'm riding Peace Offering in the Welsh National. Just give me some painkillers.'

The doctor gave her a sympathetic look. She picked up Frankie's mud-spattered helmet by the chinstrap.

'Hold out your hand.'

Frankie eased her fingers straight and held out her palm gingerly. The doctor placed the helmet onto it. Immediately, it bounced to the ground and rolled under the bed as Frankie gave a gasp of pain.

'Ow.'

'You need to go to hospital.'

Panic fought its way to the fore. She *had* to ride Peace Offering. She'd bolloxed up the Becher Chase on him. If she didn't ride him now then Jack would surely convince Pippa to drop her as jockey.

'No! Please, you don't understand. I *must* ride in the next. I can do it. There's nothing wrong with me. It's a little sore, I'll give you that, but you dropped my helmet onto my hand. I wasn't expecting it.'

The doctor shook her head.

'You're not riding again today. And probably not for a while, I'm afraid. I'm signing you off for the rest of the day.'

'Shit!' Frankie cried. She slumped on her chair. A lump the size of a golf ball rose in her throat. 'Shit! Shit! SHIT!'

The doctor patted her on the shoulder.

'I'm sorry.'

Frankie's cheeks burned with frustration and she turned to glare at the woman.

'Fine, but I'm not going anywhere until the Welsh National has been run.'

32

The pervading smell of all things medical hung gloomily in the ward as Frankie sat back against the wall of Chepstow Community Hospital pillows. She looked dejectedly at her strapped wrist resting within a pile of icepacks in her lap.

'The doctor said to keep it raised, lovie,' Vanessa said.

Grudgingly, she obliged. The icepacks were freezing against her chest. She looked at her mother chewing off her lipstick then at her father. Doug was frowning at the ground.

'It could've been worse, I guess,' Frankie said.

Doug raised his eyes, troubled.

'I guess.'

Frankie hung her head. Not by much, she supposed. Peace Offering had still run in the Welsh National. Rhys had switched rides and, after a couple of early mistakes, had finished a close second to Okay Oklahoma.

'I'm sorry you came all this way just to watch me make a pig's breakfast of everything.'

'Don't be silly, Frankie,' Vanessa said. 'We'd much rather be here. We'd have been worried sick if we'd watched it on TV, not knowing what had happened.'

Frankie gave her a weak but grateful smile.

'And for being such a girl's blouse about this whole thing.' She scoffed at her immobile limb. Ow, maybe she shouldn't huff when it was up against her chest like that.

'Nonsense,' Doug said. 'You're being very brave.'

She couldn't see any sign of her father not being genuine, yet she still sunk a little lower knowing how disappointed he must be. She cursed all the times she'd bigged herself up in front of him to impress him. How could he not be disappointed when she fell flat on her face the first occasion he came to watch her ride?

'Great way to start the year, eh?'

Vanessa batted a hand at her.

'Honey, most people start the year off with a hangover. I wouldn't read too much into it. And look on the bright side. At least your horse was okay.'

'Guess so.' Only three jumps in when they'd fallen, Dory had ignored all opportunities presented to her to stop racing and had jumped the remaining fifteen with carefree abandon. 'Speaking of hangovers, how was your party last night?'

'The best. I was so hungover this morning even my eyelashes hurt.'

The door to the ward opened and Frankie looked up hoping it would be the doctor to discharge her. Instead, Rhys entered. He was dressed in warm clean clothes and his hair was still damp from the shower he'd obviously taken at the racecourse.

'Rhys!'

'Hey. Thought I'd come see how the walking wounded is doing.'

Her initial delight was punctured by the sudden realisation that Doug was in the same room. Rhys followed her wary glance towards her father. He paused before stepping forward with his hand outstretched.

'Hi. You must be Frankie's parents. I'm Rhys.'

Doug stiffened and kept his arms rigid at his sides. Frankie willed him to take Rhys's hand. Thankfully, Vanessa stepped forward and gave him a gracious smile.

'Hi, Rhys. Lovely to meet you at last,' she said. 'I'm Vanessa. This is Doug.' She gave Doug a subtle kick on the ankle and he reluctantly gave Rhys's hand a shake.

Rhys took his hand back awkwardly. There was an uncomfortable pause before he looked at Frankie optimistically.

'How're you doing?'

'I sprained my wrist. Doc says I probably tore some ligaments.'

Rhys grimaced in sympathy.

'At least nothing's broken. How long before you can ride again?'

'Isn't her health more important than riding?' Doug said frostily.

Rhys gave an embarrassed chuckle.

'Well, of course. But as a jockey, I know riding again will be the main thing on her mind.'

'And as a jockey, you'll also want to know if you have her ride in the National.'

'Dad! Please!' Frankie said, mortified by his rudeness.

Rhys's face took on a grave expression.

'It's okay, Frankie,' he said, still watching Doug. 'Your dad's probably just a bit upset after your fall. I doubt whether he means it personally.'

'Don't give yourself bloody airs!' Doug growled. 'You're precisely the reason why I'm angry.'

'Doug, behave!' Vanessa scolded him. 'For God's sake, do we have to have a scene? Frankie's hurt. Let's concentrate on getting her better.'

Doug pursed his lips, but didn't reply. With relief, Frankie turned back to Rhys.

'I've got to rest it for a few days then I can take on light duties at the yard after a week. Then depending on how fast it heals, I could be back riding in three or four weeks.'

Rhys smiled encouragingly.

'That's great.' His smile lost its potency as he glanced across at Doug again. He shifted from one foot to the other and ground his fists in his jacket pockets. 'I also came by to see if you needed a lift home, but since your parents are here...'

Frankie looked helplessly from Rhys to Vanessa and Doug. She knew her father was out of line, but like Rhys had pointed out, he was probably also worried about her. She didn't want to desert him, to throw his protectiveness in his face. At the same time, she didn't want to turn Rhys down. He'd made the effort to come to see her. How could she just fob him off?

She swallowed hard and readjusted the position of her arm.

'No, I'll come with you.'

Doug looked dissolute, but Frankie stood her ground.

'It'll save you the journey,' she said as way of conciliation. 'Rhys lives in Helensvale so it'd be easier all round.'

'Good idea, darling,' Vanessa said. 'We've got a dinner party to go tonight anyhow.'

'Do we?' Doug said, looking at her in surprise.

Vanessa gave him an exaggerated *run-with-me-on-this-one* look.

'Yes. And it's already ten to five. I've still got to get myself ready.' She stepped over to the bed and gave Frankie a quick kiss. 'Bye-bye, darling. I'll call later to see how you're getting on.'

'Okay. Thanks, Mum.'

33

Time stretched torturously slow while Frankie recuperated. Unfit to work, she wandered around the house interrupting Atticus Finch's five hour naps and worrying about her weight. Every time she looked into the fridge, she felt as if she put another pound on. Using a bag of frozen peas on her wrist didn't help either.

A few days after her fall, however, the mailman brought a nervous excitement to her boredom. Tom had left early to go racing at Huntingdon and wasn't expected back until at least six o'clock. Frankie sat in the lounge, watching *The Biggest Loser* with Atticus, but not taking any of it in. Her gaze kept straying to the letter which had landed on the mat that morning now taking pride of place on the coffee table.

At ten to six, she was roused from a doze by a scuffling at the front door. Her heart stepped up the pace and she got up to retrieve the letter addressed to Tom.

'Hey, how was racing?' she asked when he appeared in the doorway.

'You know, same ol' same ol'. Rhys had three winners today so he's gone clear of Mick Farrelly in the jockeys' championship.'

'Ah, good.' Frankie fingered the envelope behind her back. 'Something arrived in the mail for you today.'

Tom stiffened. He swallowed hard and tried to appear nonchalant.

'Oh, really? Latest issue of *Heat* I hope.'

Frankie bit her lip and brought the letter into view. Her fingers were shaking as she held it out for him to take. His name and address were written in thick loopy writing and had been smudged by raindrops. Tom turned it over and took a deep breath when he saw the return addressee: A. MANN. He cumbrously teased open the seal. He stopped, his hands shaking more than Frankie's had.

'Do you want some privacy?' she asked.

Tom shook his head.

'No, I'm glad you're here.' He reached inside the envelope and paused. 'I can't do this,' he sighed. He thrust the letter into Frankie's hand. 'Here, you read it.'

'You sure?'

Eyes closed, he nodded. She cleared her throat and shook the sheet open.

'*Dear Tom,*' she read aloud. '*Thank you for your letter, which I received just before Christmas. I am sorry not to have written sooner, however family commitments prevented me from doing so.*' She looked up to see Tom cringe and she felt a sudden rush of anger on his behalf. Family commitments? Wasn't Tom a family commitment? '*I wish I could write with the information you are looking for, but unfortunately I am unable to help.*' Frankie's heart drooped. Okay, maybe he wasn't.

Tom sagged and sat down on the arm of the sofa with a bump.

'*Although my name is Adelaide Mann, I am not the person you are trying to find. I was born and brought up in Edinburgh before moving to London twenty-two years ago with my now-ex-husband. There we raised four children. I am very sorry that I am unable to help you, but wish you the very best of luck with your search. Regards, Adelaide Mann.*'

'It's not her,' Tom said glumly.

Frankie folded the letter again and put her arm around Tom's shoulders.

'So it would seem. But she *is* out there. Somewhere.'

Tom looked up at her, his eyes doleful.

'What if it is her? What if she's lying?'

Frankie's heart ached for him.

'I don't think she is, Tom,' she said gently.

He rubbed his face with his palms and exhaled wearily.

'Back to square one again.'

'We still have her name,' Frankie tried to give him hope. 'That's more than we had before. We can still find her.'

'Yeah, whatever,' Tom muttered. He took the letter from her and scrunched it into a ball and threw it into the fire grate and strode out the room. Frankie sank back down onto the sofa and stroked an ever-hopeful Atticus.

34

Frankie was back riding work within ten days. On the one hand, when Jack announced that he wanted her to give Ta' Qali some roadwork she was relieved that her still fragile wrist could have a break (well, not literally). On the other hand, his reason for sending the string into Helensvale on market-day left her a fraction apprehensive. The trainer's attempt to conquer Ta' Qali's nerves, albeit in less demanding circumstances than on a race-day, was doing nothing for Frankie's nerves.

The main road to Helensvale didn't have much of a verge, but there was so little traffic that the riders were able to walk two abreast.

'I'm surprised to see you out doing light exercise,' Frankie teased Rhys.

'What can I say? I convinced Jack to let me come along in case Ta' Qali had a fit.'

Despite her own doubts, she gave him a playfully prim look.

'I'm quite capable of taking care of myself, thank you.'

Rhys nodded to her bandaged wrist, resting easily on her thigh.

'So I can tell.'

Ta' Qali walked with his head held high and his black ears pricked towards the sound of sheep on the other side of the hedge. He didn't look to have a care in the world. Little did he realise where they were headed for.

'At least I did it now,' Frankie said, referring to her wrist. 'Cheltenham's in a couple of months' time. It would have been awful if I'd done it right before then.'

'Don't tempt the gods. You know what it's like. There's no injury quota that means you've had your fill and can be blasé about the rest of the season.'

Frankie took that on board. As far as her job went, she'd been injury-free for the most part. She'd dislocated her shoulder once when she was nineteen, riding in a point-to-point, but besides that and her sprained wrist, that was the extent of her injuries.

'What's been your worst season for injuries?' she asked.

Rhys thought for a moment.

'Five years ago. I broke my elbow summer jumping. That was hell. Can't stand summer jumping. The ground gets so firm, it's unsafe. Anyway, that put me out until September. Then I broke my collarbone.'

'Ouch.'

Rhys shrugged, indifferent.

'Was back six weeks later, managed a month then got concussion, managed to fool the doc and ended up falling off in the next race. Dislocated my thumb.' Rhys held up his left hand and bent his thumb back to touch the back of his hand to demonstrate.

'Urgh, yuck!' cringed Frankie. 'Didn't it ever heal?'

Rhys chuckled to himself, obviously pleased that he'd grossed her out.

'No. It's something I've always been able to do. I'm very dexterous, you'll find.'

'I think I've already found actually,' Frankie conceded. Rhys put everyone else she'd slept with – all three of them – in the shade.

The hedges and sheep gradually gave way to bungalows and parked cars as they neared Helensvale's outer limits. Frankie leaned forward and scratched Ta' Qali on the crest of his neck. He tossed his head in response.

'He looks like he's trying to flick that weird marking off his nose,' Rhys said, watching.

'The first time I saw it, it reminded me of spilt salt. Maybe he's trying to toss salt over shoulder.'

'It hasn't brought him much luck so far.'

Frankie smoothed Ta' Qali's mane to the side in consolation.

'Don't be mean. I think he's being really good.'

'For now,' Rhys warned.

They turned into the High Street, a magnificent parade of seven horses clip-clopping on the road. The riders' red jackets stood out in the overcast morning and the saddle cloths bearing Jack Carmichael's initials left rubberneckers in no doubt as to where they were from. OAPs steadied themselves on their Zimmer frames to watch them pass and office workers loitering on the pavement having a cigarette break paused mid-puff. Frankie was alert, ready for Ta' Qali to start performing.

When the memory of Seth rose in her mind, she pushed it to the back. She couldn't think like that.

They neared the striped canvas stalls of the market just as the clock tower beside the bookies chimed ten o'clock. The alluring smell of fresh-baked pies drifted on the cool air and Frankie hoovered it up.

'Mmm. That smells divine.'

'Local produce doesn't equate to low-cal produce, unfortunately,' Rhys replied. 'Breathe through your mouth. It's less torturous.'

Someone was very keen on selling their rhubarb and shallots at a knockdown price. Ta' Qali snorted.

'Watch him,' Rhys murmured beside her.

Pies forgotten, Frankie concentrated on her horse's ears. They switched back and forth, absorbing the hustle and bustle of Market Day. What if he bolted? Would her wrist hold up? Behind them, a scatter of hooves on tarmac sounded as one of the other horses spooked. Frankie adjusted her seat ever so slightly, ready for Ta' Qali to take off. A gust of wind blew down the street and a plastic bag was swept from a groceries crate and into the street.

'It's just a bag,' she murmured as Ta' Qali raised his head and pricked his ears.

The bag tumbled weightlessly towards them. Ta' Qali tensed. Frankie clicked her tongue at him and held her breath. The bag cartwheeled past them and Ta' Qali relaxed. Out of sight, out of mind.

They passed the flapping canvases of the stalls and slowly the market traders' voices began to fade. Ta' Qali resumed his swinging stride. Frankie felt a tidal wave of relief wash over her. She looked across at Rhys, dubious but pleased.

'Beginner's luck,' he said, a wry smile on his face.

'Who you calling beginner?'

'*Amateur's* luck then.'

'That's more like it,' she grinned. 'One more win and I'll only be able to claim three pounds.'

'You going to go professional eventually?'

She shrugged and concentrated harder than necessary on steering her horse past an idling van. If she was to go professional, she would be the only female jump jockey in Britain to do so. And she knew it wasn't for want of other women trying. She didn't exactly see herself as being the one to pave the way though.

'I don't know,' she said. 'I've still got to ride another thirty-five winners before I lose my claim completely and I'd have to apply for a conditional license before I go professional. There seems an awful lot to be done.'

'So?' Rhys said with a laugh. 'Isn't riding professional what your ambition has always been?'

Frankie frowned to herself. She loved her job, there was no mistake about that, but she wasn't sure she didn't love the yard work more than the actual racing.

'Yeah, I guess.'

'You guess? Jesus, Frankie,' he chuckled. 'How can you be so blasé about the whole thing? This is your career we're talking about. And it'll be over before you know it –'

'Excuse me?'

'No, I didn't mean it like that. I mean *all* of our careers will be over before we know it. We're jump jockeys. On average we fall every sixth or seventh ride. Name me one jump jockey who is over forty.'

Frankie thought then reluctantly shook her head.

'I can't.'

'There you go. Come on, you're twenty-three. Your claim is going to run out in three years' time. Make hay while the sun shines, as they say.'

Frankie snorted.

'I'm twenty-four next month.'

'Even more reason to be focussed on your career.'

Frankie twisted her reins around her whip thoughtfully. Put like that, she didn't have much time left at all. Her career as a jockey would probably be over in less than ten years. It felt as if it had hardly started though! And while Rhys might be older and wiser – all twenty-eight years' worth of wisdom – his career security unsettled her. Was it so wrong that she wasn't yet convinced that being a jockey was the right job for her? She was too afraid to ask Rhys if he ever felt the same fear she did during a race. It must surely be natural to be scared when hurtling towards twenty-odd walls of birch at thirty-five miles an hour.

She stole a glance at Rhys. He wasn't your average person though. He sat on a horse as if it was the most natural place to be. And horses obviously approved of his inborn ability. Peace Offering's Welsh National placing was evidence enough of that. Frankie felt a stab of envy in her gut at the thought of how he'd got such a tune out of a horse he hadn't sat on for the best part of a year.

By the time the string of Aspen Valley horses had turned for home, that envy had evolved into guilt. Misplaced as it might be, she felt undeserving of the ride on Peace Offering when Rhys obviously knew exactly what he wanted. Not only that, but he had forgiven her for sauntering in and taking his best chance of winning the National because she 'guessed' this was the career she wanted.

Back in the warmth of Ta' Qali's stable, Frankie struggled to undo his girth.

'Here, let me give you a hand with that,' Jack's voice interrupted her from the doorway.

Frankie stepped aside with a grateful smile.

'Thanks.'

'How's it holding up?' he said, nodding to her wrist.

Frankie pulled a face.

'Holding up.'

Jack slipped Ta' Qali's saddle off his dipped back.

'Did he give you any trouble?'

'He didn't turn a hair,' she said with a proud grin. 'Quietest horse in the string. Had all the market traders shouting, plastic bags and canvases flapping in the wind but he was as good as gold.'

'Good,' Jack said. He carried on looking at the horse, studiously chewing his lower lip. Ta' Qali rolled his eye at his owner. 'So if crowds aren't the problem, what is it, big guy?' he said.

Frankie stood by Ta' Qali's head with her hand held out for him to lip at. She'd learnt that while he didn't like his head being touched, he was quite partial to having his lips rubbed. She wished she could help Jack figure him out, but she had no suggestions.

'Maybe it's you,' Jack said finally, turning to Frankie.

Frankie looked sideways, wide-eyed.

'Me?'

'Yeah. He's never been a problem with you on his back and he looks like he's getting used to being handled by you at least,' he said.

Frankie glowed with inner pride.

'A bit. I can't touch the marking on his nose yet, but he's better than he was.'

'We've seen just how good he can be on the gallops. Hell, he's the only horse that can keep Dexter company and look what Dexter's just done. I mean, this guy's obviously got the ability if he can keep pace with a Christmas Hurdle winner at home. Maybe he just doesn't like Rhys's style. He is quite a strong jockey whereas you've a more sympathetic style. Maybe that's what it is. Yeah,' he said, nodding with conviction as the idea formed in his head. 'Tell you what: next start, we'll put you up on him and see if that makes the difference. You okay with that?'

Frankie struggled not to jig on the spot. She bit her lips together, but her smile of approval still shone through. Jack nodded.

'Good. That's that sorted then.' He turned to leave, but she stopped him. His mood was too good not to take advantage of, and she'd had a rather unorthodox idea flitting around her head for the past couple of weeks.

'Jack, can I ask a favour?'

'Of course. What's up?'

'I don't know if you're aware of it, but I help run Helensvale's Girl Guide group and they've got their GFI Animal Active to do. I was wondering if they could do it here?'

'A *what?*'

'It's like a badge. I thought maybe they could learn about horse husbandry for this one.'

Jack frowned at her and she grimaced in anticipation of his answer.

'I guess it couldn't hurt,' he eventually conceded. 'But only after Cheltenham Festival. Speaking of which, I've pencilled in the Kim Muir Chase for you and Peace Offering.'

Frankie was too gobsmacked to respond. Jack winked at her expression and dropped her saddle into her limp arms. Frankie turned to her horse once he'd left.

'Did you hear that, boy? I'm going to the Festival! And you and I are gonna race together! Don't let me down, baby. Let's show them what we're made of, eh?' Overcome with excitement, she dropped a kiss on the crooked bridge of his nose, for a brief moment forgetting his shyness.

Ta' Qali's memory was not so patchy. He chucked his head up, smashing her lip into her front teeth. Tears sprung to her eyes as pain and the metallic taste of blood filled her mouth. She touched her lip tentatively and winced. Great, she was going to look like she'd been to a Botox party. On the subject of which, her thoughts turned to Cheltenham and the annual party held at the end of the four day festival.

This year she'd really feel part of the action if she and Peace Offering made it there in one piece.

Imagination running riot, she imagined Ta' Qali performing so brilliantly for that Jack wouldn't be able to resist supplementing him in the Triumph Hurdle. They could be the fairy tale which the Festival so often produced. Frankie walked on air back to the tack room and bumped into Billy on his way out.

'Ooh, Frankie, your lip's bleeding,' he cringed. 'Are you okay?'

'I'm fine. I –' She shook her head in wonder. 'Jack just came to see me and –'

'Jack did that to you?' Billy looked horrified.

'No!' she laughed. 'He just told me I can ride Ta' Qali in his next race,' she said.

'Bloody 'ell. What did you do to piss him off?'

'No, it's a good thing, see. Ta' Qali can be really good, Billy. Jack thinks a jockey change might bring out the best in him.'

'Rather you than me.'

'And he's letting me ride Peace Offering in the Kim Muir at the Festival. I can't believe it. My first Festival ride and such a high profile horse.' She took a deep breath and exhaled with excitement. 'Have you noticed Jack's in a *really* good mood today?'

Billy grinned.

'Sure he is. Haven't you heard?'

'Heard what?'

'Oh, shit.' Billy clumsily crossed himself. 'Sorry, I swore I wouldn't tell.'

35

Come the evening of the Girl Guides' Lights, Camera, Action event, Frankie still wasn't certain Rhys would show. While she'd spent a productive day schooling Aspen Valley's novices at home, he'd had a full book of rides at Taunton. She was already regretting her decision to come dressed as Lara Croft. Not only had her body not seen the sun for six months, but the temperature inside Helensvale's Community Hall bordered on Arctic. As she set up a table of DVDs, a squealing herd of Hermione Grangers and Ginny Weasleys ran by pursued by Charlotte, snarling through plastic vampire teeth. She wished she could run around with the abandon of the girls to warm up.

'Right, come along, girls!' Bronwyn, the Guider In Charge shouted, clapping her hands. 'Get into your patrols. You've got a camcorder each to make a short film and we haven't much time.'

Frankie sighed and tried to hide her disappointment. Rhys obviously wasn't going to show. When she'd reminded him that morning about tonight's Go For It, he'd only said he'd see if he could make it. He wouldn't make any promises.

The thirty girls gradually came to order and Frankie took the helm of Starfish Patrol. Charlotte was still grinning in her vampire teeth, Mischa was patting her blonde Marilyn Monroe wig alongside Harriet in a Pink Ladies jacket. All she needed was a cigarette dripping from her lip and she could have stepped off the set of *Grease*. Cassa had donned a nurse outfit, four sizes too big for her, which Frankie was struggling to place in the world of cinema.

'Have you girls thought of any ideas for a film then?' she asked once they were all settled.

'A vampire movie!' lisped Charlotte.

'Yes!' agreed Mischa. 'Then I can be the victim. Cassa can be the doctor trying to save me – who are you meant to be anyway?' she asked, wrinkling her nose at Cassa's costume.

Cassa shrank away.

'Someone from *Grey's Anatomy*?'

'Oh, okay,' Mischa said with disinterest. 'We're going to need some tomato sauce for blood.'

Frankie shook her head.

'If you're sure your mothers aren't going to complain about stains –'

In the relative quiet of the hall, the heavy entrance door slamming shut roused everyone's attention. Captain Jack Sparrow stood uncertainly in the doorway with a sack of treasures slung over his shoulder. An intake of girlish breath pre-empted a universal window-shattering shriek as the girls dropped what they were doing and stampeded over to him. The pirate limped forward, making a great show of swaying on his sea-legs.

Frankie's heart swelled. She watched with escalating pride and something resembling love as Rhys greeted the girls in character. She walked over at a more leisurely pace, silently laughing at him, while at the same time thinking how very well he pulled off the role.

'Johnny Depp, eat your heart out,' Victoria, her fellow helper, murmured in her ear. 'I'd take a trip down his gangplank any day.'

Frankie smiled like only the sexually self-satisfied can.

'Sorry, I'm the only one allowed to rock his boat.'

'Mm-hmm,' Victoria murmured in approval. 'Frankie, I'm impressed.'

Frankie grinned then turned to watch Rhys withdrawing a tripod from his contraband sack to show the eager Guides.

'Not as impressed as I am.'

The following morning was deceptively bright despite being overcast. Frankie whistled as she mucked out her boxes, warmed by the physical work and the large imposing presence of Ta' Qali overseeing her progress. She gave him a quick pat on his muscled shoulder then pushed her wheelbarrow out into the chilly yard. She noticed Jack walking her way in the company of an elderly man.

'Morning, Frankie. Is Blue Jean Baby on the horse walker?'

'No. Just about to muck her out now so she will be in a sec.'

'Hold that thought. This is her owner, Mr McCready. Ron, this is Frankie Cooper, Blue Jean Baby's lass and Aspen Valley's amateur jockey.'

Frankie wiped her palm on her jeans before shaking the man's cold gnarly hand.

'Nice to meet you, Mr McCready. Blue Jean Baby's a real character.'

Ron McCready's face creased into a smile.

'Frankie *Cooper*?' he said, directing the emphasis at Jack.

'Yup, one and the same,' Jack nodded.

'Well, well, well. It's a pleasure to meet you, Frankie,' he said with a hoarse Cornish accent. 'And good to see the next generation so involved in racing too.'

Frankie assumed the old man must have known or heard of her father. His eyes were a milky blue, kind and warm and Frankie gave him her most genuine smile.

'Would you bring Blue Jean Baby out for us to have a look at?' Jack said.

'No problem.' Frankie led them over to the last stable in her row. 'Dory? You having a lie-in?' she joked when Dory's ever-present head didn't materialise over the door. The three peered inside. Frankie's heart sank to her soles faster than an express elevator. The stable was very empty.

'Maybe you forgot that you'd put her on the walker?' Jack suggested slowly. He gave her a meaningful look. Frankie gaped. She wasn't losing her mind. She most definitely hadn't seen to Dory yet. In fact, she hadn't heard a peep from Dory's stable since she'd arrived. Frankie looked at the bolted door.

She turned to Jack and Ron McCready and laughed jovially.

'Yup. You're right again, Jack. Please excuse me – second day back. Still getting the old brain back on the job.' She knocked her knuckles against her skull and rolled her eyes. 'Why don't I go get Blue Jean Baby while you wait in the office where it's warm?'

Jack narrowed his eyes at her.

'Yes, that sounds a good idea,' he said, his voice wooden. He would make a terrible actor, Frankie reckoned. 'You go *find* Blue Jean Baby and we'll go have a cup of tea.'

With owner and trainer walking away, Frankie sprinted out of the block. It was pointless checking the walker. Unless Dory had put herself on it, she wouldn't be there.

'Maybe June or someone put her on before I arrived,' she said, skidding to a halt.

She ran back into the yard and nearly flipped over Romulus' half door in her haste. Romulus jumped in fright and June looked up from her raking.

'June, did you put Dory on the walker earlier?' Frankie said breathlessly.

'Dory?' the lass looked confused. 'No. Why?'

'She's missing. And her owner's here to see her.'

'Shit. She must have taken herself on walkabout. I'll come help you.' June collected her barrow and tools and Frankie held the door open for her.

'You check the walker. I'll check the home paddocks.'

Frankie jogged down the track separating the paddocks, her rapid breath ghosting the air in front of her. Each lush field stood empty in the cold. Tiny snowflakes began to fall.

'That's all I need when I'm looking for a grey horse,' she muttered.

At the end of the track, she stopped and leaned her hands on her thighs. A stitch twisted her side. She hoped Jack was stalling Ron McCready over his cup of tea.

'If I were Dory, where would I go?'

Useful perhaps with any other horse, but Dory was eccentric enough to gallop to London and join a West End theatre production. What if she wasn't on Aspen Valley property? What if she was on the roads? Dread dragged the air from her lungs and she ran back down the track, faster, more desperate.

At this rate, it wouldn't matter how much Jack stalled the owner, they would have to break the news that his horse was missing.

'Dory!' she called helplessly.

The snow began to fall faster, the flakes fat and dense. She could barely make out the far end of the paddocks. She reached the stables again and was met by June.

'Any luck?' she called.

June shook her head.

'Oh, God. Where is she?' Frankie groaned.

'There is one place we haven't checked. Dory spent her summer in the paddock on the other side of the hill next to Jack's house. She might have gone there.'

'Crikey, that's going to take us forever to run up that hill. Mr McCready's going to start to wonder.'

'We'll take the quad bike,' June said.

*

Riding shotgun, Frankie clung to June's waist as they bounced up the hillside track. Jack's house rose into view, a barn conversion dusted with fresh snow on its roof. June pulled up alongside the gate to a paddock nearby and Frankie scrambled up the bars to peer through the murk.

'Dory!'

Only the wind, swirling the snow into flurries, answered her call.

She and June exchanged worried looks.

'She must have got out onto the road,' Frankie said at last. 'I'm going to have to go tell Jack. Oh, why did her owner have to come see her today of all days!'

'Come on,' June said. 'Better not waste any more time. Have you got your phone on you? It'll be quicker to tell him and keep looking at the same time.'

Frankie despaired. She was just digging her mobile out of her pocket when a sound, high on the wind, made her stop.

'What was that?' She stopped to listen. For a moment only the gusting wind and steady growl of the quad bike broke the silence. Then the sound came again. Fainter. But Frankie was certain.

'It's her. DORY!' she yelled again.

'Where did it come from?'

'It sounded like it was coming from there,' she said pointing to Jack's house.

June mirrored her dubious expression.

'Let's go check it out then.'

Frankie straddled the growling bike again and the pair bounced off the main track and onto the driveway.

'DORY!' June took up the call.

A clearer whinny reached them and June hurriedly shut off the bike's engine.

'It sounds like – she can't be *inside*, can she?' Frankie said.

Jumping off the bike they ran round the side of the house. As one, they stopped dead. Slowly, they digested the scene before them.

'Fuck me,' June murmured.

'Oh, God. Dory. What the hell have you done?' Frankie strode towards the mare on the other side of the fence. Jack's entire vegetable garden was ploughed up beyond recognition. Blue Jean Baby was caked in mud, her belly distended from where she'd gorged herself and been unable to jump back out of the garden. A sheepish smile hung from her radish-tinted lips.

'Jack is going to kill us both.'

Frankie stood awkwardly in the warmth of the office facing the two men. Ron McCready was surprisingly understanding when the truth surfaced.

'Horses will be horses,' he shrugged.

'And Dory will be Dory,' Jack muttered, looking less impressed. 'I'll get the vet out just in case she develops colic.'

'Sorry about your veggie garden,' Frankie said.

'Forget it. Why don't you go clean up Dory while I give Warnock a ring? I'm sorry about this, Ron.'

The elderly owner beamed at Frankie from his seat.

'No problem at all. Makes me feel part of a yard again.'

Back in the biting cold of the yard, Frankie hurried across to Dory's stable (where the top door had now also been closed). The old man's words looped round her mind. Now that she had a moment to think, his name did sound oddly familiar.

Ron McCready. She thought back to Dory's previous racing engagements, but her owner had failed to attend any of them. No, it wasn't through Dory that the name was niggling her. He'd mentioned feeling part of a yard again. Had he been involved in racing in a different capacity? Earlier, he'd implied he'd known her father. He must have been in the game for a good few years then.

McCready, McCready.

She unbolted the stable doors and gasped. In her mind's eye, she saw her laptop screen before she'd spilt coffee over it all those months ago. Ron McCready had trained Crowbar, the horse who had won the Grand National for Alan Bradford.

In a haze of possibilities and speculations, Frankie scraped the mud from Dory's legs. Her thoughts were interrupted by a knock on the half-door. Ron McCready smiled in at her.

'Mind if I come inside the warmth? Jack's been sidetracked with vet issues so I thought I'd come pay you both a visit.'

Dory reached out and nosed his pockets for treats.

'Yes, of course.'

He snuffled into a handkerchief and Frankie hesitated.

'Are you sure you wouldn't prefer to wait in the office? It's a lot warmer in there.'

The old man waved her away.

'It's been too long since I've seen my Blue Jean Baby. Been in hospital with a chest infection that wouldn't shift. The joys of being a pensioner in winter.'

'You used to train, didn't you?'

Ron McCready responded with another warm smile.

'That I did. Didn't have quite as big a set-up as Jack does here, but we had our moments of glory.'

Frankie carried on brushing Dory. She bit her lip, summoning her courage.

'My dad rode for you, didn't he?'

He gave a wheezy cough and Frankie waited for him to answer.

'If Doug Cooper's your dad then yes, he did. A fine rider just as you are, I'm sure. Not every Tom, Dick and Harry gets a job with Jack Carmichael.'

'Thanks.'

She opened her mouth to ask another question then closed it again when she failed to compose the words. Airily brushing the mud from Dory's temples, she tried a different approach.

'Dad sometimes mentioned a horse that you trained – Crowbar, I think it was,' she said. 'He must have been some horse to have.'

'That he was. Lazy as a dog at home, but he saved his energy for when it really mattered.'

'But he had two jockeys, didn't he?'

She paused in her grooming, fearful that she was probing too deep, but Ron didn't seem to notice. He chuckled and shook his head. Even though his eyes still travelled over Dory's body, she could tell he was looking back into the past.

'Wouldn't be much of a surprise, would it? Your dad and Alan Bradford practically shared everything. Those two were inseparable.'

Frankie dropped the dandy brush.

'They were friends?'

'Well, of course. Shared a house when they were both doing their apprenticeships. Your dad was best man at Alan's wedding if I remember correctly. Poor sod. Had to stand up and do a speech in front of hundreds.' He paused to reminisce then nodded. 'That's right, I remember that day well now. Maria's parents hadn't spared any expense – mind you, they could well afford it. Your poor dad was so nervous about telling stories about Alan without getting him in trouble with the new in-laws. They were all Spanish too and – well, you know, the British sense of humour isn't universally shared.' He gave a raspy chuckle and shook his head.

Frankie stared at him, her limbs numb. She nearly lost her balance when Dory shoved her. Her assumption that her father and Alan Bradford had always been enemies lay in rubble in her brain. They'd been *friends*? And by the sounds of it, not just friends, but *best* friends.

'Is that why Alan Bradford rode Crowbar in the National then? Because they were friends?'

The old man tilted his head back to look at her curiously.

'Doug never told you they were friends, did he?' he said.

Frankie gave an ambiguous shrug and retrieved the brush from the straw. She started on combing out the clots of earth from Dory's mane.

'I know that they knew each other. There's no big secret or anything,' she said. 'I was just wondering why my dad didn't ride Crowbar in the National.'

'Why are you asking me these questions?' he said with a grey frown. His face took on the expression of someone who's realised they've said too much. 'I think you should ask your father if you've got questions. It's not my place,' he mumbled. He gestured at Dory with his hand. 'Mind you use a soft cloth on her ears now.'

Abandoning her grooming, desperation got the better of her.

'But why? All I want to know is why they fell out. If I could just understand then it would be okay. But right now, I don't know what Rhys and I are doing that's so wrong.'

'You and Rhys?'

Frankie grimaced. That one had slipped out like a fart in an elevator.

'Yeah, kinda.'

'Alan's son, Rhys? Oh, Lord. Talk to your father, Frankie. That's all I can say.'

'But –'

'Come along now. I'm sure you've got plenty of work to be getting on with without standing around chatting.'

Frankie sighed. She saw Jack walking briskly over to them from across the yard and her shoulders slumped. Theories and questions buzzed around her head like rush-hour traffic. So hers and Rhys's fathers had been best friends. Where had it all gone wrong? Did Crowbar have anything to do with the bust-up? Who was to blame? Why wouldn't Ron McCready tell her what had happened? Why did Doug Cooper still hate Alan Bradford's guts so vehemently thirty years on?

36

Fine flurries of snow were still silently falling when Frankie mounted the steps to her parents' front door that evening. The brass knocker, lit by the security lantern, burned her fingertips with cold. Vanessa answered the door, delight and surprise on her face.

'Frankie, darling. This is unexpected.' Her expression flickered in doubt. 'It's not Sunday yet, is it?'

Frankie grinned.

'No, Mum. Still Thursday.'

'That's a relief. Come on in. It's freezing out here.'

Grateful, Frankie stomped the snow from her boots on the mat and stepped into the warmth of the house.

'So, to what do we owe this treat?' her mother asked, closing the door behind her.

'Urgh, you know. Just wanted to see you guys,' Frankie shrugged.

'I've just boiled the kettle. Would you like a cuppa?'

'Yes, please.'

'Go on through. Doug!' Vanessa called ahead. 'Frankie's here!'

Frankie walked through into the lounge warily. It had been five weeks since Doug and Rhys had clashed swords at Chepstow Community Hospital. During the one brief visit she'd paid to her parents' house since then, Doug had been in bed with 'flu and hadn't been up to further argument. Three weeks on, however, he was sitting in his recliner, pulled close to the crackling fireplace, and looking as healthy as ever.

'Hello, Dad,' she ventured.

'Hello, Frankie.'

She hesitated, but when Doug gave her an appeasing smile, her confidence returned and she delivered her usual greeting kiss to his cheek.

'Your nose feels like an icicle,' he said.

'It's snowing outside.'

'So I believe. Are you staying for dinner?'

'I don't think so, thanks.' Frankie sat down on the hearth rug to welcome the delicious heat of the fire. She was still unsure how to go about confronting her father about his dealings with the Bradfords. She'd played over all the different ways she could broach the subject on the drive over, but they'd all sounded prying or interrogatory. She supposed that was because whichever way she looked at it, she *was* prying.

Vanessa returned from the kitchen with a tray and set it down on a side table, slopping the contents of the three mugs onto the cloth.

'Did I hear you're staying for dinner?' she said.

Frankie shook her head.

'Thanks, but I won't. I promised Tom I'd cook tonight.' Well, that was only half a lie. She'd been promising Tom that she'd make a meal for the past fortnight, but she'd either arrived home from racing too late or she'd been at Rhys's. Yesterday, Tom had looked less than thrilled by her absence so tonight was as good as any to get back into his good books.

'Ah, Tom,' Vanessa sighed. 'I hope you thanked him for his Christmas present. So sweet of him to think of us. How is he?'

Now there was a million-dollar question. Moody? Irritable? Depressed?

'He's been a bit down lately,' she replied.

Vanessa shook her head.

'Winter does that to some people. Short days, long nights, the cold, post-Christmas. Mind you, I don't remember him having Seasonal Affective Disorder before. Is everything okay with him?'

Tom hadn't given her license to tell anyone about his search for his birth parents so Frankie skirted the issue.

'He's just got a lot on his plate at the minute. Plus, I haven't been around much for him to talk to.'

'Aspen Valley keeping you busy?' Doug said.

Frankie swayed. It wasn't Aspen Valley so much as an Aspen Valley member of staff who was keeping her busy.

'You could say that,' she said.

Doug and Vanessa both cottoned on in the same instant. Doug's mouth disappeared in a grim line while Vanessa's formed a teasing 'ooh'. Then she gasped.

'Do you think that Tom's – I don't know, do you think he might be a little bit in love with you?'

Frankie screwed up her face.

'What? No way! Why would you think that? Tom and I are just friends, you know that.'

Vanessa gave her a knowing look.

'Yes, but darling, does *he* know that?'

Frankie looked at her parents in disbelief. Even Doug looked quite taken with the idea.

'Of course he does. We've been friends for how many years? Believe me, if Tom was in love with me, he's had plenty of time to make it known.'

'Men's minds work differently to women's, Frankie,' Doug said. 'You might think you're "just good friends", but you ask any guy honestly and he'll tell you that isn't possible.'

'How long has he been depressed?'

Frankie shrugged.

'A couple of months I guess. Ever since winter really set in.' She wasn't going to betray Tom's confidence now even when her parents' theory saw him as a love-sick pup.

'Ever since *you-know-what?*' Vanessa probed.

Frankie took an irritable sip of her tea.

'I guess so, but that's just coincidence.'

'You sure about that? Think about it, Frankie,' Vanessa said, giving her a sidelong look. 'Has Tom ever had girlfriends round?'

'No, but he's never hidden past girlfriends from me. He might just be going through a quiet patch at the minute.'

'How did he react when you told him *you-know-what?*'

'Mum, do we have to keep referring to Rhys as *you-know-what?* You make him sound like Lord Voldemort. Tom was fine. He didn't believe me at first, but he's really not fazed. Like I said, he's got other things on his mind right now.'

'I bet he wasn't exactly ecstatic about it though, was he?' Doug persisted. 'Tom's a good lad. He's got pride. If he's keeping it a secret then of course he's going to act blasé about the whole thing.'

Frankie paused to think. She had to admit Tom had never shown much enthusiasm for her and Rhys's relationship, but surely that was because he was too wrapped up in his genealogy search?

'And he's always been there for you, hasn't he?' Vanessa continued. 'Now, you show me one person – of the opposite sex – who would give that kind of support and not be after anything in return.'

Frankie frowned. Tom *was* a very loyal friend. He put up with Frankie's moods, always listened to her moaning, always seemed pleased if she suggested they go to the Golden Miller for a drink together... Her eyes widened.

'Do you really think so?' she said dubiously.

Vanessa gave an exaggerated nod.

'I don't think so. I *know* so.'

Frankie blew on her tea, trying to grasp this new bombshell in her life. She'd come here to ask her father about Alan Bradford, but had instead been persuaded that the person she thought of as her best friend might actually be in love with her. Just thinking those words though made her doubt herself. No, not Tom. Surely not. But what if they were right?

'I don't know,' she compromised. 'I'll watch him from now on, just to see how he reacts then – I don't know. I guess I'll have to talk to him about it. I mean, I love Tom, but I love him like a brother.'

Vanessa bit her lip and nodded sadly.

'I know you do, darling.'

Frankie realised just what she'd said. She shot a quick look at her father. Doug was looking into the fire, his mouth twisted in bitterness. She wished Tom could be as much like a son to him as he was a brother to her, but they had never shared that closeness.

Ironic, Frankie thought. There was Tom breaking his heart trying to trace his mother and father, while Doug sat, still mourning Seth. All of a sudden, bringing up the subject of Alan Bradford didn't seem so important. But a change in topic was definitely a good idea.

'Jack said he's going to enter Peace Offering in the Kim Muir Chase at the Festival next month,' she said brightly. 'Isn't that great?'

Doug's gaze left the fire to settle on the mantelpiece above. His eyes came to rest on the photograph of Seth winning on his one and only Cheltenham Festival ride. He was grinning from ear to ear and in his hands he held aloft the Cross Country Chase trophy.

Frankie sighed. For a brief moment, she found resentment rising up inside her as she looked at Seth's mud-splattered face.

Doug's focus flickered back to her.

'That's very good, lovie,' he said in a vain attempt to sound enthusiastic.

Frankie wanted to shake him. She wanted to shout at him: *Don't you see that I'm doing all of this for you?* but she knew she never could. He was hurting enough already.

'Yeah, isn't it?' she mumbled instead.

'That sounds very exciting, dear,' Vanessa said. Her painted smile pleaded with them both not to tumble into an argument. 'I don't think I know that race. Is it one of the big ones?'

Still the resentment simmered.

'*All* of the Festival races are big ones. That's why getting a Festival ride is such a big deal,' she said sourly. Vanessa's face fell at her bitterness and Frankie at once regretted her tone. She attempted a humble smile to compensate. 'It's one of the main amateur races of the week.'

'We'll have to come along and cheer you on then.'

Frankie downed the last of her tea and got to her feet.

'Thanks, Mum.' She gave her mother a hug then turned to Doug. 'Well, I'd better go.'

Doug nodded.

'See you soon, honey,' he said.

Frankie noticed that the words were barely out of his mouth before his gaze was drawn back to the picture of Seth. She wondered if he was reliving the day he'd died or the day he'd won the Cross Country Chase. The wistfulness in his expression made it difficult to tell. All Frankie knew was that it wasn't a wistfulness for her to win.

'Will we see you this weekend?' Vanessa asked. 'We could take you out for a birthday dinner.'

Doug snapped back into the present and Frankie couldn't help a wry smile from tugging at her lips. Her father had never been good with dates; the only one he never needed reminding about was the anniversary of Seth's death. It was with some degree of malicious pleasure that Frankie said,

'No. I'm racing at Ascot then *Rhys* and I are going to a Valentine's fireworks display.' There. That would serve him right for always putting Seth first. Doug frowned, but he didn't say anything. 'See ya,' she said and walked out the room.

37

Frankie didn't feel at all like cooking dinner and all the while trying to analyse Tom's feelings for her. But a promise was a promise and actually, the more she thought about it, the more she fancied eating bangers and mash.

Tom came down from his bedroom when he heard her arrive home.

'Hey. Good day? I see it's snowing,' he said, joining her in the kitchen with Atticus at his heels.

Frankie tensed as she peered into the fridge in search of sausages. Atticus slinked over to offer his opinion. Did other people's housemates come join them as soon as they got home? Tom appeared quite cheerful for a change too. Was that because she was home? Frankie stared hard at a tub of margarine as she tried to decide if this was natural behaviour.

'Yeah, not bad,' she said.

'Will you help me build a snowman in the park if it keeps up?'

Was that a coercive way of asking her out on a date? Frankie frowned again. Was that really how much salt was in margarine? Atticus sniffed dismissively at the lower vegetable shelf and shuddered.

'Sure. Why not.'

'You okay?' Tom said.

She looked across at him and gave him a bright smile.

'Yes, of course. Why would you think otherwise?'

'Well, you haven't bothered to take your head out of the fridge since I've walked in. What are you looking for?'

'Sausages. I'm looking for sausages.'

Tom walked over with exaggerated caution and picked up the plastic tray of sausages on clear display and handed it to her.

Frankie laughed, an octave too high.

'Think I need my eyes tested.'

'That would be a good one to start with. Are you cooking dinner for us?'

Frankie gave him an uncertain look. If she said yes, would it look like she was leading him on?

'Yeah. I figured I owe you. I mean, that's what buddies do, right? They do things for each other.'

Tom frowned at her.

'You sure you're all right?'

Frankie closed the fridge door with a forced jovial laugh.

''Course.' She directed a playful punch at his upper arm. '*Buddy*.'

'Ow,' Tom said, shying away from her and rubbing his arm. He looked at her with a wounded expression. 'What the hell's got into you?'

Frankie set the sausages down on the counter and rubbed her face wearily. Okay, she had to get a grip. She was freaking Tom out now.

'I've just got loads on my mind. It's been one of those days. You okay with bangers and mash?'

Tom still looked guarded.

'I think so. You want to talk about it?'

'What? The bangers and mash? Well, I think I'll use three big potatoes and are you happy with just two sausages?'

'No, doofus. Do you want to talk about your day?'

Oh, heck. Tom was offering her a sympathetic ear. Maybe her parents were right. Why would a guy do that if he wasn't after something more?

She picked out the three peeler-friendliest potatoes from the rack and headed for the sink.

'You don't want to hear about it.'

'Sure, I do. Come on, tell Uncle Tom.'

With her back to him, Frankie felt more at ease and there was something bizarrely therapeutic in spud-peeling.

'Tom, how do you feel about me dating Rhys?'

The short silence that followed prompted her to turn around. Tom was leaning against the kitchen table, his arms crossed and a puzzled look on his face.

'Have you and him had a fight?'

'No, no.' Frankie gave a vague wave of her hand and a slither of potato peel fell to the floor. Atticus pounced on it then turned away in distaste. He glared at Frankie. 'It was just something my parents said when I went to see them this evening.'

'Ah. They're still not happy with you dating him, eh?' He shrugged. 'I don't know. I mean I want you to be happy and everything, but –'

Frankie held her breath.

'But what?'

'Well, I don't want to see you get hurt either.'

'Why do you think I'll get hurt?' she said, a trace of defensiveness creeping into her tone. Okay, maybe if she was looking for support for her relationship, a potential admirer like Tom was perhaps the wrong person to seek it from.

'Come on, Frankie. You know Rhys, he hasn't exactly got a reputation for being a loving long-term partner, has he?'

'We've been together seven weeks.'

'I hate to break it to you, Frankie, but that's only considered long-term when you're fourteen. You'll be twenty-four on Saturday.'

Oh God, he remembered her birthday. Even her father couldn't remember her birthday.

'Okay. Well, let's just pretend then that I'm in a long-term relationship with Rhys. Would you be okay with that?'

Tom pursed his mouth in thought.

'You want an honest answer, right?'

Frankie's heart picked up the pace. She nodded.

'Well, I've hardly seen you at all this past fortnight and, don't think I'm getting possessive or anything, but I have to say I've missed your company.'

Her cheeks burned and she spun back to the sink before he could see. She heard him scrape a kitchen chair back to sit on.

'Look, Frankie, I don't know what's going on in your head or what your parents said to you, but if you're happy then I'm happy.'

Didn't people say that when they were in love? Her parents were right! How could she have been so blind?

'Would you like two sausages with your meal? I thought I would try do that chilli gravy. Or maybe I should just stick with the normal mix? What do you think? Do we have any beef stock cubes?'

'What *did* your parents say?' Tom asked.

Could she tell him? She sighed. She didn't think she could face breaking Tom's heart and cook dinner at the same time.

'Nothing much.'

'Then why are you questioning how I feel about Rhys? Did they tell you to break up with him? I know you said they're not particularly fond of him – like I said, he hasn't got the best reputation so it makes some sense – but if that's what they said then it's not very fair on you.'

Frankie hesitated. She wanted Tom's opinion so bad, but would it be like rubbing salt into a wound to unload her burdens onto him? She picked up the last potato and carefully tried to peel it in one long strip. It was no good, she needed to tell someone.

'I don't think it's because of Rhys's reputation that Dad disapproves so much,' she said. 'Years ago, when he and Rhys's father were both jockeys, there was a horse called Crowbar –'

'Oh yes. I remember,' interrupted Tom. 'Well, I don't *remember* as such. But he won the National the year I was born and you always remember those ones, don't you?'

Frankie looked round at him.

'So you knew that Alan Bradford won it on him?'

'Did he? To be honest, no, I didn't know that. Maybe if he'd won a string of Nationals or was champion jockey or something it might have stuck in my mind, but I don't think he was any great shakes. Not like Rhys, anyway. I just remember the horse's name.'

'Oh. Well, Alan Bradford won the National on Crowbar, but it was *my* dad who had ridden Crowbar in all of his races prior to that. Dad refuses to talk about any of it, but then Dory's owner pitched up at work today to see her and he's Ron McCready, Crowbar's old trainer. So I asked him why. And *he* said that Dad and Alan Bradford had been great mates. Apparently, Dad had even been best man at his wedding! I mean, Dad never said anything about them being friends! Neither did Mum. When I asked her ages ago, she made out that they had been rivals who just rubbed each other up the wrong way. But there must have been more to it than that, mustn't there?'

'What did that Ron Mc-whatever say?'

'That's the weird thing. He wouldn't tell me. Said that I should ask Dad. What do you think the big deal is?'

Tom frowned.

'Dunno. Have you asked Rhys? He might know.'

Frankie shook her head.

'No. And to be honest, I'm not sure that he *would* know. He doesn't much like talking about his father.'

'Maybe you should do what that Ron guy said and ask your dad again. Like outright. It might shock him into telling you the truth.'

Frankie pursed her lips in contemplation.

'Maybe. I've just got to find the right time.'

'Frankie, you and your dad haven't been on proper speaking terms for weeks. Is there ever going to be a right time?'

'Good point, Watson.'

38

The downside to having one's birthday on Valentine's Day was that Frankie had spent her youth picking up the pastel-coloured envelopes that had fallen through the letterbox and opening each with a trembling hope that one might be from a secret admirer. Usually they would contain birthday wishes instead. Of the five that landed on the mat that Saturday morning she was unsurprised to find that none of them were Valentine's Day cards. She hadn't expected anything from Rhys, it wasn't his style. Besides, they were going to watch a fireworks display after racing tonight and he had promised her dinner at some swanky Ascot restaurant.

Frankie sat in the changing rooms, tying and retying the red ribbon on the cap of her helmet. She could hear the commentary for the Ascot Chase in which Rhys was riding Virtuoso coming from the television and from the PA system, but she wasn't listening. She couldn't remember feeling so nervous prior to a race before. Sure, every race got to her to a greater or lesser degree, but this one – when she knew she needed to stay calmer than she'd ever done before – this one was different. In this one, she would be riding Ta' Qali.

Rhys was riding another Aspen Valley novice, Asante, in the same race and they both knew that if the Ta' Qali that impressed so much at home turned up then his stablemate would have no hope. But the chances of a calm and collected Ta' Qali making an appearance were slim. She needed to relax. For everyone's sakes.

She was roused out of her worry pit by the commentator's cries and she winced as she heard last year's Cheltenham Gold Cup winner, Zodiac, called home a neck clear of Rhys and Virtuoso.

It wouldn't be long now before the weighing room would begin to fill up again, noisy with the adrenalin-high jockeys arguing, joking and taunting each other after their race. The valets would be busy making sure saddles had the correct weight cloths for their jockeys' next race. Then it would be crunch time. Frankie closed her eyes. She prayed her time wouldn't be too crunching.

The grounds surrounding Ascot's immaculate parade ring were packed. A glimmer of sunlight had replaced yesterday's snowfall and racing fans were taking full advantage of it. She and Rhys made the short walk from the jockeys' rooms in silence. As Frankie had suspected, Rhys hadn't looked particularly pleased about losing out so narrowly on Virtuoso, but like all the best sportsmen his moody composure had changed for the better as his next challenge arose.

Frankie scanned the outer reaches of the ring for her mount. There he was. Billy was leading him, digging his elbow into the black horse's shoulder to keep him steady. Ta' Qali wore the same fluffy white noseband as before, but in addition he also wore a lip-chain.

A flutter of hope rose inside her. The lip-chain made him look like he was snarling but the pressure on his gums was obviously releasing the intended endorphins that kept a horse calm. Not that Ta' Qali was exactly the quietest of the runners, but he wasn't going berserk. Yet.

Jack was waiting for them both in the centre of the ring.

'Frankie, your guess is as good as mine about how to ride Ta' Qali, probably better. Just get him to settle. That horse over there, Raphaelite, is bound to set a good gallop so that's one good thing. Ta' Qali has the *ability* to win this, but only if he settles.'

His face was grimmer than usual, Frankie noticed. This wasn't just another runner for him. Ta' Qali was *his* horse and his horse to sell. If he lived up to his potential on such a high profile race card, Ta' Qali could be sold within a week. But if he mirrored his last two runs, it was doubtful he would get any serious offers for the rest of the season.

The bell rang for the jockeys to mount and Jack addressed Rhys.

'Asante likes to come off the pace. Don't leave him out the back though, else he'll just fall asleep. Come on, Frankie. I'll leg you up. Good luck both of you.'

Through the tunnel and onto the course, Frankie's breath evaporated. Ascot's arcing grandstand stretched all the way to the far turn and the crowds that had come to watch the clash between two Cheltenham Gold Cup winners in the last race still packed the rails a hundred deep.

Frankie shivered as Ta' Qali upped his pace and an icy wind blew through her. With his lip-chain removed, it seemed her horse's more fractious nerves had returned. But with these crowds she couldn't blame him. Helensvale Market Day couldn't hold a candle to Ascot. Frankie sat lower on her haunches, gently sawing at the reins as they galloped down to the two mile start.

'How's he doing?' Rhys asked her once they were circling behind the tape.

Ta' Qali shook his head as if he had a fly in his ear and pawed at the lush carpet of grass.

'Not great,' she replied.

'I wish I could give you some advice, but if anyone knows how to ride him, you do.'

Frankie smiled grimly and nodded. Her reins were slick from Ta' Qali's sweating neck and she tried to dry her gloves on her breeches. She followed her rivals in a haphazard circle, trying to avoid the worst of the sixteen-runner traffic. The field turned sharply, catching her unawares and carried her forward as they rushed towards the tape.

Ta' Qali stretched out his neck, pulling her out of the saddle and bounded forward. The orange tape, ribbing in the breeze, was too close. The starter wasn't even on the steps of his platform. She hauled back on the reins, but the momentum of the field continued to push them forward.

'Get back! Get back!' the starter roared. 'Take a turn! You!' he said, pointing at Frankie. 'Take a turn! Go on, all of you! Get back!'

Ta' Qali fought angrily with Frankie. Another horse shot out of the pack and nearly clothes-lined its jockey on the tape. Frankie's heart sank. What little hope she held for Ta' Qali dwindled. Groans and mutters rumbled from the others as they all turned away. More delays, more time for her horse to psyche himself up. The runners retreated behind the start and the tape was painstakingly retied across the track.

'Okay, on you go!' the starter shouted.

Ta' Qali wheeled round on his hocks and set off like a cannonball. Frankie's hands slipped on the reins. Apart from two other horses on her outside, she was out in the clear. She hadn't had much of a game plan to start with, but heading affairs had definitely not been part of it. The first of the nine hurdles bounced into her line of sight. She gritted her teeth and tried not to close her eyes. Ta' Qali was running wild. She was scared. Ta' Qali was scared. He cat-jumped over the first, rapping the top of the hurdle with his knees and pecking on landing.

'Whoa, boy. Whoa,' she tremored. 'Come on, slow it down, Ta' Qali. Please.'

Ta' Qali jinked sideways and bumped a horse coming up his inside.

'Watch it, Frankie!' the rider shouted.

She turned to see Donnie glaring at her.

'Sorry! I –' She couldn't concentrate on a reply. Ta' Qali was too much for her. He threw his head, whipping her face with his mane. She didn't feel the sting, she just felt the fear.

The second hurdle was quickly upon them and Ta' Qali stood off a stride early. He stretched out his neck and forelegs to clear it, for a moment forgetting to fight his rider, but as soon as they were on the other side and galloping into the shade afforded by the grandstand, his mind was back on the struggle. The noise of the crowd rolled in waves around her, so loud that she hardly heard the snap.

She looked down. The reins were still tight in her fists; her stirrups were still straining against their leathers. Then she saw Ta' Qali's breastplate flap around his chest.

'Damn,' she muttered. The force of Ta' Qali's erratic gallop had torn the piece of tack clean from the saddle. She tried to calm herself. It wasn't serious. Horses didn't need breastplates, they were just there as a precautionary measure to keep the saddle from slipping.

They rounded the long sloping turn that would take them up to the highest point of the course. With Donnie half a length in front of her and two others ahead, they galloped in fourth. Over the third hurdle, Frankie caught a glimpse of just how good Ta' Qali could be. Her arms ached. Lactic acid burned through her thighs as she balanced her weight in opposition to her mount's tearaway speed.

The ground began to fall away as they raced towards the next hurdle. Ta' Qali was breathing harder than Frankie yet his legs carried him faster down the descent. Frankie leaned back. Her desperate tugs garnered no response. Ta' Qali took off unbalanced and flattened the hurdle. He stumbled in the thick turf on landing. Frankie's heart leapt into her throat. She looked down between her knees. Her saddle was inching up Ta' Qali's withers with every stride he took. Panic tightened her chest but lent her strength. She pulled back on the reins. But every time she did so, she was forced to push down in her stirrups. The saddle crept higher. Frankie felt her balance begin to teeter.

'Stop, Ta' Qali!' she cried. 'Please! Whoa, boy!'

She looked up and felt her body go furnace hot with dread. Up ahead was their next obstacle – another hurdle going downhill followed by a sharp turn. She snatched at the reins, hoping the saddle wouldn't slip any further if she stopped the constant hauling.

Ta' Qali shook his head and snatched back, tearing the reins through her fingers. Frankie gasped and clutched thick handfuls of his mane to stop herself toppling over his shoulder.

She scrabbled with her reins and tried to calculate whether she had enough time to pull Ta' Qali wide and miss out the looming jump. She pulled on her left rein, careful to keep her weight balanced in both stirrups.

'Hey!' an angry voice shouted.

Frankie darted a look sideways.

Shit. She hadn't checked to see if she had a clear path. She looked round further. The chasing field of fifteen were right behind her. Blood pounded in her ears. The hurdle stretched out across the course. Frankie bit her lip and gripped Ta' Qali's black mane with her fingers. He took off. Another loud snap. One of the girth straps gave way. They landed and the saddle climbed higher.

Jolted forward, she flung her arms round Ta' Qali's neck then pushed herself back upright. Panic overcame her. She didn't know what to do. She couldn't throw herself off. Not only were they going at a breakneck pace, but she also had the cavalry on her heels. But she couldn't keep her balance for much longer. Ta' Qali's neck was a lot narrower than his back. She tried to push against him, but her centre of gravity was too far forward. Ahead was the bend. Her chest tightened. She would never stay on going round that. The heavy drum of hoofbeats and the harsh breathing of another horse loomed on her outside.

'Frankie!' Rhys's bellowing voice reached her like a life-ring to stranded swimmer.

She turned her head. Asante was drawing level, his head stretched low, his nostrils wide as he galloped flat out.

'Rhys!' she cried. 'My saddle's slipping! I'm going to fall!'

'Hang on!'

Ahead the white running rail began to curve inward. Rhys reached out and grasped her upper arm. His fingers dug into her straining muscles, but it was the most comforting pain she'd ever experienced. With it came stability. Asante bumped shoulders with Ta' Qali and Frankie teetered.

She looked across at Rhys. She knew her face was stricken with fear. She didn't care. Rhys wore a look of thunderous determination.

'Just hold on! Okay?' he shouted.

She nodded dumbly. With Rhys's arm steadying her, they skirted the turn.

'I'm slipping!' she yelled, feeling her centre of gravity shift right.

'Push down with your left foot!'

'I can't!'

'Yes, you can! Push down!' He pulled on her arm as he shouted.

Frankie tore her lip with her teeth as her balance wavered.

'Hold on to me, okay? I'm going to let go –'

'No! Don't!' she cried.

'I have to. I'm going to stop Ta' Qali. Just hold on.'

Frankie let go of her horse's mane and flung out her arm to grasp Rhys's shoulder. He leaned forward and snagged her reins. She felt the pressure of her straining hold on Ta' Qali's mouth lessen as he took up the fight. Ta' Qali shook his head. The saddle slipped further. Frankie cried out and grabbed a handful of Rhys's blue silks. The rumble of the approaching field grew louder as Ta' Qali's pace slackened. In seconds they were surrounded, Asante grunting as he took the bumps of the advance. Then the field raced on. Ta' Qali slowed to a ragged trot beside his stablemate, jarring Frankie, when the final girth strap snapped.

Her landing was relatively soft considering other falls she'd experienced. Ta' Qali's toe glanced off her shoulder but her body protector took the brunt of the force. She lay for a moment in the moist grass, looking up at the patchy sky. She was alive. She rolled onto her knees. Up ahead, Rhys was pulling up both horses. He spun Asante round and hurried back to her. Ta' Qali threw his head at Rhys's rough treatment.

'Stop it, you stupid fucker!' he growled.

Ta' Qali rolled his eyes. Rhys jumped off and rushed to Frankie's side.

'Are you okay?'

She climbed to one knee. It was trembling so much she nearly fell over again. She looked up at Rhys's desperate expression and felt like crying. Instead she reached out and let him hold her, safe, solid, secure.

39

Frankie rolled over in Rhys's bed and sleepily reached out for him. When all she felt was cold empty bedding, she opened her eyes. The room was dark and lonely apart from the ticking clock on his bedside table.

'Rhys?' she said blearily.

She craned her neck, but no, he hadn't fallen out of bed either. She winced; her shoulder was stiff and achy from Ta' Qali's ill-judged kick. Settling back into a more comfortable position, she smiled to herself as she relived their evening together. Dinner had been smooth and pleasant. Unlike so many of her previous dates, Rhys hadn't criticised her choice in menu by saying, 'Come on, you have to put some meat on those bones!' She'd used to hate that. Didn't they realise that given the choice she would much rather have chosen the roast dinner with Yorkshire puddings or battered haddock smothered in tartare sauce? But Rhys knew that dieting was part and parcel of a jockey's life. He even went so far as to seek advice from a nutritionist so that he could stay as healthy as he could on the miniscule portions he ate.

Dinner had been followed by half an hour of Sparks in the Park back in Helensvale. It had been cold and the ground was still frozen with snow, but the white carpet they'd stood on had added to the atmosphere. The green and red Catherine Wheels had lit up the ground as well as the sky. Frankie had been mesmerised. Rhys had seemed less enraptured with the display and on a couple of occasions she'd caught him watching her. The glow of glittering chrysanthemums had danced across his cheekbones and jaw, and Frankie hadn't known which was more beautiful to watch. It had been the perfect way to erase her hair-raising ride at Ascot that afternoon.

Frankie shivered as she left the warmth of the bed and left the bedroom. The flat was quiet and her socked feet padded noiselessly across the floorboards. In the lounge she found Rhys sitting with his back to her, hunched forward with his elbows on his knees, watching the television on mute. In the darkness the reflection of the screen flashed across the walls. She watched him. He was replaying a race recording. He let it play for a few seconds then paused it, rewound and slow-mo-ed each jump.

'Hey,' she said gently when she felt no longer comfortable spying on him.

Rhys leapt in the air and dropped the remote control.

'Sorry,' she said, shuffling in and sitting beside him on the sofa. 'Whatya watching?'

Rhys let the recording play on and sat back.

'Virtuoso's Ascot Chase. I couldn't sleep.'

'You never sleep.'

Rhys shrugged, not denying his insomnia. He offered Frankie some of the blanket he had slung over his knees and she gratefully pulled it over her. The silvery light cast by the television made him look even more hallowed and his eyes looked bruised with fatigue.

'Why do you torture yourself by watching it over?' she said.

Rhys looked surprised.

'I'm not torturing myself. I just wanted to see where I could've saved ground or ridden a better jump. Improve for next time. It's part of the job.'

Frankie looked at him uncertainly. Dare she admit that she hardly ever watched her races over? She hated watching herself. She always seemed to grimace over each fence. She didn't mind watching the races that she had won, but Rhys appeared to do the exact opposite. He watched the races that he'd lost and no doubt beat himself up about it.

'Second place isn't so bad though,' she said. 'Especially in a Grade One.'

Rhys looked confused.

'That's when it's the *worst*. No one remembers who comes second.'

'I wouldn't say that,' she said doubtfully.

'Who came second to Faustian in last year's Grand National?'

Frankie paused to think.

'I don't remember.'

'Exactly. Who came second in the jockey's championships?'

She shook her head in defeat. Rhys slapped his thigh.

'There you go. You see? There're no prizes for runner-up even if like today it was only by a neck. The history books aren't going to say: first, Zodiac, but only be a neck to Virtuoso. It's just going to say: first, Zodiac. Fine, so he won the Cheltenham Gold Cup last year, but Virtuoso's a much better horse.' He lay his head back against the sofa and sighed. 'Yet I can't find anything that I could've done differently.' He gestured to the screen, unaware that the race had already finished. 'The more I watch it, the more I realise he wasn't travelling well. He just wasn't himself today. I'm going to tell Jack to get some blood tests done tomorrow just to see if he's picked up something we haven't spotted.'

Frankie stayed silent. She knew Rhys was a determined man. She knew he liked to win, that he *thrived* on winning whereas she was just glad to finish a race alive and if she won, it was a bonus. She had never done this sort of research, watching and rewatching races.

Her gaze flickered back to the screen. What better time to start than now? In shot was Ta' Qali being led around the parade ring prior to the novice hurdle race. Lather dripped from his saddle cloth like soap suds and he was sweating between his hind legs.

She'd wanted to win that race, there was no doubt about that yet she hadn't thought to watch his previous races to see if she could learn by Rhys's mistakes. She'd just presumed that once she was astride she would know what to do. No wonder she was halfway down the leaderboard in the amateur jockeys' rankings. It wouldn't be so bad if she was only getting the odd average ride, but she was riding for the best stable in the country.

'No wonder Dad never pays my job any attention,' she muttered.

'What?'

Frankie looked at him in surprise.

'Did I say that out loud? Sorry, I was just thinking.'

'No, go on. You've listened to me ranting. What's on your mind?'

Frankie shrugged and fiddled with the corner of the scratchy blanket. She didn't want to appear disloyal to her father and she didn't want to sound like a whinger. But then, as she relived the other night at her parents' house, the frustration began to accumulate and she couldn't keep it in any longer.

'It's just that Dad never seems to notice me these days. I thought that would change when I got the job at Aspen Valley, but if anything, it's just got worse. The other day, I told him that I was riding Peace Offering in the Kim Muir at the Festival and all he did was gaze at the photos of Seth winning at Cheltenham. Then only when he realised how rude he was being did he say "oh, that's very good".' A long forgotten memory weaved itself into her mind – her father joyous, ecstatic, slapping Seth on his back with pride and ushering Vanessa to get the camera out. She sighed. 'And really, who can blame him? Look at Seth – he won the amateurs' championship in his first year and that was *before* he even started riding for Jack.'

It was Rhys's turn to sigh, but his was impatient.

'Jesus, Frankie. Seth wasn't perfect.'

'What do you mean?'

Rhys pulled himself closer on the sofa to where Frankie was sat cross-legged. She held the blanket up against her chest protectively, suddenly scared by the seriousness of his expression. He placed his hand on her knee.

'I mean you talk about Seth like he could do no wrong, but look what's really going on. Everyone's made him into this beaming ray of sunshine and left you completely in the shadows.'

'Seth *was* a ray of sunshine,' she replied, her voice shaking. 'He never made me feel like I was in the shadows. I wasn't. He made sure I was always happy. Seth was wonderful. He was brilliant.'

Rhys's hand tightened over her knee. He shook his head. He looked at Frankie with a pained expression.

'No, he wasn't. I'm sorry. I'm not trying to upset you.'

Frankie hitched her knee out of Rhys's grasp.

'Then why are you saying this?' she said, accusingly.

'You remember Gracie? Seth's girlfriend?'

She nodded hesitantly. She felt like she was speeding down a twisty road in the dark without headlights. Where was he going with this?

'Did you know that he was cheating on Gracie?'

Frankie stared at him then scrambled to her feet. The iciness of the room only accounted for part of the chill which spread through her body.

'What? No – stop saying that. It's lies.'

'No, it's not. It's the truth. Seth was sleeping with June – you know, June from the yard – right up until the day he died.'

She looked down at him, wide-eyed, searching for some glimpse of dishonesty. But his face was solemn.

'Why are you telling me this?' she whispered.

'Because you and your folks have created this golden Adonis boy who never made any mistakes. I bet your parents haven't said a bad thing about Seth since he died. I doubt whether they can even remember a moment when he wasn't excelling. But that wasn't him. He did occasionally fuck up.'

Frankie's eyes welled and she shook her head. She tried to fight off this dark shadow from dimming her mental image of Seth. He looked so beautiful, any hint of darkness lessened her pleasure at remembering him. With a cry, she turned and ran back to the bedroom. She didn't want to know any more.

'Frankie! Wait!'

She heard his uneven footsteps following her and she looked around the darkened room, crazily trying to find a place to hide.

'Go away!' she said when he appeared in the doorway. She threw a pillow at him and he ducked. Frankie threw herself onto the bed and covered her head with another pillow, blocking her ears.

'I'm not trying to upset you –'

'Then why are telling me these things?' she said through a mouthful of cotton and goose feathers.

'He was human,' he went on. 'Like you, and like me.'

She felt the bed sag as he sat down beside her. She raised herself to a sitting position, but still clutched the pillow to her chest.

'Seth was *good*,' she whispered.

'He was good. But he wasn't perfect. I look at you and I see you trying your damnedest to live up to him, to make your parents as proud of you as they were of him. But you and your parents have made him into some sort of god, and you're never going to equal a god.'

Frankie crumbled. She felt the sheets crunch as Rhys moved closer. His arms folded around her, strong and comforting, just as he had done earlier that day.

'Listen, Frankie, Seth was great. Everyone loved him and maybe that's where he went wrong. June loved him too, yet because she was the Other Woman, nobody knew to ask her how she was doing after he died.'

'Poor June,' she murmured. Rhys handed her a Kleenex and she mopped her eyes. Suddenly, all the wooden conversations she'd had with the stable lass made sense. June didn't really want to be close to her, she just wanted to feel close to Seth.

'She was there when he died too,' Rhys continued. 'And I never knew how scared she must have been – not until today.'

Frankie gave him a questioning look.

'I love you,' he whispered. 'I mean I care for you a lot. I just don't want to see you hurt yourself.'

Frankie stopped mid-nose-blow.

'What did you say?'

Rhys's body tensed against hers.

'I said I don't want to see you hurt yourself,' he said guardedly.

She pulled away so she could see him properly.

'No, before that.'

Rhys swallowed.

'I care for you?' he said dubiously.

Her heart pounded in her chest.

'Before that. Did you say you love me?'

'Maybe. Actually, yes,' he said, nodding with more conviction. 'Do you think you could not hate me after everything I've said?'

'You weren't lying? Even if it was to make me feel better in some weird sadistic way?'

He shook his head sadly. Frankie's heart palpitated. *He loved her.* He, being Rhys Bradford and her, being Frankie Cooper. He leaned forward to kiss her, his breath tickling her lip. She let him draw her towards him against the pillow. With a calloused but tender hand he stroked her hair behind her ear.

'When I saw what was happening with you on Ta' Qali, it scared me to death. I could see what would happen if you fell. It made me realise what you mean to me.'

Lying beside him, Frankie felt the enormity of that chaotic race.

'You saved me,' she said with a faint smile. 'Like a guardian angel.'

Rhys's shoulder rose and fell beneath her cheek as he sighed.

'I'm no angel, Frankie.'

They lapsed into silence, her thoughts twisting and turning, trying to get a grasp on everything that had happened today. As she got used to the idea that her idol had stumbled – he hadn't quite fallen – she began to question her own aspirations. She questioned her father's expectations. Rhys loved her. She mightn't be certain enough to echo his words, but she could do the next best thing.

40

'You sure?'

It felt like a sack of horse nuts had been lifted off Frankie's shoulders.

'Yes, I'm sure, Pippa.'

Sat in her and Jack's spacious lounge, Pippa continued to stare at her in surprise. Her hand remained lodged in a Pringles tube.

'But why? I – I don't understand. Isn't this the sort of opportunity that all jockeys dream of?'

Frankie half-nodded, half-shook her head.

'I'm sorry to have messed you around,' she said with genuine regret. 'You gave me an incredible opportunity. I really am grateful to you, but I realise now that I don't deserve it.'

Pippa let out a shocked laugh.

'Frankie, you don't have to worry about that. Let me decide if you deserve the National ride on Peace Offering or not.'

'I *don't* deserve it though. This is for the best. Honestly, it is. Rhys deserves it more. He works harder than me, he's a much better rider than I am. He really has earned the right to ride Peace Offering in the Grand National.'

Pippa looked at her with suspicion.

'Did he ask you to give up the ride?'

'No! Oh, no. He doesn't even know I'm here talking to you.' She allowed herself a small smile. 'I wanted to surprise him.'

Pippa slumped in her armchair and blew a curly lock of hair off her forehead.

'Wow. Rhys doesn't know how lucky he is to have you.'

'I'm lucky to have him. Look how he saved me yesterday. Will you let him ride?'

'I guess I'll have to. I don't mean that horribly. I offered you the ride because I thought you deserved it, not so I could spite Rhys. Now that you don't want it, I can hardly go out of my way to put a different jockey up.'

'Rhys is a good guy,' Frankie said. 'And he really is the best rider around.'

Pippa looked mildly discomforted.

'I don't want to say anything because I know he's your boyfriend. But okay, he is growing on me. I can't really claim to know him all that well.'

'Not many people do,' she replied. Hell, wasn't she still finding out little things about him every day?

'We're going to have to tell Jack,' said Pippa.

Frankie grimaced. She'd especially picked a time when Jack and Rhys were on their way to Market Rasen Racecourse – far far away – to tell Pippa.

'Do you think he'll be mad? I feel like a bride who's cancelling her wedding a week before the ceremony.'

'He might not be particularly happy to begin with,' Pippa said, crunching into another crisp. 'But then again, he wanted Rhys to ride Peace Offering from the get go so it shouldn't take him too long to get used to the idea.'

'I'm really sorry to have messed you – and Jack – around like this. But I know it's the right decision.'

Pippa looked sympathetic.

'You sure? There's still time to change your mind.'

Frankie clasped her hands and took a deep breath. After this, there would be no going back.

'I'm sure.'

'Your call. Pringle?' Pippa held out the tube and Frankie hesitated. She could sneak one, surely? She hesitated again.

'Uh – there aren't any left,' she said.

Pippa looked dubiously into the empty tube then shrugged her shoulders happily.

'Ah, well. We've both got excuses then.'

With no rides that afternoon, Frankie pulled up outside her parents' house in time for lunch. Glorious wafts of her favourite roast chicken teased her nostrils when she opened the front door. Doug and Vanessa were in the lounge chatting with the television turned on low.

Vanessa was first to notice her arrival and her face brightened.

'Happy birthday, darling!' she said, getting up and holding her arms out to Frankie. 'Oh, my baby girl is growing up so fast!'

'Thanks, Mum. Don't remind me.' She returned Vanessa celebratory kiss and hug.

'Don't remind you? How do you think it makes *me* feel? I can't believe it was twenty-four years ago that I popped you out.'

'Happy birthday, lovie,' Doug said, climbing to his feet. He too wore a smile on his face and hugging her, he rocked her from side to side. Frankie breathed in the comforting smell of his woollen sweater. It felt so reassuring to be in his good books for a change. Not that it would last long, of course. Not after the news she would inevitably have to break.

'I made roast chicken especially,' Vanessa said. 'With parsnips and butternut.'

Frankie's mouth watered at the mention of all her favourite foods. It was moments like these that she resented her job. Injuries she could handle, but the tempting smell of succulent roasting meat and vegetables was torturous.

'Ooh, lovely, Mum. Dad'll have to dish mine otherwise I'll load my plate with far too much.'

'Rubbish. There're hardly any calories in white meat and parsnips are vegetables.'

Doug shook his head.

'I'll dish out for you, Frankie, don't worry.'

Considering they were in one another's company for the next hour and a half, Frankie thought she and her father were both doing well to steer conversations clear of Rhys (Doug's doing) and Peace Offering (Frankie's doing). Vanessa had helped, relaying the latest gossip passed on by Valerie "The Voice" Banks during her hair appointment the previous afternoon.

With lunch put away and her birthday presents revealed – a book voucher and matching necklace and bracelet – Frankie felt she couldn't postpone it any longer. It was a shame to potentially ruin the mood, but she felt her parents needed to hear it from her rather than via the *Racing Post*.

She helped her mother clear the table of empty plates while Doug opened a fresh bottle of white wine. Once they were all relaxing in the lounge, allowing their food to digest, Frankie didn't feel quite so sure of herself.

'There's something I've got to tell you,' she began.

The blood drained from Vanessa's face. Her mother broke eye contact to look at Frankie's stomach.

'You're not –'

'No! No! Nothing like that.'

She swallowed hard and turned her gaze to Doug. He was sitting very still, unblinking. Guarded. Frankie bit her lip. He was going to be so disappointed, she could feel it already. She looked down at her lap, unable to meet his eyes.

'I went and spoke to Pippa Taylor earlier. I'm giving up the ride on Peace Offering.'

Silence greeted her. Surprisingly, Doug almost looked relieved. Maybe he was expecting Frankie to announce her and Rhys's engagement or something.

'You're not riding Peace Offering in the Grand National?' Vanessa said.

Frankie shook her head.

'No.'

'Why not? Who are you going to ride then?'

'Nobody. I'm not going to ride in the Grand National.'

Doug looked at her curiously.

'Why've you changed your mind?'

Frankie paused before answering. Tact wasn't high on her list of social skills so she took her time to choose her words.

'I thought Peace Offering would have a better chance of winning with Rhys aboard.'

'Rhys is riding him now?' Doug's tone changed in an instant.

Oh, crikey, Frankie despaired. Why was she even born with vocal cords?

'It's best for everyone. I don't think I would've been up to it, Rhys is a much better rider and –'

'Is this what he's told you?' Doug's voice rose with his temper. 'Did he tell you he was better than you?'

'No, Dad. This was my decision –'

'Like hell!' he snapped. 'I don't believe that for one minute. Rhys is a Bradford. I knew right from the start that he was up to something. I knew it! I just knew it!'

A ball of tears swelled painfully in Frankie's throat.

'No, Dad! You're wrong! Rhys had nothing to do with me changing my mind. It was my choice!'

'He's a scumbag, just like all the other Bradfords!'

Frankie jumped to her feet and glared at her father through glistening eyes. Her hands trembled in rigid fists by her sides.

'He's not! You don't know him. Why do you find it so hard to believe that Rhys is a decent person?' she cried. 'Is that how much you think of me? You think that's the only way I can get a guy as successful as Rhys to be interested in me?'

Doug stood up as well and pointed a finger at her.

'He's using you, Frankie!'

'No, he's not! He's not, he's not, he's not! He loves me. You're not there! You don't see it! You don't know him!'

'I know his type,' Doug spat.

Frankie's breath shuddered out of her. Even the tips of her ears burned with fury.

'His type?' she echoed. 'His type being the Bradford type? What is it about the Bradfords which gets you so mad?'

Doug's eyes flashed from her to a stupefied Vanessa sitting on the sofa.

'That's beside the point –'

'Bullshit, Dad!' Frankie shouted. Her parents looked at her in horror. Had she ever sworn at her father before? She very much doubted it, but right now she didn't care. 'It is exactly the point. What is the big secret? Why won't you tell me what you've got against the Bradfords? I know you've got history. I met Ron McCready the other day.'

'Ron McCready?' Doug was jerked out of his rage into surprise.

'Yeah. Remember him? Because he certainly remembers you. He also remembers Alan Bradford and how you were best man at his wedding.'

'We are not going to talk about this, Francesca!'

'Yes, we are! Because unless we get this sorted out, I am never going to understand why you are so against Rhys. Rhys has done absolutely nothing to you.'

'Yes, he has,' Doug said, shaking his head. 'He's conned my daughter out of her Grand National ride. Why am I not surprised?' He gave a mirthless laugh. 'Those Bradfords are all the same. I should've known right off when you said you two were involved that he was up to something.'

'Then tell me why you should've known!'

'Doug, darling,' Vanessa spoke up for the first time. 'Let's just tell Frankie. This is hardly fair on her.'

'No, no, no!' Doug boomed. 'I refuse to talk about that – that – *rat*, Alan Bradford. Ever!'

Frankie crossed her arms over her chest.

'I'm not going anywhere until you do.'

'Well, you're in for a long wait, sweetheart. Why can't you just take my word for it that Alan Bradford is a scumbag and be done with it?'

'It's not your opinion of Alan Bradford that gets to me, Dad. It's the way you treat Rhys.'

Doug clutched his head and growled in frustration.

'I don't want to talk about either of them!'

Vanessa stood up and placed her hand on his shoulder.

'Then let me tell Frankie.'

Doug shrugged her off like her hand was a tarantula and stomped past them both out of the lounge.

'Where are you going?' Vanessa called after him.

'Out,' he yelled back. 'You tell Frankie whatever the hell you want. I'm not going to sit there and relive it all.' The front door slammed in finality, making the windows tremble.

Frankie felt tears rise in her with a gusto she hadn't felt since she was about ten. She turned to her mother and stamped her foot.

'Why is he being like this?' she cried. 'Why does he hate Rhys so much? He wants me to take his word for it that Rhys's dad is a scumbag. Then why can't he take my word for it that Rhys isn't like that!'

Vanessa heaved a sigh and sent Frankie a sympathetic look.

'I'm sorry, darling. You're right, he is overreacting a bit, but try not to be too hard on him. He's had a tough day – he's been putting on a brave face for you all afternoon.'

'*He's* having a bad day?'

'Yes. That racehorse that he's so fond of – Caspian, is it? The one that won that French race. It was on the news this morning that he injured himself in training. Had to be retired.'

On any other day, Frankie would have received this news with a healthy dose of remorse, but now her blood was up and Caspian was the least of her concerns.

'And that's his excuse for insulting Rhys? For walking out after telling me that my boyfriend is using me?'

Vanessa shook her head.

'No, you're right.' She looked around her. 'Where did he put that wine? I have the feeling we're going to need it.' She spotted it on a side table and took an enthusiastic slug straight from the bottle.

41

Frankie sat opposite her mother on the sofa, balling a damp wad of kitchen roll in her hands. She waited impatiently for Vanessa to take another swig.

'So,' Vanessa said, putting the bottle down and taking a deep breath, 'how much do you already know?'

'Hardly anything. Only what you've told me and what I've already said about Ron McCready.'

'Okay, let's start from the beginning then. Doug was a jockey the same time as Alan. Things were different thirty years ago. They shared a house with a bunch of other boys while they were doing their apprenticeships.' Vanessa looked unseeingly at the muted television. 'Your dad went pro around the same time he and I got a house together in Gloucester. Alan was engaged to Maria, but she was still studying for her degree in Madrid or Barcelona, I can't remember which. So Alan moved in with us. That was all fine. We were all great mates. Maria was okay, but she wasn't around a lot and Alan wasn't very good at making her feel at ease.'

'Did you like Maria?'

'There was nothing wrong with her,' Vanessa said, frowning as she thought back. 'Quiet type, very pretty. But different culture, different upbringing.'

'If Alan was such a bastard, why was she marrying him?'

'Oh, Alan wasn't always a bastard, darling. He and your dad were best friends at one time, remember. And he wasn't bad looking either. He was fun, he was confident, the life of a party.' She smiled, obviously reliving happier times. 'Maria was from a very wealthy Catholic family, quite a conservative family I would say if she was anything to go by. Maybe it was the rebel in Alan that attracted her? Anyway, they were married. It was a beautiful wedding. Maria's family shipped us all out to Spain for it, must have cost them a small fortune.' She shook her head and gave a small laugh at whatever memory had surfaced. 'But then it was back to work after that. Doug and Alan both rode for Ron McCready even though it wasn't a big yard. That's when things started to go downhill a bit. Your dad was having a great season with that horse, Crowbar. I don't think he was in the same league as – I don't know, Red Rum or Desert Orchid, but for such a small stable, he was a superstar. Things were looking good for us, but Alan was having a bit of a tough time. He thought that once he and Maria were married then they'd be able to buy their own house and make a good dent in her inheritance. But apparently that wasn't happening just yet. So they were still living with us – well, *Alan* was still living with us. Maria still had to finish her Masters or whatever it was she was studying. I don't know why she couldn't have just transferred to Bristol or somewhere. Maybe that sort of thing wasn't done. I don't know. I never did a proper degree for hairdressing. Funny how these days you need a degree just to pack shelves – '

'Mum,' Frankie interrupted. She gave her a pained look.

'Oh, sorry. I digress. So Alan wasn't happy, and between you and me I don't think it was just because his wife was never there. I think he was a little jealous of your dad, who was busy winning all the big races on Crowbar. Then this girl from New Zealand walked into town. Heidi, her name was. She was doing this round-the-world trip and wasn't planning on staying for long. She was great fun and so brave travelling by herself. But then Heidi and Alan met and she decided to stick around. She got a job behind the bar at the local pub, and one thing led to another and before long they were having an affair.'

'What a bastard,' Frankie gasped.

'You're not to tell Rhys this, okay?' Vanessa warned.

Frankie crossed her heart and her mother nodded approvingly.

'Good. So this went on for a few weeks, I can't remember how long exactly. I was doing a stylist course in Bristol so I don't know how often she was at the house, but eventually, with the spotlight on Dad so much, what with Crowbar and the Grand National coming up, Heidi was snapped sneaking out of the house at some ungodly hour. Well, when the papers got hold of this, they had a field day, but of course they couldn't say who Heidi was there visiting. Alan was shitting himself – 'scuse my language, because if Maria and her family found out, then he was *guaranteed* not to get any of their money. So he asked Doug and me if Doug would take the rap for it.'

'And Dad agreed?' Frankie said, with mounting surprise.

'Well, he took a bit of persuading, but they were best mates. They looked out for each other back then. I knew what was going on, so there was never any risk of your father and I splitting up. But the one condition made was that Alan and Heidi stop seeing each other.' Vanessa stopped for another couple of gulps of wine then arched her back in a stretch.

Frankie took the brief respite to try get a handle on what her mother was telling her. So Alan had had an affair with a bargirl and her father had taken the blame to protect his friend. Okay, so it wasn't a very saintly scenario, but was it enough for Doug to bear a grudge for the next thirty years?

'Is that why Dad doesn't like Alan then?'

'It might have been the start of it, but worse was to come,' explained Vanessa. 'Heidi and Alan agreed to stop seeing each other. Heidi moved on with her travels, but as soon as word got out that Doug was the one having the affair, Crowbar's owners took exception to his "philandering" I think is what they called it. Even though your father had won all of those races for them, they said they didn't want to associate with a cheat like him.'

Frankie's eyes widened as it dawned on her.

'So, *that's* why Alan rode Crowbar in the National!'

Vanessa nodded.

'He was the stable's other jockey so it made sense. It was just ironic that the successor just so happened to be the real cheat.'

'But he didn't have to accept it, surely? Why didn't Dad speak up and say something? The ride was his.'

'Well, that's when things began to go sour. Alan could have turned the ride down. Perhaps *should* have turned it down. But he didn't. Maybe it was pride? Maybe he wanted a piece of the pie which your father had been scoffing all season? Who knows? Whatever his reasons he took it and he won.'

'But why didn't Dad say anything?'

'Because by that stage, Maria was pregnant. With Rhys, as it happens. It would've been selfish. He could've broken up their marriage. And while she was pregnant? All for a race, which he was bound to ride in again? No, Doug couldn't do that. Besides, who would believe him?'

Frankie sat back on the sofa and looked at her in wonder.

'So that's why Dad hates him so much,' she mused.

Vanessa wagged her forefinger and gave Frankie a sad smile.

'It doesn't end there. As soon as Alan took the National ride on Crowbar, Doug threw him out. But luckily for Alan, now that Maria was going to have a son, her family did what he'd wanted right from the start.

They gave them a shed-load of dosh and bought them a house, and as far as we were concerned, they were out of our lives. Then who comes back, but Heidi. Came to our house to see Alan. She'd been in Brighton or somewhere and hadn't heard about the big fall out over the National. She was in a right state, said that she was pregnant with Alan's child; she didn't have anywhere to go, no money or anything. Alan wouldn't believe her at first, and to be honest, neither did we. Heidi'd gone down on everything bar the Titanic by the time she got to Gloucester. Nevertheless, she threatened to tell all if Alan didn't help her out. So that's what Alan did. He paid for her to have an abortion and gave her a good bundle of his wife's money to keep her quiet. It must have worked because we never saw or heard from her again, but that was the final straw for Doug. There must have been something in the water around that time because I then got pregnant with Seth. And well, you can just imagine your dad. He couldn't wait to be a father and the idea of getting rid of a baby just repulsed him. He and Alan never said a word to each other ever again.'

Frankie was aware that her mouth was hanging open, but she was incapable of closing it.

'My God,' she breathed. 'Alan Bradford really is a scumbag. Dad was right.' A thought then struck her. 'But Alan and Maria must have got divorced eventually. She's living in Spain with Rhys's stepfather.'

'Well, yes. One would've hoped that a scare like that might have stopped him from having more affairs. You'd even think that becoming a father might've stopped him, but he had other affairs, I believe.'

'Wow. And you've kept this secret all those years?'

'What was the point in telling anyone? The damage was already done.'

'But what about Dad's reputation?'

Vanessa shrugged.

'It didn't suffer all that bad. All of the jockeys in those days were a bit promiscuous; it was almost expected of them. It just so happened that when Doug took the blame, it was at the wrong time with the wrong owners. It wasn't like he was shunned by the racing community. He got other good rides in other good races. But he never won the Grand National, and the year that he should've won it, Rhys's father stole the ride from him.'

Frankie sunk into the cushiony depths of the sofa as she saw everything from her father's perspective.

'Poor Dad. God, no wonder he was upset I'd given the ride on Peace Offering to Rhys. It must have been like déjà vu for him.'

Vanessa nodded sadly.

'So, now do you understand that he wasn't really directing his anger at you? He was shouting at Alan. When something like this has been simmering for thirty years, it can become very ugly, uglier than it possibly was at the start.'

Frankie sighed.

'I know, but it still doesn't mean that Rhys is like that too. Rhys doesn't even like his father. He and Dad would probably get on really well considering they've already got that in common.'

'You would think so, wouldn't you?' Vanessa tipped the last of the bottle down her throat before continuing. 'But also remember, you're Daddy's little girl. He's just looking out for you.'

Frankie gave a frustrated laugh.

'And I appreciate that, but how am I going to convince him that Rhys isn't this evil cheat?'

Vanessa shrugged.

'I don't know, honey. Maybe he just needs time. If Rhys can prove over time that he's as you claim, then Dad won't have a choice.'

42

It was past ten by the time Rhys returned from the races and stopped by Frankie's house. She opened the door to let him and the cold night breeze in. Rhys greeted her with a kiss and a raised eyebrow.

'I got your text. What was so important that it couldn't wait until morning?'

'Come in. I'll tell you inside,' Frankie said, her heart hammering with anticipation.

She led the way into the kitchen where she and Atticus Finch had been sat attempting a crossword puzzle. She hadn't got further than the sixth clue. Not only was she hopeless at word games, but the words 'Rhys' and 'Grand National' didn't fit into any of the boxes.

Rhys sat down, glanced at the puzzle and immediately filled in two more clues. Atticus, stretched out on the table, smiled at him in approval. Frankie clasped her hands and gave him a nervous grin.

'I've some news for you.'

Like Vanessa had done before, Rhys's gaze immediately dropped to her stomach. She really needed to rethink her opening lines.

'No, don't worry. You're not going to be a father,' she laughed.

Rhys looked relieved.

'I spoke to Pippa earlier,' she continued. 'And you are now Peace Offering's new jockey in the National!' She cinched her tongue between her teeth, so eager to see his reaction.

Rhys's face fell, the blood draining from his cheeks.

'What?'

'I told Pippa I wanted you to ride him instead of me!'

Rhys continued to stare at her. He even looked a little horrified. She smiled even wider at him, trying to ignite some celebration in him. She'd hoped he'd yell the house down then spin her round in happiness. But he wasn't doing any of that. He was just staring at her with his mouth open. 'Aren't you pleased? You're going to ride Peace Offering! In the Grand National,' she added, just to clarify.

Rhys closed his eyes and put his face in his hands.

'Frankie, no,' he groaned.

Her smile faltered. Okay, she could take a less than exuberant response. This was Rhys, after all. But getting a negative response hadn't even occurred to her.

'Don't you want to ride him? I-I thought that was what you wanted?'

Rhys looked up.

'It is, but –' He shook his head. 'But not like this, not at your expense. I can't do this to you. Riding in the National was what *you* wanted as well.'

Frankie bit her lip. She'd been so looking forward to telling him, all the while thinking it would make up for her earlier meeting with her parents. She couldn't help a trace of annoyance seep into her voice.

'It was, but I know you want it more. Rhys, I'm *giving* you the ride on Peace Offering.'

'Oh, God,' he groaned. 'I don't know what to say. I mean, yes, you're right, I do want to ride Peace Offering, but Frankie –' He paused, his eyes pleading with her. 'This was *your* opportunity. Don't make me the one who takes it away from you.'

'You're not listening to me, not really. I don't *want* to ride Peace Offering in the National,' she said slowly so it would sink in. 'It's all done. I've spoken to Pippa. You're now his new jockey. You're going to Aintree. You're going to ride in the Grand National.'

Rhys looked around the kitchen, shell-shocked then a small laugh escaped from him. He looked at Frankie again with a dazed expression.

'Really?'

Frankie bit her lips together to stop herself from beaming again and nodded. Slowly, Rhys's capsized mouth righted into a wide smile. In an instant, he was out of his chair and had scooped Frankie into his arms. He kissed her hard on the lips then pulled back. Cupping her shoulders, he looked solemnly into her eyes.

'Thank you, Frankie. Thank you, thank you.' He gave her shoulders a gentle squeeze with each thank you. 'You've no idea what this means to me.'

At last, getting the response that she wanted, Frankie grinned. He might not be climbing the walls with joy, but in his own way, Rhys looked thrilled.

'I'm happy if you're happy,' she said, simply.

'Oh, I'm happy. You've no idea. I'll win it. I'll ride like I've never ridden before. I'll win it for you.'

Frankie met his deal-sealing kiss with a new warmth in her veins. If only her father could see them now, he'd see straight away that Rhys wasn't using her. He'd see that he loved her for *her*, not for any conniving scheme. Then she could love Rhys unstintingly. She was pretty sure she already loved him, but it was an insecure emotion which didn't mix well with her self-doubt.

'You know that giving up the ride on Peace Offering in the National is going to have a wider effect, don't you?' Rhys said cautiously.

'Yeah, I know. He's bound to go favourite again now.'

'Maybe, but it also means you probably won't get to ride him in any prep races beforehand as well.'

'Ah, yes,' she said, realising what he meant. 'I'm not going to ride him at Cheltenham, you mean?'

Rhys nodded with an expression of anguish on his face.

'Yeah. I'm sorry. I know you were looking forward to having your first Festival ride.'

Frankie chewed her lip in deliberation. She hadn't thought further than the Grand National ride. Losing her one and only Cheltenham ride was a bit more disappointing.

'Is it too late to change my mind?'

'You being serious?'

'No, silly. Sure, it would've been nice to ride at Cheltenham, but I can't have it all, I guess.'

'God, your father is going to hate me even more than he already does,' Rhys groaned.

'He doesn't hate you.'

'Really?' Rhys sounded doubtful.

She bit her lip. She wished she could tell Rhys what Vanessa had told her earlier, just so he knew that it wasn't him that Doug disliked. But she knew she couldn't. Even if Rhys didn't get on with his father, it still wouldn't be right to tell him just what a sleaze Alan Bradford had been.

'Does your dad know about us?' she asked.

Rhys shook his head.

'No. I tell him as little as I possibly can about my private life.'

She wondered if Alan Bradford hated Doug as much as Doug hated him. If he did, and Rhys told him about he and Frankie dating, would his reaction be the same? Would he try to dissuade Rhys for fear of his scandalous past being exposed? A new fear gripped her chest. What if he was successful?

'He'd have to find out eventually, wouldn't he?' she said apprehensively.

Rhys looped his arms around her and gave her a bemused smile.

'Hey, what's wrong? You scared he won't like you? You know I couldn't care less about what my father thinks. Besides, how can he not like you?'

Frankie smiled weakly, feeling little comfort in his words or his arms. Rhys might claim not to care what his father thought of him, but wasn't it because of his father that he was so determined to win the Grand National? She knew too much now. Alan Bradford had killed his unborn child to protect his secret. When he discovered Rhys was dating the daughter of the only people who knew of his past, as he must surely do, he would have to assume the worst. What lies and what lengths would he go to to ensure Rhys never found out?

43

Frankie's Girl Guides meeting midway through the week was usually a time for her to escape whatever problems she might have elsewhere in her life. This week, however, her problems continued to encroach on her. Tonight was the Chocolate Go For It, which had Frankie slavering at the mouth as the girls tasted all the different confectionery with little care to the amount of calories involved. But also the Golden Miller was also hosting the semi-final of their singing competition. She knew what was coming towards the end of the meeting when Cassa sidled up to her.

'Frankie, can you give me a lift home tonight?'

Frankie regarded her with a sceptical eye.

'You know you don't have to ask me every time, Cassa. 'Course I can. I can have you home in twenty minutes.'

Cassa fiddled with the hem of her T-shirt and looked up at Frankie with doleful eyes.

'There's no rush to get home. I mean, it'd only mean I sit and watch TV all night.'

Frankie grinned at her as she stacked the last of the plastic chairs in the corner of the community hall.

'Somewhere you'd rather be?'

'Please, Frankie, it's the semi-final tonight,' Cassa begged, bouncing up and down on her knees. 'The *semi-final*.'

Frankie gave an exaggerated sigh of defeat.

'Which means if you get through tonight, I only have to do this once more?'

'Wouldn't it be amazing if I made the final?' squeaked Cassa.

'Your mum would kill me if she knew, you know that?'

'She won't find out, I promise. She's always at work. She still doesn't know anybody in Helensvale. All of the friends she's made live near the hospital in Bristol.'

This small reassurance only partly settled the niggling concern in Frankie's stomach.

'But what if you win, Cassa? And I honestly believe you can. You realise what we're doing is cheating, don't you? You're underage.' The more she thought about it, the less sure she was about the whole thing. They'd both be in a muck heap of trouble if they were found out.

She shook her head. This was a bad idea. On the other hand, seeing Cassa bloom with a confidence which had been absent prior to the singing competition, was just so satisfying. Was it worth losing her Girl Guiding job over?

'Nobody has to know,' Cassa pleaded.

'But –'

'What are you two scheming about?' a voice interrupted them.

Cassa gasped and stood frozen to the spot. Mrs Preston walked across the room from the door. She laughed at Cassa's shock. 'Surprise! Matron had double-booked my shift so I thought I'd come surprise you. What does nobody have to know about?'

Judging by her cheery chatter, Frankie reckoned she hadn't overheard any more of their conversation.

'It was the Chocolate Go For It tonight,' she said, her brain whirring. 'Cassa was concerned you mightn't approve of the amount of chocolate she ate.'

Cassa looked at her without confidence. Was that the best she could do? Mrs Preston gave a puzzled laugh.

'Sweetie, you must learn to relax,' she said, giving Cassa's shoulder a squeeze. 'I know I like you to eat healthily, but I don't mind the occasional pig out. We all do it, don't we?' She looked at Frankie expectantly.

Frankie's food binges haunted her sleep, nevertheless she smiled in agreement.

'Are you ready to go?' Mrs Preston asked Cassa.

Cassa looked from her mother to Frankie in desperation.

'But-but Frankie was going to give me a lift home.'

'But I'm here now. I'm sure Frankie will be relieved to not chauffeur you home for once.'

Watching Cassa's eyes fill with disappointment made Frankie's heart ache. Even if they did manage to persuade Mrs Preston otherwise, they would then have to explain the hour in between leaving the community hall and getting home.

'Sorry, Cassa,' she said.

Cassa's shoulders drooped and she turned away, dragging her feet. Frankie felt even worse.

'I'll see you next week, okay?' she called after the departing pair.

'Yeah, see you next week,' came Cassa's gloomy reply.

Frankie watched them exit the building before turning back to the plastic chairs. She knew what it felt like to be thirteen and have something that felt so big cave in. It made her long for next week to arrive so she could reassure Cassa that pulling out of this singing contest wasn't the end of the world. Before that though, she would have to go over to the Golden Miller and tell them their young superstar wouldn't be performing anymore.

The pub was warm with the crush of customers. Frankie squeezed through to Tom's Corner, and her housemate raised a hand in greeting.

'I'm here!' she said, raising her voice above the babbles of conversation. 'What are your other two wishes?'

'You want a drink?' he said.

Frankie shook her head.

'I just popped in to tell Joey that Cassa's not singing tonight.'

'Really? Why?'

Frankie opened her mouth to explain then hesitated. Not even Tom knew of her and Cassa's deception.

'Long story.'

'Well, good luck with trying to get his attention. He's been rushing around like a headless chicken all night. I've been waiting for a refill for ten minutes.'

Frankie squeezed between Tom and other bar-propping customers to try catch Joey's eye. Pressed up against Tom's thigh as she waited, she became more and more aware of their contact. She was practically sat on his lap. Tom wasn't making any effort to move his leg. Oh dear, maybe her jokey pick-up line had been misconstrued. She glanced discreetly sideways at him as her mother's theory of Tom's singleton status came back to her. He was gazing across the bar into the void with a small smile on his face. Frankie stiffened. Was he enjoying this? She tried to edge away from him but only succeeded in jogging the man next to her. He glared at her while making a show of wiping the spillage from his hand.

'Sorry,' she said half-heartedly. She turned to Tom again. 'Busy in here tonight, isn't it?'

'Of course, it's the semi-final. We'd all come to hear your Girl Guide singing sensation.'

Frankie felt a ripple of guilt. It seemed Cassa wasn't the only one to be disappointed tonight. She caught Joey's attention and he strode over to her. Beneath the heat of the bar lights, his forehead shone with perspiration.

'Hey, Frankie! Where's our star?'

'She couldn't make it, I'm afraid.'

'You're joking! No? Now, that's a shame. Everyone's turned out to watch her. This is the busiest night I've had since we opened. What's up with her?'

'Laryngitis or something,' she lied, surprised at the ease with which it rolled off her tongue. Probably because of the relief that she was ending their treachery. What harm could one more lie do?

Joey pulled a sympathetic face.

'Poor love. I had her marked down to win. Never mind. *C'est la vie*, right? I'll go tell the judges.'

'Hey, what do I have to do to get served around here?' Tom said, holding up his empty beer glass.

Joey winked at him.

'You like yours with a bit of head, don't you?'

Tom snorted and waved him away. Joey laughed and ducked under the bar flap without serving him.

A couple of minutes later the piercing whine of a microphone being switched on silenced the pub. Joey stepped up onto the stage.

'Sorry to interrupt, folks. I've just been informed that Cassa won't be taking part in the semi-final tonight –'

A wave of disgruntled mutterings rumbled through the crowd accompanied by a couple of boos.

'I know, I know,' Joey tried to placate them. 'Unfortunately, she's ill so is out of the competition. That means tonight won't be a double elimination. But before we come to all that, please give it up for Russell!'

A few cheers went up from a corner, obviously the Russell camp, as Joey handed the mic over to the first contestant and jumped off the stage.

'Well, I'm going to head off home,' Frankie told Tom. 'I'll see you later.'

'Actually, I don't fancy sticking around. Cassa's not singing and I can't get a drink. Mind if I catch a lift with you?'

'Sure. No problem.'

'Great. I'll just say goodbye to Joey.'

*

The car journey home was barely five minutes, yet Frankie felt she could almost make sand art with the tension in the small confines of the Mini. She searched for a neutral but interesting subject, but could only think of Rhys and giving him the ride on Peace Offering. If Tom did have a crush on her, she didn't want to rub it in.

'So, have you had any luck with your search for Adelaide Mann yet?' she asked instead.

Tom shook his head.

'I'm just about ready to give up. I've put my name down on all the forums and registers. There's not much else I can do.'

'Pity. You must be disappointed.'

He shrugged.

'Like Joey always says, *c'est la vie.*'

'Does Joey know?' she asked in surprise.

Tom hesitated.

'Kinda. You know how it is when you've had too much to drink.'

'Gosh.' Frankie blinked at the dark road in front of them. 'I didn't realise you and Joey were such good mates.'

Tom gave a wry chuckle.

'Well, I don't have you around so often these days. Since you've been dating Rhys, you're hardly ever at the house.'

'Oh, sorry.'

'Forget it. It's no big deal.'

The resignation in his voice caused a surge of compassion inside her.

'Don't say that. Of course it's a big deal if you need someone to talk to.'

'I have someone to talk to. Joey.'

'Yes, but that's not the same as having a friend to talk to.'

'Frankie, being a barman doesn't stop him from being a friend.'

'I'm sorry. I-I didn't mean it like that. It's just that you and I have been friends for so long. You've been having such a rough time lately, and I haven't helped matters by going out with Rhys...' The words died on her lips.

Pulling up at a Give Way, she saw Tom looking confused.

'I know it can't be easy,' she went on. 'And I'm really sorry, Tom. I never knew you felt that way and when it finally dawned on me - well, it was too late. I'd never hurt you on purpose.'

'What are you talking about? When did you find out?' Tom's tone shook with panic. Frankie decided it best not to tell him that her parents also knew about his crush.

'A few weeks ago when you started spending so much time down at the pub. It'd never occurred to me that you never went out on dates or anything.'

'Frankie, no one must know, you hear me!'

Surprised by his vehemence, she nodded profusely.

'Of course, of course. If that's what you want. There's no shame in it though. Friends fall for each other all the time.'

Tom groaned and leant back in his seat.

'I didn't mean for it to happen. I didn't even realise it *was* happening until Joey practically spelt it out to me.'

'Wow, you do tell Joey an awful lot,' Frankie said with a strangled laugh.

Tom shifted in his seat so he was facing her. With the glow of passing street lights, his face was lit with fear.

'Frankie,' he said breathlessly, 'if you love me then you won't tell anyone. I could lose my job.'

Frankie balked. Tom was being a bit over-dramatic, even by her standards.

'I *do* love you, Tom,' she said gently. 'But I love you like a brother. And I know that it must feel pretty serious, but even if people did find out you had a crush on me, you wouldn't lose your job. Rhys isn't that revered in the weighing room.'

'What?'

'What?'

'You think I've got a crush on you?'

Frankie shrugged, embarrassed.

'Or in love with me, whichever you think you feel.'

Tom gave a harsh laugh of disbelief. Frankie pulled up in a parking space and switched off the engine. She looked at him properly for the first time. Something in his expression told her that hadn't been the right thing to say.

'You think I'm in love with you?' Tom spluttered.

Doubt loomed.

'Aren't you?'

'No, Frankie!' he cried. 'I'm gay!'

This time it was Frankie's turn to be gobsmacked.

'I thought that was what we were talking about,' Tom said. 'I thought you knew!'

'You're gay?'

'Yes!'

'But how? I mean, since when? Have you always been gay? You used to date girls when we were teenagers.'

Tom fell back against the door and laughed. He dragged his fingers through his hair and shook his head at her.

'I was confused back then. I didn't know what I wanted. But then I met Joey, and well, then I knew.'

Frankie gasped as realisation hit her.

'That's why you were always at the Golden Miller! You weren't drowning your sorrows because I was dating Rhys. You were there because of Joey!'

'Pretty much, yeah.'

Frankie slapped her hand over her mouth.

'Oh, my God. I'm such a fool.'

She giggled and Tom snorted.

'Are you guys, you know, *dating*?'

Tom shrugged.

'Yes and no. I haven't exactly "come out" as they say. And you can't tell anyone. Can you imagine the response I'll get from the weighing room? There I am, valet to all these male jockeys, who have no qualms about getting naked in front of each other. But they might not be so indifferent if they knew I was gay.'

'They don't mind getting naked in front of me either, and I'm a girl.'

'Yeah, but that's different. Some guys might feel - I don't know, *threatened* by a gay man being around while they're getting changed.'

Frankie took a moment to imagine the scenario. The first person's point of view she visualised was Rhys's. She didn't think he would be bothered which team Tom batted for, so long as he had clean breaches and the correct boots and saddles.

'They might surprise you,' she said. 'They're not a bad bunch of guys. The odd one, maybe, might be a bit of a drama queen - oops, sorry - but on the whole I'd say they probably wouldn't care.'

Tom chewed his lip and continued to stare at her. She could see the desperate glint of his eyes in the darkness.

'I don't want to live a lie,' he said. 'I don't want to pretend to be someone I'm not. I've spent my entire life not knowing who I am and now I've found Joey, it's like the start of a new life, a *real* life. But it's – it's scary, you know? You don't know what kind of response you might get. Hell, I haven't even told my folks.'

Frankie reached out and rubbed his arm in sympathy. She didn't know what else to do.

'I'm sorry, Tom. I wish I'd known so I could've given you more support. Instead, you've had to shoulder this whole thing on your own.'

'I have had Joey,' he pointed out.

'Oh, yeah. If it makes any difference, I'm glad it's him. I think he's lovely.'

Tom smiled bashfully.

'He is, I know.' He took a deep breath. 'And maybe you're right about the guys in the weighing room. Maybe I've overthought this. Maybe I've become paranoid. I've got to come out at some point.'

'And I'll be there to back you up when you do.'

Tom leaned over and gave Frankie a rare kiss on the cheek and a hug which said he really appreciated it.

44

With the pressure of her Grand National date relieved and the direction of Tom's affections resolved, it felt as if the wind was whooshing Frankie faster through the remaining weeks of the season. March's Cheltenham Festival began with a bang for Aspen Valley with Rhys winning the Champion Hurdle on Dexter and notching up three other placings on the first day. Frankie watched the following two days on the television in the yard's office, a stone in her stomach yearning to be one of those jockeys onscreen to lift a victory flag over her shoulders as they were led into the winner's enclosure.

As she watched a fellow amateur jockey punch the air in a victory salute after sealing victory in the Kim Muir Chase, a kindling of regret crackled inside her.

'Weren't you meant to ride Peace Offering in that race?' Billy said, as they strolled back out into the yard.

'Yeah. That went down the pan when I gave up the National ride on him though.'

Billy tutted in sympathy. He kept step with her as they headed over to the feed room to finish off evening stables.

'But it's not all bad,' she continued. 'Jack's given me the ride on Bold Phoenix tomorrow. I think he's let me ride as a consolatory gesture. He never really wanted me to ride Peace Offering in the National.'

'Ah, well, don't take it personally. Rhys is the best. I mean, look at him back there,' he said, tossing a thumb in the direction they'd just come from. 'He's got the pink armband on for being leading rider and he's still got Virtuoso in the Gold Cup tomorrow.'

Frankie's grin was less forced as she swelled with pride.

'I'll never hear the end of it. I hope Virtuoso's back to his old self.'

'Sure he is. Those blood tests he had after the Ascot Chase came back normal. With the sun shining like it is, the ground is going to be perfect for the old boy.'

'I hope Bold Phoenix likes it too,' she replied, her thoughts straying back to her own task ahead. She picked up a couple of freshly prepared feed buckets and waited for Billy to find his.

'Pah,' he said with a fob of his hand. 'He'll be cool. How did Donnie take being sidelined? It would've been him aboard originally, wasn't it?'

Frankie shifted in her boots.

'I don't know. I have won on Bold Phoenix before. But he probably wasn't too chuffed all the same. I haven't really spoken to him lately. Then again, we're not exactly favourite for the race so he might not be missing out on anything.'

They wandered back into the yard to be greeted by its impatient and hungry residents.

'I've heard a rumour,' Billy said, lowering his voice and sidling a couple inches closer to her. 'You know your friend, Tom?'

Frankie bit back a smile. She could see where this was heading.

'Yes, I know him.'

'Well, I heard that – and this is only a rumour, like – but I heard that he's *gay*.'

She laughed at Billy's uncertain expression. Tom had "come out" about a week ago, and while the whispers on the grapevine hadn't been especially audible, there had been a definite hum. Billy was the first person to ask her, in fact.

'That's right,' she said.

Billy stopped in his tracks and nearly tipped out one of his buckets.

'Wow,' he said. 'I've got nothing against queers or anything, but bloody hell, he's been hiding this for how long?'

'He's twenty-eight.'

'Poor guy.'

'He's happier now that he doesn't have to hide it anymore. He's just worried about how the weighing room are going to take it.'

Billy shook his head sadly.

'Poor guy,' he said again. 'Anyway, good luck tomorrow, Frankie. We'll be cheering you on.'

'Thanks, Billy. Appreciate it.'

Frankie carried on down the concourse, the first few butterflies taking flight in her stomach. Tomorrow, Billy wouldn't be the only one cheering. It was Gold Cup Day. That meant seventy thousand others would be cheering too. Oh, how she prayed she wouldn't fuck up in front of seventy thousand onlookers.

*

Rhys, who had been staying in a Cheltenham hotel for the past few days, greeted Frankie with a kiss when she arrived at the racecourse early the next morning.

'Ready for the masses?'

'No,' she shuddered, watching keen spectators already trickling onto the misty infield. 'How about you?'

'Okay,' he shrugged. 'Are your parents coming to watch you?'

She nodded. Despite their strained relationship, Doug was still loyal enough to attend her Festival debut.

'Yeah. I just hope I don't disappoint them like I did at New Year.' An icy thought occurred to her. 'Is your dad going to be here?'

'So he says.'

Already nauseous with nerves, Frankie's stomach gave an uneasy lurch. Rhys hadn't mentioned before that he'd spoken to his father. What else had they talked about? She studied Rhys's face. Black circles beneath his eyes betrayed his lack of sleep, but that was nothing new. Rhys hardly ever slept anyway. With the excitement of Cheltenham all around him she doubted whether he'd managed eight hours' rest this entire week.

'Did you tell him about us?' she ventured.

Rhys stopped and regarded her studiously.

'Do you want him to know about us?'

Frankie broke eye contact and shrugged, tunnelling her fists deeper into her coat pockets to ward off the chilly wind. It was so cold her fingernails felt like they were becoming detached.

'I don't know,' she lied. 'It's not like he needs to know or anything.'

She carried on walking and Rhys limped to catch up.

'You're right, I haven't told him,' he said. 'But it's not because I'm ashamed of us or anything. It's because I prefer to keep my affairs private from him.'

Frankie masked her breath of relief.

'Affairs?' she teased. 'That's what this is?'

'You know it's not.'

Despite his words, Frankie couldn't help reaching for more reassurance.

'But he's got to find out sooner or later. What if he doesn't like me?'

'What? You mean how your father doesn't like me?'

She grimaced.

'Sorry. And don't mind my dad. It's - it's nothing personal.'

Rhys chuckled. He spun her round and tipping her backwards in his arms, gave her a sultry look.

'Frankie, my dear, I don't give a damn.'

She giggled beneath his kiss.

'*Oh, Rhett,*' she whispered dramatically.

Rhys cocked an eyebrow.

'Not quite. But we've the same initials.'

As the hours slipped by, Frankie felt more and more like a pressure cooker about to explode. Dressed in Bold Phoenix's yellow racing colours, she watched the run-up to the Gold Cup from the confines of the weighing room on the mounted television. It was still another half hour before her race, but she hadn't been able to resist donning her silks. Just to be doing *something*. At least with the Gold Cup about to begin, she had something to distract her.

The minutes passed agonisingly slowly. Tom walked past, busy setting up silks and saddles ready for his jockeys in the next race. He winked at her as he passed.

Frankie's gaze left him to settle on Donnie McFarland making his way over to her. Without a ride in the next, courtesy of Jack's last minute jockey change, he was showered and dressed in a white towel around his waist. It might have just been her imagination, but he looked to give Tom a wide berth.

Frankie ground her teeth. She turned her attention back to the screen. The horses were milling around at the start, gradually forming two rows. Her stomach clenched in anticipation. Her eyes never left Rhys on Virtuoso, even when Donnie plonked himself down beside her.

'I see you're all dressed up for your party,' he said.

Frankie glanced at him, distracted.

'Not much else to do.'

'It's more than some of us.'

Frankie scowled as she recognised the trace of bitterness in his tone. Tom appeared from behind them to watch the race and Frankie noticed Donnie pull his towel more securely over his legs. She heard Tom sigh and walk away.

Onscreen, Virtuoso was acting mulish. Rhys flapped his legs and flicked his whip as they lost their position in the front line of horses.

Nerves frayed and her defences up, Frankie turned on her fellow jockey.

'What's your problem, Donnie? For God's sake, he's gay, not a pervert.'

Donnie gave her a sour look.

'A gay valet?' he scoffed. 'I'd say Peeping Tom's had plenty opportunity to perve.'

'Oh, come on. You can't be serious,' she laughed. 'Not everybody is as interested in your body as you are, you know.'

Donnie leant over in a conspiratorial fashion.

'Frankie, the guy's gay,' he hissed. 'He's been helping me get dressed for years. How can he not have been perving?'

She shook her head.

'You don't have a problem bearing all in front of me.'

'You're different.'

'Oh, don't be so ridiculous,' she snapped. 'Do you have any idea how much guts it took for him to come out?'

'Goddamn pansy,' muttered Donnie.

Frankie exhaled in exasperation and turned back to the television. The horses were trotting towards the tape with purpose now, yet the Aspen Valley contender was baulking. She winced. The tiny figure of the starter on his rostrum waved the horses away to take another turn. One of the handlers ran forward and tugged at Virtuoso's bridle.

'What's wrong with him?' she said, to no one in particular.

'You can lead a horse to water...' Donnie murmured.

With the runners lined up again, the starter called them forward once more. The handler at Virtuoso's head pulled the bridle like he was heaving a cart up a hill. Rhys let his whip fall on his horse's flank. Virtuoso switched his tail. Panic began to swirl in Frankie's stomach. This was not looking good for the Gold Cup winner of two seasons ago.

How much patience would the starter show? The starter shouted at the other runners to slow and the disgruntled jockeys pulled up in a ragged line before the orange tape. Virtuoso's handler was almost running on the spot.

From the microphone positioned somewhere close by, she could hear him and Rhys growling and shouting at Virtuoso. Rhys gave him another smack, this one more demanding. The horse bounded forward, nearly sending the handler sprawling. Seizing the moment, the starter released them. The runners bounded forward. All except one. Rhys's desperate growls were drowned out by the customary roar of the Cheltenham crowd. But Virtuoso was having none of it. He slowed to a walk before digging in his toes again and locking his knees. He didn't care how humiliated his jockey looked flapping on his back. He was going nowhere.

Frankie groaned. As the camera swept along the running rail to keep pace with the rest of the field, Rhys on an immobile Virtuoso disappeared from shot. She slumped in her chair, all interest in the race evaporated. Forgetting for a moment that she was annoyed with Donnie, she glanced at him to see his reaction. He looked just as nonplussed. He met her look of disbelief with a crooked eyebrow.

'Like I said, you can lead a horse to water, but you can't make him drink.'

'But – but, that's Virtuoso we're talking about,' she exclaimed. 'He's one of the best chasers around! He's meant to like Cheltenham. Hell, most of his wins have come here.'

Donnie shrugged.

'Guess it's an early bath for your man.'

Frankie moaned in pity.

'Oh, God. Poor Rhys.'

Donnie gave a mirthless snort and shook his head.

'Damn, he really has done his job well.'

'It wasn't his fault,' she said. 'You could see him doing everything to get that mule to move.'

Donnie leaned back in his chair and crossed his arms across his bare chest. Frankie didn't like the sneery smile on his twisted face.

'Frankie, you're so naive,' he chuckled.

'What are you talking about? Are you implying Rhys made Virtuoso refuse to start like that? If so, then you and I have been watching different races.'

'God, maybe it's not naivety, maybe it's stupidity.'

'Hey!' Frankie glared at him. 'What the hell's your problem? Are you having a go because Jack is letting me ride Bold Phoenix in the next?'

Donnie didn't contradict her.

'If I'd had a bit more warning, maybe I could've done Rhys's trick and seduced it back off you.'

Swallowing became impossible. Frankie stared at him, not breathing. She could hear the blood pumping through her body like a death drum. Her tongue stuck to her palate as she tried to speak.

'What are you talking about?'

'Come on, Frankie. It's so obvious. Do you really believe that Rhys bedded you because he *fancied* you? He hated your guts! You stole his National ride, for God's sake! That's like the Holy Grail to him. Do you really think he was just going to say "Oh, go on then, you have it"?'

Frankie shook her head and got to her shaky legs to back away.

'That's not true.'

Donnie raised his eyes to the ceiling before giving her a look of disdain.

'Yes, Frankie, it *is* true. I was there. Remember? At the Christmas party? You came over practically gagging for it. Rhys saw his opportunity to get his ride back... and get another into the bargain,' he added with an evil twinkle.

Heat washed over Frankie's face. She couldn't speak. She couldn't think. Fear curled around her body until it held her in a vice-like grip. She'd never realised how isolating the feeling of betrayal was.

'He wouldn't – Rhys wouldn't do that,' she stammered. 'Not to me.'

Donnie raised a challenging eyebrow then nodded to the open doorway. Rhys, looking thunderous after his void ride, limped into the room with his saddle over his arm.

'Might just as well have stayed in here with you guys,' he muttered, dumping his saddle on the bench. 'Bloody Virtuoso figures he just wanted to go for a look at the countryside rather than contest the Gold Cup. Fucking animal.'

When neither Frankie nor Donnie replied, he looked up.

'What's up with you two?' he said.

Frankie felt numb, her legs, her arms, her brain seemed to have switched to some sort of survival mode. She couldn't answer him.

Rhys narrowed his eyes, his dark eyes switching from her to Donnie and back again.

'What –'

'Rhys, is it true?' Her words were strangled.

'Is what true?'

'Did you – did you –' She moistened her lips, summoning the courage to ask the question. 'Did you seduce me to get the ride on Peace Offering?'

In desperation, she watched his face for his reaction, a reaction that would ease the panic rising inside her.

A pause.

'No, of course not,' Rhys said.

She sucked in her breath, gulping in air to fill her lungs. His words sounded genuine, but his expression was all wrong. He was glaring at Donnie. And that pause... Frankie staggered backwards. The expression on his face during that pause had said a thousand words. And they weren't the words which were uttered from his mouth.

45

Rhys had lied.

Frankie's body was numb as Bold Phoenix jogged onto Cheltenham's centre stage. She heard the amassed crowd like she was underwater. Her mind swirled. Rhys wasn't whom he'd claimed to be. Yet she'd felt like she had learned so much about herself through being with him. If he was a fraud, did that mean she wasn't whom she thought she was either? Bold Phoenix broke into canter and she automatically rose in her stirrups. She shook her head to clear it. There she'd been, asking herself – seriously questioning herself as a mature adult – if she was in love with Rhys. But that Rhys hadn't existed. It'd all been for show. An act.

'I can't believe it.' The words fell from her lips and were swept away by the wind. They remained the only response in her mind though. Thinking in coherent sentences was impossible. 'I-I can't believe it.'

Down at the start, Bold Phoenix slowed on his own accord to join the other horses circling. Frankie looked at them without actually seeing them. The usual ball of trepidation before a race was strangely absent. She had no idea what Jack might have said in the parade ring. She couldn't even remember him saying anything at all.

The runners were called forward. With no instruction from his rider, Bold Phoenix happily followed at the rear.

Rhys had lied.

Like a genie from a lamp, the loving boyfriend in whose arms she'd spent so much of the season, had vanished in a puff of smoke. Frankie became more aware of the race when her horse launched into a gallop. How long was this race? How many jumps were there? Was it a hurdles race or a steeplechase? Who was she riding again?

She looked down, her brain taking a sabbatical before matching her yellow sleeves to the chestnut neck. Bold Phoenix, that was who she was on. Was this how people felt after an accident when you saw them wrapped in foil with a "Have I left the oven on" expression on their faces? Was this full-blown shock, which numbed the brain to protect it from the psychological trauma of the event? She'd only once felt like this before.

When she'd been told Seth was dead. Was this so dissimilar? She'd lost someone close to her, someone, she dared say it, she loved?

The first fence registered when she saw the front runners rising over it. Five lengths off the pace, Bold Phoenix took the jump in his own time. Frankie didn't notice the gap begin to widen. Neither did she notice the next three fences nor the hollering crowds when they passed the grandstands.

Rhys had lied.

What a fool she'd been! She cringed as she recalled how blissfully happy she'd been. All that time he'd probably been laughing at her. Had he been keeping Donnie updated with his progress? Had they chuckled at her gullibility? Despite the fresh wind blowing in her face as the field rounded the far turn, her cheeks burned with humiliation.

She was jolted back to her race when Bold Phoenix cat-jumped over the water and dragged his hindlegs. In a daze she looked up. Apart from a horse pulling up on the wide outside, the rest of the field were a good ten lengths clear. The skeletal trees bordering the course scratched the slate sky. Distractedly, she pushed her mount on and Bold Phoenix quickened his stride.

Rhys had lied.

Had he though? Or had she created a fantasy? She thought she'd gone into the relationship with her eyes wide open, yet she might just as well have been wearing Ta' Qali's sheepskin noseband over them.

As the ground ahead rose up the side of the hill, a faller brought Frankie's mind sharply back to the job. She switched wide to avoid the crumpled heap of silks on the landing side. The rest of the field had reached the top of the hill and were now picking up speed on the descent. They were pulling further and further clear.

Rhys had lied.

Frankie frowned to herself. That could well have been her on the floor back there. She *had* to concentrate. She clucked in Bold Phoenix's ear and once again, he responded to her urging. Hell, she was three quarters of the way through her first Cheltenham Festival ride and she'd taken absolutely nothing of it in. Rhys's bombshell had completely decimated every scrap of enjoyment, all the nerves, all the adrenalin. Not only had he managed to seduce her Grand National ride off her, but he was about to ruin her Festival debut too.

'Bastard,' she muttered.

She gave Bold Phoenix an unnecessarily violent kick over the next open ditch on the downhill slope. He pitched on landing. She pushed herself back in the saddle to counterbalance his momentum. The chestnut found a footing. The cheering of the crowds drifted over to her on the wind. She had heard that the cheers at Cheltenham were like nowhere else on earth. They made the hairs on people's arms stand on end. And here she was, lagging fifteen lengths behind the field, about to let Rhys steal this opportunity away from her as well?

'Not bloody likely,' she growled.

She kicked Bold Phoenix on, letting caution depart on the south-westerly. Filled with a fury completely foreign to her, Frankie felt no fear. She urged her mount towards the third from home. Her blood boiled in a cauldron of anger. Bold Phoenix spring-heeled the jump. The leaders were now just ten lengths clear. They galloped flat out around the long turn into the home straight, the noise of the crowd building. Frankie imagined her parents somewhere in that pebbledash of yelling punters. Her father! A new rage flooded her face. She'd turned her back on him, had shouted him down every time he'd warned her that Rhys was bad news. And all the while, he had been right! How could Rhys allow her to ruin her relationship with her father? A wave of guilt mixed uncomfortably with her anger. She'd let him down so many times in the past. Discovering he'd been right about Rhys was just the icing. How could he ever look at her again without thinking she had been the child that was a constant disappointment? Tears stung her eyes and she blinked them away.

Rhys had lied.

She looked ahead. The field were coming back to them and a blob of red in the distance marked the Finish lollipop.

'Come on, Phoenix!' she shouted. 'Come on! You bastard, Rhys! I'm not going to let you take this away from me too!'

Her renewed urgings surprised Bold Phoenix into running faster than he'd ever done before. The second last fence loomed. He took confidence from his determined rider and hurdled it like it was a practice jump at home.

The roar of the grandstand hit them in a wave of jubilant sound. They could have been shouting for any one of the ten runners in front – River Train, the favourite was leading – but at that moment, Frankie felt they were all for her. Bold Phoenix was gaining, galloping like he'd just joined the race. They picked them off, tenth, ninth, eighth, seventh. They took the last in joint fifth position. Just the infamous Cheltenham run-in opposed the horses.

'Come on, Phoenix!' Frankie shouted, the roar in her tone emanating from somewhere deep deep within. She ducked her head between her shoulders and shoved forward for all she was worth. 'We are going to do this! Come on!'

Bold Phoenix stretched out his neck, straining his legs to run faster, to reach further. They passed the fourth then third horses in a flash of muddied silks and chestnut and blonde manes. The horizon bobbed as she raised her head. Two horses up ahead, to her left. River Train leading. A heaving black mass of tweed and corduroy to her right. A hundred yards to that lollipop.

Frankie pushed. Frankie shoved. Frankie's blood boiled at the thought of Rhys. Bold Phoenix could go no faster. Rocking back and forth in her saddle, Frankie glimpsed the front two horses slowing, the lactic acid burning in their muscles too unbearable to see out the Cheltenham hill.

'Come on! We can do this!'

Bold Phoenix dug deep. With an extra spurt, he quickened. Three, four, five strides; they drew level. Six, seven, eight; they galloped in sync. Nine, ten... Exhaustion overruled his willingness to please. Frankie closed her eyes. She rested her face against his mane and wrapped her arms around his neck, bobbing on his back as he changed down into a rattling trot. She looked back down the course at an upside down world. There behind them was that red lollipop. There also behind them was River Train. They'd done it. Frankie slumped.

But Rhys had still lied.

A hammering on the front door roused Frankie from her daze. She lay on her bed looking up at the ceiling. What little comfort the darkness afforded was jarred out of her as a second hammering sounded. She heard Tom descending the stairs.

'Don't answer it, Tom,' she called.

His footsteps stilled.

'You sure?'

'Yes, I'm sure.'

'Okay, then.' He sounded uncertain. Nevertheless, his footsteps returned to his bedroom.

'Frankie!' Rhys shouted from outside.

She closed her eyes, trying to block out the sound of his voice.

'Frankie, let me in!'

She wrenched the pillow from beneath her head and blocked her ears with it.

'Come on, Frankie! It's me, Rhys!'

Like a match to kindling, rage erupted inside her. She flung the pillow aside and flew to the window. Struggling with the latch for a moment in her haste, she shoved it wide and leaned out.

'I know it's you, goddammit! And that is exactly why I'm ignoring you!'

Rhys stepped back from the front door's overhang to look up at her. The security light lit the anguish on his face.

'Frankie –'

'Just go away!'

'If you could just let me explain.'

Frankie's hands trembled on the window frame and she sucked in a lungful of cold air to keep her voice from going the same way.

'What is there to explain, Rhys? Don't tell me that Donnie was lying. I could see that he wasn't.'

'I wasn't –'

'Did you or did you *not* sleep with me at the Christmas party just to get the ride on Peace Offering?' A new iciness crept into her tone.

Rhys lifted his hands and let them fall in exasperation.

'Yes, but –'

The knife that had been wedged in her heart for the past four hours twisted deeper.

'Then there's nothing to explain, Rhys!' she screamed. 'Just fuck off! I don't want to see you again. Dad was right about you – you are just like your father!'

Rhys stepped back as if she'd physically assaulted him.

'Don't!' he yelled in reply. 'Don't you *ever* say that! I'm nothing like my father!'

'Yes, you are. You're a lying, cheating son of a bitch. Dad said right from the start not to trust you.' She bit her lip and her voice quavered. 'I turned my back on him for you. I trusted you –'

'I never asked you to turn your back on your dad.'

Frankie gripped the window frame until her fingertips hurt. She felt like hurling herself out of the window and punching Rhys.

'You never *what?*' she said. 'Of course you bloody did! You-you *seduced* me. Dad told me you were up to no good, that the Bradfords never change, but I didn't listen to him.' She laughed in ridicule at herself. 'The fool that I am, I actually believed that you wanted to be with me because of who I am, not for what I could give you.'

'I hate my father,' he said deliberately. 'I am *not* my father.'

Frankie shook her head, watching Rhys clench his fists by his sides. A wild hysterical laugh gathered inside her. He might have more layers to him than an onion in Antarctica but she still knew how to hurt him.

'Take a good look in the mirror, Rhys,' she spat. 'A *good* look. Because from where I'm standing, you are exactly like your father.'

She slammed the window closed, making the photo frame on her bedside table fall flat.

'Frankie?' Rhys's voice was muffled but still clear. '*Frankie!*'

'Go away!' she shrieked. She picked up the photograph. With the glow of the outside light shining through the window, she didn't see Seth leading the string of horses though. All she saw was the black-jacketed figure in the background. She flung the photo at the wall, but screamed in frustration when the shattering glass did nothing to assuage her anger.

'Goddammit!' Rhys yelled from below. 'Stupid fucking – RRRR!' The wheelie bins parked out the front received the brunt of his frustration.

Frankie stood in the middle of her room, shaking. Her trembling breaths filled the void. She listened for Rhys to cut through her heart again, but there was only silence. A few seconds later, the security light, with no movement to trigger it, clicked off.

A gentle tap on the door made her jump.

Tom peeped in.

'Sorry, I couldn't help overhearing.'

Frankie sat down on her bed with a bump.

'Yeah, I know. Sorry about that.'

'Hey, don't be,' he said, joining her on the bed and putting his arm around her.

She leaned her head against his shoulder, the fight drained from her. A thick painful ball of tears swelled at the back of her throat.

'Tom, I've been such a fool.'

'No, you haven't.'

'Yes, I have. I've never felt so – so humiliated before. All those months, I was merrily under the impression I had a boyfriend who loved me for me. And now, now I find out he was lying the whole time. He was probably laughing at me behind my back, just like Donnie was, thinking how gullible I was and congratulating himself on making me give him the National ride.' Frankie choked on a sob and Tom squeezed her closer to him.

'Ah, sweetheart. I know, I know. But it wasn't just you he fooled. He had us all going.'

'Except Dad,' she sniffed. 'Oh God, how am I going to tell him? Do you think he'll forgive me for being such a bitch towards him?'

'Of course he will. And you haven't been a bitch. You were just defending Rhys. If anything, I'd be more concerned for Rhys's safety than anything else because your dad is going to kill him.'

46

Frankie had never felt less like going to work than the next morning. When everyone met her with cheery congratulations for riding her first Cheltenham winner, another surge of resentment towards Rhys rose within her. Not only had he taken away her chance for a National winner, but he'd ruined her enjoyment of Bold Phoenix's triumph. Cheltenham winners were supposed to be celebrated for the great achievement they were, yet for Frankie it was like drinking a chocolate milkshake that didn't have any chocolate in it.

Jack met her outside her row of stables with a pat on her back and a rare smile.

'I know I said it yesterday, but I'm going to say it again,' he said. 'That was a bloody fantastic ride you gave old Bold Phoenix.'

'Thanks,' she replied. 'And thanks for letting me ride.'

Jack shrugged.

'It was the least I could do considering-' He stopped mid-sentence and looked down at his feet.

An uneasy feeling began to form in her stomach. Had Jack been in on Rhys's connivery?

'Considering what?'

'Well, considering you were going to ride Peace Offering in his National trial but lost out.'

'Did you know what Rhys was doing all along?'

Jack held up his hands and took a step backward.

'Whoa, Frankie. I heard you and Rhys split up, but that's as far as my knowledge of your relationship goes. I don't want to know who's to blame, who's the bad guy in all this. Okay?'

Frankie nodded reluctantly and half-hid her embarrassment by receiving Blue Jean Baby's head-butt greeting with a pat.

'Yeah. Sorry.'

'So am I. I'll do my best to give both of you space away from each other. Rhys can go back to riding out just a couple of times a week, but I'll be honest. I'm not going to do this forever. Whatever differences you and Rhys have, sooner or later you're going to have to put it behind you if you two are going to work alongside one another.'

Frankie tried to imagine working with Rhys a year from now. She failed, but she could see Jack's reasoning. She nodded again.

'Okay, I know. Thanks for understanding.' She fiddled with the grotty lead rope in her hands, feeling uncomfortable having this type of conversation with her boss. 'How's Virtuoso?' she asked.

Jack shook his head.

'Finished.'

'For the season, you mean?'

'Nah. We decided to retire him after yesterday's debacle.'

For a moment, Frankie was jolted out of her own mournful world.

'Seriously? Just like that?'

Blue Jean Baby stuck her nose forward and Jack stroked her mindlessly.

'He's been telling us for a while. We couldn't figure out why he ran so lethargic in February then when he refused to start yesterday, he made it clear. He's had enough. He doesn't want to do it anymore.'

'But he's got so much talent,' Frankie said.

'Yeah, three King Georges and a Gold Cup aren't to be sniffed at. But come on, Frankie. You know horses. People think we force them to race, whip them into submission, but the simple truth is when they don't want to do it anymore, they'll just stop. Virtuoso's an eleven year old now. He probably would've raced for only two more seasons anyway.'

'So what's going to happen to him now?'

'We'll think of something. Eventing maybe. Or show jumping. Who knows?'

Frankie gnawed her lip in regret.

'It's a shame. All that ability, all that promise and now it's gone to waste.'

Jack gave her a sympathetic look.

'It hasn't gone to waste, Frankie. Just remember the good times.'

The tone of his voice made her look up abruptly. Something in his expression told her he wasn't talking about Virtuoso anymore. How could she remember the good times when they had all been a farce? She took a deep breath and gave him a brave smile.

'Sure.'

Jack patted her awkwardly on the shoulder.

'Right. Let's get a move on. You're due at Newton Abbott later and I'm off to Kempton and we've still got horses to work.'

Sunday lunch at her parents was rescheduled to dinnertime the next day after a full book of rides at Ffos Las. Frankie steeled herself as she walked in the door. She knew she must apologise to her father, but just the thought of Rhys's deception made her want to cry. She didn't want to cry in front of Doug.

He greeted her with wide arms and an even wider grin on his face.

'Hello, honey. How's my favourite Festival-winning daughter?'

A rush of pride warmed her blood. At last. She'd made him proud.

'Okay, thanks,' she said as a matter of habit. She hugged him tight.

'Darling!' Vanessa said, appearing from the hall. 'I didn't hear you come in. Congratulations!'

'Thanks,' she replied, transferring her hug to her mother.

'Where did you disappear to after the race though? We wanted to congratulate you.'

'She was probably at the Festival after-party. Am I right?'

Frankie looked down at her trainers.

'No, I went home. I was tired,' she mumbled.

'I'm not surprised,' chortled Doug. 'Bold Phoenix certainly made you work for your money. An inspired ride though, beautifully timed. Such a clever girl!'

Hearing Doug's praise made Frankie's cheeks burn more. If he was this proud over a Cheltenham winner – and not even one of the more prestigious Festival races – then how proud would he have been if she'd kept the ride on Peace Offering and ridden *him* to victory?

She twisted her fingers together, summoning the courage to apologise.

'Can we sit down?' she said.

Doug laughed and waved her over to the sofa.

'You can't still be that tired.'

'No, not quite. There's something else I need to tell you,' she said, sinking into the sofa and dumping her handbag at her feet.

Hearing the seriousness in her tone, her parents both sat and looked at her with concern.

'What is it, darling?' Vanessa said gently.

'I owe Dad an apology – both of you, really.'

'What for?'

Frankie opened her mouth to speak and felt a familiar wave of emotion rise up again. She swallowed hard.

'Rhys and I broke up,' she said in a stilted voice.

'Oh, Frankie,' Vanessa said sympathetically.

Frankie looked at Doug and her eyes filled.

'You were right, Dad. I'm sorry, I should've listened. You were right about him.'

Doug stiffened.

'What did he do to you?'

It hurt to even think about it; the pain was still so fresh.

'I found out on Friday that - that what we... *shared* hadn't meant the same thing to him as it did to me. It was all a ruse to make me give him the National ride on Peace Offering.'

'I knew it!' muttered Doug. 'The son of a bitch.'

'I'm sorry, Dad.' She hung her head. 'You told me right from the start that he was up to no good. I didn't listen. He-he played me so well. He saw that I was a fool and he took advantage of it.'

'Darling,' Vanessa said reaching out her hand to squeeze Frankie's knee. 'You mustn't blame yourself.'

Frankie's gaze flickered between her parents. In contrast to Vanessa's sympathy, Doug's face was turning purple with anger.

'You know,' he said through gritted teeth, 'I was even beginning to doubt myself. That maybe I was overreacting, living in the past, but now...'

'I know. I'm so sorry.'

Doug shook his head and gave a cheerless laugh.

'It's like history repeating itself all over again.' He looked at Frankie helplessly. 'What is it about those Bradfords that makes us sacrifice our own?'

Frankie sighed.

'An incredible power of persuasion? Manipulation? I don't know. He never asked me outright that I give him the ride, but it was in everything he did, everything he said. He made me think he deserved it more than I did. Even when I told him Peace Offering was his to ride, he still played along, tried to refuse it.' Frankie's voice faltered. 'He said that he'd win it for me, that he loved me.'

'And all the while I bet he was congratulating himself,' Doug sneered. 'Useless pile of shit. Are you going to try get the ride back?'

Frankie shrugged, feeling hopeless.

'How can I? The National's only three weeks away. Rhys has ridden Peace Offering in just about all of his prep races. I couldn't ask Pippa and Jack to change everything back just because he's an arsehole, especially not at this late stage.'

Doug sucked his teeth and looked across the room to the mantelpiece. Frankie squeezed her eyes shut. She could imagine his thoughts, how Seth would never have been so foolish.

'I'm sorry I let you down, Dad,' she said in a small voice.

'What?' Doug's eyes flashed back to her, but she couldn't hold his gaze.

'I know how much the National means to you. I wanted to ride in it - to win it for you. I wanted to make you proud. I -'

'What are you talking about, Frankie?'

Frankie couldn't help herself. She burst into tears, overcome by shame and humiliation.

'I know I'll never measure up to Seth. I'll never be as good a jockey as he was.'

'Don't say that.'

'But it's true. You were always so proud of him. Nothing I could do could compare. So I thought by winning the National you'd be proud -'

'But I am proud of you!'

Frankie looked at him helplessly.

'But how can you be? Every time I have the opportunity to win a big race I fall flat on my face. I know you're just trying to make me feel better, but I can see it, Dad. When I got the job at Aspen Valley, when Pippa gave me the ride on Peace Offering, you hardly even acknowledged those things.'

'Frankie -'

'I didn't know what else to do to make you proud. Then I kept messing things up. Every time you came to watch me race I either made a complete hash of things or ended up in hospital. Then Peace Offering didn't take to me, Rhys was working his magic on me. I just despaired. And I was angry at you because you wouldn't accept Rhys so I gave up the one thing which I knew would make you proud. I -'

'Frankie! Stop!' Doug exclaimed.

Frankie halted mid-blub.

Doug got up and kneeled in front of her. He mopped her wet cheeks with his handkerchief then took her hands in his.

'Frankie, honey. I am proud of you. Not because of what you do or how many races you win, but of who you are.'

Her eyes stung as she looked up at him.

'But why?'

'You're a good person. You're generous, kind, helpful. How could I not be proud of you?'

Frankie crumpled again and she clenched her fingers in his.

'Then why have you always made me feel second best to Seth?'

'I never meant to make you feel that way.'

'Of course I felt that way. Look around, Dad. Why are there photos everywhere of Seth and none of me? They're everywhere! Seth winning this, Seth winning that. I'm invisible.'

Doug looked at the mantelpiece with a new sadness.

'Oh, Frankie. I'm sorry. We never thought you'd see it like that.' He sighed. 'I suppose we surround ourselves with photos of Seth because it's all we have left of him. Whereas, I guess with you here, living, breathing, there was never any need to remind ourselves. I could be proud of you in the moment, so to speak.'

A bitterness seeped into her mouth and she scowled at her father.

'Then why haven't you ever told me? Why haven't you ever shown it?'

Doug hesitated, summoning the courage to continue the conversation.

'After what happened to Seth, I was just so scared of losing you too. I thought that if I didn't encourage you then maybe you wouldn't want to be a jockey. It wasn't because I wasn't interested. I just didn't want the same thing happening to you as it did Seth.' His voice cracked and he bit his lips together.

Frankie stared at him, her mouth agape. She really did need to work on her people-reading skills.

'You mean that? You don't want me to ride? Why've you never said anything?'

Frankie was distracted from her father's anguished face by her mother leaning forward beside her.

'Your father and I never wanted to stand in the way of what you wanted to do with your life,' Vanessa said. 'We'd never have forbidden you from your chosen career – well, except if you'd wanted to be a hooker or a drug dealer. It's your life. It isn't for us to say how you should live it.'

Frankie looked at her, dumbstruck.

'Seriously?' was all she could muster.

'Yes,' Doug sniffed.

Frankie looked back at her father.

'You don't want me to ride?'

'I know you love to ride, Frankie. I wouldn't ask you to quit, but racing is just so dangerous. You could be killed. I don't know what I'd do if you were – were –'

Frankie looked away distractedly. What was happening? What was she doing? She remembered that night snuggled in Rhys's bed when he'd asked her what she dreamed about and she'd answered making her father proud. The only way she'd ever considered this possible was by winning races. Yet now, in contrast, Doug was saying that he didn't want her to race-ride. She'd built an entire career on a delusion.

She looked back at him, feeling dazed. Her father's blue eyes searched hers desperately.

'I – I have to think about it. I don't know what else to say,' she stammered. 'Racing's my job. It's the only thing I know how to do.'

Vanessa patted her thigh and got to her feet.

'We can't ask for more than that. I'd better go check on the food.' She made a move to the kitchen then paused. She held up an inspired finger. 'On second thoughts, while I'm busy in the kitchen...' She trotted out of the room in the opposite direction to the kitchen.

Frankie and Doug looked at each other.

'What do you reckon she's up to?' Doug said.

'Beats me.'

A moment later, Vanessa reappeared with a stack of photo albums piled in her arms. She dumped them on the table beside Frankie.

'Here you are. I think now is a good opportunity for you two to catch up on some good times. Show Frankie the times you've been proud of her.'

Frankie opened the first album and gasped. Behind the laminate, a six-year-old Frankie sat in front of the Christmas tree; presents which were now old and tired looked sparkling and new. She flipped through the pages, gazing at the pictures which so often showed her on Doug's shoulders, of the two of them playing in the surf in Cornwall.

Doug grunted as he got off his knees and came and sat beside her. Frankie tore her eyes away from the pictures to look at him.

'Where've these been? I'd forgotten about these times.'

Already feeling cheerier, she giggled at the photo of herself and Seth burying Doug in beach sand, with ten-year-old Seth moulding two lumpy breasts onto his father's chest.

With Vanessa excusing herself to the kitchen, they sat together, reliving Frankie's childhood. Frankie felt Doug was being particularly brave about not baulking from the memories of Seth. She reached for the last album, dog-eared and more old-fashioned than the ones they'd already looked at. The photographs had long lost their sticky backs and were gathered haphazardly along the inner spine of the album. Frankie picked up one and snorted.

'You had a moustache, Dad?'

Doug took the photo and shook his head with a wry smile.

'God, this was a lifetime ago. I only had the moustache for a short while. Your mother fancied Tom Selleck so I grew it to impress her, but she didn't like it on me.'

Frankie giggled and flicked through the loose photos – photos of Doug riding racehorses, eighties hairstyles and superhero-esque shoulder pads. She studied a Polaroid of a young dark-haired Doug with his arm around an equally young good-looking blond man. They were sat in a pub and both held up pints of lager in a toast. Her interest piqued by the friend's good looks, she turned to her father.

'Who's this?'

Doug gave her a bemused look.

'Don't you know?'

Frankie looked closer. She mentally ran through all her far-flung uncles, but none of them matched the man in the photo.

'I don't think so. Should I?'

'It's Alan Bradford. Rhys's dad.'

She gasped. His hair was blond and straight and his face fuller, but with closer scrutiny, she recognised the man's crooked, teasing smile.

'My God,' she breathed. Her attention flickered to a woman to the right of the picture, standing behind the bar counter.

'Who's that?' she asked. 'Do I know her?'

'Wouldn't have thought so. She was gone long before you were born. That was Heidi.'

Frankie threw him a wary glance.

'Heidi, as in the one Rhys's dad was having an affair with?'

'Yup.' He shook his head with a heavy sigh. 'The one and the same.'

Frankie's reply was interrupted by her mobile bursting into song from her jeans pocket. She squirmed under her tray of photo albums to retrieve it. It was Tom.

'Hey, Tom. You okay?'

'Frankie. Thank God you answered,' Tom said breathlessly.

'What's wrong? Have you locked yourself out the house?'

'No. I'm inside. I've just got home. It's Atticus, Frankie. I think he needs to go to the vets.'

Frankie sat bolt upright.

'Atticus?'

'Yeah. He doesn't look well. I think there's something wrong with him.'

Panic swelled inside her.

'Like what? Is he vomiting? What?'

'No, he's just lying here like – like – I don't know. But he doesn't look good, Frankie.'

'Okay, I'm on my way.'

She cut the call with a trembling finger.

'It's Atticus. He's sick. I've got to get him to the vet.' She stood up in a rush, spilling the photo albums all over her bag and the floor. 'Oh!' Her knees shook as she scrabbled to pick up all the loose photos.

'Leave it, honey. Let me deal with this. You go on.'

'God, I'm sorry, Dad. Thanks.' She looped her bag over her shoulder and made for the door. 'Tell Mum I'm sorry.'

47

The surgery waiting room's deathly silence was punctuated by Atticus Finch's less than complimentary yowls as Frankie and Tom waited to be called.

'He's not sounding pleased,' she said, peering into the cat carrier.

Atticus glared at her with yellow eyes.

'Let's hope his vocalising's a good sign then,' Tom replied.

A door opened and Mr Warnock, Aspen Valley's regular vet, stepped out.

'Atticus Finch?'

Frankie leapt to her feet and grabbed Atticus's carrier.

'I'll wait here for you,' Tom said, picking up a *Your Pet* magazine and making himself comfortable.

Mr Warnock smiled at Frankie and stepped aside to let her into the examination room.

'Hello, Frankie. Not often I see you outside the yard.'

'Thankfully,' Frankie said, lifting the cat carrier onto the table. Realising how that sounded she clapped her hand over her mouth. 'Sorry, I didn't mean it like that.'

Mr Warnock laughed.

'I know what you meant. Now what's the problem with Atticus Finch?'

'We're not entirely sure. Tom came home tonight and found him lying in the kitchen, yowling like he was in pain. He's not the liveliest cat, but he's acting more lethargic than usual. And he's fifteen years old so we thought it best to have him checked out.'

'Quite right,' Mr Warnock said, unclipping the carrier and extracting a rigidly reluctant Atticus.

Chewing her lips, Frankie watched as the vet's gentle hands prodded and probed the elderly cat. He lifted him onto a weighing tray then checked his teeth.

'He's got a good set of gnashers for his age. What's his appetite like?'

'Very healthy. He's always hungry.'

'Hmm. Well, he's a little underweight. Worming up to date?'

Frankie nodded. Atticus scowled as the vet probed his intestines.

'...Feels like he's got a stool waiting to pass. Okay, okay, old boy, I'll let you keep your dignity.' He took a thermometer and contrary to his words inserted it in Atticus's most undignified orifice. Atticus's eyes bulged at this violation. Frankie would have laughed if she hadn't been so concerned.

With temperature and heart rate checked, Mr Warnock gave Atticus a consolatory pat on the head.

'Well, there's nothing obviously wrong with him. It might just be that he's eaten something which he's struggling to pass. It's not unusual for older cats to have digestive problems. But since he's as underweight as he is, I'd like to keep him in, do some blood tests. We'll have a much better idea of what might be troubling him after that. Do you have pet insurance?'

'Yes.'

'Jolly good. Just let Ali know at reception and give us a call on Thursday.'

'So he'll be okay?'

'I can't say for sure until we have the blood tests done, but he doesn't appear to be on his death bed. He might just be feeling a little lethargic like we all do sometimes. Nothing to worry about, I'm sure.'

Relief that Atticus wasn't on the last of his nine lives flooded through her.

'Oh, thank God.' She fondled Atticus's bony back, but thought better of the kiss she was about to drop on his head. He looked about as thrilled as a turkey on Christmas Eve.

The house felt empty without the arthritic bag of grey fur wandering around and Frankie plonked down at the kitchen table and stared glumly at the opposite wall.

'He'll be okay,' Tom said. 'I probably over-reacted by calling you like I did.'

Frankie gave him a grateful smile.

'I'm glad you did. Thank you.'

'Don't mention it. You had anything to eat?'

She shook her head.

'I'm not hungry.'

Tom extracted a tin of chocolate digestives and came to sit opposite her. Frankie closed her eyes, shutting out the image of the creamy chocolate biscuits, but her mouth still watered.

'How did it go at your folks'?' he mumbled through a mouthful of crumbs.

'I told them,' she shrugged. 'Dad wasn't best pleased, as you can imagine.'

'Should Rhys think about getting police protection?'

Frankie gave a half-hearted laugh. It would be a good long while before she could make jokes about Rhys.

'Nah. In a way, it turned out to be quite a good evening. Well, maybe not *good*,' she said when Tom raised an eyebrow. 'Productive, more like. I learnt a few things about Dad that I didn't know before.'

'Oh?'

'Yeah. I discovered he doesn't really want me to be a jockey.'

Tom spat out biscuit crumbs.

'What?'

Frankie raised a wry smile.

'I know. Ironic, wouldn't you say? I spend my time trying to impress him by becoming a jockey, while all the time he wanted me to quit.'

'Why did he never say anything?'

'Mum and Dad have always been very good about letting me choose my own path. They thought this was what I wanted.'

'And is it?'

Frankie lifted her hands in a gesture of defeat.

'I don't know. Honestly, I really don't. I mean it just seems that all my goals, all my ambitions have suddenly disintegrated.'

'Are you considering quitting?'

She grimaced, her loyalties torn.

'I don't want to quit Aspen Valley,' she said. 'I love it there – well, I did until me and Rhys split. It's all a bit egg-shelly now.'

'But the racing side of things? Come on, Frankie, do you really enjoy it that much?'

Frankie wrinkled her nose. She watched Tom munch through another biscuit.

'Probably not as much as I should. But I couldn't quit. How could I do that to Jack? He's done so much for me this season. I'd look so ungrateful if I just jacked it all in after only one season.'

'I'm sure he'd appreciate it a lot more if he knew he had a jockey who actually wanted to be a jockey.'

Frankie sighed. Her thoughts turned to Ta' Qali and Dory, Bold Phoenix and Asante, all the horses at Aspen Valley that she'd grown so attached to.

'I don't want to leave though. I do love Aspen Valley. And I love working with the horses. But what if Jack decides he doesn't want another work rider, that it's this or nothing? Then there's Rhys and... I don't know. It's too complicated.'

Tom shrugged.

'It looks pretty simple from where I'm sitting. You could work as a groom and exercise rider. That's the stuff you enjoy doing. What's so great about being a jockey anyway? You put yourself in the line of fire, risk death and injury, starve yourself, make yourself ill. And for what? Just another winner. And since you're an amateur you don't even get any prize money.'

'And I'm not even that competitive.'

'Exactly. The only reason you've stayed in the game this long is because you thought this was what your dad wanted. Now he's given you a get-out clause, what's stopping you from doing what you really want to do?'

Frankie paused to think. She scratched at the table with a dirty fingernail.

'Nothing, I guess. Apart from disappointing Jack and forever being in danger of running into Rhys.'

'Hey, if it was an easy job everyone would be doing it.'

Frankie smiled, meagrely reassured.

'Yeah, you're right. I - I'll think about it. I'm not going to make any drastic decisions now. Not with so much going on. I might end up regretting it.'

Tom slid the biscuit tin across the table to her.

'Go on,' he whispered. 'Take that first step.'

She eyed the biscuits and swallowed. She licked her lips. Gingerly, she reached forward and picked up the top biscuit. She bit into it. She closed her eyes at the explosion of flavour in her mouth and moaned. Tom laughed. Frankie opened one eye and wagged a finger at him.

'You're a bad influence on me, Tom Moxley.'

'Rubbish. See me as your guiding light instead.'

Frankie snorted and reached for a second biscuit.

48

Tom might have claimed to be her guiding light, but come Wednesday, as she walked away from Haydock Park's winner's enclosure with her saddle looped over her arm, Frankie was beginning to wonder if there wasn't some greater force at work. A television crew loitered outside the weigh-in steps and the presenter, Sarah Swann, was quick to stop her.

'Frankie! Well done on Blue Jean Baby back there. You must be pleased with the way she reversed the form with Faulkner. Can we have your thoughts on the race?'

Frankie paused. Was she allowed to say that the only thought going through her head all the way up to the line was that she'd beaten Rhys?

'I let Blue Jean Baby down when I rode her on New Year's Day, so yes, I'm very pleased that she got to show her class today,' she said instead. 'She handled the soft going very well and hardly put a foot wrong the whole way round.'

Sarah nodded in eager agreement.

'It's very modest of you to give her all the credit when your form since Cheltenham has been inspired. This is your fifth win in how many rides?'

Frankie shifted her saddle to her other arm uncomfortably.

'Nine if you include Bold Phoenix.'

'We certainly are. Bold Phoenix was your one and only ride at the Festival and I'm sure viewers don't need to be reminded of the terrific victory you enjoyed on Gold Cup Day. It strikes me that your partnership with Aspen Valley has really taken off. Jack Carmichael must also be very pleased.'

Frankie eyed the doorway and edged towards it. She really didn't want to discuss her job at Aspen Valley. For fear of being sacked on the spot, she still hadn't told Jack of her plans to quit as amateur jockey. She tensed when, in the fading light of the early spring day, she saw Rhys returning from his runner-up ride. Sarah Swann's face lit up when she too saw him and she beckoned him over.

'Rhys, do you mind having a quick word with us?'

Frankie tried to make a quick exit but Sarah (out of camera shot) closed her hand over her arm in a vice-like grip. Rhys reluctantly stopped and he and Frankie exchanged guarded glares. Sarah beamed at the camera.

'I'm here talking to two of Aspen Valley Stables' retained jockeys, Frankie Cooper and Rhys Bradford – a great team if the last race is anything to go by. They are also the most familiar with the Grand National favourite, Peace Offering.' She turned to address Rhys. 'With the big race just a few short weeks away, can you tell us how he's doing?'

'He's okay,' Rhys mumbled.

'And how do you rate his chances over the Aintree fences?'

Frankie bit her lip. She'd had dentist appointments more enjoyable than this.

'He's been working well at home,' Rhys said, keeping a wary eye on her. 'He's got as good a chance as any.'

'That's very reassuring for the punters at home to hear, I'm sure. Now, I must ask: Frankie, it was a pleasant if unexpected turn of events when you were given the ride on Peace Offering back in October. Yet only a month ago, we were told that another switch had been made and now Rhys is back aboard. What prompted this late jockey change?'

Even though the question was directed at her, Frankie raised an eyebrow at Rhys. He could talk his way out of this one.

Rhys swallowed and his eyes flittered guiltily away from hers.

'The decision was made in Peace Offering's best interests.' He licked his lips nervously and sent Frankie a wary glance. 'Frankie very generously gave up the ride so he could have the best possible chance of winning. Frankie's a very good jockey but I have more experience over the National fences. And while a certain amount of luck is involved in the race, experience can come in handy.'

Frankie ground her teeth, so tempted to turn their interview into a soap-opera. She was speechless that he had the gall to stand there, live on television, and say nothing but his superior skill had anything to do with her decision.

'And now that you seem to have struck form-gold, Frankie, are you having any second thoughts?' joked Sarah. 'Being the first woman to win the Grand National would write your name well and truly into the history books.'

She heard Rhys hold his breath. She measured her own with control.

'It's too late now for second thoughts,' she replied. She gave Rhys an evil smile. 'Don't you agree?'

Rhys opened his mouth to reply but nothing came out. Sarah Swann looked at them, confused.

'Well, as Rhys said, it was very generous and unselfish of you to make the sacrifice. And while I'm certain you would love to win the National, I'm sure Rhys would too. And since you're a couple, it shouldn't really be any surprise that you would be willing to compromise for the sake of your other half's happiness.'

Rhys shot Frankie a warning look, but Frankie had had enough.

'We're not a couple anymore,' she said flatly. She nodded a farewell to the camera and at Sarah. 'Excuse me.'

Walking into the warmth of the building, Frankie heard the presenter trying to regather her interview. She hoped Rhys was squirming in his boots.

49

Perhaps because of Frankie's streak of good fortune on the racecourse, Jack was more accommodating when she approached him the next morning to remind him of her Girl Guides GFI Animal Active that he'd promised to host.

'Okay, just so long as they don't run around like hooligans. God forbid. I don't know how good I'd be at giving a talk, but June has said she'll help out.'

Understanding how far out on a limb he was going, she grinned.

'Thank you. And you never know. Some of them might be so impressed they'll be asking for a job in a few years' time.'

'As flattered as I am, we're not short of staff, Frankie. The CV pile is about as high as Becher's Brook. Just – just keep them under control.'

Now the following week, and with all her duties completed by a quarter to six, she waited at the yard entrance for the troops to arrive. June came over to join her.

'Thanks for staying on and helping out tonight,' Frankie said.

'My pleasure. I've nothing else to do. No man to rush home to look after,' she said with a wink.

Frankie replied with a half-smile, suddenly reminded of how June had once had a man in her life. Perhaps not one she could rush home to, but a man nonetheless.

'We watched Bold Phoenix's race on TV,' June went on. She paused before continuing. 'Seth would've been proud.'

'Thanks.' Frankie turned away to search the dusk for headlights. The main road at the bottom of the hill lay dark and undisturbed. Would Seth have been proud? Or would he have been worried sick like Doug always was? Would it have been different if Seth was still alive?

'And I-I'm sorry to hear about you and Rhys,' June said hesitantly. 'It can't be easy.'

Frankie snapped back to attention.

'Er – yeah. Um, it's not.'

'If you ever need anyone to talk to...' June's voice faded and she dropped her gaze. 'I know what it's like to bottle things up.'

Frankie looked at her with a newfound sympathy. She might be mourning the loss of Rhys, but at least he wasn't dead, and at least she had friends and family that she could talk to. June had had none of that when Seth had died.

'I know about you and Seth,' she said gently.

June looked up sharply.

'What?'

'I know you and Seth were having a – *thing*.'

June's eyes were wide, glistening in the darkness.

'You don't hate me for it?'

Frankie shook her head with a small chuckle.

'On the contrary. It allowed me to realise Seth wasn't perfect. It was a bit of a relief in a way.'

'How did you find out though? Nobody knew.'

A wave of sadness broke over her. That night Rhys had told her, he'd sounded so genuine, that he'd had her best interests at heart. Obviously, it had just been another ploy to break her confidence and doubt herself.

'It doesn't matter. But, you know –' Frankie shifted awkwardly, '– if you ever want to talk about him, you can come to me. I don't mind. In fact, it'd be quite nice to talk about him. My parents don't like talking about him so much.'

June gave her an uncertain smile.

'Um, thanks. That'd be nice.' She gave a small laugh. 'He always spoke about you, you know.'

An inner warmth dissipated the chilled night air.

'He did?'

'Yes. He used to tell me how talented a rider you were. The pony that you shared – Toffee, was that it?'

'That's right.'

'Yeah, he told me how you were the one who put in all the hard work schooling her and he felt bad that he was the one that used to take her to shows and collect all the prizes. He said you never got the plaudits you deserved.'

Frankie smiled at his memory, vaguely aware of two sets of headlights now bouncing up Aspen Valley's long driveway.

'I didn't mind,' she said.

The two minivans crunched to a stop in the gravelled car park and June shifted off the wall she'd been leaning against.

'He was proud of you, you know.' She took her hands out of her pockets and rubbed them together to generate some warmth. 'Now, I take it these are your Girl Guides, are they?'

Dusk turned to night unnoticed as Frankie and June led the twenty girls around the stables, explaining to them the differences between feeds and haylage and the nutrients in each source. Under the glare of a security light, June led Peace Offering out of his stable for the girls to pat. Being one of the quieter horses in the yard, it was a bonus that he was also their Grand National hope.

'Peace Offering nearly won it last year,' Frankie said. 'Just like you have favourite places to hang out, horses sometimes have favourite courses, and Peace Offering really sparkles at Aintree.'

'Like Edward Cullen in *Twilight* sparkles when the sun shines on him?' Charlotte piped up.

Frankie took a patient breath.

'No, Charlotte. Not quite.'

'Has anyone heard the expression "No foot, no hoss"?' June said, stepping forward. 'That's because if a horse has sore feet he can't run fast.' She ran her hand down Peace Offering's shoulder and down his leg. He lifted his foot obligingly. 'Although his hoof looks hard on the outside, it's soft on the inside and this cushiony bit here is called the frog.'

A chorus of 'eurghs' greeted this and the girls crowded round to see Peace Offering's foot. Frankie grinned, pleased with their curiosity. Her smile faded though when she took the time to consider what she'd given up. Was she that upset that she was no longer going to ride the Grand National favourite? Honestly, no, she wasn't. As she got her head round this, her anger towards Rhys quietened. Yes, he'd conned her out of the ride, but since it wasn't something she'd wanted as bad as all that, she felt the resentment she'd been harbouring quell. Could she forgive him? Frankie turned away from Peace Offering with a sigh. Rhys had still betrayed her, and that she couldn't quite get over.

Half an hour later, June was leading the tour around the remainder of the yard. Frankie walked at the rear, making sure no stragglers wandered off. In the darkness though, she almost missed Cassa Preston stopping outside Ta' Qali's stable. The gelding had his head over the door, his ears pricked forward at the little people.

'Hey, Cassa.'

Cassa stopped stroking Ta' Qali's cheek.

'Hi.'

'I see you've made friends with Ta' Qali. He's one of my horses that I have to look after every day.'

'He's so soft,' she murmured. 'Is he a nice horse?'

Frankie threw the question from side to side in her mind.

'Yes and no. He's a lovely horse here at home, but he – he gets stage fright when he goes racing, so he doesn't always do very well.'

'I know how he feels.'

'But you still love to be on stage, don't you?'

'I love to sing,' Cassa said simply. 'Does he love to gallop?'

'It's hard to say,' Frankie considered. 'He's very good at it here at home so I guess he enjoys it.'

'How did he get hurt?'

'He hasn't hurt himself, has he?' she said, peering closer at the horse.

Ta' Qali waffled Cassa's palm, enjoying her soft fingers on his lips.

'Here, on his nose. He has a scar.'

'Oh, that,' Frankie said with a wave of her hand. 'That's just a marking. Horses can have all sorts of markings.'

Cassa sunk into silence and Frankie sighed.

'I'm sorry about the singing competition, Cassa. It was just too risky. You must see that, don't you?'

'I guess so,' she said with a shrug. 'It-it's just that when I sing, I forget everything else. It makes me feel happy. Not like happy when Mum takes me places, but something deeper – I don't know how to explain it. And at the competition, there were people there that I could tell were happy too when I sang.'

Frankie squeezed Cassa's shoulder.

'You do make people happy when you sing. And it might not seem it now, but soon you'll be old enough to do what you want and if you want to sing then that's what you should do.'

'But Mum thinks it's a bad thing. Not my voice, she says my voice is quite good, but she says the people in the music business are bad, that there's too much drugs and stuff going on.'

'Well, she's probably not wrong,' Frankie said, her loyalties tilting. 'Have you asked your mum if you can be a singer?'

'No. But it's obvious she doesn't want me to be one. She wants me to be a nurse, like her.'

'Has she told you this?'

'Well, no. But I can tell.' Cassa turned back to Ta' Qali as he nuzzled her pockets. 'She's always dropping hints and telling me I should start doing voluntary work because it looks good on a CV.'

'You're a bit young to be thinking about CVs, aren't you?'

'Mum says you're never too young to help people.'

'I suppose so,' Frankie said grudgingly. 'But even though it seems clear as daylight that she wants you to be a nurse or a doctor, maybe you should talk to her about it. I had the same thing with my dad only recently and we found out that we were completely off-track when it came to knowing what each of us wanted.'

'Really?'

'Yes, really.'

Cassa twisted her mouth into a reluctant smile.

'I'll see.'

50

Newbury Racecourse played host to Frankie's attention the next afternoon. Rhys would be there with a full book of rides. For once, Tom wasn't busy and Frankie sent a glare in Donnie's direction.

'You're cutting it fine,' Tom said as she passed.

'Trying to spend as little time in this company as I can,' she replied, keeping a guarded eye on Rhys.

'You're not the only one,' Tom replied.

Frankie sent him a quizzical frown.

'The boys haven't really taken to my new image,' he explained in a muted voice. 'A few of them have dumped my valeting services.'

'Oh, for God's sake. Really? Let me guess. Donnie's one of them.'

'He was the first,' he nodded. 'Now a bunch of the other, younger guys have changed valets.'

'Bunch of homophobes,' growled Frankie.

Tom shrugged.

'They're just following Donnie's lead. With him being one of the top jocks, they're impressionable. I doubt whether most of them are actually homophobes.'

'How has Rhys reacted to you coming out?'

'In his usual way. He's kept himself to himself. Hasn't condemned me or the others. I guess he's got other things on his mind.'

She longed to ask him if Rhys had asked about her, but knew she couldn't. She couldn't make everything about herself. The searching look Tom sent her made her drop her gaze for a brief moment.

'You're right,' she said, lifting her chin. 'He's riding in the Grand National in a couple of weeks' time. He's got plenty to think about.'

'And so do you. Come on. Get your skates on, Frankie. I've just got to get this helmet to Rhys. He got a hoof through the last one in the first.'

Frankie pulled up sharp.

'Is he okay?'

Tom raised an eyebrow.

'He's fine. Or rather he says he is. You can never really tell since he hardly says anything to anyone.'

'Ain't that the truth,' Frankie scoffed.

Out in the spring air, Jack waited for her and Rhys to join him. Frankie kept her head down and avoided Rhys's eye. Instructions were brief and Jack legged her up onto Media Star. Jogging out onto the course, she was about to breathe a sigh of relief when Rhys appeared at her flank. She pushed her mount into canter and stood up in her stirrups.

'Is this how it's going to be?' Rhys growled, keeping pace.

She pushed Media Star faster.

'How long are you going to keep ignoring this?' He stuck like a bramble to her side.

'Go away, Rhys,' she managed to mutter. 'This is neither the time nor the place.'

'Well, when is the time and where is the place?'

She turned swiftly in her saddle to glare at him.

'I don't know. Okay? All I know is that I don't want to talk to you.' Media Star quickened his pace.

'But I want to talk to you,' Rhys snarled.

Recognising the impatience in his tone, she shook her head.

'What for, Rhys? What would be the point? You've admitted to using me to get Peace Offering. You've got what you wanted. Now bloody well leave me alone.'

'You haven't let me explain though!'

'Explain?' she spluttered. 'Explain the finite details of how you slept with me, lied to me, made me look like a fool? Excuse me for not wanting to know.'

She kicked Media Star on, not caring that he was travelling faster than was sensible down to the start. Rhys didn't attempt to follow.

51

Frankie's ear was still burning when she arrived at the veterinary surgery that evening. Thanks to her tearaway warm-up prior to Media Star's race, her mount had arrived at the start in a muck sweat, had fought her throughout the race and she'd pulled him up exhausted before the end.

Atticus Finch greeted her with loud indignant yowls through the cage door of his carrier.

'How is he?' she asked Mr Warnock, hope mingling with trepidation.

'Well, the good news is that what was troubling him in the first place appears to have been just a case of constipation. He's pooing just fine now.'

'Oh, that's a relief,' she breathed.

'The bad news, however,' Mr Warnock said, making her stomach muscles clench, 'is that the blood tests showed up a bit of a problem with his thyroid.'

Frankie stared at him.

'Wh-what does that mean?'

'It means his thyroid isn't working as well as it should be. It's not uncommon in older cats and it might explain why he's always so hungry yet doesn't put on any weight.'

Frankie's gaze flickered from the vet to Atticus who was vainly trying to claw his way out of the carrier.

'I-I thought he was just getting old and senile,' she stammered. 'I didn't think it was anything serious.'

'Well, it doesn't have to be serious. To look on the positive side, we seem to have caught it quite early. The negative is that he'll need an operation.'

'An operation? Oh, God. Can he still have an operation at his age?'

Mr Warnock smiled sympathetically.

'There's always a risk involved, especially with older animals, but it is the recommended treatment.'

'Is there an alternative? Like medication or something?'

'I'm afraid not. Operating is the only option we have. Otherwise he's very healthy and there's no reason, if everything goes smoothly, that he shouldn't be around for a good few more years.'

Atticus meowed and Frankie poked her fingers through the carrier to scratch him under his chin.

'Poor old boy. I guess if you think an operation is the way to go then we have to do it. When would he have to have it?'

'As soon as possible. I'd be inclined to keep him here and do it on Saturday. That's the earliest we can schedule it for.'

Frankie gulped. She'd been so looking forward to taking him home tonight.

'Okay, I guess.'

'We'll schedule it for Saturday morning then. You've made the right decision.'

'Yes,' she replied weakly. 'I know.'

Atticus wailed as she walked away and she turned back. 'I'm sorry, Atticus. We'll make you better, I promise.'

The Golden Miller was quiet when Frankie walked in an hour later. Tom was sitting in his corner of the bar watching Joey serve customers. She wandered over to him and hoisted herself onto a neighbouring barstool.

'Hey.'

'Hey yourself. How did it go at the vets?'

'They're keeping Atticus there. He needs an operation on his thyroid.'

'Christ. Is he going to be okay?' he said, wiping beer froth from his top lip.

'Mr Warnock was pretty confident he would be. Fingers crossed anyway.'

Joey walked over, having finished serving his other customer.

'Evenin', Frankie,' he said with a wide smile. 'What can I get you?'

She was about to answer when the opening of the pub's doors distracted her. Rhys stopped in his tracks in the entrance as he too saw her. Frankie's heart stopped. Like a masochist, she couldn't drag her eyes away from him. Drinking in his haunted dark eyes and masonic features, she was filled with the pain of the betrayed mixed in a heady cocktail of pleasure at his presence. Rhys's lips tautened, his fists looked to tremble and he spun on his heel and strode out of the pub.

Frankie sucked in a lungful of beer-stale air. He'd walked away. Frankie's heart sank even lower. Before she'd had a vague sense of meaning something to him, even if it was just her forgiveness that he'd wanted. Yet now, it seemed he didn't even want that. An empty pit inside her yearned to feel needed, to feel wanted by him. Even now. Even after all he'd done to her.

Joey clicked his fingers in front of her face and she blinked back to the present.

'You want a drink, Frankie?'

She'd only been planning a single drink to take the sting out of Mr Warnock's verdict, but now she felt the need for something more.

'A double vodka and orange, please.'

'Coming up.' He deftly measured her drink and placed it on the bar for her. 'Hey, Frankie. I've decided to see what this racing lark is all about. I'm going racing at Warwick this weekend. Got any tips?'

'Don't ask me, Joey. I couldn't tip a wheelbarrow.' She downed half the glass in one go.

'Blimey, you look like you needed that,' he said, resting a languid elbow on the counter.

Suddenly, getting completely shit-faced seemed a very attractive idea to Frankie. Just for one night, she could numb her brain from the complications in her life.

'Can I start a tab?'

'Sure you can.'

'What are you doing, Frankie?' Tom shook his head.

'Dealing with things.'

'With alcohol? Come on, it's not going to solve anything.'

'Hey,' Joey said, teasing a finger at him. 'My livelihood depends on her solving her problems through alcohol. Let her do it if she wants to.'

'And if I start to make a fool of myself then I've got you two to stop me.'

Joey raised his hands and looked around.

'Honey, there's no one here for you to make a fool of yourself in front of.'

Taking another large gulp of her drink, she followed Joey's gesture. In the ever so slightly tilting room, she noticed for the first time just how empty the pub was. She hadn't seen it this sparse since before Christmas.

'Where is everyone?'

'We've got a mutiny going,' Joey replied. 'It's the singing contest final next week and we've just had one disaster after another. First, your lovely friend Cassa pulled out, now the one of the other three finalists has decided to go on holiday next week. We're having to invite back that guy who Cassa beat last time round.'

'That's a bit shit.'

'Tell me about it. If he sings another Chris de Burgh song, I'm going to hang myself. Loads of people turned up last time to see Cassa and I think they're still a bit sore that she didn't pitch. She was everyone's favourite.'

'What a shame. She really wanted to sing, it's a pity she can't come back for the final, but I guess that's life.'

'*C'est la vie*, as I always say,' Joey said. 'Can I get you another?'

She gave him a grateful smile and nodded.

'What's the story with Cassa, anyhow?' Tom said.

Frankie shrugged. What did it matter now?

'She wasn't meant to be singing. She was underage.'

Tom choked on his beer.

'Seriously?'

'Yup, and her mother didn't know she was competing.'

'Jesus Christ, Frankie!'

Joey returned with a fresh double vodka and orange and looked curiously at Tom's expression.

'What have I missed?'

'That girl, Cassa,' Tom spluttered. 'Frankie was sneaking her in. How old is she really?'

'Thirteen.' Unabashed, she twirled the liquid around her glass, marvelling at how much easier it was making things. Confession wasn't half as difficult with a few units put away.

Joey tutted at her, still wearing a teasing smile. Frankie grinned.

'Sorry,' she said. 'It all got blown out of proportion a bit. But we don't have to worry anymore. She's out of the competition.'

Tom shook his head.

'Frankie, you're such a fraud.'

She paused, not drunk enough yet to have forgotten how she'd called Rhys a fraud. Wasn't what she'd done no better than what he'd done? Of course not, she told herself. She hadn't broken anyone's heart, and all she'd done was to let Cassa follow her dream.

Frankie shifted on her seat, uncomfortable with her thoughts. Tiny slurring voices kept popping into her head. She'd broken Cassa's heart – but it hadn't been her fault. If Mrs Preston hadn't pitched up, they would still probably be in the competition. What Rhys had done to her was selfish and wrong.

But hadn't her and Cassa's ploy also been that? Of course not, Cassa had sung for the right reasons. *You would think that though*, that annoying voice argued. *Rhys might be thinking the same thing*. Maybe the way he had gone about things hadn't been particularly righteous, but wasn't him riding Peace Offering in the Grand National the right decision? And given how desperate he was for the ride, how else could he have secured it other than by seducing her?

Frankie shook her head to clear it and glared at her half empty glass. Maybe she shouldn't take up alcoholism as an escape. She had a full-scale debate going on inside her head of which she was just a spectator.

'Cassa could still sing at the final,' Joey piped up.

Frankie and Tom both looked at him in surprise. The barman leaned forward on his elbows.

'As a special guest, like. That way people wouldn't be disappointed and she wouldn't be breaking any rules because she wouldn't be competing.'

'It's a nice idea, but there's her mother to think of,' Tom pointed out. 'She still doesn't know that Cassa was in the competition.'

'Oh, but we could so use the customers,' Joey grimaced. 'Can't you sneak her in just one more time?'

Frankie thought of Cassa's sullen demeanour these past few weeks. It would raise her spirits sky-high if Frankie told her the Golden Miller was asking for her to do a special performance. But of course, there were the risks involved. Mrs Preston would probably kill her if she found out. And that crazy mental debate she'd just had – if she was so right and Rhys was so wrong then surely going along with Joey's idea was just as fraudulent, if not worse?

'She's too young,' she said.

'Well, since the stage is in the restaurant area, which is also the family area, she wouldn't be.'

'But she's too young for the competition.'

Joey's smile sparkled.

'But she'd be a special guest, not a contestant. Come on, Frankie. Where's your sense of adventure?'

Frankie swayed, both mentally and literally.

'She would really love to come back,' she agreed.

'Who? Your sense of adventure or Cassa?'

'Both,' she grinned.

'I hate to put a dampener on your plan, but the final's barely a week away,' Tom said. 'How are you going to let everyone know that Cassa's going to be performing? All your usual customers are packed into The Plough so you can't even tell them when they come in.'

Joey's smile turned upside down and he slumped his face into his palm.

'Could we put it in the paper?'

'No!' Frankie cried. 'God, Mrs Preston would definitely find out if we did that.'

'Shall we sky-write it while Cassa's mother is at work?' Joey suggested.

Neither Tom nor Frankie bothered to answer.

'I guess she'd just have to show up on the night and we could hope that word of mouth gets round,' Tom said.

At Tom's words, a light pinged inside Frankie's brain. She pulled her mobile phone out of her pocket and dialled her mother's number.

'Who are you ringing?' Tom said.

Frankie held up a finger as the call connected.

'Hi Mum,' she said, grinning at Tom's confused expression. 'Just a quick question, is Valerie Banks coming in on Sunday for her usual hair appointment?'

52

With a rare Saturday off from the races, for once Frankie wished she had the distraction of race nerves to take her mind off Atticus's operation. After tipping her last bucket of evening feed into Dory's manger, she felt her mobile phone vibrate in her pocket. Her blood ran cold when she recognised the veterinary practice number on the screen. Did vets usually ring pet owners if an operation had gone well? Surely not. What would be the point? She'd find out this evening when she dropped in. Her finger trembled as she pressed Connect.

'Hello?' Her voice quivered and she cleared her throat, aware that she sounded like a victim in a horror film who answers the call from her murderer.

'Hello, Frankie?' Mr Warnock's deep gentle voice lent her little reassurance. Bad news was always broken with that sympathetic tone.

'Yes.'

'It's Mr Warnock from Helensvale Veterinary Practice. Are you free to talk?'

Frankie's stomach plummeted down to her boots into the straw bedding of Dory's stable.

'Yes.' She squeezed her eyes shut and clenched the bucket handle with her free hand. 'How did Atticus's surgery go?'

'Like clockwork. He's a little groggy from the anaesthetic, but I thought you'd like to know that it all went fine.'

Frankie exhaled and dropped the bucket.

'He's okay? Everything's fine?'

Mr Warnock chuckled.

'Yup. No problem whatsoever. He's got to wear a protective collar for a while, but he should be good to go home tomorrow.'

Frankie dissolved into relieved laughter.

'Oh God. Thank you. Oh, that's so good to hear. I thought you were ringing me up to tell me bad news.'

'Not at all. Aspen Valley Stables is a favourite of mine so I thought I'd ring just to let you know how it went.'

*

Frankie let herself out of Dory's stable still gushing her thanks. The racing lorry was just pulling up in the car park, brake lights aglow in the dim light of dusk. She walked across the yard to put away her bucket, but was intrigued to see an unfamiliar dark bay horse being led down the ramp. He skittered across the gravel, dragging Billy behind him. Preoccupied with the new arrival, she didn't notice the motorbike being dismounted nearby, nor did she register Rhys's presence until he had removed his helmet and begun limping in her direction.

Frankie shot into the nearest hideaway, the tack room. The smell of leather, horse sweat and saddle soap mixed in a heady cocktail for her to breathe in. She stood tense beneath the single electric bulb darting panicked looks around for more sheltered cover. Her gaze stopped on a pile of rugs beside a cabinet. Could she hide under those? What if someone else came in and found her? She'd look a right plonker. But she couldn't face Rhys now. What was he doing here? How long would she have to hide in here before she could make an escape?

She leapt out of her skin, overturning a line of saddles as the door was opened, and nearly gored herself on a bridle peg. Jack jumped back in fright.

'Jesus Christ, Frankie! What are you trying to do, give me a heart attack?'

'Sorry, I - I -' Her gaze flittered past her boss to the darkened yard beyond. Rhys was nowhere to be seen, but she wished Jack would close the door. Just in case.

Jack caught her looking over his shoulder and shook his head. He swung the door closed and walked over to the opposite wall to hang up the bridles he carried.

'He's having dinner with me and Pippa tonight,' he said.

Frankie blushed.

'Sorry, I wasn't expecting to see him, that's all.'

'You're going to have to at some point,' Jack said, not unkindly.

'I know. Just -' She cringed, hating that she was having this conversation with her boss. Not only her boss, but Jack Carmichael, champion trainer who would probably have the mob running scared if he chose. 'I just need time.'

Jack gave her a withering glance.

'Well, I might have something to distract you. We've just come from the sales. Picked up a couple of good looking novices for you to work on,' he said.

'That's great,' she replied brightly, trying to buck herself up.

'I probably shouldn't have got them both, what with Ta' Qali still under Aspen Valley's ownership, but fingers crossed he'll be sold by the end of the season.'

'Oh? Do you have a buyer?'

Jack shrugged.

'Maybe. A syndicate got in touch. Apparently they'd heard that he was Dexter's work companion, and with Dexter winning the Champion Hurdle, they were keen to find a bargain.'

'He'd certainly be that,' Frankie said. 'If we could only figure out how to get him to settle though.'

'Exactly. It's not a done deal by any means. They want to see him race again before they commit to the sale. And if he doesn't step up then I'm going to have pie on my face for buying too many novices.'

'Are the new ones total greenies or are they ex-flat horses too?'

'Both ex-flat. A filly by a Derby winner and a colt that doesn't have much going for him, but he looks like he could be something when he matures. We'll have him gelded soon enough though. He's a bit of a boy-o as he is. Needed one of those to lead him from the lorry to his stable,' he said, jabbing a thumb in the direction of a curb chain hanging from a peg.

Frankie frowned at the chain, noticing the short dark hairs pinched between its links. She hadn't had much experience using curb chains, but knew they were often used on boisterous, usually ungelded horses, looping over the bridge of their nose to allow the handler more control. It wasn't something she agreed with entirely, but if she were a colt and she had the choice of having one's knackers chopped off or a sore nose, she'd opt for the latter every time. Even if she was a woman. And speaking of balls...

She took a brave breath. She had to tell him of her plans.

'Jack, I - I can't continue as a jockey here.'

Jack's eyes nearly popped out of his skull.

'What?'

'This season has been a real wake-up call for me; the opportunity you've given me, the experience working the horses at home and also racing them. It's made me realise where I see myself career-wise.'

'You're quitting?'

'No, no! Well, kinda.' She grimaced. 'I mean I can't be a jockey *anywhere*, not just here. I thought I knew what I wanted in my life, but it turns out I didn't.'

Jack's frown deepened and his mouth set into a grim line.

'Do you know how many amateurs would kill for your job – how many are serious about their careers?'

'I know and I'm sorry. I didn't set out to mess you around. When you gave me the job, I seriously thought it was what I wanted.'

'So is that it? You said you weren't quitting. How is this not quitting?'

Suddenly, Frankie didn't feel quite so confident about Jack letting her change her job description.

'Well, I was sort of hoping that I could stay on working here. At the yard. This season I've learnt not only what I *don't* want to do, but also what I *do* want to do. And you letting me ride all of the novices has made me realise that is where I'm happiest – on the gallops, schooling the babies, bringing them on. I find it much more rewarding than riding in races.'

Jack's blue eyes darkened.

'And you just presumed that I can simply alter your job just like that?' he said, snapping his fingers.

Frankie quailed. She could tell saying yes would unleash Jack's inner dragon, but wasn't he right in thinking she was being presumptuous?

'Hopeful more than anything,' she said.

'Frankie, I'm not made of money. If you quit as jockey, I will have to replace you with another amateur, who will be expected to carry out the same stable duties as you've had. I know we employ plenty of staff here, but no one is superfluous. I'm sorry, but I'm not going to employ someone just for the hell of it.'

Panic began to form in Frankie's gut. This was not how things were meant to turn out. If she was honest with herself, she hadn't reckoned on it being a problem at all. Perhaps a temporary inconvenience, but certainly not a deal-breaker.

'But I can't leave here completely,' she cried.

'Well, you obviously don't want to be a jockey and there's not enough work to warrant keeping you on full-time as stable staff.' He shook his head. 'My God, Frankie, you haven't half fucked us around this season. First, you wanted the ride on Peace Offering, then you don't, then you get involved with Rhys, then you split. How can I trust that this isn't another thing which you're going to change your mind about in a few months' time?'

A flame of annoyance pinked her cheeks.

'I didn't mean to mess you around, Jack,' she said through clenched teeth. 'I'm not proud of my mistakes, but every decision was made to last. If you want to know why Rhys and I split, then you ask Rhys. And while you're at it, you can ask him why I gave up the ride on Peace Offering too. He certainly knows the answer to both of those.'

'Frankie, to be honest with you, I don't care. I don't care about the whys and what fors. All I know is that they've been a thorn in my side and now you're coming out with this nonsense about being a work rider instead of a jockey.' He regarded her for an angry moment. 'I don't owe you anything. Give me one good reason why I shouldn't fire you right now?'

The panic flooded to Frankie's feet at the mention of that dreaded word. God, why had she even opened her mouth to begin with? She should have compromised. Isn't that what everyone said life was about? She should have remained in her role as amateur jockey. At least then she'd be staying at Aspen Valley. How could she bear to leave this place? The set-up was so magnificent, traditional yet modern, relaxed yet efficient. She'd never been prouder of any job she'd had. She was a fool to have told Jack she wanted to quit. What about the horses? Ta' Qali and Dory, even that bugger Dusty Carpet whose day wasn't complete without throwing her off at least once. Faced with the threat of losing it all, she realised just how much the horses completed her too.

Jack still glared at her. Maybe that question hadn't been rhetorical. Maybe he was giving her a chance – if she could think of *one good reason*. Her eyes darted around the room as she tried to think of something, anything.

'Ta' Qali,' she blurted. 'That's why you should keep me on. Let me work with him. If I can find the key to unlock that potential then I'm worth keeping on, aren't I?'

'And how do you intend to "unlock" him? Not five minutes ago you were just as clueless as me.'

Her gaze alighted on the curb chain which Jack had hung up. An idea began to take shape in her mind and she swallowed the doubts that surrounded it.

'Just give me a few weeks. If I'm right about him then you'll probably end up getting the sale you wanted. Not only that, you'll probably also end up with a champion if his work at home is anything to go by. With Virtuoso retired now, you've really only got Dexter flying the flag for Aspen Valley. You're going to need your novices to step up. I'm good with them, you've said so yourself. Let me stay and bring on the youngsters.' She gestured outside. 'You've even got two more today which will need schooling.'

A muscle pulsed in Jack's jaw. Frankie could imagine his brain whirring through the possibilities, holding up her suggestions, tossing them into the fire.

'Please, Jack,' she whispered.

'There are riders who could be just as good bringing on the novices,' he said.

'Perhaps, but none of them have figured out Ta' Qali.'

'And neither have you, may I remind you.' He regarded her thoughtfully. 'Fine. But you've got two weeks. No more. We're taking him to Aintree. There's a decent novice hurdle earmarked for him.'

'On the Grand National card?' quailed Frankie.

'You said it yourself, Ta' Qali has the potential. If you manage to "unlock" him then that race should be a doddle for him. If he performs.'

Frankie swallowed. Jack was no push over, that was for certain.

'And if he doesn't?'

'Then you're out. Deal?'

It might not be very secure, but it was a lifeline. She had to have faith. She nodded.

'Deal.'

'We're not going to mention this to anybody right now, okay? And I mean no one. I don't want any more press stress with the National in just a fortnight. You're to stay on as amateur jockey until the end of the season. And now, I'm going home. I'm late and I'm hungry.'

Frankie sunk back against the wall as Jack strode out of the room. She closed her eyes and prayed, really prayed that her theory would prove not as whimsical as it sounded in her head.

53

Rhys's absence from Frankie's everyday life had settled into a dull ache, made especially poignant in the evenings when she had little else to occupy her thoughts. So it was with a temporary relief that she attended her Girl Guides meeting the following Wednesday. At last, as the girls began filtering out of the hall, squealing as they dashed through the rain to their waiting parents, Frankie grasped a moment alone with Cassa.

'Cassa, have you got a minute?' she stage whispered, one eye still on Bronwyn, their matriarch Guider In Charge. 'How are you getting home tonight?'

'Taxi,' Cassa replied with a shrug.

'How about I give you a lift?'

'Thanks, but I don't think so.'

'Is your mum at work?'

'Yeah.'

Frankie bit back her grin of excitement.

'You remember the Golden Miller singing competition?'

Cassa looked wounded at the thought.

'Yeah.'

Frankie leaned in closer so absolutely no one could overhear.

'It's the Final tonight and they've asked me to ask you if you'll make a special appearance.'

Cassa's eyes bulged.

'Seriously?'

'Shh. Yes, seriously. So I ask again, how about I give you a lift home?'

Cassa giggled and covered her mouth, darting a quick look in Bronwyn's direction.

'Okay,' she nodded. 'But why do they want me back? Am I back in the competition?'

'No, you're out of the competition, but there was a bit of a mutiny when the customers heard you weren't in it. Then one of the other finalists withdrew so they had to ask the person who got voted off in favour of you to step in. You're to be their special guest.'

'Oh my God,' squeaked Cassa. 'Why didn't you tell me earlier?'

'I do have some sensibilities. If I told you earlier you wouldn't have been able to concentrate on your GFI Circus Skills. Do you think you could sing without having a song prepared?'

Cassa grabbed Frankie's hand and dragged her towards the exit.

'I've got loads of songs prepared! Come on! Let's go!'

Pulling up outside the pub, Frankie simultaneously went cold with dread at seeing it so packed any self-respecting sardine would have objected, but also giddy with relief that her hints about Cassa's appearance dropped in Mrs Banks's company on Sunday had not been in vain.

With the rain still lashing down, the pair sprinted to the doors. Gripping Cassa's hand in hers, Frankie weaved through the masses to the bar. She was surprised to see Tom in his usual corner in conversation with Pippa and Emmie and Billy.

'Hiya, Frankie!' Pippa waved, raising her fruit juice and her voice above the anticipatory hum of the crowds.

'Hey, Pippa. Haven't seen you here in a while.'

'Tell me about it. I heard tonight was going to be a blast so Jack gave me the night off.'

Frankie smiled at Emmie.

'Back at the scene of the crime, are you?'

'I'd say the crime had been committed a good few months earlier and certainly not here, thank God,' she replied with a wry grin.

'This is Cassa, everyone.' Frankie manoeuvred the teenager in front of her. 'She's going to sing the opening number tonight. Hey, Joey!'

Pausing in mid-pull of a Guinness, Joey cheered when he saw Cassa.

'The diva's back! Good to see you here, Cassa. Thanks for stepping in at the last minute.'

Perhaps overwhelmed by the bustling crowds, Cassa's greeting was little more than a squeak.

'You're on in about ten minutes. I'll just finish this order then let the judges know you're here.'

'Thanks, Joey,' Frankie said.

'No, thank you,' he replied. 'I don't know how you did it, but this place is heaving. Everyone's been asking about Cassa.'

Frankie beamed with pride and turned back to her party.

'Have you heard Cassa sing?' she asked them.

'No, but I'm really looking forward to it,' Pippa said to Cassa. 'I've heard great things about you.' She turned her attention back to Frankie. 'There's also another reason I'm here tonight. It's to give you these.' She dipped into her handbag and held out a couple of coloured badges.

Frankie turned them over on her palm and looked at Pippa questioningly.

'Owners' badges?'

'Yes. For the Grand National.'

Frankie stood, frozen to the spot. Was this a sick joke?

'Sorry, Pippa. I can't accept these.'

'No, please take them. Really, I feel bad about what's happened. You were meant to ride Peace Offering. Since you gave it to Rhys, Jack has become so much easier to live with.'

'I-I can't take these,' Frankie stammered. She tried to give them back, but Pippa pushed her hands away.

'Please take them. There's only two, I'm afraid. That's all I could spare. But I remember you saying the Grand National meant a lot to your father, so I thought he might like to come along too, to act as owner for a day.'

Frankie opened and shut her mouth. On the one hand, going along to Aintree and watching Rhys ride Peace Offering would be torturous. On the other hand, it would be rather pleasant to mill around the parade ring without feeling nauseous with nerves. She hesitated again. Ta' Qali's race would be just prior to the National. What if her theory failed and she lost her job? How awkward would that be?

'Take them, Frankie!' Billy said in exasperated tones. 'For God's sake, how many people get to do the whole la-di-da with the National favourite?'

'I know, and it's very kind of you, Pippa, but –'

'But what?'

'Your dad will enjoy it,' Tom piped up.

'D'you think?' Frankie was doubtful.

'Yeah. You said he always wanted to win the National. If Peace Offering wins, then as acting owner, he will have.'

She swayed. In a bizarre way, it did make sense.

'Well...'

'Oh, go on. Don't make me beg,' Pippa urged.

'Okay then,' she said with a weak smile. She dropped the badges into her handbag. 'Thank you.'

'My pleasure,' Pippa beamed. She looked beyond Frankie and frowned. 'Um, I think the barman's trying to get your attention.'

Frankie swivelled round. Joey was up on the stage at the far end of the restaurant area, waving like a windscreen wiper. He motioned her and Cassa to come join him.

'You ready?' she said, gripping the girl's shoulders.

Cassa gulped and nodded.

Head down, Frankie shouldered the way clear to the stage with Cassa on her heels. With her eyes fixed on the floor, she didn't notice the person attached to a pair of flatties until she'd bumped straight into them.

'Sorry, excuse –' Her apology evaporated on her lips as her eyes met Mrs Preston's. 'Oh, God.'

Mrs Preston, dressed in a starched uniform, stood rigid with rage.

Cassa bumped into Frankie from behind and shrunk back when she saw her mother.

'What in God's name do you think you're doing?'

Cassa gawped. Frankie gawped.

'I didn't believe it was true when the A&E receptionist congratulated me on your – your *shenanigans*.' She shook her head at her daughter. 'I said my Cassa isn't a pub singer, she's at Girl Guides. Now, I see I was wrong. I'm so disappointed in you, Cassa. What on earth were you thinking? Singing in a bar like some sleazy lounge singer? You're thirteen!' She turned her laser glare onto Frankie. 'And you. As a Girl Guide leader, you are meant to be responsible! Sensible! A good influence on young girls! What do you call this? You ought to be ashamed!'

Frankie was. Very. A heat wave blush burned across her face and neck.

'I'm sorry, Mrs Preston.'

'I don't want to hear your apologies!' She grabbed Cassa by the wrist. 'Come on, I'm taking you home. And don't think this is the end of it. You're grounded, young lady. And as for you, Miss Cooper,' she said her name with distaste. 'I'll be straight onto the phone to Bronwyn about this. You're not fit to be in charge of young girls.'

Cassa wrenched her arm out of her mother's grasp.

'It's not Frankie's fault, Mum!' she cried.

Frankie saw Mrs Preston's nostrils flare as she sucked in her breath. At this rate Cassa wouldn't be allowed out of the house until her eighteenth birthday.

'It's okay, Cassa. Your mum's right. I should've known better.'

'But it was my idea! I made you enter me in the competition.'

Mrs Preston looked dumbstruck by her outburst. Cassa took advantage.

'Frankie was just giving me a ride home. It was me who saw the sign for the competition. I was the one who entered.'

Mrs Preston's lip curled in disgust.

'But why would you want to do such a thing? I don't understand. Is this some sort of teenage rebellion – trying to get my attention?'

'No, Mum.' Cassa looked pained. 'I just want to sing. It's what I've always wanted to do.'

'This is just a phase, Cassa. You can sing at home. Concentrate on your schoolwork so you can go to nursing school. That is what you should be doing. Not singing in some karaoke competition like this.'

'Mrs Preston, if I may just interrupt you. This isn't just some poxy karaoke competition. Cassa's really good. She would've got through to tonight's final round if we hadn't pulled out in the semis. *But they asked her to do a special appearance.* She's that good, honestly.'

'I don't care!' Mrs Preston snapped. 'I'm not going to fill her head with nonsense when she should be concentrating on her education. If Cassa wants to work in medicine like her father and I, then she has to work hard to get the grades.'

'But *does* she want to work in medicine? Have you asked her?'

'I don't need to ask her. I'm her mother.'

Frankie bit her lip, saddened. Sad for Cassa, but a new sympathy mounted for Mrs Preston. She wasn't curbing Cassa's dreams on purpose, she really did think working in medicine was the right thing.

'Mum, I don't want to be a nurse. I see the long hours you do, how tired it makes you. Look how it ruined yours and Dad's marriage. I don't want that.'

'But singing, Cassa? Why can't you want some reliable career? Why does it have to be singing?'

'She has a real talent for it,' Frankie said.

'Please let me sing tonight, Mum.'

The mixed feelings which had been on Mrs Preston's face vanished with the tight set to her mouth.

'This is ridiculous, Cassa. I don't know why we're even discussing this. Singing in a bar at your age! I'm surprised they even let you enter this competition.'

Frankie and Cassa exchanged uneasy glances.

'They didn't know. Then we withdrew before they found out,' Frankie said. She didn't expand on the reason for their withdrawal. Some things were best left unsaid.

'I suppose that's something,' scoffed Mrs Preston. 'But it's still out of the question. Your father would have a fit if he knew.'

'Little chance of that happening,' Cassa said bitterly. 'He'd have to be in contact to find out. When was the last time he rang?'

Mrs Preston's face softened.

'I know it doesn't seem fair, darling. But he's very busy at work.'

'Exactly. Can you understand why I don't want to be a doctor now?'

'Let's go home and talk about it, shall we?'

'Just let me sing first.'

'No, Cassa.' Mrs Preston's tone was authoritative. Frankie closed her eyes, garnering all her bravery cells together.

'Mrs Preston, I think it's a good idea that you and Cassa have a chat. But look around you. You see all these people? They haven't come to watch the finalists. They've come to see Cassa. That's how good she is. You should be proud of your daughter, not disappointed in her.' She held her breath, waiting for the woman's response. Cassa's sweaty hand slipped into hers.

'Just ten minutes, Mum. And I'll sing your favourite song.'

A hint of a smile flickered over Mrs Preston's lips.

'You know Sarah McLachlan's *Angel*?'

'You play it often enough.'

Frankie looked over to the stage, just a few metres away, yet with the crush of people, it seemed further. Joey sent her a questioning gesture. She raised an eyebrow in Mrs Preston's direction.

'They're ready for her.'

Mrs Preston sighed then reluctantly nodded.

'Okay, then. Just this once. I do love that song.'

Frankie grinned and gave Joey the thumbs up.

*

Mounting the stage, Cassa smiled shyly as she was greeted with applause. The first gentle piano notes quietened the pub and as Cassa began to sing, pint glasses stilled. Her voice, melancholy and pure, wrapped around Frankie like cool silk, giving her goose-bumps. Frankie stole a glance at Mrs Preston. The woman's eyes glistened with unshed tears.

'This song was playing when I first met Cassa's father,' she murmured to Frankie. 'He asked me to dance. I felt like I was in the arms of an angel for real.'

Frankie tried to smile. As Cassa sang the chorus, she couldn't help but remember how she'd lain in Rhys's arms, called him her angel. There, she'd found peace; there, she'd found comfort. His touch had been as tender as the melody that now surrounded her. Her heart ached. His scent, his warmth, his strength tugged her back to that night.

'I'm no angel, Frankie,' he'd said.

She squeezed her eyes shut to stem the tears. Hindsight was so bittersweet. She looked around the pub. It was as if they were all playing a game of musical statues and the music had stopped. No one fidgeted, drinks were forgotten. Everyone stood transfixed by Cassa's voice.

A figure standing outside the glass doors caught her eye. Her heart double-bounced into her throat. Rhys stood in rain that shimmered gold in the glow of the street lamp. His hair clung to his forehead in rats' tails, his jacket plastered sodden to his hunched shoulders.

'Rhys.' His name tore from her lips like a knife withdrawing from her chest.

Unable to move for the crush of people, she watched him helplessly. He stared desolately back. The knife plunged back in. He looked so completely bloody. There was no trace of his usual cocksure arrogance, just a cold damp misery. Cassa's sorrowful tones made his stance seem all the more alone.

The last piano chord was met with deafening applause, jolting Frankie back into the room. Mrs Preston clapped furiously. Cassa stood, awkwardly accepting the ovation. Frankie turned back to look at Rhys and her heart drooped. Where he had stood there was now an empty space, made lonelier still by the veil of gold-tinted rain. Frankie closed her eyes. So this was the final goodbye.

54

Like grumbling thunder rolling in, anticipation for the Grand National meeting built until at last with a deafening clap, it had arrived. On the eve of the jumps season's grand finale, Frankie sat with Doug in the demure coffee lounge of their hotel.

'So if Ta' Qali wins tomorrow in the novice hurdle, you get to stay on at Aspen Valley, is that right?' Doug said over the rim of his coffee cup.

'As a work rider, yes.'

'And if he doesn't?'

Frankie exhaled.

'Then I guess I'll have to leave.'

Doug shook his head sadly.

'I'm sorry, lovie. I hope you haven't done this just because of me.'

Frankie grinned.

'No, this time I'm doing this for me. I don't think I ever really wanted to be a jockey. I was too shit-scared most of the time. But being a work rider and bringing on the youngsters is definitely more satisfying.'

'So Ta' Qali is your trial run?'

'Quite literally, yes.'

'D'you think you've nailed him?'

She shrugged.

'We'll find out tomorrow one way or another.'

'Have you got our badges?'

Frankie held up her handbag.

'Right here. Do you want see?'

Doug looked undecided then he smiled sheepishly.

'Go on then. It's not every day you get owners' badges for the National favourite.'

Chuckling, Frankie rummaged through her handbag. Although she had mixed feelings about tomorrow, Doug had been positively glowing since Frankie had told him she was quitting as a jockey and had given him his owners' badge a week ago. In the side pocket of her bag, as well as the badges, her fingers touched on a smooth flat surface. Frowning to herself she pulled out the unfamiliar object.

'How did this get in here?'

Doug leaned forward.

'What is it?'

'It's that picture of you with Alan Bradford and his mistress – it must have fallen into my bag when I dropped all the albums that night Tom called about Atticus.'

She let Doug take the photo from her. He leaned back in his armchair, a sigh escaping and held it long-sightedly to study it. On the back of the photo, Frankie recognised her mother's handwriting, younger and neater. *"Doug and Al at The Goat's Head. Adelaide in background."*

Frankie frowned.

'I thought her name was Heidi?'

'Hmm?' Doug looked across, distracted.

'On the back, Mum's put you and Alan Bradford and Adelaide. I thought her name was Heidi?'

Doug shrugged and tossed the photo onto the table between them.

'Heidi, Adelaide, same thing. Heidi's short for Adelaide apparently and she didn't like her real name.'

A thought occurred to Frankie, but she dismissed it immediately. It would be too much of a coincidence. Nevertheless, she picked up the photo and examined it again. Her heart began to pound. Was this her just wanting to believe what she was seeing, or could it be true?

'What was her surname, can you remember?'

'God, I don't know. She was just Heidi – oh no, wait. I do remember. She was a big fan of that pop group, Manfred Mann.' Doug chuckled. 'She was always singing *Pretty Flamingo*. She claimed that she was related to Manfred Mann because they had the same surname, so she must have been Heidi Mann.'

Frankie's mouth fell open.

'You're sure?'

Doug's brow furrowed at her serious tone.

'Pretty sure. She might have been lying, I don't know. I doubt she was really related to Manfred Mann. Why?'

Frankie licked her lips and tried to regulate her breathing.

'When did she get pregnant?'

'Why?'

'Just answer the question, Dad! This is important.'

'Hell, I don't know exactly. It was a couple of weeks before Crowbar's National that she came back knocking on the door. I don't think she'd known about it long so maybe January? I don't know.'

Blood pounded in her ears as she furiously flicked through her mental calendar.

'So the baby would have been born around September, October?'

'If she'd kept it,' Doug said bitterly. 'She had an abortion.'

'Do you know that for definite?'

'Well, presumably she did. We never heard from her again. Alan paid her off. Why are you so interested in this now?' Doug looked bemused.

Frankie swallowed, scratching her dry throat. She looked down at the photo. Her gaze flickered between the two smiling faces of Alan Bradford and Adelaide Mann.

'I've got to go find Tom,' she breathed.

'What on earth?' Doug said, watching Frankie fumbling the photo into her handbag. 'Why do you have to go see Tom? Frankie, what is going on?' His tone was commanding.

A dumbfounded smile pinked her cheeks.

'What if she kept the pregnancy? What if she had the baby and gave it up for adoption?'

Doug's jaw dropped.

'Are you saying what I think you're saying?'

Frankie nodded.

'I think so.'

The bed and breakfast house Tom was staying at proved further away than she'd imagined. It took her numerous attempts to explain to the hostess in breathless gasps who she was after. The woman eventually understood enough to call Tom's room and he was quick to appear.

'Frankie, is everything okay?'

'Tom, I need to speak to you,' she glanced at the hostess sat in a nearby armchair pretending to read a magazine. 'In private,' she added.

Tom gave her a quick frown and ushered her towards a corridor.

'Come to my room. Don't worry, she won't be staying,' he said when the hostess opened her mouth to object.

Tom's room looked like someone had gone Laura Ashley mad. Floral frills bedecked the single bed, the curtain rails and even the wastepaper bin. Frankie shrunk away in disgust.

'My God, how can you sleep in here? It'd give me nightmares.'

Tom hooked a chair closer – or was it a flower bush, Frankie wasn't sure – then sat down on the bed.

'Have you really come over here to criticise the interior decorating?'

Frankie sat down and refocused.

'Tom, you're not going to believe this, but – oh, God, how do I even begin to say it? Are you still trying to find Adelaide Mann?'

'You came all this way to ask me that?'

'Just answer the question!'

Tom clasped his hands and blew his fringe off his forehead.

'You've found something out, haven't you?'

'Yes!' squealed Frankie. 'I found her! I found *him* too!'

'My father as well?' Tom looked taken aback.

'Yes! My God, Tom, it's such a small world, you wouldn't believe it. Adelaide Mann was –'

'Wait, Frankie,' he interrupted her, holding up his hand. He rubbed his face and sighed. 'I-I don't think I want to know.'

'But –'

'No, listen. I know it might sound bizarre considering the lengths I went to before, but that was then.'

Frankie stared at him in disbelief.

'But what's changed? Don't you want to know who your parents are?'

'I know who my parents are. They are Charles and Ruth Moxley.' Noting Frankie's confusion he carried on. 'They might not be my biological parents, but they've given me all the love that any son could wish for, and more.'

'I get that,' Frankie replied. 'But then why did you start looking for Adelaide Mann in the first place?'

Tom chewed his lip in consideration.

'I was in a strange place in my life, I guess. I was trying to find myself and I thought I could find the answer by finding my real parents. It happened round about the time I met Joey. I was confused. I didn't know who I was or what I was. I thought that by tracing my roots – by confirming my foundations – I would know where I stood. As it happens, I didn't need to find Adelaide Mann. Joey – and you – gave me the courage to face up to who I am. My parents stood by me when I came out. They were wonderful. I don't need to find my biological parents anymore; I don't *want* to find them. Does that make any sense?'

Frankie looked at him doubtfully. Okay, so this had all been a subconscious ploy to find his own identity, but surely, with her sitting here, knowing what she did, he must be a little curious?

'I think so.' She looked down at her hands still clutching her bag where the photo of Tom's parents lay in hiding and consciously loosened her grip.

Perhaps sensing her disappointment, Tom leaned forward and squeezed her knee.

'I know it's hard to understand. And a part of me does want to know how you managed to find out. But consider this: what can of worms might we be opening if you told me?'

That much was true, Frankie granted. She nodded and smiled.

'So you're okay now?'

Tom winked at her.

'Yeah. Things aren't as bad as they first seemed. I'm not living a lie any more, I've found someone to love, and work is picking up again.'

'It is?' Frankie said, cheered at the news.

'I've got most of my old jockeys back to valet. And I hate to say this to you, but I owe Rhys for it.'

Frankie's neck muscles sprung taut.

'How come?'

'He and Donnie had a set-to not so long ago. Rhys called him a homophobic idiot then turned round and shouted to everyone there that they would be too if they carried on the way they were.'

Frankie didn't know what to feel. Her heart ached with Rhys's betrayal yet at the same time it soared with pride that he'd stood up for Tom. A thought occurred to her and a small smile touched her lips. Little did either men realise they were actually half-brothers. It would have made things a whole lot more complicated if Rhys had reacted the same way as Donnie.

'I know this might be hard for you to hear, especially after what you've gone through, but he's really not such a bad guy.'

Frankie wanted to cry. Missing Rhys like she did, she desperately wanted to believe Tom, but it would never change the fact of what he had done.

'He used me,' she said staunchly.

'He made a mistake. We all make mistakes, right?'

'Yes, but there are mistakes and then there are *mistakes*.'

'Exactly, some mistakes work out for the best. Look at me, I'm a mistake – Adelaide Mann's mistake. But if she hadn't done it, I wouldn't be here. In Rhys's case, by getting you to give up the ride on Peace Offering he gave you a get-out clause. You only wanted to ride in the National to please your dad and your dad's admitted he never wanted you to be a jockey anyway. So wasn't it for the best?'

'Rhys didn't know that though. Stop making him sound like the good guy.'

'That's not what I'm saying and you know it,' Tom said with an impatient sigh. 'Can't you just forgive him? I know you miss him. I see it every day on your face.'

Frankie grimaced.

'I do miss him, you're right. And I do want to forgive him, but there's something – I don't know what – something that won't allow me to. Why should I forgive him? What has he done to redeem himself?'

'Remember, this is Rhys we're talking about. He doesn't have much to say on a good day. And he's not short on pride either. He knows what he did was wrong, but admitting it would be especially hard for him. Having said that, he has tried and each time you've pushed him away. He's a jockey, he has to watch what he eats, and there's only so much humble pie a jockey can stomach.'

A drizzle began to fall as Frankie trudged back to her hotel. It was past midnight by the time she at last pushed open the entrance door, yet still people were about, out-of-towners here for the weekend, looking alert and excited about the National tomorrow.

'Today,' she corrected herself. Another sixteen hours and it would all be over.

She took the elevator to the fourth floor where, by comparison, the corridors were quiet. She let herself into her room and threw her bag onto a chair. Her clothes and her hair were damp, but she didn't have the inclination to do anything about it. She fell back onto her bed and stared up at the ceiling.

Tom and Rhys were *brothers*. If Tom was still concerned about going bald she supposed she could always keep an eye on Rhys from afar and give him the head's-up if she saw his hairline receding. She couldn't imagine Rhys going bald, perish the thought. Maybe, if Ta' Qali fell short tomorrow and she lost her job, it might be for the best. Best that she leave

Aspen Valley – leave Helensvale if necessary. She didn't want to see Rhys grow old, to see him move on with his life.

A gentle tap on her door roused her from her thoughts. Doug had probably heard her arrive back from the room next door and would want to be filled in on all the details of Tom's "situation".

'Coming,' she said, heaving herself off the bed.

She unlocked the door and swung it open. She gaped. It wasn't Doug standing there, and it wasn't housekeeping either. Her voice escaped in a gasp.

'Rhys.'

55

Had she conjured him up out of wishful thinking? Maybe she should try it with lottery numbers next time.

'Don't slam the door on me,' he said.

In a daze, Frankie looked at the door then back to him. She hadn't got that far in thought processing.

'Wh-what are you doing here? How did you know where to find me?'

Rhys looked like he'd rather be anywhere else. He held out an appeasing hand.

'I – er, bumped into someone who told me. Listen, can we talk? Please?'

Remembering Tom's encouragement that she give Rhys a chance, she nodded.

'All right,' she said uncertainly.

He swallowed and took a deep breath.

'Okay. Right. First up, you have every right to hate me. I've been a bastard and an idiot and I'm sorry it's taken this long for me to say what I'm about to say. God – I'm terrible at these conversations. It's just that it's hard to ask you to take me back when I hate myself for what I did. I don't deserve you.'

He paused. She wanted to say something to make this easier for him, but what to say? He *had* been a bastard, even if it was a bastard she missed. She stayed silent, her hand still clutching the door handle.

'When I read in the papers that Pippa had given you the ride on Peace Offering in the National, I was furious,' he went on. 'Livid. This was going to be my year, my best chance of winning it and instead it got handed to you, the new kid. The amateur. And at the Christmas party I seduced you. I didn't much care if I hurt you in the process. All I could think about was getting back my National ride.'

Frankie squeezed her eyes shut and leant her head against the door. Would the pain ever lessen? When she opened them again, Rhys was looking desperately at her.

'But then as we carried on, I started to – to have *feelings* for you. I didn't want it to end, I didn't want to hurt you. I thought if I just kept quiet then you'd never be any wiser and we could just carry on. Then you gave me the ride on Peace Offering.' He looked at her helplessly. 'What could I do? You were offering it to me on a plate, the thing which meant the most to me. I didn't want to accept it, but I let you convince me that you'd made the decision off your own head. So I accepted it.'

A noisy group of guests, staggering out of the elevator, interrupted him, and he stepped forward to avoid being trampled. Once the raucous laughter disappeared round the corner, Rhys moistened his lips and refocused. Beneath the corridor lighting, beads of sweat clung to his forehead. Frankie almost wished the guests had carried him away on their wave of high spirits. Rhys's explanation didn't make the hurt any easier. No amount of excuses could undo the damage.

'Then you found out and everything went to shit,' he continued. 'I completely destroyed your trust in me, what I did was unforgiveable. But that's what I want: your forgiveness. So I want you to take back the ride on Peace Offering.'

Frankie's mouth fell open. Now *that* had come from left field.

'But –'

'Please, Frankie. When you'd gone, I tried for a while to console myself with the fact that I still had the National ride, I still had the thing which meant most to me. But it didn't work. It made me realise that the National isn't the most important thing to me. You are.' He searched her face for a reaction, but faced with her frozen expression, he stepped forward again. 'You are what means the most to me.'

Frankie felt hollow.

'I can't...'

Rhys looked panicked. He grabbed her hand.

'Please, Frankie. Yes, you can.'

'I can't. It's too late.'

'No, it's not. We can start again, do it properly this time.'

She looked down at his hand grasping hers and carefully removed it.

'I can't take the ride on Peace Offering because I don't want it. I don't want to ride in any races because I don't really want to be a jockey.'

Rhys looked horrified.

'But I've nothing else to offer you! What more do you want?'

Frankie looked long and hard at Rhys. To forgive or not to forgive? Rhys's black eyes bore into hers, his lips were pink from being bitten.

'I want the past to be undone,' she whispered.

'But I can't do that,' Rhys despaired.

She smiled sadly.

'I know. I'm sorry, Rhys. There's nothing you can do. I can't go back.'

For a moment, Rhys didn't respond. Then with a grimace, he spun around and stalked away. Once again, tears welled in her eyes, but this time they represented a new emotion. She wept for Rhys – compassionate tears that admired his courage and his sacrifice. And she wept for herself – angry tears frustrated at her inability to forgive.

56

Fifteen hours on, Frankie could barely breathe. Circled by the runners for the two-mile novice hurdle, she stood in the centre of the parade ring beside Jack.

'Sorry, Frankie,' he said. 'Whatever plan you had for Ta' Qali doesn't appear to have made much difference.'

Frankie cringed and turned to watch Ta' Qali hop, skip and jump around the paddock. The jockeys trooped out from the weighing room and she caught her breath. Rhys walked over, his expression hard, his demeanour tense. Frankie avoided his eyes.

'Wait,' she said to Jack. 'Just bring Ta' Qali over here before you send them off.'

Jack gave her a puzzled glance but assented.

'Your call.' He motioned to Billy and the lad wrestled Ta' Qali into the centre of the ring. The gelding's nostrils flared and he rolled his eyes at Aintree's fanfare. The bell rang for jockeys to mount and he twirled around in a flurry of black mane and tail.

Frankie took a deep breath and reached out to unbuckle the horse's sheepskin noseband.

'What the hell are you doing?' Rhys demanded.

'Just go with me on this one,' she said through gritted teeth. Ta' Qali threw his head as she tugged the noseband free from the bridle.

'What are you doing, Frankie?' Jack said.

'It's a long shot,' she replied hesitantly. 'But when you let me show my Girl Guides around the yard, one of them asked how he'd hurt his nose.' She gestured to the white marking on Ta' Qali's face. 'Then when you brought home those new novices, you said that you'd had to use a curb chain on one –'

'This is a waste of time,' muttered Rhys. 'Can you just leg me up so we can get on with it?'

'No, wait. Listen. I know it might sound ridiculous. But what if Ta' Qali had been a handful in his youth? What if he'd had a curb chain used on him and something had gone wrong? We know he's head shy. Maybe it's the pressure on his nose that upsets him? We don't ride him in a

329

noseband at home and he's quiet as a lamb then.' She looked timidly at Jack, waiting for him to ridicule her. Jack's attention wavered between her and the horse. Ta' Qali stood, his head high and his nostrils still blown wide, but nevertheless quieter than he had been moments earlier.

'You're right,' the trainer said at last. Frankie exhaled. 'It does sound ridiculous.' She grimaced and her hand clenched the fluffy noseband in her hand in disappointment. 'But it's not implausible,' he went on. Frankie looked at him with renewed hope. 'His nose does look like it could've been broken before. Come on, Rhys. Let's get you aboard. We'll know if Frankie's right in a few minutes. If you're wrong...' He fixed her with a stern look. '...then you're through with Aspen Valley. That was the deal.'

'What?' Rhys said. 'You're going to fire her because of this psychopath?'

'That was the deal. Right, Frankie?'

Frankie nodded. Jack boosted Rhys into the saddle and she rubbed her fingers over Ta' Qali's lips.

'Don't let me down, boy,' she whispered.

If Ta' Qali had time to understand her, he didn't have time to show it. With Rhys on his back, he wheeled round at his bidding and joined the string of horses exiting the ring.

In the crush of grandstand punters, Frankie joined Doug to watch the runners and riders mingling behind the two mile start in Aintree's infield. Frankie's eyes never left Ta' Qali. With mounting dread she noted his flicking head and uneasy side-stepping.

Doug patted her arm.

'Don't be so worried. Aspen Valley's on a roll. They've won two of the three races so far,' he said.

Frankie peeled her tongue from the roof of her mouth.

'I wish they'd get on with it. What's the delay?'

Doug gave her a sympathetic smile.

'They're running to time, there's no delay. They'll be off in a minute.'

Frankie's gaze left Ta' Qali to scan the horizon. A fine persistent drizzle fell, shrouding the course in half-light. Maybe she'd been too hasty in betting her job on Ta' Qali. Everything looked set against them, the weather, the large field of twenty-one runners, all of a higher class than those he'd raced against previously. And she wasn't so confident about her noseband theory now either. His initial calm appeared to have evaporated. He was still acting like a skittish filly.

She breathed deep as the horses jogged onto the main course. They bustled together, bumping shoulders and throwing their heads to get a clear view. For a moment, she lost sight of Ta' Qali as he was swallowed up in the thick of it.

The tape snapped back and the horses were away. With only nine hurdles to jump, there was a long run to the first. Frankie chewed the lipstick from her lips and a grimace clawed her face when she saw Ta' Qali take a hefty bump around the turn. He ran in snatches, leaping out from Rhys's hands then bobbling when he ran into the horse in front. Rhys sat quietly on his back, a firm hold on the reins. They raced to the first flight.

Frankie bounced on her knees as horse and rider knocked the hurdle flat. The second hurdle wasn't far beyond and Rhys was still trying to rebalance Ta' Qali when they met it. Again, they rapped it hard.

The crowd cheered extra hard as the runners neared the grandstand for the first time, but Frankie was too tense to even whisper her support. Over the third, still packed deep in midfield, Ta' Qali galloped past the finish post. A squeak escaped from Frankie when she saw Rhys increasing his hold on the reins.

'What is he doing?' she cried.

'Beats me. Looks like he's pulling up. Maybe he's lame,' Doug replied.

Frankie snatched the binoculars hanging round her father's neck and ignoring his gasps for air, trained in on the Aspen Valley duo. Rhys's severe restraint on his mount was dragging him back through the field. She looked for an inconsistency in the horse's stride, but despite it being curbed, he looked sound as a bell. Was this his way of avenging her rebuttal of him last night? When Ta' Qali's head was almost in his chest, Rhys stretched forward and looked to almost go to hit him on his head. Instead he brushed his gloved hand down Ta' Qali's nose, as if to rid the horse of the spilt salt marking on his nose. Instinctively, Ta' Qali shied away from his hand and bounced into the inside rail.

'What the hell?' Doug said, watching the jockey's antics on the big screen.

A small smile warmed Frankie's face and she let Doug have full use of his airways again.

'I think I know what he's doing,' she said. 'Ta' Qali still thinks he's got a noseband on because he associates race-days with nosebands. I think Rhys was trying to show him he doesn't have a noseband on.'

Doug nodded to the track, his expression grave.

'Well, he'd better hurry up about it. Slowing him down like that might have cost him the race.'

Cringing away, Frankie saw he was right. Ta' Qali was now stone cold last going into the final circuit. On the other hand, he looked to be quietening down. She knotted her hands together in prayer. If ever there was a time for Ta' Qali to prove his potential, now was it.

Rhys let him out a notch and with half a circuit before the next hurdle, set about closing the gap. Frankie didn't doubt he would catch them, but whether he could get to the front and sustain his run right to the finish was an unknown.

'Come on, my boy,' she murmured. 'Come on, Rhys. Work your magic.'

They galloped in solitude down the back straight, a murky blur of black mane and red silk. Frankie darted a quick look to see how the other horses were faring. The pace was brisk. A couple were already being pushed along by their jockeys. Her heart began to thump extra hard.

Ta' Qali jumped the next three hurdles straight as a bullet. This wasn't the horse who'd run wild in all twelve of his previous starts. This was the horse she rode on the Aspen Valley gallops every morning. Rounding the last long sweeping turn of the course, she saw Rhys nudge him forward again, commanding, yet as gentle as if he was kneading dough. The response was immediate, but was it too little too late?

'Ooh!' wailed Frankie.

Her voice was drowned out by the roar of the crowd welcoming the field back into the home turn. They were strung out like washing. All the jockeys were hard at work. Whips rose and fell, glossy boots pumped, shoulders shovelled like butterfly swimmers.

Ta' Qali winged his way round the turn as the others took the third last hurdle. Rhys's body was low, a cat hunting its prey. Frankie knew that look and a new wave of excitement crashed over her.

'Come on, Rhys!' she cried. 'COME ON!'

Fleetingly, she saw Doug's look of bemusement beside her. She didn't have time to care. Ta' Qali picked off the stragglers and the inherent speed which had carried his sibling to Doncaster and Goodwood Cup victories shone with his every movement. The leaders jumped the second last. Ta' Qali chased them ten lengths shy.

Roused even higher by the commentator's excited call as he too saw Ta' Qali's pursuit, Frankie screamed in urgency. The feeling was contagious. As the horses neared the last hurdle, Doug, too, bellowed his support. The crowd's crescendo reverberated around their ears. The leaders landed over the last, tired but genuine. Ta' Qali skimmed over on their heels and without loss of stride, began to move past them.

Frankie stopped breathing. She stopped leaping up and down. Her muscles felt paralysed, so mesmerising was her horse's speed. The furlong lollipop flashed the horses by. Ta' Qali drew level with the leader and for a moment, the horses lent in on each other. They bumped apart and Rhys threw his reins at Ta' Qali. Ta' Qali stretched out his head. His muscles strained as he sought to gain the lead. The half furlong lollipop counted them down to the finish line. Rhys used his whip, counting four strides, waiting for his mount to respond, used it again, four strides. He lifted it once more, but there his arm stayed in a victory salute as Ta' Qali galloped over the line a length clear.

Frankie felt like she was going to explode. She wanted to yell the grandstand down, but couldn't unclench her teeth. She would burst into tears if she did. Turning to Doug, she raised her bunched hands to her face and shook.

Doug laughed.

'And you did that? You brought on that tearaway horse and taught it to jump and run like that?' he said.

Frankie had never felt so proud. This was the job for her. She could never have felt this amount of satisfaction just being a jockey. Looking down to the front of the stands, she saw Billy hurtling along the walkway doing bojangle kicks as he ran.

'It was a team effort,' she said with a smile.

With no attempt at gentleness, Doug slapped her on the back and pulled her into a rough hug.

'That's my girl,' he laughed.

Frankie's world glowed.

57

The drizzle was still falling steadily an hour later. Aintree's parade ring was bursting at the seams as crowds gathered at the ringside to watch the horses walk around. Such was the lottery of the Grand National, no particular attention was paid to any one horse. Cameras and mobile phones clicked at every one of the forty runners, their photographers knowing not to ignore even the hundred-to-one shots. Within the ring, forty groups of owners chattered nervously among themselves, their eyes flitting between their surroundings to their runners.

Frankie stood beside her father, feeling strangely like a fish out of water. She'd been in the parade ring countless times before, but never in the capacity of owner. Doug fidgeted beside her.

Jack stood a few feet away, immobile and outwardly calm – to Frankie a dead giveaway that he was just as nervous as everyone else. His earlier high spirits that had assured Frankie of her place at Aspen Valley had vanished. For that brief moment, when he'd winked at her, he'd become less of a businessman and more of a human. But now, the businessman was back. There was a hunger in his eyes as he sought to win the Holy Grail of National Hunt racing. Pippa fidgeted beside him and her friend, introduced to Frankie as Tash, gave her a reassuring pat on her shoulder.

'Hey, don't stress, sweets. I don't want to become an auntie just yet.'

Frankie looked at her in surprise.

Tash baulked at everyone's silence.

'Oops, hasn't it been announced yet?'

Frankie stared at Pippa.

'You're pregnant?'

Pippa squirmed.

'Fourteen weeks.'

A bubble of laughter rose in Frankie's throat.

'That's wonderful, but...' She looked at Jack. '...I thought after our trip to Southmead with Emmie that you weren't –'

Jack threw his hand, cross and embarrassed.

'Things have changed. Baby Sam really is quite cute.'

Frankie grinned.

'Congratulations.'

'Thanks,' he muttered. 'Now though, we've got more immediate things to think about.'

A few cheers went up as the jockeys spilled into the ring. Rhys walked over to them in Peace Offering's red silks, his stride long and confident. Frankie marvelled at his composure. How was he not bricking it? He greeted them all with his customary nod, although his gaze lingered a second longer on Frankie. She wished she could thank him for his brilliant ride on Ta' Qali, for saving her job, but now wasn't the time.

'Now, remember they've modified the jumps since you last rode in the National,' Jack said to him, his tone sombre. 'Since they've levelled off the landing at Becher's Brook there's no brave man's route any more. Everyone's going to pile in on the inside. There are going to be fallers. Peace Offering's not the fastest out of the blocks, as you well know, but get as close to the front as you possibly can. We don't want a repeat of last year and get brought down.' Jack paused, his words making them all realise this was going to be far from a walkover. 'Just get round the first circuit, and if you get that far, ride to win if you can.'

Rhys's black eyes never left Jack's as he received his instructions. He gave a brief nod of assertion. The bell for jockeys to mount rang, and the whole parade ring seemed to take in a deep breath. Pippa grasped Rhys's hand and squeezed it.

'Good luck,' she said, as if he was being sent to war.

Frankie's stomach dropped to her feet when he turned to her. His face was paler than usual, his expression still and focussed, a chiselled stone sculpture. He walked away with Jack to be legged up and Frankie bit her lip.

'Please God, bring him home safe.'

The tape went up and, to the roar of the crowd, the horses thundered away from the grandstand. Standing in the shelter of the owners and trainers stand, Frankie clenched her fists by her side. Rhys had Peace Offering in a handy position four or five off the rail. A fan of mud flicked up as the horses galloped over the Melling Road. They headed for the first in a line of six daunting obstacles which stretched far into the gloom. Peace Offering shortened then soared over, brushing his forelegs through the top of the spruce branches. Frankie squeezed her eyes shut. The voice of commentator, Nick Stone, filled her ears.

'And we lose Voila Ici at the first. Voila Ici is a faller. The rest are over safely...'

She opened her eyes again. Rhys and Peace Offering were about ten lengths shy of the lead, and, on the screen opposite the stand, looked calm and collected. She braced herself as the horses tackled the second. She lost Rhys in the jumble of coloured silks.

'We've lost two more at Fence Two,' droned the commentator. 'It looks like Sleepy Earl has parted company with his jockey and I can't quite see the other...'

Frankie leaned forward, her eyes peeled on the curled up jockey on the ground. She let out a sigh of relief when she saw his yellow silks. It wasn't Rhys. Her nails cut half-moons into her palms as the horses tackled the big open ditch. As if attached to an invisible cord, the horses streamed over, one after the other.

Two more plain fences, each bigger than the last, followed, and just as Frankie was starting to relax into the rhythm of the race, Nick Stone announced Becher's Brook and its skyscraper drop. She gave a silent moan. There were still thirty-seven horses left in the race, all full of running, all packed together. And barring a few safety-conscious jockeys, they were all angling for the inside line. Desperately, she checked Peace Offering's position. He had four rows of horses in front of him. She cringed. Directly in front was Blanca Peak, renowned for his dodgy jumping. But with Becher's fast approaching and the field bunching up, there was nowhere for Rhys to go except in Blanca Peak's wake.

The longshot put in a false stride and took off. Peace Offering followed. Blanca Peak landed short and nodded, his nose scraping through the turf. He scrambled a couple of strides to stay upright, but his momentum dragged him down. Frankie clutched Doug's arm. Peace Offering landed, solid and balanced. With Blanca Peak in their path, Rhys pulled him sideways. Doug, Frankie, Pippa, Tash and Jack all leaned with him and gave a collective sigh of relief when half-stepping, half-jumping, their horse avoided the faller.

Doug looked at Frankie and puffed out his cheeks.

'Is it wrong that I'm so relieved that you are not the one out there?' he shouted above the roar of the crowd.

Frankie shook her head.

'No. I can't think of anything scarier.'

*

The field rounded the far turn and jumped Foinavon. Another faller. Not Peace Offering. Peace Offering was making ground on the leaders and now there were just three rows in front of him. Next, the Canal Turn.

'Oh, I hate this one!' Pippa cried on Frankie's right. 'It's suicidal the way they jump it at that angle!'

As if to prove her theory correct, the horses swung wide before tacking back towards the inside and streaming over the fence at a forty-five degree angle. In the lead, the fancied Irish horse, Thar Farraige, jumped fast but lost ground on the sharp turn. Another two jockeys were bounced over their horses' heads and out of the race. Valentine's Brook loomed, five foot high with a brook on landing wider still. Rhys and Peace Offering had cut the corner and made up ground and now galloped in an easy rhythm.

Frankie allowed herself to breathe. They were going well. In fact, the whole field now seemed to have found a rhythm and the next three fences bore no casualties. Surprisingly, the simplest and smallest of all the Grand National fences caught out three.

Frankie felt her fear creep back as the depleted field galloped closer to the grandstands and The Chair. The leaders soared over the canyon-like ditch, scraping through the six foot wall of spruce. Her nerves weren't helped by Pippa's wail of dread beside her. Rhys saw a stride and kicked Peace Offering into action. They cleared it well, looking the epitome of a seasoned steeplechaser.

'I don't understand it,' yelled Pippa as all the remaining horses landed safely. 'That's the biggest fence in the race and they all clear it. Yet the one before is the smallest and there are three fallers.'

With one eye trained on the horses as they galloped past the stands, Frankie yelled back,

'It's for that precise reason. The bigger the fence, the more respect horses give it. Bigger sometimes is better.'

'Amen to that!' Tash chortled.

The next jump was the water and Frankie gripped her father's arm. This was the fence, where in the Becher Chase all those months ago, she and Peace Offering had come to grief. If Rhys shared her trepidation, he didn't show it. Quietly determined, he pushed for a big effort. Peace Offering responded with gusto – too much gusto as his leap landed him dangerously steep on his forehand. He pecked, kicking up clods of turf.

Frankie lurched back, inadvertently willing horse and rider to find their balance. Rhys did the same and Peace Offering found his legs again. They galloped away and onto their last lap. Frankie took a couple of measured breaths. Just one more circuit. Just fourteen more fences to jump.

By the time the field reached the Canal Turn for a second time, their numbers had been reduced to barely half. The fancied Okay Oklahoma led to Irish raiders Ficara and Thar Farraige, followed by the previous year's winner, Faustian in company with the French trained Cascadeur then Peace Offering.

Frankie groaned as a loose horse forced Peace Offering wide around the turn. Her eye was caught by the ominous screens being erected on the landing of a fence yet to be jumped. A steward bravely stepped out and waved a chequered flag, signalling the runners to bypass the fence.

'Ooh, I hate it when you see this,' Pippa groaned. 'Which horse is it that's down?'

'It's for a jockey, not a horse,' Jack said.

'Thank God, that's all right then,' she replied.

Frankie and Jack both gave her sidelong looks.

Nick Stone's voice went up a decibel as he called them over the third last fence.

'And it's Thar Farraige now who takes the lead. Okay Oklahoma is beginning to drop away. Faustian is being driven along in second with Cascadeur and Peace Offering making up the leading group. Now approaching two out – Peace Offering is down on his nose! Rhys Bradford had to sit tight there!'

Frankie sucked in her breath until her lungs hurt. She watched in torturous excitement as Rhys gathered his mount together again and set off with the leaders in his sights. The cheers from the crowds all around deafened her. They seemed to all be Irish as they rallied with Thar Farraige over the last. Faustian plugged on wearily behind. Cascadeur jumped tired and landed awkwardly, and unshipped his rider. Peace Offering, too, was far from tidy, but Rhys kept the partnership intact.

There were no more jumps to be tackled. They'd defied danger thirty times. Yet, it wasn't enough. Thar Farraige and Faustian still led. They were so close. The run-in was a stamina-sapping five hundred yards long. Frankie prayed there was still time.

'Go on, Rhys!' she yelled. 'Go on Peace Offering!'

Her shouts were drowned out by the rest of the Aspen Valley quintet. Even Doug was bellowing himself hoarse. Thar Farraige wobbled round the Elbow, maintaining his four length lead over Faustian. Peace Offering, his neck low, his jockey moulded against him, galloped as hard as his weary legs would carry him in pursuit. Whether Faustian was slowing or Peace Offering was quickening, Frankie wasn't sure, but the gap was closing. She darted a quick glance at the finish. Peace Offering was gaining, but with barely two hundred yards left. Time was not on their side.

'Come on Peace Offering! Come on, come on, *come on!*' she yelled.

Faustian threw in the towel – he couldn't emulate his victory from last year's race. The Irish looked to lift the roof off Aintree's grandstand as Thar Farraige kept stoically on. Peace Offering plugged past Faustian, his white blaze muddied and his lean body slick with sweat and rain. A new wave of sound crashed against the Irish supporters as Peace Offering, carrying the hopes of the British, edged closer and closer to the leader.

One hundred yards to go.

An inferno of adrenalin coursed through Frankie's body. Peace Offering nodded his head beside Thar Farraige's flank. She no longer had the ability to form words; all that came out was a senseless yell of support *'Gwan! Gwan! Gwan!'* Rhys never looked up, never took the time to soak up the historicism he'd once described with such longing. He pumped his arms and legs to the rhythm of Peace Offering's stride. Driven. Determined. They drew level with Thar Farraige.

Twenty yards to go.

The two horses bumped against one another, then bumped wearily apart. Each strained for the right to have their name stencilled in gold on the Grand National winners' board. Neither gave way. Their strides synchronised, their courage equal. In a flash, they were past the finishing post. Still so absorbed in the race, Rhys didn't stop riding for another four or five strides. Frankie sagged against her father.

'Did they do it?' she croaked.

Doug shook his head, bewildered.

'I-I don't know. I really don't.'

She looked over at the rest of their party. Pippa looked traumatised, clinging to Jack, whose jacket sleeve was torn at the shoulder. By the look on their faces, they didn't know either. She squinted down to the course where, in the drizzle, Rhys was pulling up a thankful Peace Offering. He patted the horse, but was not celebrating.

Frankie felt as if she'd been punched in the gut. If anyone knew the result, it would be Rhys. She looked at Thar Farraige's jockey. He wasn't celebrating either. On the other hand, he was accepting an Irish flag from a supporter by the rails, ready to lift it high above his shoulders should he be called into the winner's enclosure.

The tanoy whined, prompting the crowds to quieten, then Nick Stone's voice rang out, true and clear.

'First, Number Seven, Peace Offering...'

The rest of his sentence was lost as the grandstands erupted into cheers. Spinning hats and fluttering newspapers flew high. Down on the course, Rhys punched the air and a rare grin split his mud-spattered face. Pippa burst into tears and Frankie felt close to doing the same. Doug snatched her up in a bear hug, jostling her with his laughter.

For the briefest of moments, Frankie wondered about the "what ifs". What if she had been the one riding? What if she'd kept the ride? Would she now have been a Grand National-winning jockey? The first female jockey in history to win the Grand National?

She dismissed those questions. Not only were they redundant, but something inside her told her no one other than Rhys could have ridden Peace Offering to victory like he had. Her eyes brimmed with tears at the sacrifice he had been prepared to make.

'You okay, Frankie?' Her father's voice was hoarse.

She nodded and wiped her eyes with her sleeve.

'Just feeling a bit... regretful,' she sniffed.

'Regretful that you weren't the one riding or regretful about something else?'

'Something else,' she nodded.

Doug pinched her chin and gave her a sad smile.

'Don't make the same mistake I did, honey. Life's too short to bear grudges.'

'I'm not bearing a grudge, Dad. It – it's complicated.'

Doug nodded.

'Then learn to forgive. It's the bravest thing a person can do. Don't be a coward like me.'

Frankie gulped. If only she had that courage.

*

'And please put your hands together for winning jockey, Rhys Bradford!' Aintree's chairman said into his microphone. Stood to the side of the trophy presentation circle, Frankie swelled with pride as Rhys jogged forward, shaking hands and accepting people's congratulations as he went. Skipping up onto the podium, he shook the sponsor's hand and accepted his prize, a heavy bronze statue of two horses jumping Canal Turn. He lifted it high above his head and everyone cheered. He blinked as camera flashes burst in his face.

Just behind her, Frankie's attention was caught by a television reporter doing an interview.

'Alan Bradford, it's been thirty years since your Grand National victory on Crowbar. Now your son, Rhys, has won it, how does it compare?'

Frankie froze. She felt Doug stiffen beside her. They exchanged wary glances before turning around. Alan Bradford was holding court to a group of reporters.

Frankie looked at him in amazement. Sure, the photo she had seen of him had been about thirty years old, and if one looked closely, there was still a suggestion of his former good looks. But a suggestion was as far as it went. Alan Bradford was enormous. Rolls of blubber packed around his neck and his stomach drooped low and heavy over his belt and braces. Taking little notice of his son receiving his prize, the man beamed at his audience.

'Nothing quite compares to winning the National for yourself, I'll be honest, but sure I'm proud of Rhys. What father wouldn't be? Mind you, the Grand National we watched today is not the same Grand National from thirty years ago. We didn't have all those safety precautions you have now.'

Frankie curled her lip at him in disgust. How awful to have a father like that.

'God, am I glad I've got you for a dad,' she drawled.

Doug smiled and looked smug.

Rhys, with Jack and Pippa behind him, stepped off the podium with his trophy. The media immediately fell upon him like vultures on a fresh kill.

'Rhys!' Alan called. 'Rhys, over here!'

Hearing his father's voice, Rhys scanned the sea of heads, microphones and dictaphones. His eyes rested on Frankie for a moment before he caught sight of his father. The press, perhaps sensing the sudden tension, made a passage for him. Rhys stopped before his father, thought about it, then he walked on to Frankie and Doug. Alan Bradford's mouth fell open. His jaw was cranked a notch wider when he saw whom he was being ignored in favour of.

Frankie's heart hammered in her chest as Rhys halted in front of them.

'Mr Cooper, I'd like you to have this –' He paused and swallowed. '– To replace the one which should've been yours. The one which is now standing on my father's shelf.'

Frankie caught her breath. The circle of reporters stopped fidgeting and talking. Like tennis spectators, they transferred their shocked gazes from Rhys to Doug then finally to Alan. Doug reached out to run his hand over the bronze-work, now dotted with raindrops. His hand trembled then he pushed the trophy back to Rhys.

'No, son. You earned this. You keep it.'

Watching Rhys, Frankie's heart ached with joy. So this was what love was. There was no doubting it. It was undisputed. Rhys' eyes sought redemption in hers.

'I said I'd win it for you.'

Frankie threw her arms around him and, feeling the cold press of his nose against her cheek, she kissed him.

'I love you,' she whispered in his ear.

His grip around her tightened and his familiar breath was warm on her skin.

'I love you too,' he murmured.

The click of cameras and remembering that her father was standing right there, Frankie pulled back, suddenly self-conscious. Holding Rhys's hand, she looked at Doug a little timidly for his reaction. A muscle jumped in Doug's jaw. He looked like he was working very hard at controlling his emotions. At last he summoned a smile and nodded in approval. Frankie lurched out of Rhys's embrace and flung her arms around her father and buried a kiss in his cheek.

'Thank you, Dad.'

'You're welcome, honey,' Doug said. 'Now go on with you.' He untangled her arms from around his neck and nodded to Rhys. 'Go on, the both of you. Go celebrate.'

Rhys held out his hand and Frankie gladly took it. As they walked away, Alan's blustering voice drifted over.

'I don't know what he's talking about. I earned my National just like everyone else...'

The media stayed with Alan and Doug, leaving Rhys and Frankie to walk away relatively undisturbed.

'So where do we go from here?' she ventured.

Rhys looked at her from beneath heavy lids. His eyelashes clumped together in the fine rain. A teasing smile rerouted the raindrops dripping from his cheekbones.

'Back to the beginning. And this time we're going to do it right.' He hesitated then took the signet ring he had been awarded and held it before her ring finger. 'Frankie, will you marry me?'

Her body trembled like an earthquake and rational thought evacuated.

'Marry you? M-marry me?'

He grinned.

'Yes. I want to marry you. No ulterior motives. I just want to spend the rest of my life waking up next to you.'

Frankie paused, but it was only to savour the moment. She pushed her finger through the ring. It was a winner's ring. A ring to remind them of where they'd begun and a ring that promised a future full of hope.

THE END

Printed in Great Britain
by Amazon.co.uk, Ltd.,
Marston Gate.